Blackmailed the Rich Man

Bedded by blackmail! But for how long?

Three powerful, glamorous romances from three bestselling Mills & Boon authors!

In December 2008 Mills & Boon bring you two classic collections, each featuring three favourite romances by our bestselling authors…

BLACKMAILED BY THE RICH MAN

In the Millionaire's Possession
by Sara Craven
Blackmailed Into Marriage
by Lucy Monroe
Bedded by Blackmail by Julia James

ONE PASSIONATE NIGHT

His Bride for One Night by Miranda Lee
One Night at Parenga by Robyn Donald
His One-Night Mistress by Sandra Field

Blackmailed by the Rich Man

IN THE MILLIONAIRE'S POSSESSION
by
Sara Craven

BLACKMAILED INTO MARRIAGE
by
Lucy Monroe

BEDDED BY BLACKMAIL
by
Julia James

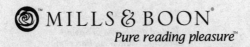
MILLS & BOON®
Pure reading pleasure™

Harlequin Mills & Boon Limited,
Eton House, 18-24 Paradise Road, Richmond, Surrey TW9 1SR

BLACKMAILED BY THE RICH MAN
© by Harlequin Enterprises II B.V./S.à.r.l 2008

In the Millionaire's Possession, Blackmailed Into Marriage and Bedded by Blackmail were first published in Great Britain by Harlequin Mills & Boon Limited in separate, single volumes.

In the Millionaire's Possession © Sara Craven 2005
Blackmailed Into Marriage © Lucy Monroe 2005
Bedded by Blackmail © Julia James 2004

ISBN: 978 0 263 86138 9

05-1208

Printed and bound in Spain
by Litografía Rosés S.A., Barcelona

IN THE MILLIONAIRE'S POSSESSION

by

Sara Craven

100 Reasons to Celebrate

We invite you to join us in celebrating
Mills & Boon's centenary. Gerald Mills and
Charles Boon founded Mills & Boon Limited
in 1908 and opened offices in London's Covent
Garden. Since then, Mills & Boon has become
a hallmark for romantic fiction, recognised
around the world.

We're proud of our 100 years of publishing
excellence, which wouldn't have been achieved
without the loyalty and enthusiasm of our
authors and readers.

Thank you!

Each month throughout the year there will
be something new and exciting to mark the
centenary, so watch for your favourite authors,
captivating new stories, special limited
edition collections…and more!

Sara Craven was born in South Devon and grew up surrounded by books in a house by the sea. After leaving grammar school she worked as a local journalist, covering everything from flower shows to murders. She started writing for Mills & Boon in 1975. Apart from writing, her passions include films, music, cooking and eating in good restaurants. She now lives in Somerset.

CHAPTER ONE

HELEN had never been so nervous in her life.

The starkness of her surroundings did not help, of course.

This was, after all, the London headquarters of Restauration International—an organisation supposedly devoted to historical conservation projects.

She'd expected panelled walls hung with works of art, antique furniture, and possibly a Persian carpet. Something with the grace and charm of the past.

Instead she'd been greeted by a receptionist with attitude, and dumped in this glass and chrome box with only a water cooler for company as the long, slow nerve-racking minutes passed.

And although she had to admit that the arrangement of canvas slats that formed her chair was surprisingly comfortable, it couldn't make her feel at ease mentally.

But then, in this life or death situation, what could?

Her hands tightened on the handle of her briefcase as she ran a silent check on the points she needed to make once she came face to face with the directors of Restauration International.

They're my last hope now, she thought. Every other source has dried up. So I need to get it right.

Suddenly restless, she walked across to the cooler and filled a paper cup. As she moved, she saw the security camera become activated, and repressed a grimace at the idea that unseen eyes at some control point might be watching her.

'Look businesslike,' her friend Lottie had advised her. 'Get out of those eternal jeans and put on a skirt. Remember you're making a presentation, not mucking out the ruins. You've had a lot of help over this,' she added with mock sternness. 'So don't blow it.'

And Lottie was quite right, Helen thought soberly. So many people had rallied round with quite amazing kindness. Checking the draft of her written report and making suggestions. Providing quick facelifts to the outside buildings and grounds with painting and weeding parties, in case the committee came to see the place for themselves. And even offering films of various events held at Monteagle over the past couple of years to use in the video, itself the result of a favour that had been called in by Lottie.

But now, at last, it was all down to her. She'd taken her friend's advice and put on her one good grey skirt, teaming it with a demure white cotton blouse and her elderly black blazer. Hopefully they wouldn't look too closely and see the shabbiness of her attire, she thought.

Her light brown hair—which badly needed cutting and shaping, when she had the time and the money—had been drawn back severely from her face and confined at the nape of her neck by a black ribbon bow, and there were small silver studs in the lobes of her ears.

Not much there for the hidden spectator to criticise, she thought, resisting the impulse to raise her cup in salute.

She made the trip back to her chair look deliberately casual, as if she didn't have a care in the world and there was nothing much riding on the coming interview.

Only my entire life, she thought, as her taut throat accepted the cool water. Only everything I care most about in the world now at the mercy of strangers.

Apart from Nigel, of course, she amended hastily.

Somehow I have to convince them that Monteagle is worth saving. That I'm not going to give up the struggle like my father and Grandpa and watch the place slide into total oblivion. Or, worse still, into the hands of Trevor Newson.

She shuddered at the memory of the fleshy, complacent face awaiting with a smile the victory that he thought was inevitable. Counting the days until he could turn Monteagle into the gross medieval theme park he'd set his heart on.

It had been those plans, as outlined to her, that had sent her on this last desperate quest to find the money for the house's urgently needed repairs.

All the other organisations that she'd doggedly approached had rejected her pleas for a grant on the grounds that Monteagle was too small, too unimportant, and too far off the normal tourist trails.

'Which is why it needs me,' Trevor Newson had told her. 'Jousting on the lawns, pig roasts, banqueting in the great hall…' His eyes glistened. 'That'll put it on the map, all right. The coach parties will flock here, and so will foreign tourists once I get it on the internet. And don't keep me waiting too long for your answer,' he added. 'Or the price I'm offering will start to go down.'

'You need not wait at all,' Helen said with icy civility. 'The answer is no, Mr Newson.'

'And now you're being hasty,' he chided in the patronising tone she so resented. 'After all, what choice have you got? The place is falling down around you, and it's common knowledge your father and grandfather left little but debts when they died.'

He ticked off on his fingers. 'You've got the rent from the grazing land and a bit of income from the handful of visitors who come when you open the place up each summer, and that won't get you far. In fact, it's a wonder you've hung on as long as you have.'

He gave a pitying shake of the head. 'You need to sell, my dear. And if you really can't bear to leave and move away I might even be able to offer you some work. These tournaments used to have a Queen of Love and Beauty presiding over them, apparently, and you're a good-looking girl.' He leered at her. 'I can just see you, properly made-up, in some low-cut medieval dress.'

'It's a tempting offer,' Helen said, controlling her temper by a whisker. 'But I'm afraid the answer's still no.'

'Ghastly old lech,' Lottie had commented. 'Better not tell Nigel, or he might deck him.' She'd paused. 'Is he going with you to confront this committee?'

'No.' Helen had resolutely concealed her disappointment.

'He's incredibly busy at work right now. Anyway,' she'd added, 'I'm a grown up girl. I can cope.'

As Nigel himself had said, she recalled with a pang. And maybe she'd simply taken too much for granted in counting on his support today. But they'd been seeing each other for a long time now, and everyone in the area presumed that he'd be fighting at her side in the battle to save Monteagle.

In fact, as Helen admitted to no one but herself, Nigel had been pretty lukewarm about her struggles to retain her home. He wasn't a poor man by any means—he worked in a merchant bank, and had inherited money from his grandmother as well—but he'd never offered any practical form of help.

It was something they would really need to discuss—once she got the grant. Because she was determined to be self-sufficient, and, while she drew the line at Mr Newson's theme park, she had several other schemes in mind to boost the house's earning power.

Although lately they hadn't had the opportunity to talk about very much at all, she realised with a faint frown. But that was probably her fault in the main. Nigel's work had kept him confined to London recently, but she'd been so totally engrossed in preparing her case for the committee that she'd barely missed him.

What a thing to admit about the man you were going to marry!

But all that was going to change, she vowed remorsefully. Once today was over, win or lose, it was going to be permanent commitment from now on. Everything he'd ever asked from her. Including *that*.

She knew she was probably being an old-fashioned idiot, and most of her contemporaries would laugh if they knew, but she'd always veered away from the idea of sex before marriage.

Not that she was scared of surrender, she thought defensively, or unsure of her own feelings for Nigel. It was just that when she stood with him in the village church to make her vows she wanted him to know that she was his alone, and that her white dress meant something.

On a more practical level, it had never seemed to be quite the right moment, either.

Never the time, the place, and the loved one altogether, she thought, grimacing inwardly. But she couldn't expect Nigel to be patient for ever, not when they belonged together. So why hold back any longer?

She was startled out of her reverie by the sudden opening of the door. Helen got hurriedly to her feet, to be confronted by a blonde girl, tall and slim, with endless legs, and wearing a smart black suit. She gave Helen a swift formal smile while her eyes swept her with faint disparagement.

'Miss Frayne? Will you come with me, please? The committee is waiting for you.'

'And I've been waiting for the committee,' Helen told her coolly.

She was led down a long narrow corridor, with walls plastered in a Greek key pattern. It made her feel slightly giddy, and she wondered if this was a deliberate ploy.

Her companion flung open the door at the far end. 'Miss Frayne,' she announced, and stood back to allow Helen to precede her into the room.

More concrete, thought Helen, taking a swift look around. More metal, more glass. And seven men standing at an oblong table, acknowledging her presence with polite inclinations of their heads.

'Please, Miss Frayne, sit. Be comfortable.' The speaker, clearly the chairman, was opposite her. He was a bearded man with grey hair and glasses, who looked Scandinavian.

Helen sank down on to a high-backed affair of leather and steel, clutching her briefcase on her lap while they all took their places.

They looked like clones of each other, she thought, in their neat dark suits and discreetly patterned ties, sitting bolt upright round the table. Except for one, she realised. The man casually lounging in the seat to the right of the chairman.

He was younger than his colleagues—early to mid-thirties, Helen judged—with an untidy mane of black hair and a swarthy face that no one would ever describe as handsome. He had a beak of a nose, and a thin-lipped, insolent mouth, while eyes, dark and impenetrable as the night, studied her from under heavy lids.

Unlike the rest of the buttoned-up committee members, he looked as if he'd just crawled out of bed and thrown on the clothing that was nearest to hand. Moreover, his tie had been pulled loose and the top of his shirt left undone.

He had the appearance of someone who'd strayed in off the street by mistake, she thought critically.

And saw his mouth twist into a faint grin, as if he'd divined what she was thinking and found it amusing.

Helen felt a kind of embarrassed resentment at being so transparent. This was not how she'd planned to begin at all. She gave him a cold look, and saw his smile widen in sensuous, delighted appreciation.

Making her realise, for the first time in her life, that a man did not have to be conventionally handsome to blaze charm and a lethal brand of sexual attraction.

Helen felt as if she'd been suddenly subjected to a force field of male charisma, and she resented it. And the fact that he had beautiful teeth did nothing to endear him to her either.

'Be comfortable,' the chairman had said.

My God, she thought. What a hope. Because she'd never felt more awkward in her life. Or so scared.

She took a deep breath and transferred her attention deliberately to the chairman, trying to concentrate as he congratulated her on the depth and lucidity of her original application for a grant, and on the additional material she'd supplied to back up her claim.

They all had their folders open, she saw, except one. And no prizes for guessing which of them it was, she thought indignantly. But at least she wasn't the object of his attention any longer. Instead, her swift sideways glance told her, he seemed to be staring abstractedly into space, as if he was miles away.

If only, thought Helen, steadying her flurried breathing. And, anyway, why serve on the committee if he wasn't prepared to contribute to its work?

He didn't even react when she produced the videotape. 'I hope this will give you some idea of the use Monteagle has been put to in the recent past,' she said. 'I intend to widen the scope of activities in future—even have the house licensed for weddings.'

There were murmurs of polite interest and approval, and she began to relax a little—only to realise that he was staring at her once again, his eyes travelling slowly over her face and down, she realised furiously, to the swell of her breasts against the thin blouse. She tried to behave as if she was unconscious of his scrutiny, but felt the betrayal of warm blood invading her face. Finally, to her relief, the dark gaze descended to her small bare hands, clasped tensely on the table in front of her.

'You plan to marry there yourself, perhaps, *mademoiselle*?' He had a low, resonant voice which was not unattractive, she admitted unwillingly, still smarting from the overt sensuality of his regard. And his English was excellent, in spite of his French accent.

She wondered how he'd taken the section of her report which stated that the fortified part of Monteagle had been built at the time of the Hundred Years War, and that the Black Prince, France's most feared enemy, had often stayed there.

Now she lifted her chin and met his enquiring gaze with a flash of her long-lashed hazel eyes, wishing at the same time that she and Nigel were officially engaged and she had a ring to wear.

'Yes,' she said. 'As a matter of fact, I do, *monsieur*. I thought I might even be the first one,' she added with a flash of inspiration.

Of course she hadn't discussed this with Nigel, she reminded herself guiltily, but she didn't see what objection he could have. And it would make the most wonderful setting—besides providing useful publicity at the same time.

'But how romantic,' he murmured, and relapsed into his reverie again.

After that questions from the other committee members came thick and fast, asking her to explain or expand further on some

of the points she'd made in her application. Clearly they'd all
read the file, she thought hopefully, and seemed genuinely interested in what she had to say.

The door opened to admit the tall blonde, bringing coffee
on a trolley, and Helen was glad to see there was mineral water
as well. This interview was proving just as much of an ordeal
as she'd expected, and her mouth was dry again.

When the blonde withdrew, the Frenchman reached for his
folder and extracted a sheet of paper.

'This is not your first application for financial assistance towards the repair and renovation of Monteagle House,
mademoiselle. Is this an accurate list of the organisations you
have previously approached?'

Helen bit her lip as she scanned down the column of names.
'Yes, it is.'

'But none of your efforts were successful?' The low voice
pressed her.

'No,' she admitted stonily, aware that her creamy skin had
warmed.

'So how did you become aware of us?'

'A friend of mine found you on the internet. She said you
seemed to be interested in smaller projects. So—I thought I
would try.'

'Because you were becoming desperate.' It was a statement,
not a question.

'Yes.' Helen looked at him defiantly. Her consciousness of
her surroundings seemed to have contracted—intensified. There
might just have been the two of them in the room, locked in
confrontation. 'By this stage I will explore any avenue that
presents itself. I will not allow Monteagle to become derelict,
and I'll do whatever it takes to save it.'

There was a silence, then he produced another sheet of paper.
'The surveyor's report that you have included in your submission is twenty years old.'

'Yes,' she said. 'I felt that the recommendations made then
still apply. Although the costs have obviously risen.'

'Twenty years is a long time, *mademoiselle*. Having commissioned such a report, why did your family not carry out the necessary works at that time?'

Helen's flush deepened. 'My grandfather had every intention of doing so, but he was overtaken by events.'

'Can you explain further?' the smooth voice probed.

She took a breath, hating the admission she was being forced to make. 'There was a crisis in the insurance industry. My grandfather was a Lloyds' name in those days, and the calls that were made on him brought us all to the edge of ruin. He even thought Monteagle might have to be sold.'

'That is still a possibility, of course,' her adversary said gently, and paused. 'Is it not true that you have received a most generous offer for the entire estate from a Monsieur Trevor Newson? An offer that would halt the disintegration of the house, *mademoiselle*, and in addition restore your own finances? Would that not be better than having to beg your way round every committee and trust? And deal with constant rejection?'

'I find Mr Newson's plans for the estate totally unacceptable,' Helen said curtly. 'I'm a Frayne, and I won't allow the place that has been our home for centuries to be trashed in the way he proposes. I refuse to give up.' She leaned forward, her voice shaking with sudden intensity. 'I'll find the money somehow, and I'll do anything to get it.'

'Anything?' The dark brows lifted mockingly. 'You are a most determined champion of your cause.'

'I have to be.' Helen flung back her head. 'And if achieving my aim includes begging, then so be it. Monteagle is well worth the sacrifice.'

And then, as if a wire had snapped, parting them, it was over. The Frenchman was leaning back in his chair and the chairman was rising to his feet.

'It has been a pleasure to meet you, Miss Frayne, and we shall consider your proposals with great care—including the additional information and material you have supplied.' He picked up the video, giving her a warm smile. 'We hope to come to our decision by the end of the month.'

'I'm grateful to you for seeing me,' Helen said formally, and got herself out of the room without once glancing in the direction of her interrogator.

In the corridor, she paused, a hand pressed to her side as if she had been running in some uphill race.

What in hell had been going on there? she asked herself dazedly. Were they running some good cop/bad cop routine, where the upright members of the committee softened her up with their kindly interest so that their resident thug could move in for the kill?

Up to then it had been going quite well, she thought anxiously, or she'd believed it had. But her audience might not appreciate being regarded as the very last resort at the end of a long list of them, as he'd suggested.

God, but he'd been loathsome in every respect, she thought vengefully as she made her way back to the reception area. And to hell with his charm and sex appeal.

Quite apart from anything else, she knew now what it was like to be mentally undressed, and it was a technique that she did not appreciate. In fact, she thought furiously, it was probably a form of sexual harassment—not that anyone whose spiritual home was obviously the Stone Age would have heard of such a thing, or even care.

All the same, she found herself wondering who he was exactly and how much influence he actually wielded in Restauration International. Well, there was one quick way to find out.

The blonde was in the foyer, chatting to the receptionist. They both glanced up with brief formal smiles as Helen approached.

She said coolly, 'Please may I have a copy of the organisation's introduction pack?'

Brows rose, and they exchanged glances. The blonde said, 'I think you'll find you were sent one following your original enquiry, Miss Frayne.'

'Indeed I was,' Helen agreed. 'But unfortunately it's at home, and there are a few details I need to check.' She paused. 'So—if it's not too much trouble…?'

There was another exchange of glances, then the receptionist opened with ill grace a drawer in her large desk, and took out a plastic-encased folder, which she handed to Helen.

'One per application is the norm, Miss Frayne,' she said. 'Please look after it.'

'I shall treasure it,' Helen assured her. As she moved to put the pack in her briefcase, she was suddenly aware of footsteps crossing the foyer behind her. And at the same time, as if some switch had been pulled, the haughty stares from the other two girls vanished, to be replaced by smiles so sweet that they were almost simpering.

Helen felt as if icy fingers were tracing a path down her spine as instinct told her who had come to join them.

She turned slowly to face him, schooling her expression to indifference.

'Making sure I leave the building, *monsieur*?'

'No, merely going to my own next appointment, *mademoiselle*.' His smile mocked her quite openly. He glanced at the pack she was still holding. 'And my name is Delaroche,' he added softly. 'Marc Delaroche. As I would have told you earlier, had you asked.'

He watched with undisguised appreciation as Helen struggled against an urge to hurl the pack at his head, then made her a slight bow as upbringing triumphed over instinct and she replaced it on the desk.

She said icily, 'I merely wanted something to read on the train. But I can always buy a paper.'

'But of course.' He was using that smile again, but this time she was braced against its impact.

'*A bientôt*,' he added, and went, with a wave to the other two, who were still gazing at him in a kind of dumb entrancement.

'See you soon', Monsieur Delaroche? Helen asked silently after his retreating back. Is that what you just said to me? She drew a deep breath. My God, not if I see you first.

She was disturbingly aware of that same brief shiver of ice along her nerve-endings. As if in some strange way she was being warned.

* * *

Marc Delaroche had said he had an appointment, but all the same Helen was thankful to find him nowhere in sight when she got outside the building.

She'd thought her nervousness would dissipate now that the interview was over, but she was wrong. She felt lost, somehow, and ridiculously scared. Perhaps it was just the noise and dirt of London that was upsetting her, she thought, wondering how Nigel could relish working here amid all this uproar.

But at least she could seize the opportunity of seeing him while she was here, she told herself, producing her mobile phone. Before she got her train back to the peace of the countryside and Monteagle.

He answered at once, but he was clearly not alone because she could hear voices and laughter in the background, and the clink of glasses.

'Helen?' He sounded astonished. 'Where are you ringing from?'

'Groverton Street,' she said. 'It isn't too far from where you work.' She paused. 'I thought maybe you'd buy me lunch.'

'Lunch?' he echoed. 'I don't think I can. I'm a bit tied up. You should have told me in advance you were coming up today, and I'd have made sure I was free.'

'But I did tell you,' Helen said, trying to stifle her disappointment. 'I've just had my interview with Restauration International—remember?'

'Oh, God,' he said. 'Yes, of course. I've been so busy it completely slipped my mind.' He paused. 'How did it go anyway?'

'Pretty well, I think—I hope.' Helen tried to dismiss the thought of Marc Delaroche from her mind.

One man, she thought. One dissenting voice. What harm could he really do?

'They seemed interested,' she added. 'Sympathetic—for the most part. And they said I'd know by the end of the month, so I've less than ten days to wait.'

'Well, I'll keep my fingers crossed for you,' Nigel said. 'And maybe—under the circumstances—I could manage lunch after all. Celebrate a little. It's certainly the most hopeful result you've had.' He paused again. 'I'll need to pull a few strings, change things around a little, but it should be all right. Meet me at the Martinique at one clock.'

'But I don't know where it is,' she protested.

'But the cab driver will,' he said with a touch of exasperation. 'It's new, and pretty trendy. Everyone's going there.'

'Then will we get a table?' Helen asked, wondering, troubled, whether she could afford the price of a taxi.

He sighed. 'Helen, you're so naïve. The bank has a standing reservation there. It's not a problem. Now, I must go. See you later.'

She switched off her phone and replaced it slowly in her bag. It sounded rather as if Nigel had gone to this Martinique place already. But then why shouldn't he? she reminded herself impatiently. Entertaining the bank's clients at smart restaurants was part of his job. It was all part of the world he inhabited, along with platinum cards, endless taxis, and first-class tickets everywhere.

Yet she'd travelled up on a cheap day return, needed to count her pennies, and most of her entertaining involved cheese on toast or pasta, with a bottle of cheap plonk shared with Lottie or another girlfriend.

Nigel belonged to a different world, she thought with a pang, and it would require a quantum leap on her part to join him there.

But I can do it, she told herself, unfastening the constriction of the black ribbon bow and shaking her hair loose almost defiantly. I can do anything—even save Monteagle. And nothing's going to stop me.

Her moment of euphoria was brought to a halt by the realisation that lack of funds might well prevent her from completing even the minor mission of reaching the restaurant to meet Nigel.

However, with the help of her *A to Z* and a copy of *Time Out*, she discovered that the Martinique was just over a mile away. Easy walking distance, she decided, setting off at a brisk pace.

She found it without difficulty, although the search had left her hot and thirsty.

Its smart black and white awning extended over the pavement, shading terracotta pots of evergreens. Helen took a deep breath and walked in. She found herself in a small reception area, being given a questioning look by a young man behind a desk.

'*Mademoiselle* has a reservation?'

'Well, not exactly—' she began, and was interrupted by an immediate shake of the head.

'I regret that we are fully booked. Perhaps another day we can have the pleasure of serving *mademoiselle*.'

She said quickly, 'I'm joining someone—a Mr Nigel Hartley.'

He gave her a surprised look, then glanced at the large book in front of him. 'Yes, he has a table at one o'clock, but he has not yet arrived.' He paused. 'Would you like to enjoy a drink at the bar? Or be seated to wait for him.'

'I'd like to sit down, please.'

'*D'accord.*' He came from behind the desk. 'May I take your jacket?' He indicated the blazer she was carrying over her arm.

'Oh—no. No, thank you,' Helen said, remembering with acute embarrassment that the lining was slightly torn.

'Then please follow me.' He opened a door, and what seemed like a wall of sound came to meet her, so that she almost flinched.

Nigel had not exaggerated the restaurant's popularity, she thought. She found herself in a large bright room, with windows on two sides and more tables crammed into the rest of it than she would have believed possible. Every table seemed to be occupied, and the noise was intense, but she squeezed through the sea of white linen, crystal and silver after her guide and discovered there were a few remaining inches of space in one corner.

She sank down thankfully on to one of the high-backed wooden chairs, wishing that it were possible to kick off her shoes.

'May I bring something for *mademoiselle*?' The young man hovered.

'Just some still water, please,' she returned.

She had no doubt that the Martinique was a trendy place—somewhere to see and be seen—but she wished Nigel had chosen something quieter. She also wished very much that it wasn't a French restaurant either. Too reminiscent, she thought, of her recent interrogation.

She wanted to talk to Nigel, but the kind of private conversation she had in mind could hardly be conducted at the tops of their voices.

He clearly thought she'd enjoy a taste of the high life, she decided ruefully, and she must be careful not to give him a hint of her disappointment at his choice.

Besides, they would have the rest of their lives to talk.

He was already ten minutes late, she realised, and was just beginning to feel self-conscious about sitting on her own when a waiter appeared with a bottle of mineral water and a tumbler containing ice cubes. The tray also held a tall slender glass filled with a rich pink liquid, fizzing gently.

'I'm afraid I didn't order this,' Helen protested, as he placed it in front of her. 'What is it?'

'Kir Royale, *mademoiselle*—champagne and *cassis*—and it comes with the compliments of *monsieur*.'

'Oh,' she said with relief. Nigel must have phoned through the order, she thought, as a peace offering for his tardiness. It was the kind of caring gesture she should have expected, and it made her feel better—happier about the situation as a whole.

She drank some water to refresh her mouth, then sipped the kir slowly, enjoying the faint fragrance of the blackcurrant and the sheer lift of the wine.

But she couldn't make it last for ever, and by the time she'd drained the glass Nigel still hadn't arrived. She was beginning to get nervous and irritated in equal measure.

She beckoned to the waiter. 'Has there been any further message from *monsieur* to say he's been delayed?' she asked. 'Because, if not, I'd like another kir.'

He looked bewildered. 'There is no delay, *mademoiselle*. *Monsieur* is here at this moment, having lunch. Shall I consult him on your behalf?'

Helen stared at him. 'He's *here*? You must be mistaken.'

'No, *mademoiselle*. See—there by the window.'

Helen looked, and what she saw made her throat close in shock. It was Marc Delaroche, she realised numbly, seated at a table with two other men. He was listening to what they were saying, but, as if he instantly sensed Helen focussing on him, he glanced round and met her horrified gaze. He inclined his head in acknowledgement, then reached for his own glass, lifting it in a swift and silent toast.

She disengaged from him instantly, flushed and mortified. She said, 'You mean he—that person—sent me this drink?' She took a deep breath, forcing herself back to a semblance of composure, even though her heart was racing unevenly. 'I—I didn't know that. And I certainly wouldn't dream of having another. In fact, perhaps you'd bring me the bill for this one, plus the water, and I'll just—leave.'

'But you have not yet had lunch,' the waiter protested. 'And besides, here comes Monsieur Hartley.'

And sure enough it was Nigel, striding across the restaurant as if conducting a personal parting of the Red Sea, tall, blond and immaculate, in his dark blue pinstripe and exquisitely knotted silk tie.

'So there you are,' he greeted her.

'It's where I've been for the past half hour,' Helen told him evenly. 'What happened?'

'Well, I warned you I was busy.' He dropped a cursory kiss on her cheek as he passed. 'Menus, please, Gaspard. I'm pushed for time today. In fact, I won't bother with the *carte*. I'll just have steak, medium rare, with a mixed salad.'

'Then I'll have the same,' Helen said. 'I wouldn't want to keep you waiting.'

'Fine.' He either ignored or didn't notice the irony in her tone. 'And a bottle of house red, Gaspard. Quick as you can. Plus a gin and tonic.' He glanced at Helen. 'Do you want a drink, sweetie?'

'I've already had one,' she said. 'Kir Royale, as a matter of fact.'

His lips thinned a little. 'Rather a new departure for you, isn't it? Did the waiter talk you into it?'

'No,' she said. 'But don't worry. One is more than enough.'
She was ashamed to hear how acerbic she sounded, and it was
all the fault of that—that *creature* across the room. But she
was sharing precious time with the man she loved, and she
wouldn't allow it to be spoiled by anyone or anything.

She made herself smile at Nigel, and put her hand on his.
'It's so great to see you,' she said gently. 'Do you realise how
long it's been?'

He sighed. 'I know, but life at work is so hectic just now I
hardly have any time to spare.'

'Your parents must miss you too.'

He shrugged. 'They're far too busy planning Dad's retirement and giving the house a pre-sale facelift to worry about
me.' He shot her a swift glance. 'You did know they're moving
to Portugal in the near future?'

'Selling Oaktree House?' Helen said slowly. 'I had no idea.'
She gave him a blank look. 'But how will you manage? It's
your home.'

'Off and on for the past ten years, yes,' Nigel said with a
touch of impatience. 'But my life's in London now. I'm going
to stop renting and look for somewhere to buy. Ah, my drink
at last. My God, I could do with it. I've had a hell of a morning.' And he launched himself into a description of its vicis-
situdes which was still going strong when their food arrived.

Not that Helen was particularly hungry. Her appetite, such
as it was, seemed to have suddenly dissipated. Nor was she
giving her full attention to the vagaries of the financial markets
and the irresponsible attitude of certain nameless clients, as
outlined by Nigel. Her mind was on another track altogether.

Something had happened, she thought numbly. Some fundamental shift had taken place and she hadn't noticed.

Well, she was totally focussed now, because this involved
her life too. She'd assumed that Nigel would live with her at
Monteagle once they were married, and commute to London.
After all, she couldn't move away, use Monteagle as a weekend
home. Surely he realised that.

But there was no way they could talk about it now. Not with

Nigel glancing at his watch every couple of minutes as he rapidly forked up his steak.

Eventually she broke into his monologue. 'Nigel—this weekend, we have to talk. Can you come over—spend the day with me on Sunday?'

'Not this weekend, I'm afraid. It's the chairman's birthday, and he's celebrating with a weekend party at his place in Sussex, so duty calls.' His smile was swift and light. 'And now I have to dash. I have a two-thirty meeting. The bill goes straight to my office, so order yourself a pudding if you want, darling, and coffee. See you later.' He blew her a kiss, and was gone.

Once again she was sitting alone, she thought as she pushed her plate away. A fact that would doubtless not be lost on her adversary across the room. She risked a lightning glance from under her lashes, and realised with a surge of relief that his table was empty and being cleared. At least he hadn't witnessed her cavalier treatment at Nigel's hands. Nor would she have to grit her teeth and thank him for that bloody drink. With luck, she would never have to set eyes on him again. End of story.

She'd wanted this to be a great day in her life, she thought with a silent sigh, but since she'd first set eyes on Marc Delaroche it seemed to have been downhill all the way.

And now she had better go and catch her train. She was just reaching for her bag when Gaspard arrived, bearing a tray which he placed in front of her with a flourish.

'There must be some mistake,' Helen protested, watching him unload a cafetière, cups, saucers, two glasses and a bottle of armagnac. 'I didn't order any of this.'

'But I did,' Marc Delaroche said softly. 'Because you look as if you need it. So do not refuse me, *ma belle, je vous en prie.*'

And before she could utter any kind of protest, he took the seat opposite her, so recently vacated by Nigel, and smiled into her startled eyes.

CHAPTER TWO

'I THOUGHT you'd gone.' The words were out before she could stop herself, implying that she took even a remote interest in his actions.

'I was merely bidding *au revoir* to my friends.' He filled her cup from the cafetière. 'Before returning to offer you a *digestif*.' He poured a judicious amount of armagnac into each crystal bowl, and pushed one towards her. 'Something your companion should consider, perhaps,' he added meditatively. 'If he continues to rush through his meals at such a rate he will have an ulcer before he is forty.'

'Thank you.' Helen lifted her chin. 'I'll be sure to pass your warning on to him.'

'I intended it for you,' he said. 'I presume he is the man you plan to marry at Monteagle with such panache?' He slanted a smile at her. 'After all, it is a wife's duty to look after the physical well-being of her husband—in every way. Don't you think so?'

'You don't want to know what I think.' Helen bit her lip. 'You really are some kind of dinosaur.'

His smile widened. 'And a man with a ruined digestion is an even more savage beast, believe me,' he told her softly. 'Just as a beautiful girl left alone in a restaurant is an offence against nature.' He raised his glass. *Salut.*'

'Oh, spare me.' Helen gritted her teeth. 'I don't need your compliments—or your company.'

'Perhaps not,' he said. 'But you require my vote on the committee, so maybe you should force yourself to be civil for this short time, and drink with me.'

Smouldering, Helen drank some of her coffee. 'What made you choose this restaurant particularly?' she asked, after a loaded pause.

23

His brows lifted mockingly. 'You suspect some sinister motive? That I am following you, perhaps?' He shook his head. 'You are wrong. I was invited here by my companions—who have a financial interest in the place and wished my opinion. Also I arrived first, remember, so I could accuse you of stalking me.'

Helen stiffened. 'That, of course, is just *so* likely.' Her tone bit.

'No,' he returned coolly. 'To my infinite regret, it is not likely at all.'

Helen felt her throat muscles tighten warily. 'Why are you doing this? Buying me drinks—forcing your company on me?'

He shrugged. 'Because I wished to encounter you when you were more relaxed. When you had—let your hair down, as they say.' He leaned back in his chair. 'It looks much better loose, so why scrape it back in that unbecoming way?'

'I wanted to look businesslike for the interview,' she returned coldly. 'Not as if I was trading on my gender.'

'Put like that,' he said, 'I find it unappealing too.'

'So why are you ignoring my obvious wish to keep my distance?'

He lifted his glass, studying the colour of the armagnac. He said, 'Your fiancé arrived late and left early. Perhaps I am merely trying to compensate for his lack of attention.'

She bit her lip. 'How dare you criticise him? You know nothing at all about him. He happens to be working very hard for our future together—and I don't feel neglected in any way,' she added defiantly.

'I am relieved to hear it, *ma mie*,' he drawled. 'I feared for your sake that his performance in bed might be conducted at the same speed as your lunch dates.'

She stared at him, shocked into a sudden blush that reached the roots of her hair.

Her voice shook. 'You have no right to talk to me like that— to speculate about my private relationships in that—disgusting way. You should be ashamed of yourself.'

He looked back at her without a glimmer of repentance. 'It was prompted solely by my concern for your happiness, I assure you.'

She pushed back her chair and got to her feet, fumbling for her jacket. She said jerkily, 'When I get the money to restore Monteagle I shall fill the world with my joy, *monsieur*. And that is the only affair of mine in which you have the right to probe. Goodbye.'

She walked past him and out of the restaurant, her face still burning but her head held proudly.

It was only when she was outside, heading for the tube station, that she realised just how afraid she'd been that he would follow her—stop her from leaving in some unspecified way.

But of course he had not done so.

He's just a predator, she thought, looking for potential prey and testing their weaknesses. He saw I was alone, and possibly vulnerable, so he moved in. That's all that happened.

Or was it?

If only I hadn't blushed, she castigated herself. I just hope he interprets it as anger, not embarrassment.

Because she couldn't bear him to know that she didn't have a clue what Nigel or any other man was like in bed. And she'd certainly never been openly challenged on the subject before—especially by a man who was also a complete stranger.

She knew what happened physically, of course. She wasn't that much of a fool or an innocent. But she didn't know what to expect emotionally.

She hoped that loving Nigel would be enough, and that he would teach her the rest. It was quite some time since he'd made a serious attempt to get her into bed, she thought remorsefully. But she couldn't and wouldn't delay the moment any longer. It was long overdue.

Perhaps it was the fear of rejection which had kept him away so often lately. She'd been so wrapped up in her own life and its worries that she hadn't truly considered his feelings.

I've just been totally insensitive, she thought wearily. And the tragedy is that it took someone like Marc Delaroche to make me see it.

But from now on everything's going to be different, she promised herself firmly.

*   *   *

I still can't believe you're back already,' Lottie said, as she put a shepherd's pie in the oven. 'Your phone call gave me a real jolt. I wasn't expecting you until tomorrow at the earliest.' She threw Helen a searching glance over her shoulder. 'Didn't you meet up with Nigel?'

'Oh, yes,' Helen said brightly. 'We had an amazing lunch in one of the newest restaurants.'

'Lunch, eh?' Lottie pursed her lips. 'Now, I had you down for a romantic dinner *à deux*, then back to his place for a night of seething passion. Supper with me is a pretty dull alternative.'

Helen smiled at her. 'Honey, nothing involving you is ever dull. And, to be honest, I couldn't wait to get out of London.'

Lottie gave her a careful look as she sat down at the kitchen table and began to string beans. 'Your interview with the committee didn't go so well?'

Helen sighed. 'I honestly don't know. Most of them seemed pleasant and interested, but perhaps they were humouring me.'

'And is this Marc Delaroche guy that you phoned me about included in the 'pleasant and interested' category?' Lottie enquired.

'No,' Helen returned, teeth gritted. 'He is not.'

'How did I guess?' Lottie said wryly. 'Anyway, following your somewhat emotional request from the station, I looked him up on the net.'

'And he was there?'

'Oh, yes,' Lottie nodded. 'And he's into buildings.'

'An architect?' Helen asked, surprised.

'Not exactly. He's the chairman of Fabrication Roche, a company that makes industrial buildings—instant factories from kits, cheap and ultra-efficient, especially in developing countries. The company's won awards for the designs, and they've made him a multimillionaire.'

'Then what the hell is someone from that kind of background doing on a committee that deals with heritage projects?' Helen shook her head. 'It makes no sense.'

'Except he must know about costing,' Lottie pointed out

practically. 'And applying modern technology to restoration
work. The others deal with aesthetics. He looks at the bottom
line.'

Helen's lips tightened. 'Well, I hope the ghastly modern eye-
sore we met in today wasn't a sample of his handiwork.'

'I wouldn't know about that.' Lottie grinned at her. 'But I've
printed everything off for you to read at your leisure.' She
paused. 'No photograph of him, I'm afraid.'

'It doesn't matter,' Helen said quietly. 'I already know what
he looks like.'

And I know the way he looked at me, she thought, remembering her sense of helpless outrage as his gaze had moved
over her body. And that glinting smile in his eyes...

She swallowed, clearing the image determinedly from her
mind. 'But thanks for doing that, Lottie. It's always best to—
know your enemy.'

'Even better not to have an enemy in the first place,' Lottie
retorted, rinsing the beans in a colander. 'Especially one with
his kind of money.' She went to the dresser to fetch a bottle
of red wine and a corkscrew. 'Did you tell Nigel how your
interview went?'

Helen hesitated. 'Some of it. He was really pushed for time,
so I couldn't go into details.'

'And you'll be seeing him this weekend, no doubt?'

'Actually, no.' Helen made her voice sound casual. 'He's
got a party to go to. A duty thing for his chairman's birthday.'

Lottie stared at her. 'And he hasn't asked you to go with
him?' She sounded incredulous.

'Well, no,' Helen admitted awkwardly. 'But it's no big
deal. It will be a black tie affair, and Nigel knows quite well
I haven't anything to wear to something like that.' She gave
a little laugh. 'He probably wanted to save me embarrassment.'

'For the same reason he might have considered buying you
an evening dress,' Lottie said with a touch of curtness. 'He can
certainly afford it.'

Helen shrugged. 'But he didn't,' she said. 'And it really

doesn't matter.' She paused. 'Of course it will be different when we're officially engaged.'

'I hope so,' Lottie agreed drily, filling their glasses.

'And what about you?' Helen was suddenly eager to change the subject. 'Have you heard from Simon?'

Her friend's face lit up, her blue eyes sparkling. 'The dam's nearly finished, and he's coming home on leave next month. Only two weeks, but that's better than nothing, and we're going to talk serious wedding plans. He says from now on he's only accepting contracts which allow accompanying wives, so I think he's missing me.'

Helen smiled at her teasingly. 'You can't leave,' she protested. 'How are the locals to give dinner parties without you to cook for them?'

'I promise I won't go before I cater for your wedding reception,' Lottie promised solemnly. 'So can you please fix a date?'

'I'll make it a priority,' Helen returned.

She was in a thoughtful mood when she walked home that night. There'd been a shower of rain about an hour before, and the air was heady with the scent of damp earth and sweet grass.

She was delighted at Lottie's obvious happiness, but at the same time unable to subdue a small pang of envy.

She wished her own life was falling so splendidly and lovingly into place.

Yet Nigel seems to be managing perfectly well without me, she thought sadly. If only we could have talked today—really talked—then maybe we'd have had Lottie's romantic kind of evening—and night—after all. And he'd have bought me a ring, and a dress, and taken me to Sussex. And he'd have told everyone, 'This is my brand-new fiancée. I simply couldn't bear to leave her behind.'

She'd started the day with such optimism and determination, yet now she felt uneasy and almost frightened. Nothing had gone according to plan. And miles away, in a glass and concrete box, her fate had probably already been decided.

I need Nigel, she thought. I need him to hold me and tell me everything will be all right, and that Monteagle is safe.

She walked under the arched gateway and stood in the court-yard, looking at the bulk of the house in the starlight. Half-seen, like this, it seemed massive—impregnable—but she knew how deceptive it was.

And it wasn't just her own future under threat. There were the Marlands, George and Daisy, who'd come to work for her grandfather when they were a young married couple, as gar-dener and cook respectively. As the other staff had left George had learned to turn his hand to more and more things about the estate, and his wife, small, cheerful and bustling, had be-come the housekeeper. Helen, working alongside them, de-pended on them totally, but knew unhappily that she could not guarantee their future—specially from Trevor Newson.

'Too old,' he'd said. 'Too set in their ways. I'll be putting in my own people.'

You'll be putting in no one, she'd told herself silently.

I wish I still felt as brave now, she thought, swallowing. But, even so, I'm not giving up the fight.

Monteagle opened to the public on Saturdays in the summer. Marion Lowell the Vicar's wife, who was a keen historian, led guided tours round the medieval ruins and those parts of the adjoining Jacobean house not being used as living accommo-dation by Helen and the Marlands.

Her grandfather had been forced to sell the books from his library in the eighties, and Helen now used the room as her sitting room. It had a wonderful view across the lawns to the lake, so the fact that it was furnished with bits and pieces from the attics, and a sofa picked up for a song at a house clearance sale a few miles away, was no real hardship.

If the weather was fine Helen and Daisy Marland served afternoon teas, with home-made scones and cakes, in the court-yard. With the promise of warm sunshine to come, they'd spent most of Friday evening baking.

Helen had been notified that a coach tour, travelling under the faintly depressing title 'Forgotten Corners of History' would be arriving mid-afternoon, so she'd got George to set up wooden trestles, covered with the best of the linen sheets, and flank them with benches.

Placing a small pot of wild flowers in the centre of each table, she felt reasonably satisfied, even if it was a lot of effort for very moderate returns. However, it was largely a goodwill gesture, and on that level it worked well. Entries in the visitors' book in the Great Hall praised the teas lavishly, particularly Daisy's featherlight scones, served with cream and home-made jam.

For once, the coach arrived punctually, and as one tour ended the next began. Business in the courtyard was brisk, but evenly spaced for a change, so they were never 'rushed to death', as Mrs Marland approvingly put it. The weather had lived up to the forecast, and although Monteagle closed officially at six, it was well after that when the last visitors reluctantly departed, prising themselves away from the warmth of the early-evening sun.

The clearing away done, Helen hung up the voluminous white apron she wore on these occasions, today over neatly pressed jeans and a blue muslin shirt, kicked off her sandals, and strolled across the lawns down to the edge of the lake. The coolness of the grass felt delicious under her aching soles, and the rippling water had its usual soothing effect.

If only every open day could go as smoothly, she thought dreamily.

Although that would not please Nigel, who had always made his disapproval clear. 'Working as a glorified waitress,' he'd said. 'What on earth do you think your grandfather would say?'

'He wouldn't say anything,' Helen had returned, slightly nettled by his attitude. 'He'd simply roll up his sleeves and help with the dishes.'

Besides, she thought, the real problem was Nigel's mother Celia, a woman who gave snobbishness a bad name. She liked the idea of Helen having inherited Monteagle, but thought it should have come with a full staff of retainers and a convenient treasure chest in the dungeon to pay the running costs, so she had little sympathy with Helen's struggles.

She sighed, moving her shoulders with sudden uneasiness

inside the cling of the shirt. Her skin felt warm and clammy, and she was sorely tempted to walk round to the landing stage beside the old boathouse, as she often did, strip off her top clothes and dive in for a cooling swim.

That was what the thought of Nigel's mother did to her, she told herself. Or was it?

Because she realised with bewilderment that she had the strangest sensation that someone somewhere was watching her, and that was what she found suddenly disturbing.

She swung round defensively, her brows snapping together, and realised with odd relief that it was only Mrs Lowell, coming towards her across the grass, wreathed in smiles.

'What a splendid afternoon,' she said, triumphantly rattling the cash box she was carrying. 'No badly behaved children for once, and we've completely sold out of booklets. Any chance of the wonderful Lottie printing off some more for us?'

'I mentioned we were getting low the other evening, and they'll be ready for next week.' Helen assured her, then paused. 'We have had a good crowd here today.' She gave a faint grin. 'The coach party seemed the usual motley crew, but docile enough.'

Mrs Lowell wrinkled her brow. 'Actually, they seemed genuinely interested. Not a hint of having woken up and found themselves on the wrong bus. They asked all sorts of questions—at least one of them did—and he gave me a generous tip at the end, which I've added to funds.'

'You shouldn't do that,' Helen reproved. 'Your tour commentaries are brilliant, and I only wish I could pay you. If someone else enjoys listening to you that much, then you should keep the money for yourself.'

'I love doing it,' Mrs Lowell told her. 'And it gets me out of the house while Jeff is writing his sermon,' she added conspiratorially. 'Apparently even a pin dropping can interrupt the creative flow. It's just as well Em's got a holiday job, because when she's around the house is in turmoil. And it's a good job, too, that she wasn't here to spot the coach party star,' she went on thoughtfully. 'You must have noticed him yourself during tea, Helen. Very dishy, in an unconventional way, and totally

unmissable. What Em would describe as ''sex on legs''—but
not, I hope, in front of her father. He's still getting over the
navel-piercing episode.'

Helen stared at her, puzzled. 'I didn't notice anyone within
a hundred miles who'd answer to ''dishy''—especially with
the coach party. They all seemed well struck in years to me.'
She grinned. 'Maybe he stayed away from tea because he felt
eating scones and cream might damage his to-die-for image.
Perhaps I should order in some champagne and caviar instead.'

'Maybe you should.' Mrs Lowell sighed. 'But what a shame
you missed him. And he had this marvellous accent, too—
French, I think.'

Helen nearly dropped the cash box she'd just been handed.
She said sharply, 'French? Are you sure?'

'Pretty much.' The Vicar's wife nodded. 'Is something
wrong, dear?'

'No—oh, no,' Helen denied hurriedly. 'It's just that we don't
get many foreign tourists, apart from the odd American. It
seems—strange, that's all.'

But that wasn't all, and she knew it. In fact it probably
wasn't the half of it, she thought as they walked back to the
house.

She always enjoyed this time after the house had closed,
when they gathered in the kitchen to count the takings over a
fresh pot of tea and the leftover cakes. And today she should
have been jubilant. Instead she found herself remembering that
sudden conviction that unseen eyes had been upon her by the
lake, and it made her feel restive and uneasy—as well as seriously relieved that she hadn't yielded to her impulse by stripping off and diving in.

Of course there were plenty of French tourists in England,
and their visitor might well turn out to be a complete stranger,
but Helen felt that her encounter with Marc Delaroche in the
Martinique had used up her coincidence quota for the foresee-
able future.

It was him, she thought. It had to be…

As soon as Mrs Lowell had gone Helen dashed round to the

Great Hall and looked in the visitors' book, displayed on an impressive refectory table in the middle of the chamber.

She didn't have to search too hard. The signature 'Marc Delaroche' was the day's last entry, slashed arrogantly across the foot of the page.

She straightened, breathing hard as if she'd been running. He might have arrived unannounced, but his visit was clearly no secret. He wanted her to know about it.

She simply wished she'd known earlier. But there was no need to get paranoid about it, she reminded herself. He'd been here, seen Monteagle on a better than normal working day, and now he'd gone—without subjecting her to any kind of confrontation. So maybe he'd finally accepted that she wanted no personal connection between them, and from now on any encounters they might have would be conducted on strictly formal business lines.

And the fact they'd been so busy today, and their visitors had clearly enjoyed themselves, might even stand her in good stead when the time came for decisions to be made.

At any rate, that was how she intended to see the whole incident, she decided with a determined nod, then closed the book and went back to her own part of the house, locking up behind her.

Helen awoke early the next morning, aware that she hadn't slept as well as she should have done. She sometimes wished she could simply turn over and go back to sleep, letting worries and responsibilities slide into oblivion. But that simply wasn't possible. There was always too much to do.

Anyway, as soon as the faint mist cleared it was going to be another glorious day, she thought, pushing aside the bedcover and swinging her feet to the floor. And, as such days didn't come around that often, she didn't really want to miss a moment of it.

She decided she'd spend the day in the garden, helping George to keep the ever-encroaching weeds at bay. But first she'd cycle down to the village and get a paper. After all, they might finish the crossword, earn some money that way.

George was waiting for her as she rode back up the drive.
'All right, slave driver,' she called to him. 'Can't I even have
a cup of coffee before you get after me?'

'I'll put your bike away, Miss Helen.' George came forward
as she dismounted. 'Daisy came down just now to say you've
a visitor waiting. Best not to keep him, she thought.'

Helen was suddenly conscious of an odd throbbing, and realised it was the thud of her own pulses. She ran the tip of her
tongue round her dry mouth.

'Did Daisy say—who it was?' she asked huskily.

He shook his head. 'Just that it was someone for you, miss.'

She knew, of course, who it would be. Who it had to be,
she thought, her lips tightening in dismay.

Her immediate impulse was to send George with a message
that she hadn't returned yet and he didn't know when to expect
her. But that wouldn't do. For one thing it would simply alarm
Daisy and send her into search-party mode. For another it
would tell her visitor that she was scared to face him, and give
him an advantage she was reluctant to concede.

Surprised, cool, but civil, she decided. That was the route to
take.

Of course there was always an outside chance that it could
be Nigel, returned early from Sussex for some reason—because
he was missing her, perhaps. But she couldn't really make herself believe it.

In a perverse way she hoped it wasn't Nigel, because she
knew what she looked like in old jeans, with a polo shirt sticking damply to her body and her hair bundled into an untidy
knot on top of her head and secured by a silver clip, and knew
that he disliked seeing her like that.

But, no matter who was waiting for her, she owed it to herself and no one else to make herself slightly more presentable,
even if it was only a matter of washing her face and hands and
tidying her hair.

She supposed reluctantly that she'd better sneak in through
the kitchen and go up the back stairs to her room.

But he'd forestalled her—the intruder—because he was already there in the kitchen, sitting at the table and tucking into

a bacon sandwich with total relish while Daisy fussed round him, filling his cup with more coffee.

Helen halted abruptly. 'What are you doing here?' She heard the note of aggression in her voice and saw Daisy glance at her, her lips pursed.

Marc Delaroche got to his feet. In casual khaki pants and a short-sleeved black shirt, he looked less of a business tycoon and more of a tough from the back streets of Marseilles.

'As you see, *mademoiselle*, I am having some breakfast.' He slanted a smile at Daisy. 'Your housekeeper is an angel who has taken pity on me.'

Helen forced herself to amend her tone slightly. 'I meant surely you saw everything you needed to yesterday, so why are you still around?' She pushed a dusty strand of hair back from her face. 'After all, a village is hardly your kind of place.'

'I still had some unfinished business here,' he said softly. 'So I decided to spend the night at the Monteagle Arms.'

She raised her brows. 'They don't do breakfast?'

'Of course,' he said. 'But after the dinner they served last night I was not tempted to try the *petit dejeuner*.' He gestured at his plate. 'May I continue?'

'Coffee, Miss Helen?' Daisy placed another mug on the table and waited, coffeepot poised, her expression indicating that her employer had breached quite enough of the laws of hospitality already.

'Please.' Helen gave her a swift conciliatory smile, and subsided unwillingly on to the chair opposite him.

She was bitterly aware that she'd neglected to put on a bra that morning—a fact that would not be lost on her unwanted guest, she thought angrily, burning her mouth on an unwary gulp of coffee.

'You mentioned unfinished business?' she said after a pause. 'I presume it's something to do with the house?' She forced a smile. 'After all, why else would you be here?'

'Why indeed?' he agreed cordially.

'So...' Helen gestured awkwardly. 'If I can help...?'

'I was not able to see all the rooms in the house during the tour yesterday, because your charming guide told me they are the private living quarters of yourself and your staff.' Marc Delaroche paused. 'Perhaps you could show them to me presently?'

Helen put down her mug. 'Is that strictly necessary?'

'It is,' he said. 'Or I would not have asked. Your application to the committee covered the entire building, not merely selected sections, as I am sure you understand. And your accommodation includes rooms of historic importance—the library, I believe, and the Long Gallery, and also the State Bedroom.' He gave her an enquiring look. 'Is that where you sleep, perhaps?' He added gently, 'I hope you do not find the question indelicate.'

'I have never slept there,' Helen said coldly. 'It was last occupied by my grandfather, and I wasn't planning to make it available to the public.'

'Even though one of your kings used it for a romantic rendezvous? Charles the First, I think?'

'Charles the Second,' Helen corrected. 'He's supposed to have come here to seduce the daughter of the house, who'd fled from court to escape him.'

His brows lifted. 'And did he succeed in his quest?'

'I haven't the faintest idea,' Helen said shortly. 'And, anyway, it's just a legend. I don't believe a word of it even though I was named after her!'

'*Quel dommage,*' he murmured.

'Well, Sir Henry always said it was true,' Daisy interposed from the stove.

'My grandfather liked to tease people,' Helen said stonily. 'He said the room was haunted, too, if you remember.'

'And you thought if you slept there you might wake to find a ghost in your bed?' The dark eyes were dancing.

'Not at all,' Helen denied. 'I simply prefer my own room.'

'Until you are married, *hein*?' Marc Delaroche said carelessly. 'When you have a living man beside you at night, *ma belle*, there will be no room for ghosts.'

'Thank you,' Helen told him, biting her lip. 'You paint such a frank picture.'

He shrugged. 'Marriage is a frank relationship.' He paused.

'But, legend or not, the State Bedroom and its romantic associations should be available to your public. I hope you will allow me to be its first visitor.'

Helen finished her coffee. 'Just as you wish, *monsieur*. Would you like to begin now?'

'*Pourquoi pas?*' he said softly. 'Why not?'

Oh, Helen thought wearily as she led the way to the kitchen door, I can think of so many reasons why not. And having to be alone with you, Monsieur Delaroche, heads the list every time.

And, heaven help me, I'm not even sure whether it's you I don't trust—or myself.

CHAPTER THREE

HELEN was still recovering from that unwelcome piece of self-revelation when they entered the library together. She pushed her hands into the pockets of her jeans, trying to compose herself for the inevitable inquisition, but at first there was only silence as Marc Delaroche stood looking round with a frown at the empty oak shelves that still lined the walls.

'It was a valuable collection?' he asked at last.

'Yes—very.' She hesitated. 'My grandfather was forced to sell it in the eighties, along with a number of pictures. It almost broke his heart, but it gave Monteagle a reprieve.'

He shook his head slightly, his gaze travelling over the motley collection of shabby furniture, the peeling paintwork, and the ancient velvet curtains hanging limply at the windows. 'And this is where you spend your leisure time?'

'Yes, what there is of it,' she returned. 'There's always some job needing to be done in a place like this.'

'You do not find it—*triste*? A little gloomy.'

'In winter it's quite cosy,' she retorted defensively. 'There's plenty of wood on the estate, so I have an open fire, and I burn candles most of the time.'

'Certainly a kinder light than a midsummer sun,' he commented drily. 'Shall we continue?'

She supposed they must. The truth was she felt totally unnerved by her physical consciousness of his presence beside her. Although he was deliberately keeping his distance, she realised, and standing back to allow her to precede him through doorways, and up the Great Staircase to the Long Gallery. But it made no difference. The panelled walls still seemed to press in upon them, forcing them closer together. An illusion, she knew, but no less disturbing for that.

She thought, I should have made some excuse—asked Daisy to show him round.

Aloud, she said, 'This is where the family used to gather, and where the ladies of the house took exercise in bad weather.'

'But not, of course, with holes in the floorboards,' he said.

She bit her lip. 'No. The whole floor needs replacing, including the joists.'

He was pausing to look at the portraits which still hung on the walls. 'These are members of your family? Ancestors?'

She pulled a face. 'Mostly the ugly ones that my grandfather thought no one would buy.'

Marc Delaroche slanted an amused look at her, then scanned the portraits again. 'Yet I would say it is the quality of the painting that is at fault.'

She shrugged, surprised at his perception. 'No, they're not very good. But I guess you didn't pay the fees of someone like Joshua Reynolds to paint younger sons and maiden aunts.'

'And so the sons went off, *sans doute*, to fight my countrymen in some war,' he commented, his mouth twisting. 'While the aunts had only to remain maiden. My sympathies are with them, I think.' He paused. 'Is there no portrait of the beauty so desired by King Charles?'

'Yes,' she admitted reluctantly. 'My grandfather wouldn't part with it. It's in the State Bedroom.'

'I cannot wait,' he murmured. *En avant, ma belle.*

'Do you mind not calling me that?' Helen threw over her shoulder as they set off again. 'What would you say if I greeted you with, Hey, good-looking?'

'I should advise you to consult an eye specialist,' he said drily. 'Tell me something, *mademoiselle*. Why do you object when a man indicates he finds you attractive?'

'I don't,' she said shortly. 'When it's the right man.'

'And I am by definition the wrong one?' He sounded amused.

'Do you really need to ask? You know already that I'm engaged to be married.'

'Of course,' he said. 'But where is your fiancé?'

'He couldn't come down this weekend.' Helen halted, chin
lifted in challenge. 'Not that it's any concern of yours.'

'This weekend?' he said musingly. 'And how many week-
ends before that? It is a matter of comment in the village, you
understand.'

'The public bar of the Monteagle Arms anyway,' Helen said
tersely. 'You really shouldn't listen to idle gossip, *monsieur*.'

'But I learned a great deal,' Marc Delaroche said gently.
'And not merely about your missing lover. They spoke too
about your fight to keep this house. Opinion is divided as to
whether you are brave or a fool, but none of them thought you
could win.'

'How kind of them,' she said between her teeth. 'That must
have done my cause a lot of good.' She paused. 'Did they know
who you were—and why you were here?'

'I said nothing. I only listened.' He shrugged. 'They spoke
of your grandfather with affection, but not of your parents. And
you do not mention them either. I find that strange.'

Helen bit her lip. 'I hardly knew them. They left Britain
when I was still quite small, and my grandfather brought me
up with the help of various nannies. That's why we were so
close.'

Marc Delaroche frowned swiftly. 'My father's work took
him abroad also, but I travelled with him always. He would
never have considered anything else.'

'My father didn't work—in the accepted sense.' Helen
looked past him, staring into space. 'He'd been brought up to
run Monteagle and the estate, but after the financial disasters
we'd suffered that no longer seemed an option. Also, he knew
he would never have a son to inherit what remained. My
mother, whom he adored, was very ill when I was born, and
needed an immediate operation. The name was going to die
out.'

'He had a daughter. Did he not consider that?'

Helen's smile was swift and taut. 'I never had the chance to
ask him. There's always been a strong gambling streak in our
family—fortunes won and lost down the centuries—and my
father was a brilliant poker player. He had a load of friends

among the rich and famous, so he travelled the world with my mother, staying in other people's houses and making a living from cards and backgammon.' Her mouth twisted wryly. 'At times he even earned enough to send money home.'

'But then his luck ran out?' Marc Delaroche asked quietly.

She nodded, and began to walk along the corridor again. 'They were in the Caribbean, flying between islands in a private plane with friends. There was some problem, and the aircraft crashed into the sea, killing everyone on board. My grandfather was devastated. Up to then he'd always believed we would recoup our losses somehow, and carry out the restoration work he'd always planned. That we'd be reunited as a family, too. But after the crash the fight seemed to go out of him. He became—resigned. Instead of winning, he talked about survival.'

She stared ahead of her, jaw set. 'But Monteagle is mine now, and I want more than that.'

'Has it hurt you to tell me these things?' His voice was oddly gentle.

'It's all part of Monteagle's history.' She hunched a shoulder. 'So you probably have a right to ask. But that's as far as the personal details go,' she added, giving him a cool look. 'You're here on business, and I feel we should conduct ourselves in a businesslike manner.'

Oh, God, she groaned inwardly. Just listen to yourself. Miss Prim of the Year, or what?

'Ah,' he said. 'And therefore all matters of gender should be rigorously excluded?' His grin was cynical. 'How do you do that, I wonder?'

She bit her lip. 'That is your problem, *monsieur*. Not mine.'

She reached the imposing double doors at the end of the corridor and flung them open. 'And here, as you requested, is the State Bedroom.'

The curtains were half drawn over the long windows, and she walked across and opened them, admitting a broad shaft of dust-filled sunshine.

It was a big room, the walls hung with faded brocade wallpaper. It was dominated by the huge four-poster bed, which

had been stripped to its mattress, although the heavily embroidered satin canopy and curtains were still in place.

'As you see,' she added woodenly, 'it has not been in use
since my grandfather died.' She pointed to a door. 'That leads
to a dressing room, which he always planned to convert to a
bathroom.'

Her companion gave it a cursory glance. 'It is hardly big
enough. One would need to include the room next door as
well.'

'Just for a bath? Why?'

He grinned lazily at her. 'A leading question, *ma mie*. Do
you really wish me to enlighten you.'

'No,' she said. 'Thank you.'

Marc Delaroche took a longer look around him, then walked
over to the fireplace and studied the picture hung above it. The
girl in it looked steadily, even a little shyly back at him, a
nimbus of warm-toned ringlets surrounding her face. She was
wearing pale yellow satin, cut decorously for the fashion of the
time. There was a string of pearls round her throat, and she
carried a golden rose in one hand.

He whistled softly. 'I wonder how long she fought before
she surrendered to your king?' he said, half to himself.

'You think she did surrender?'

'Eventually. As all women must,' he returned, ignoring her
small outraged gasp. 'Besides, there is no question. You have
only to look at her mouth.' He held out an imperative hand.
'*Viens.*'

In spite of herself, Helen found she was crossing the worn
carpet and standing at his side. 'What are you talking about?'

'She is trying hard to be the virtuous lady, but her lips are
parted and the lower one is full, as if swollen from the kiss she
longs for.'

'I think you have a vivid imagination, *monsieur*,' Helen retorted, her voice slightly strained.

'And I think that you also, *mademoiselle*, are trying much
too hard.' His voice sank almost to a whisper.

Before she could guess his intention and move away, out of
range, Marc Delaroche lifted a hand and put his finger to her

own mouth, tracing its curve in one swift breathless movement, then allowing his fingertip delicately to penetrate her lips and touch the moist inner heat.

In some strange way it would have been less intimate—less shocking—if he'd actually kissed her.

She gasped and stepped backwards, the blaze in her eyes meeting the mockery in his. Her words became chips of ice. 'How dare you—touch me?'

'A conventional response,' he said. 'I am disappointed.'

'You're going to have more than disappointment to deal with, Monsieur Delaroche. You'll live to regret this, believe me.' She drew a deep breath. 'Because I, too, shall be making a report to your committee, informing them how you've abused their trust while you've been here, conducting enquiries on their behalf. And I hope they fire you—no matter how much money you have,' she added vindictively.

'I am desolate to tell you this, but you are in error, *ma belle*,' he drawled. 'The committee is not concerned with my visit. It was my decision alone to come here.'

She looked at him, stunned. 'But—you've asked all these questions...'

He shrugged. 'I was curious. I wished to see this house that means so much to you.'

The breath caught suddenly, painfully in her throat. She turned and marched to the door, and held it open. 'And now the tour is over. So please leave. Now.'

'But that was not all.' He made no attempt to move. 'I came most of all because I wanted to see you again. And ask you something.'

'Ask it,' Helen said curtly. 'Then get out.'

He said softly, 'Will you sleep with me tonight?'

Helen was rigid, staring at him with widening eyes. When she could speak, she said hoarsely, 'I think you must have taken leave of your senses.'

'Not yet,' he drawled. His eyes went over her body in lingering, sensuous assessment. 'For that I shall have to wait a little, I think.'

She pressed her hands to the sudden flare of hot blood in her face.

'How dare you speak to me like this?' she whispered jerkily. 'Insult me in this way?'

'Where is the insult? I am telling you that I desire you, and have done since the first moment I saw you. And please do not insult me by pretending you did not know,' he added silkily, 'because I did not hide it.'

It seemed altogether wiser to ignore that. Helen struggled to control her breathing. 'You—you seem to have forgotten that I'm about to marry another man.'

'He is the one who has forgotten, *ma belle*,' he said, a touch of grimness in his voice.

'And you imagined that because he's not here I would turn to you for—consolation?' Her voice rose. 'Oh, God—how dare you? What do you take me for? I love Nigel, and I intend to belong to him and no one else. And I'll wait for him for ever if necessary. Not that someone like you could ever understand that,' she added, her voice ringing with contempt.

There was an odd silence as he studied her, eyes narrowed. Then, 'You are wrong, *ma mie*,' he said softly. *'Parce que, enfin, je comprends tout.'* He gave a brief, harsh sigh. 'I see I shall have to be patient with you, Hélène, but my ultimate reward will make it worthwhile.'

'Damn you,' she said violently. 'Can't you see I'd die rather than let you touch me again?'

He reached her almost before she had finished speaking, and pulled her against him, crushing the breath from her as his lips descended on hers.

Nothing in her life had prepared her for the heated relentlessness of his kiss, and he took all the time he needed, exploring deeply, draining every drop of sweetness from her startled mouth.

Tiny fires were dancing in the dark eyes when, at last, he released her.

'You see,' he told her ironically, 'you still live. So learn from this, and do not issue ridiculous challenges that you cannot hope to win.' He took her hand and raised it to his mouth, palm uppermost, and she cried out in shock as his teeth grazed the soft mound beneath her thumb.

'*Au revoir, ma belle,*' he said softly. 'And remember this— on my next visit I shall expect to spend the night.'

And he left her standing there, mute and shaken as she stared after him, her tingling hand pressed to her startled, throbbing mouth.

A lot of those weeds you're pulling out are plants, Miss Helen,' George told her reproachfully.

Helen jumped guiltily, looking at the wilted greenery in her trug. 'Oh, Lord,' she said dismally. 'I'm sorry.'

She'd hoped that some intensive gardening would calm her down and restore her equilibrium, but it wasn't working out like that.

The thought of Marc Delaroche was interfering with her concentration at every level, and this infuriated her.

She had tried to call Nigel and beg him to come down, even if it was only for a couple of hours, so she could talk to him. But his mobile phone was permanently switched off, it seemed.

And even if she had managed to contact him, what could she have said? That she needed him to hold her and kiss her and take away the taste of another man's mouth?

The only other man, in fact, who had ever kissed her in passion.

Her mouth still seemed swollen and faintly tingling from the encounter, but maybe she was just being paranoid. Someone had made a pass at her, that was all. The sort of thing that she should have been able to take in her stride if she'd possessed an ounce of sophistication. She could even have laughed about it, telling Nigel, You'd better stake your claim, darling, because I'm being seriously fancied by someone else.

And he would have laughed too, because he knew she'd never looked at anyone but him since she was thirteen, and that they belonged together.

Anyway, her best plan would be to put the whole thing out of her mind. Marc Delaroche had simply been amusing himself, she thought, and he probably had his next target already lined up. Quite apart from his admittedly diabolical attraction, he was rich enough to ensure that he didn't get many refusals. And he wouldn't waste time repining over any of the few women who resisted him. Or risk another rejection by returning.

He'd called her *'ma belle'*, but that had to be just a seduction ploy, because she wasn't beautiful at all. Moderately attractive was the best she could honestly claim, and he knew it. He'd probably thought she would fall into his arms through sheer gratitude, she told herself, viciously slicing her trowel through a dandelion root.

All the same, she wished desperately that he hadn't sought her out and forced this confrontation on her.

She might not like him, and she certainly didn't trust him, but she could have done with him on her side when the committee came to make their decision.

No chance of that now, of course. And she still couldn't understand what had possessed him. Yes, she'd been aware of him too, she admitted defensively, but only because she'd had no choice. During the interview he'd hardly taken his eyes off her. But she certainly hadn't offered him any encouragement to—pursue her like this. Quite the opposite, in fact.

At the same time she felt oddly depressed. She absolutely didn't want him as a lover. She probably wouldn't choose him as a friend, but she surely didn't need him as an enemy either, she thought, and sighed without quite knowing why.

The sun went down that evening behind a bank of cloud, and the following day brought grey skies and drizzle and the temperature dropping like a stone.

Outside work had to be halted, and if the miserable conditions persisted to the weekend, the tourists would stay away too, Helen fretted.

She caught up on the household accounts—a depressing task at the best of times—helped Daisy bake for the freezer, and waited feverishly for the mail van to call each day. The committee chairman had said she would hear before the end of the month, and that was fast approaching. All she could hope was that no news might be good news.

Thankfully, Marc Delaroche had made no attempt to contact her again. Maybe he'd decided to cut his losses and retire from the fray after all. But the thought of him still made her uneasy, and her attempts to blot him from her memory did not appear to be working too well.

It would have made things so much easier if she'd been able to talk to Nigel, she acknowledged unhappily. But there'd been no reply from his flat after the weekend, so she'd gritted her teeth and made the unpopular move of phoning him at work— only to be told that he was working in Luxembourg all week. And when she'd asked for the name of his hotel, she'd been told briskly that the bank did not give out that sort of information.

Back to square one, she realised without pleasure. Unless he called her instead, of course, and how likely was that?

She stopped herself right there. She was being critical, which was only one step removed from disloyal. Especially when she knew from past experience that these trips were often landed on him at ridiculously short notice. And he was bound to be home at the weekend, she told herself, because this time it was his mother's birthday.

Helen didn't know what kind of celebration was being planned, but she'd managed to find a card with a Persian cat on it that was the double of the bad-tempered specimen occupying its own special chair in Mrs Hartley's drawing room. She'd signed it 'Best wishes' rather than 'Love from', in tacit acknowledgement that her relationship with Nigel's mother had always been tricky. That was one of the reasons they'd delayed making their engagement official.

'She'll be fine,' Nigel had said. 'She just needs a bit of time to get used to the idea. And to you.'

But she's known me since I was thirteen, Helen had thought, troubled. And even then I don't think I was ever on her A-list.

Thought it—but hadn't said it.

Still, Mrs Hartley's sensibilities couldn't be allowed to intrude any longer—or any further. Helen suspected she was the kind of mother, anyway, who believed no girl would ever be good enough for her only son. Nothing useful would be achieved by putting off the announcement any longer.

Because, whether the committee's decision was for or against the restoration of Monteagle, she was going to need Nigel's love and support as never before. And surely, in spite of the demands of his career, he would understand that and be there for her—wouldn't he?

It irked her to realise that Marc Delaroche, however despicable his motives, had actually taken more interest in the house than Nigel had ever shown. And he was right about the State Bedroom, too. Her grandfather wouldn't have wanted it left untouched, like some empty shrine.

Instead, it should be top of her refurbishment list and opened to the public. She might find the Charles the Second legend distasteful, but a lot of people would think it a romantic story, and let their imaginations free on the use that giant four-poster had been put to during the King's visit.

She went up there with a notebook and pen and took a clear-eyed look round. The ornamental plaster on the ceiling was in urgent need of restoration in places, and there were timbered walls waiting to be exposed underneath layers of peeling wallpaper. The ancient Turkish carpet was past praying for, but it was concealing wooden floorboards that the original surveyor's report had declared free of woodworm or dry rot, and she could only hope that was still the case.

The silk bed hangings and window curtains were frankly disintegrating, and couldn't be saved, but their heavy embroidery was intact, and still beautiful.

Helen recalled that Mrs Stevens at the village post office, who was a skilled needlewoman, had told her months ago that if the elaborate patterns were cut out carefully they could be transferred to new fabric. She'd suggested, too, that the embroidery group at the Women's Institute, which she chaired, might take it on as a project.

First catch your fabric, Helen thought, doing some rueful calculations. But at least she knew now what her first priority should be, even though it was galling that she'd been alerted to it by Marc Delaroche.

But if I get the money from the committee I might even feel marginally grateful to him, she thought. Maybe.

She was sitting at the kitchen table on Friday evening, going over some of the estimates her grandfather had obtained and trying to work out the inevitable percentage increases for the intervening period, when Lottie arrived with the new batch of guidebooks.

'Hey, there.' She gave Helen a quizzical glance. 'Got any good news for me?'

'Not yet.' Helen gave a sigh. 'And I was so sure I'd hear this week.'

'Actually,' Lottie said, 'I was thinking of something more personal than the grant application.' She looked around. 'All on your own?' she enquired, with clear disappointment.

'Not any more.' Helen pushed her papers aside and got up to fill the kettle. 'Who were you expecting?'

'I thought Nigel might be here and had my speedy exit all planned,' Lottie explained. 'So—where is he?'

Helen shrugged as she got down the coffee jar. 'Arriving tomorrow, I guess. I haven't heard yet.'

Lottie frowned. 'But his car was in the drive at his parents' place earlier. That's when I put two and two together about the party.'

Helen stared at her. 'Lottie—what on earth are you talking about?'

'Oh, hell,' her friend groaned. 'Don't tell me I've put my foot in it. I was so sure...' She took a deep breath. 'It's just that Ma Hartley rang me this afternoon, all sweetness and light, wanting me to quote for catering a 'very special buffet' next month. She was so pleased and coy about it that I jumped to the obvious conclusion. I'm so sorry, love.'

Helen spooned coffee into two beakers with more than usual care. 'Nigel's probably planning it as a big surprise for me,' she said calmly, ignoring the sudden churning in her stomach. 'Although I can't really imagine his mother turning cartwheels over it. She must like me better than I thought,' she added, without any real conviction.

'I shouldn't have said anything,' Lottie said ruefully as she stirred her coffee.

'No, it's fine,' Helen assured her. 'And when I do see him I swear I'll be the world's most astonished person.'

That would be an easy promise to keep, she thought, when Lottie had gone. She was already bewildered and disturbed by his failure to contact her when he must know how she was longing to see him.

Well, she could do something about that at least, she thought, and she dialled the number of his parents' home.

She'd hoped Nigel himself would answer, but inevitably it was his mother.

'Oh, Helen,' she said, without pleasure. 'I'm afraid this isn't a terribly convenient moment. You see, we have guests, and we're in the middle of dinner.'

'I'm sorry,' Helen said. 'But I do need to speak to him.'

'But not this evening.' There was a steely note in Mrs Hartley's voice. She sighed impatiently. 'Oh, well. Perhaps if there's something particular, he could call you tomorrow?'

Oh, nothing special, thought Helen. Only the rest of my life.

'Thank you,' she said quietly. 'I look forward to hearing from him.'

But it wasn't true, she realised as she put down the phone. She had a feeling of dread, not anticipation. And once again Nigel's mother had succeeded in making her feel excluded— as if she had no place in their lives.

When she and Nigel finally managed to talk, Mrs Hartley's attitude was going to be one of the topics of conversation, she thought grimly.

When she awoke next morning, it was to intermittent sunshine and scudding clouds driven by a sharp breeze.

Unpredictable, she thought as she dressed. Rather like my life. But a good day for touring historic houses rather than going to the beach, so let's hope the queues start forming like they did last week.

Well, not quite, she amended hastily. At least this time Marc Delaroche would not be part of them.

She was on her way to the kitchen when she saw the post

van disappearing down the drive. At the door she paused, and drew a deep, calming breath before entering.

'Any phone calls for me?' she enquired, making her tone deliberately casual.

'Nothing so far,' Daisy told her, putting a fresh pot of tea on the table.

'What about mail?'

'A couple of bills,' Daisy said. She paused. 'And this.' She held out an imposing cream envelope embossed with the committee's logo.

Helen's stomach lurched frantically. She wiped her hand on her jeans and took the envelope, staring down at it. Reluctant, now that the moment had come, to learn its contents, slowly she pushed the blade of a table knife under the flap and slit it open.

The words 'We regret' danced in front of her eyes, making it almost unnecessary to read on. But she scanned them anyway—the brief polite lines that signified failure.

George had come into the kitchen and was standing beside his wife, both of them watching Helen anxiously.

She tried to smile—to shrug. 'No luck, I'm afraid. They try to help places that have suffered some kind of terrible devastation, like earthquake sites. It seems that rising damp, leaky roofs and dry rot aren't quite devastating enough.'

'Oh, Miss Helen, love.'

She sank her teeth into her lower lip at the compassion in Daisy's voice, forbidding herself to cry.

'Does this mean you'll have to sell to that Mr Newson?' George asked, troubled.

'No,' she said. 'I'm not going to do that. I'm never going to do that.' There was something else in the envelope, too. A note in the chairman's own hand, she discovered, wishing her well. 'Mr VanStratten and Monsieur Delaroche argued very persuasively on your behalf,' the note added, 'but eventually it had to be a majority decision.'

Her hand clenched round the paper, crushing it. That—lecherous hypocrite, speaking up for her? she thought incredulously. Dear God, that had to be the final blow.

Aloud, she said, 'There'll be something else I can do. Someone else I can turn to. I'll call Nigel. Ask for his advice.'

'He hasn't been so helpful up to now,' George muttered.

'But now the chips are down,' Helen said with more confidence than she actually felt. 'He'll find some way to rescue us.'

Rather than run the gauntlet of his mother's disapproval again, Helen rang Nigel's mobile number.

'Yes?' His voice sounded wary.

'Nigel?' she said. 'Darling, can you come round, please? I really need to see you.'

There was a silence, then he said, 'Look, Helen, this isn't a good time for me.'

'I'm sorry to hear that, but please believe that it's a far worse one for me,' she told him bluntly. 'Something's happened, and I need your advice.' She paused. 'Would you prefer me to come to you instead?'

'No,' he said hastily. 'No, don't do that. I'll be about half an hour, and I'll use the side gate into the garden. I'll meet you by the lake.'

'Bringing your cloak and dagger with you, no doubt,' Helen said acidly. 'But if that's what you want, then it's fine with me.'

She'd spoken bravely, but she rang off feeling sick and scared. Suddenly her entire life seemed to be falling in pieces, and she didn't know why, or how to deal with it.

Whatever, facing Nigel in working clothes wasn't a good idea. She dashed upstairs and took another quick shower, this time using the last of her favourite body lotion. From her scanty wardrobe she chose a straight skirt in honey-coloured linen, with a matching jersey top, long-sleeved and vee-necked.

She brushed her hair loose and applied a touch of pale rose to her mouth.

War paint, she thought ironically, as she took a last look in the mirror.

Nigel was already waiting when she arrived at the lakeside. The breeze across the water was ruffling his hair and he was pacing up and down impatiently.

'So there you are,' he greeted her peevishly. 'What the hell's the matter?'

'I think that should be my question.' She halted a few feet away, staring at him. 'You don't tell me you're coming down, and then you avoid me. Why?'

His eyes slid away uncomfortably. 'Look, Helen—I know I should have spoken before, but there's no easy way to say this.' He paused. 'You must know that things haven't been good between us for quite a while.'

'I've certainly realised we don't see as much of each other, but I thought it was pressure of work. That's what you told me, anyway.' She clenched her shaking hands and hid them in the folds of her skirt.

'And what about you?' he asked sharply. 'Always fussing about that decrepit ruin you live in—scratching round for the next few pennies. You've had a good offer for it. Why not wise up and get out while it's still standing?'

She gasped. 'How can you say that—when you know what it means to me?'

'Oh, I know all right,' he said bitterly. 'No one knows better. I discovered a long time ago I was always going to play second fiddle to that dump, and you took it for granted that I'd settle for that. No doubt that's what you want to talk about now. What's happened? Deathwatch beetle on the march again?'

'I do have a serious problem about the house, but that can wait,' she said steadily. 'What we obviously need to discuss is—us.'

'Helen, there is no 'us', and there hasn't been for a long time. But you refuse to see it, for some reason.'

Her nails dug painfully into the palms of her hands. 'Maybe because I'm in love with you.'

'Well, you've got a weird idea of what love's about,' Nigel commented sourly. 'Frankly, I'm sick and tired of this 'hands off till we're married' garbage. I've tried everything to get you into bed, but you've never wanted to know.'

She bit her lip. 'I—I realise that now, and I—I'm sorry.' She looked at him pleadingly. 'I thought you were prepared to wait too.'

'No,' he said brutally. 'Men only beg for so long, then they lose interest.' He shook his head. 'There's only ever going to be one passion in your life, Helen, and that's Monteagle. No guy stands a chance against a no-win obsession like that.'

She said carefully, 'You mean—you don't want me any more?'

He sighed. 'Let's be honest. It was a boy-girl thing at best, and it certainly didn't make it into the grown-up world. Although I hope we can stay friends,' he added hastily. 'Face it, you've never been interested in sex—or even curious. A couple of kisses have always been enough for you. But now I've met someone with a bit of warmth about her and we're getting married. I brought her down this weekend to meet my parents, so I really don't need you ringing up every five minutes.'

'I see.' Helen swallowed. 'You know, I had the strangest idea I was engaged to you myself.'

He shrugged. 'I know we discussed it,' he said awkwardly. 'But there was nothing definite. For one thing, I'd have had a hell of a fight on with my parents.'

'Oh, yes,' Helen said unevenly. 'I always knew they didn't like me.'

'It wasn't that,' he told her defensively. 'They felt we were wrong for each other, that's all. And they didn't want me tipping everything I earned down that money pit of yours, either.'

He paused. 'I have ambition, Helen, and I'm not ashamed of it. I want a wife who can help with my career—someone who likes entertaining and can provide the right ambience. Let's face it, you'd hate that kind of life.'

The wind was cold suddenly—turning her to ice.

She said quietly, 'And I haven't any money—to make up for my other deficiencies. Isn't that part of it?'

He gave her an irritated look. 'Money matters. Are you pretending it doesn't?'

'No,' she said. 'Particularly when I've just been turned down for my grant.'

'Well, what did you expect? Clearly they don't want to

throw good money after bad,' he said. 'That's not good business practice.'

She winced painfully. 'Nigel,' she said urgently, 'I—I'm trying to save the home I love. I thought you might be able to suggest something—someone who could help. Who might be prepared to invest in the estate…'

'This is a joke—right?' His tone was derisive. 'I suggest you look round for a rich husband—if you can find someone as frigid as you are yourself. And how likely is that?'

The pain was suddenly more than she could bear. She took a step towards him, lifting her hand, driven by a half-crazy need to wipe the sneer from his face.

Nigel retreated, throwing up an arm to ward her off, his smart brogues slipping suddenly in the mud created by the recent bad weather.

Helen saw his face change from alarm to fury as he overbalanced, teetering on the edge of the lake for a moment before he fell backwards into the water with a resounding splash.

He was on his feet instantly, dripping and crimson with rage. 'Bitch,' he shouted hoarsely, as Helen turned her back and began to walk, head bent, towards the house. 'Bitch.'

She was trembling violently, her breathing an agony, every nerve in her body striving to continue putting one foot in front of another so that she could reach sanctuary before she fell on her knees and howled her hurt and misery to the sky.

She was too blinded by his cruelty even to see that someone was standing in front of her until she collided with a hard male body and recoiled with a cry.

'Tais toi,' Marc Delaroche said quietly. 'Be calm.' His arm round her was like iron, holding her up. 'I have you safe. Now, walk with me to the house.'

And, too numb to resist, Helen could only obey.

CHAPTER FOUR

HE'D said 'walk', but Helen was dazedly aware she was being half-led, half-carried into the house. Warmth surrounded her, and a feeling of safety as its walls closed round her.

She heard Daisy's shocked exclamation, and his quiet reply.

When she could think clearly again she found she was sitting on the sofa in the library, with a mug of strong, hot tea clasped in her icy hands.

Marc Delaroche was standing by the fireplace, an elbow resting on the mantelshelf, looking contemplatively into the blue flames of the small twig fire that she supposed he'd kindled in the grate.

He was wearing jeans and a matching blue shirt, its top buttons undone and the sleeves rolled back, revealing the shadowing of dark hair on his chest and forearms.

He turned his head slowly and met her accusing gaze.

She said huskily, 'You knew, didn't you? I mean about Nigel. Somehow, you knew.'

There was a pause, then reluctantly he nodded. 'I regret, but, yes.'

'And is that why you're here—to gloat?' She took a gulp of the scalding brew in her beaker.

'No,' he said. 'Why should I do that?'

'Who knows,' she said, 'why you do anything? Yet here you are—again.'

'Among other things, I came to warn you. But I was too late.'

'How can this be?' Helen said, half to herself. 'How can you have guessed that Nigel didn't love me when I was still in the dark about it?'

He shrugged. 'You were in the dark, *ma mie*, because you had closed your eyes to what was happening—perhaps deliberately. Also,' he added, 'I had an advantage, because you were not sitting in the window of the Martinique that day when your supposed fiancé arrived. He came by taxi, not alone, and his companion was most reluctant to let him go. That was how I came to notice him—because their leavetaking was quite a spectacle. Each time he tried to say *au revoir* she wound herself round him the more. She behaved with *une ardeur etonnante*,' he added with a faint whistle. 'I almost envied him.'

He paused. 'And then I watched him join you at your table, and realised who he must be, and it was no longer so amusing.'

'So you took pity on me,' Helen said bitterly.

'Perhaps,' he said. 'But for a moment only. Because I could see that you were strong and would survive your disappointment.'

'Disappointment?' she echoed in angry incredulity. 'My God, I've just been dumped by the man I've loved all my life. The only man I'll ever love. And you talk about it as if it were a minor inconvenience.'

She paused. 'Why didn't you tell me there and then?'

'Because I already knew that the committee's decision would go against you,' he said. 'I did not wish to overburden you with bad news.'

'So instead you let me stew in my fool's paradise,' she said. 'Thank you so much.'

'Shall we agree it was a no-win situation for us both?' he suggested.

'I don't believe this,' Helen said raggedly. 'My life's in ruins, I'm falling apart—and you sound so bloody casual.'

She gave him an inimical look. 'And, for the record, there is no "both". There's myself alone, and no one else.'

'Are you so sure of that?'

'What are you saying? That he'll dump this new lady too, and come back to me?' She shook her head. 'I don't think so. And do you know why that is, Monsieur Delaroche? It's because I lack the necessary social skills. Also, I'm frigid—and she isn't,' she added, her voice cracking. Then stopped, horrified at what she'd let him see.

'He told you that?' Marc Delaroche raised his eyebrows. 'But how can he possibly know?'

She stared at him in silence, almost paralysed with shame as she interpreted what he'd just said to her. Oh God, she thought, he—he *knows* I'm still a virgin. And I wish I'd died before he told me so.

But you were the one who told *him*, said a small cold voice in her head. You let it slip the last time he was here. And *he* said he'd be patient. How could you have forgotten that?

She'd tried to block out every detail of their previous encounter, but that was something she should have remembered. Because it spelled danger.

'I understand now why you pushed him into the lake,' Marc added.

'I didn't push him,' Helen said icily. 'He slipped.'

'Quel dommage,' he murmured. 'And, no—he will certainly not come back,' he went on calmly. 'But for a reason far removed from the ones you have given.'

She said, 'Oh?' her voice wooden.

The dark eyes studied her. 'He did not tell you, *peut-être*, the identity of his new fiancée? Then I shall. Her name is Amanda Clayburn.'

'Clayburn?' Helen repeated, bewildered. 'You—you mean she's related to Sir Donald Clayburn, the chairman of the bank?'

'His only daughter.' His grin was cynical. 'Your Nigel is an ambitious man, *ma mie*. He has chosen money and the fast track to the boardroom.'

'No,' she said. 'He couldn't. He *wouldn't*. And, anyway, he doesn't need to do that. He has money of his own.'

'Which he prefers to keep, *sans doute*.' He bent and added another handful of twigs to the fire. 'But it is all true. I have a colleague with contacts at the bank, and he informs me their *affaire* has been an open secret for weeks. She is wild and spoiled, this Amanda, and her father, they say, is glad she is marrying before she disgraces him openly.'

'Obviously a marriage made in heaven.' The words cut at her, but she refused to wince. Instead, she threw back her head.

'Monteagle and Nigel—the two things I care most about in the world—I've lost them both.'

'I notice,' he said, 'you place the house before your fiancé.'

'Yes,' she said. 'Nigel said that too. He said that because of Monteagle I would never be capable of loving anyone properly. All in all, it was a pretty comprehensive condemnation. And do you know the worst of it, Monsieur Delaroche? You—you were here to watch it happening.' She almost choked on the words. 'You—of all the people in the world. You're like some terrible jinx—do you know that?—because each time you appear in my life, everything goes wrong.'

She punched her fist into the palm of her other hand. 'Well, you've had your fun, *monsieur*, if that's what you came for, so now you can go. I need to be on my own. Even you should be able to appreciate that,' she added burningly.

His own glance was cool. 'You have a strange idea of how I choose to amuse myself, *ma chère*,' he drawled. 'And, although I am desolate to grieve you further, I must tell you I have no intention of leaving yet. Because I came not just to warn you, but also to offer my help.'

'Oh, of course,' she said. 'You spoke up for me at the committee—you and your Dutch colleague. I—I suppose I should thank you.'

'If we had succeeded, perhaps,' he said. 'But as matters stand I do not expect you to torture yourself with an attempt to be grateful.'

'But why should you do that?' she asked. 'When you knew what the verdict would be? You don't look like someone who supports lost causes.'

He shrugged. 'Perhaps I felt you did not deserve to lose yet again.' He gave her a measured look. 'So—what do you plan to do now? Will you take advantage of Monsieur Newson's offer—if it still stands?'

'I'd rather burn the place to the ground.'

'The insurance company might find that suspicious,' he murmured.

'Probably—if we were insured,' Helen said shortly, and for the first time saw him look taken aback.

'You like to take risks,' he said.

'Sometimes I don't have a choice in the matter. I found my grandfather had let the premiums lapse.' She drank the rest of her tea and put down the mug. 'And now please leave. I've answered enough questions, and you have no further excuse to be here.'

'Except my own inclination,' he told her brusquely. 'And I ask again—what will you do next?'

'I shall open the house up for visitors, as I do every Saturday.' Her smile was swift and hard as she rose to her feet.

'I think no one would blame you if, for once, the house remained shut.'

'I'd blame myself,' she said. 'Because Monteagle needs every penny I can earn. And, anyway, I'd rather have something to do.' She paused. 'Please don't feel you have to take the tour again, or pay any more visits here,' she added pointedly. 'I'm sure you have places to go and people to see, so let's both of us get on with our lives. Shall we?'

But he ignored that. 'Is that truly how you see your future?' His brows lifted. 'Welcoming crowds of the curious and the bored *pour toujours*? Serving them tea?'

She met his gaze. 'Yes,' she said. 'If I have to. I told you— I'll do anything to save Monteagle.'

'Will you?' he asked softly. 'I wonder, *ma mie*. I very much wonder. For example, will you have dinner with me this evening?'

Her lips parted in sheer astonishment. She said unevenly, 'My God, you never give up, do you? Do you think I'm in any mood to listen to another of your insensitive—tasteless invitations? Can't you understand that I've just lost the man I love?'

'You are planning to starve to death as an act of revenge?' He had the gall to sound faintly amused.

'No,' Helen said stormily. 'But I'd rather die than have dinner with you.'

He was laughing openly now, to her fury. 'A fate worse than death, *ma belle*? I always thought that involved far more than simply sharing a meal.'

She marched to the door and held it open. 'Just get out of my house and don't come back.'

'Your house,' Marc said softly, unmoved and unmoving. 'And how much longer will you be able to call it that, unless you find financial support—and quickly? You said you would do anything to save Monteagle. So, can you afford to reject my offer of assistance unheard?'

There was silence in the room, broken only by the crackle of the burning wood and the swift flurry of her own ragged breathing.

She felt like a small animal, caught in the headlights of an approaching juggernaut. Only she'd been trapped, instead, by her own words, she realised bitterly.

She said thickly, 'What—kind of help?'

'We will not discuss that now. Your mood is hardly—receptive. Also,' he added silkily, 'you have work to do. We will speak again later.'

He walked past her and she shrank backwards, flattening herself against the thick wooden door as she remembered, only too well, his last leavetaking. The hardness of his body against hers. The touch—the taste of his mouth.

He favoured her with a brief, sardonic smile. *À tout à l'heure!* he told her quietly, and then he was gone.

Did you take an order from the people in the far corner, Miss Helen?' asked Daisy, entering the kitchen with a stacked tray of dirty dishes. 'Because they're playing up at having to wait.'

Helen, lost in thought at the sink, started guiltily. 'Oh, Lord,' she muttered. 'I forgot all about them. I'll serve them next,' she added hurriedly, collecting one of the larger teapots from the shelf.

'Your mind's not on it today, and no wonder. You should have gone for a nice lie-down in your room,' Daisy said severely. 'I'd have got George to do the waiting on.'

'I'm fine,' Helen said untruthfully. 'And I really prefer to be busy,' she added placatingly.

Daisy sniffed. 'There's busy and busy,' she said. 'You've just put cream in the sugar basin.'

Swearing under her breath, Helen relaid the tray and carried it out into the sunshine.

Once again she'd been astonished at the number of visitors, but they hadn't been as easy to handle as last week's selection.

'You don't see much for your money,' one man had complained.

'We're hoping to extend the tour to other rooms in the house quite soon,' Helen had explained, but he'd glared at her.

'Well, that's no good to me,' he'd said. 'I've already paid.'

And a large family party had demanded why there were no games machines for kiddies, or even a playground, and why they couldn't play football in an adjoining field.

'Because my tenant wouldn't like it,' Helen had said, in a tone that brooked no further argument.

It had been an afternoon of moans and niggles, she thought wearily, and from the look of strained tolerance she'd glimpsed on Marion Lowell's face at one point, she wasn't the only sufferer.

Altogether, this was the day from hell, she thought. And she still couldn't decide what to do about Marc Delaroche and his dinner invitation.

Instinct told her to refuse. Reason suggested that if Monteagle's welfare was involved she should at least give him a hearing. But not over dinner, she thought. That was too much like a date rather than a business meeting.

'And about time.' Helen was greeted truculently by a red-haired woman as she reached the corner table and set down the heavy tray. She and her glum-looking husband peered suspiciously at the plates of scones and cakes. 'Is this all we get? Aren't there are any sandwiches? Ham would do. We've got a growing lad here.'

Growing outwards as well as upwards, Helen noticed with disfavour, as the child in question dug a podgy finger into the bowl of cream.

She said quietly, 'I'm sorry, it's a standard tea. But everything is home-made.'

The little boy glared at her. 'Aren't there any crisps? And where's my drink?'

'He doesn't like tea,' his mother explained in a tone that invited congratulation. 'He wants orange squash.'

Helen repressed a sigh. 'I'll see what I can do.'

Back in the kitchen, she halved oranges from the fruit bowl, squeezed out their juice, and put it in a glass with a pinch of sugar and some ice cubes.

Improvisation, she told herself with mild triumph as she took the drink outside.

'What's that?' The boy stabbed an accusing finger at it. 'I want a real drink. That's got bits in it.'

'They're bits of orange—' Helen began.

'Yuck.' The child's face twisted into a grimace. 'I'm not drinking that.' And he picked up the glass and threw the contents at Helen, spattering her with the sticky juice.

She gasped and fell back, wiping her face with her hand, then felt hands grip her shoulders, putting her to one side.

'Go and get clean,' Marc directed quietly. 'I will deal with this.'

She hadn't even been aware of his approach. She wanted to tell him she could manage, but she wasn't sure it was true.

She turned away, walking quickly back to the house, stripping off her ruined apron as she went, her colour rising as she became aware of sympathetic smiles and murmurs from other customers.

She looked back over her shoulder and saw Marc talking to the husband. Noticed the other man rise uncomfortably to his feet, his face sullen, gesturing to his family to follow.

When she reached the kitchen she found Lottie waiting, her face grave and troubled. 'Honey,' she said, 'I'm so sorry.'

Helen bit her lip. 'I see you've heard the news.' She ran cold water into a bowl and put her stained apron to soak.

Lottie nodded unhappily. 'It's all round the village. I still can't quite believe it.'

'It's perfectly true.' Helen lifted her chin. 'Nigel is being splendidly conventional and marrying his boss's daughter. I haven't worked out yet whether he ever meant to tell me to my face, or if he hoped I'd simply—fade away and save him the trouble.'

'Bastard,' said Lottie, with some force. 'But it certainly explains the special buffet episode.' She snorted. 'Well, I've rung his poisonous mother and told her to find another caterer.'

Helen smiled wanly. 'It's a lovely thought,' she said. 'But it's also the kind of gesture you can't afford any more than I could.' She glanced round her. 'Where's Daisy?'

'She said she had something to do upstairs and that she'd ask Mrs Lowell to collect the tea money. She probably thought we'd want to talk in private.'

'I don't think I have much privacy left,' Helen said ruefully. 'Not if the whole village knows.' She paused. 'I also found out this morning that I'd been turned down for that grant.'

'Oh, no,' Lottie groaned. 'That's really evil timing.' She gave Helen a compassionate look. 'Well—they say bad luck comes in threes, so let's hope your final misfortune is a minor one.'

Helen bit her lip as she refilled the kettle and set it to boil. 'No such luck, I'm afraid. It's happened—and it's another disaster.'

Lottie whistled. 'Tell me something—is there some gruesome family curse hanging over the Fraynes that you've never thought to mention?'

'If only.' Helen grinned faintly. 'Good business, a family curse. I'd have given it a whole page in the guidebook.'

Lottie started to laugh, and then, as if some switch had been operated, the amusement was wiped from her face, to be replaced by astonishment bordering on awe.

Helen turned quickly and saw Marc in the doorway, completely at his ease, arms folded across his chest and one shoulder propped nonchalantly against the frame.

He said, '*Je suis désolè*. I am intruding.'

'No,' Lottie denied with something of a gulp, getting quickly to her feet. 'No, of course not. I'm Charlotte Davis—Lottie—a friend of Helen's from the village.'

He sent her a pleasant smile. '*Enchanté, mademoiselle*. And I am Marc Delaroche—*à votre service*.'

To her eternal credit, Lottie didn't allow herself even a flicker of recognition.

Helen swallowed. 'What—what did you say to those people just now?' she asked a little breathlessly.

'I suggested only that they might prefer the Monteagle Arms. They accepted my advice.' He walked across to the table and put down some money. 'They also paid,' he added laconically. He paused. 'Tell me, *ma mie*, are many of your customers like that?'

'Not usually.' She went over to the stove and busied herself with the kettle. 'I'm just having a generally bad day, I think.' She hesitated. 'Would you like some coffee?' she offered unwillingly—as he instantly detected.

'*Merci.*' He slanted a faint grin at her. 'But I will leave you to talk in peace to your friend.' He added softly, 'I came only to say that I have reserved a table for eight o'clock at the Oxbow. I hope you will feel able to join me.'

He gave them both a slight bow and walked back into the sunshine, leaving a tingling silence behind him.

It was broken at last by Lottie. 'Wow,' she said reverently. 'Don't pretend even for a moment that he's your third disaster.'

'Oh, you're as bad as Mrs Lowell,' Helen said crossly, aware that her face had warmed. 'She was rhapsodising about him last week.'

'You mean this is his second visit?' Lottie's brows shot skywards. 'Better and better.' She eyed Helen. 'So, what are you going to wear tonight?'

'Nothing!'

Lottie grinned wickedly. 'Well, it would certainly save him time and effort,' she said. 'But a little obvious for a first date, don't you think?'

Helen's colour deepened hectically. 'I didn't mean that—as you well know,' she said, carrying the coffee back to the table. 'And it's not a date. In fact, I have no intention of having dinner with Monsieur Delaroche—tonight or any other time.'

'Nonsense,' Lottie said briskly. 'Of course you're going. Why not?'

Helen sank limply on to the nearest chair. 'You seem to have forgotten about Nigel.'

'Unfortunately, no,' said Lottie. 'But I'm working on it, and so should you.' She gave Helen's arm a quick squeeze. 'And what more could you ask than for a seriously attractive man to wine and dine you?'

'You really think that a meal at the Oxbow could console me in any way for Nigel?' Helen shook her head. 'Lottie—I'm really hurting. He's always been part of my life—and now he's gone.'

'Helen—be honest. You had a crush on him when you were thirteen and decided he was the man of your dreams. He went along with it for a while, but he's spent less and less time here for over a year now. Some love affair.'

'No,' Helen said, biting her lip. 'It never was. That's the trouble. I—I wanted to wait. So it wasn't an affair at all, in the real meaning of the word.'

'Oh,' said Lottie slowly. 'Well—that's one less thing to regret.'

'But I do regret it,' Helen told her miserably. She sighed. 'Oh, God, what a fool I've been. And I've lost him. So do you see now why I can't go out tonight? It would be unbearable.'

'Then stay here and brood,' Lottie told her robustly. 'And why not have "victim" tattooed across your forehead while you're about it?'

Helen gave her a bitter look. 'I didn't know you could be so heartless. How would you like to face people if you'd been dumped?'

'Darling, I'm trying to be practical.' Lottie drank some coffee. 'And I'd infinitely prefer to be out, apparently having a good time with another man, than nursing a broken heart on my own. Who knows? People might even think you dumped Nigel rather than the other way round. Think about it.' She paused. 'Anyway, why did you say it wasn't a date with Marc Delaroche?'

'Because it's more of a business meeting.' Helen still looked morose. 'He's got some plan for helping Monteagle now the grant's fallen through. Or he says he has.'

'All the more reason to go, then.'

'But I don't want to feel beholden to him,' Helen said passionately. 'I—I don't like him. And I don't know what you all see in him,' she added defiantly.

'Helen—' Lottie's tone was patient '—he's incredibly rich and fabulously sexy. You don't think that you're being a mite picky?'

Helen said in a low voice, 'It's not just that. I—I think I'm frightened of him.' Her laugh cracked in the middle. 'Isn't that ridiculous?'

Lottie's expression was very gentle. 'A little, maybe. But there's not much he can do in a crowded restaurant.' She frowned. 'I wonder how the hell he managed to get a table at the Oxbow, it being Saturday and all.'

Helen shrugged listlessly. 'He's someone who likes to have his own way. I don't suppose he gets many refusals.'

Lottie gave her a wry grin. 'Then meeting you might be good for his soul.' She paused, then added thoughtfully, 'Or he might even be good for yours.'

She picked up her beaker and rose. 'Now, let's have a quick scan through your wardrobe and see what might be suitable for the best restaurant in miles.'

This is still such a bad idea, Helen thought a few hours later as she looked at herself in the mirror.

The dress she was wearing was in a silky fabric the dark green of a rose leaf, and made in a wrap-around style, with a sash that passed twice round her slender waist and fastened at the side in a bow.

It made her skin look exotically pale, and her newly washed hair glint with gold and bronze lights.

Lottie had spotted it at once, of course. 'So, what's this?' she'd asked, taking it from the rail. 'Clearly never worn, because it's still got the price tag. How long have you had it?'

'Not that long.' Helen moved a shoulder restively, her voice slightly husky. 'I—I bought it for my engagement party.' She forced a smile. 'Counting my chickens again. Stupid of me, wasn't it?'

'Not at all.' Lottie's tone was comforting. 'And you can put it to good use tonight instead,' she added, spreading it across Helen's bed.

'No,' Helen said sharply. 'I got it for Nigel. I won't wear it for anyone else. I can't.'

'What will you do with it, then? Wrap it in lavender and shed tears over it, like a latter-day Miss Havisham?' Lottie gave her a swift hug. 'Babe, you can't waste the only decent thing you've got—especially when you need to make a good impression.'

'And why should I want to do that?' Helen lifted her chin.

'Monteagle, of course,' Lottie told her with a cat-like smile. 'Did you get shoes as well?'

'Green sandals.' Helen pointed reluctantly. 'They're in that box.'

'You'll have to paint your toenails too,' Lottie mused. 'I'd better pop home and get my manicure stuff, because I bet you haven't any. And you'll need a wrap. I'll lend you the pashmina Simon sent me. But don't spill vintage champagne all over it.'

The promised wrap was now waiting on the bed, together with the small kid bag that matched the sandals.

I was so sure, Helen thought, her throat muscles tightening. So secure in my dreams of the future. And so blind…

And now she had to work towards a totally different kind of future.

She'd had plenty of time to think after Lottie had completed her ministrations and departed.

Lying back in a scented bath, she'd reviewed her situation and come up with a plan. She could not afford to pay for the restoration of the entire house, of course, but perhaps Marc Delaroche might help her raise sufficient capital to refurbish the bedrooms at least, so that she and Daisy could offer bed and breakfast accommodation. Possibly with a few extra refinements.

Spend the night in the haunted bedroom! she'd thought, with self-derision. See the ghost of the first Helen Frayne, if not the second.

I could even rattle a few chains outside the door.

Joking apart, the scheme had a lot to recommend it, she told herself. It could supply her with just the regular income she needed.

And if she could prove herself, even in a small way, the conventional banking system might be more ready to back her.

But first she had to persuade Marc that it was a workable plan, and an alternative to whatever assistance he was prepared to give.

And therefore it was—just—worth making an effort with her appearance.

Only now the moment had come. Daisy had tapped on her door to say that he was waiting downstairs, causing all her concerns and doubts to come rushing back.

Because she was taking a hell of a risk. She'd said it herself—Marc Delaroche was a man who liked his own way—so what on earth made her think she could manipulate him into doing what she wanted?

Besides, she already knew he had his own agenda. *On my next visit I shall expect to spend the night.*

She'd tried to block that out of her mind—as with so much else that had passed between them.

But now the words were ringing loud and clear in her head, especially as she'd spent some considerable time getting herself dressed and beautified for him—like some harem girl being prepared for the Sultan's bed, she thought, and grimaced at the analogy.

Her skin was smooth and scented. Her eyes looked twice their normal size, shaded, with darkened lashes, and the colour of her dress had turned them from hazel to green. Her mouth glowed with soft coral, as did the tips of her hands and feet.

She picked up her wrap and bag, and went along the Gallery to the broad wooden staircase.

Marc was below her, in the entrance hall, pacing restlessly, but as he looked up at her he checked suddenly, his entire attention arrested and fixed on her, his eyes widening and his mouth suddenly taut.

She felt a strange shiver of awareness rake her body, and for a moment she wanted to turn and run—back to her room, to safety. Back to the girl she really was.

Because for the first time it occurred to her that she was not simply scared of Marc Delaroche.

I'm frightened of myself, she whispered silently. And of the stranger I've just become—for him.

She drew a deep shaking breath, then very slowly she walked down the stairs to meet him.

CHAPTER FIVE

THE restaurant was just as crowded as Lottie had predicted. Apart from their own, Helen could see only one vacant table, and that was reserved too.

She was conscious of a surprised stir as they entered, and knew that she'd been recognised by at least half the people in the room, and that the rumour mill had been functioning well. She tried to ignore the speculative looks and whispered comments as, with Marc's hand cupped under her elbow, she followed the head waiter across the room.

But a shock wave was preferable every time to a ripple of sympathy, she thought, straightening her shoulders. Lottie had been right about that too.

And it was difficult to feel too humiliated over Nigel when she'd been brought here in a chauffeur-driven car and was now being seated at a candlelit table in an alcove where a bottle of Dom Perignon on ice and two glasses were waiting for them.

And also when she was being accompanied by the most attractive man in the room, she acknowledged reluctantly.

Tonight, as she'd noticed in the car, he was freshly shaven, and the dark mane of hair had been combed into a semblance of order. Close-fitting dark pants set off his long legs, and his well-laundered white shirt was enhanced by a silk tie with the colour and richness of a ruby. The light tweed jacket, slung over his shoulder, shouted 'cashmere'.

Certainly there'd been no escaping the frank envy in some of the female eyes as they watched her progress.

Oh, God, she thought, swallowing, I must be unbelievably shallow to find all that even a minor comfort.

'It has a good reputation, this place,' her companion commented as the champagne was poured and the menus arrived.

'Yes,' Helen agreed, glad of a neutral topic. 'Lottie reckons

71

it's the best food in miles. And they do rooms as well,' she added, her mind returning to Monteagle and its problems.

'*C'est vrai?*' he queried softly. 'You wish me to reserve one for later, perhaps?'

Her head lifted from the menu she was studying as if she'd been shot, her mouth tightening indignantly as she saw the wicked amusement in the dark eyes.

She said between her teeth, 'Will you—please—not say things like that?'

'Forgive me,' he said, showing no obvious signs of repentance. 'But you are so easy to tease, *ma mie*, and you blush so adorably. Calm yourself with some champagne.'

'Is there something to celebrate?' She picked up her glass.

'Who knows?' He shrugged. 'But, anyway, let us drink to Monteagle—and its future.'

'Actually,' Helen began, 'I've been giving that some thought and—'

He lifted a silencing hand. 'Later, *cherie*,' he told her softly. 'You must learn how the game is played. And also accept that a man rarely grants favours on an empty stomach,' he added drily.

'But it's not a game,' she protested. 'Not to me.'

'*Quand même,*' he said. 'We will eat first.'

His rules, Helen thought resentfully, transferring her attention back to the list of food. A man who likes his own way. And just how far is he prepared to go in order to achieve it? she wondered, and shivered slightly.

But in the meantime she might as well enjoy the food, as this would probably be her first and last visit. She chose potted shrimps for her first course, following them with a rack of lamb, roasted pink, with grilled vegetables.

Marc ordered *tournedos* of beef, with *foie gras* and dark-gilled mushrooms, served with a Madeira sauce.

The Burgundy he picked to accompany the meal seemed to caress her throat like velvet.

'Will you tell me something?' Helen said, once they'd been served and the waiters had departed.

'If I can.'

'Why did the committee bother to hear me if they meant to turn me down?'

'We interview every applicant, or those that represent them. Mainly we concentrate on projects that will revive the tourist industry in former trouble spots, or attract it to areas entirely off the beaten track.' He shrugged. 'Your application was thought to be interesting, but not particularly deserving. Unluckily for you, *cherie*, you do not have to walk ten miles to find water each day, and your home is lit by the flick of a switch,' he added drily.

'Only,' she said, 'if I can afford to pay the bill.'

They ate in silence for a moment or two, and she was just nerving herself to mention the bed and breakfast idea when he said, 'Hélène—in an ideal world, what would you wish for Monteagle?'

'That's simple. I'd like it to be my home again, but with the money to maintain it properly, of course.' She sighed. 'No tour parties, no cream teas. Just peace, comfort and privacy. The way it once was. And the way a home should be, don't you think?'

'I would not know,' he told her drily. 'I have an apartment in Paris and a hotel suite in London. When I was a child my father never settled in any place for very long,' he added with a faint shrug. 'Only when he retired did he find somewhere— a vineyard in Burgundy with a small dilapidated château, close to the village where he was born. He planned to live there and make wine, but he died very suddenly before it was even habitable.'

'What happened to it?' she asked.

'I sold it to an English family in search of *la vie douce*.' He smiled faintly. 'Only God knows if they ever found it.'

'You weren't tempted to live there yourself?'

'And tend my vines in the sun?' He shook his head. 'I have factories to produce, and a world to travel in order to sell them.'

As he spoke he looked past her, and Helen saw him stiffen slightly, the dark brows snapping together. 'Ah,' he said softly. '*C'est complet.* The last table is now occupied—and by people you know, *ma belle.*'

She said, bewildered, 'People…?' And then stopped, staring at him, appalled.

'Oh, God,' she said unevenly. 'It's Nigel, isn't it? And his new lady?'

'And an older couple—*ses parents, sans doute*,' Marc drawled. Then, as Helen began to push her plate away, he reached across the table and captured her hands in his, holding them firmly. *'Doucement, cherie,'* he ordered softly. 'You are going nowhere.'

'But I must,' she whispered frantically. 'I can't stay here and see them together. I can't…'

'But you do not have to,' he said. 'It is all quite simple. You just look at me instead.' He lifted her hands to his lips, brushing light kisses across her white knuckles, nibbling gently at the tips of her trembling fingers, while she sat as if mesmerised allowing it to happen.

His eyes smiled into hers. 'Think, Hélène,' he urged quietly. 'If you run away, then they will know they have the power to make you suffer—and so they win. Better that you remain here—with me—and we finish our meal, *hein*?'

He released her hands and refilled her glass, wincing slightly as she took an unguarded panicky gulp of the precious wine.

She said huskily, 'Have they seen me?'

'I notice a certain *chagrin*, yes.' His mouth twisted. '*La mère*, I think, wishes to go, but her husband—*c'est un homme inflexible*, and he will get his way.'

'And Nigel?' She swallowed. 'How—how does he look?'

He shrugged. 'He seems to have survived his wetting in the lake.'

'Oh, God,' she said miserably. 'He'll never forgive me for that.'

'Perhaps,' he said. 'But that can no longer be allowed to matter to you.' He paused to let that sink in, then nodded at her plate. 'Now eat, *ma mie*, and take your time. After all, we still have the dessert to come. The apricot soufflés, I think, which have to be cooked to order, and will prove, therefore, that we are in no particular hurry.'

He cut off a sliver of beef and proffered it to her on his fork. 'In the meantime, try this, and—smile at me a little.'

'It's all right for you.' Unwillingly she did as she was told. The fact that he was talking sense made his advice no more palatable. 'You're not the one whose heart is being broken.'

He gave her a sardonic look. 'And nor are you, *cherie*, although you may not believe it at this moment.'

'How can you say that? How can someone like you possibly understand?' Helen asked passionately.

His brows lifted. 'You speak as if I was something less than human. Yet, *je t'assure*, I share all the normal emotions.' He smiled at her coolly. 'You wish me to demonstrate?'

'*No!*' Her face warmed. 'I meant that you've obviously never loved someone all your life as I've loved Nigel.' She shook her head. 'Why, I've never even looked at another man.'

'Perhaps because you have never had the chance to do so,' he said, unmoved. 'And your life is far from over. Now, eat something, *ma belle*, before your lack of appetite is noticed.'

Helen shot him a mutinous look from under her lashes, then reluctantly complied.

As they ate, Marc chatted to her lightly, asking mainly questions about the history of Monteagle, encouraging her to expand her monosyllabic replies into real animation as she warmed to her subject.

Making it almost possible, she realised with a sense of shock, for her to believe that she was there with him because she wished it, and not as a matter of expedience.

But she had to convince him of her enthusiasm, and her will to work, she thought, if she was to persuade him to lend her the money for the guest house scheme.

If only Nigel hadn't been there she'd have been able to outline her plan by now—have a proper business discussion, she thought with vexation. As it was, her companion had taken advantage of the delay while they waited for the soufflés, and taken her hand again, and was now playing gently with her fingers.

She glanced up, a muted protest already forming on her lips, but as their eyes met, and she saw the frank desire that smoked his gaze, she forgot completely what she was going to say.

She looked away swiftly, hating the involuntary colour that warmed her cheeks, trying unavailingly to release her hand from the caress of his long fingers.

She said haltingly, 'I—I don't know how you can—pretend like this.'

His faint smile was crooked. 'But I am not pretending, *cherie*,' he told her quietly. 'I want you. I have made no secret of it.'

She stared down at the tablecloth. 'Then you're due for a serious disappointment, Monsieur Delaroche. Even if I was in the market for an affair—which I'm not—you'd be the last person on earth I'd choose.'

'Then at least we agree on something,' Marc drawled. 'Because I do not want an *affaire* either. *Au contraire*, I wish you to become my wife.'

Helen was very still suddenly. She could feel her throat muscles tightening in shock. The blood drumming crazily in her ears.

'If—this is some kind of joke,' she managed hoarsely, 'then it's in very poor taste.'

'There is no joke,' he said. 'I am asking you to marry me, *ma belle*, and I am completely serious.'

She said, 'But you don't know anything about me. We've met three times at most.' She shook her head. 'We're strangers, for heaven's sake. You must be mad even to think of such a thing.'

'I do not suggest that the ceremony should take place next week.' He smiled at her. 'I intend to court you, Hélène. Give you some time to accustom yourself to the idea.' He paused. 'To all kinds of ideas,' he added drily.

He meant sleeping with him, she realised dazedly. She would have to face the prospect of him making love to her. With a sense of shock she found herself remembering their last encounter—the hard strength of his arms and the relentless heated urgency of his mouth on hers. Even though they'd both been fully dressed, she'd still been aware of every inch of his lean body against hers. And the thought of being held—touched—without the barrier of clothing, sent her mouth dry with panic.

He wanted her. He'd said so. Therefore he would not expect to be fended off—kept waiting until after the wedding.

Except there would be no wedding, she told herself with sudden fierceness. So why was she treating his outrageous proposal as if it was all cut and dried?

She said, 'You're wasting your time, *monsieur*. Did you think I'd be so terrified of being a spinster that you could catch me on the rebound?' She shook her head. 'You're wrong. Nothing on earth could persuade me to marry you.'

'Not even Monteagle?' he challenged. 'You wish it to become a home again. You said so.' He shrugged. '*Moi aussi*. Become my wife, and I will make funds available for the whole house to be restored in the way that you want.'

'No,' she said huskily. 'That's impossible. I couldn't—I can't.'

'Yet you said at the interview that you would do anything to save it.' He sat back in his chair, watching her from under half-closed lids. 'Clearly your devotion to your house is not as profound as you claim.'

'When I said that I was desperate.' Helen lifted her chin. 'But now I have a plan.'

'*D'accord,*' he said. 'A plan that you wish to share with me. But after we have finished our desserts,' he added calmly, apparently unfazed by her refusal, just as a waiter bore down on them with the soufflés, tall as chefs' hats, in their porcelain dishes.

She said unsteadily, 'You think I could eat anything else—after that bombshell?'

'*Mais, j'insiste.* One spoonful at least. To calm you,' he added, his mouth twisting wryly.

Unwilling, totally unnerved, she obeyed. The delicate flavour and texture melted deliciously on her tongue, and was impossible, she discovered, to resist.

So,' Marc said at last, putting down his spoon, 'what is this plan, and how will it save Monteagle?'

Helen took a breath. 'I want to restore and refurbish all the bedrooms so that I can offer bed and breakfast to tourists,' she said baldly.

His face gave nothing away. 'And you have costed this scheme? You have taken into your calculations the price of supplying each room with a bathroom *en suite*? Also refurbishing the dining room so that your guests have somewhere to eat this *petit dejeuner* without the ceiling falling on their heads? And, of course, there will be the updating of the kitchen to be considered, so that it meets the demands of Health and Safety regulations.'

'Well, no,' Helen admitted, disconcerted. 'Not entirely. Because I've only just thought of it. But I'll get proper estimates for all the work for you to approve first.'

'For me?' he queried, brows lifted. 'How does this concern me?'

She bit her lip, suddenly wishing that her earlier rejection of his proposal had been a little less forceful. 'I was hoping that— you would lend me the money.'

There was a silence. 'Ah,' he said. 'But you have forgotten that there is an offer already on the table, where I give you all the money you need and you become my wife.'

She said breathlessly, 'But if you gave me a loan we wouldn't need to be married. And I'd have thought you were the last man on earth in the market for a wife.'

The dark eyes glinted at her. 'It does not occur to you, *ma mie*, that, much like yourself, I might be deeply and irresistibly in love?'

Helen felt as if all the breath had suddenly been choked out of her lungs. She stared at him, her eyes widening endlessly.

She said in a small, cracked voice, 'I don't—understand...'

'No? But you have only yourself to blame, *ma chère*. If you had not written and spoken about Monteagle with such passion, then I would not have been tempted to come and see it for myself. *Et voilà*. The rest, as they say, is history.'

She clutched at her reeling senses. She said huskily, 'You— mean that what you really want—is Monteagle. *Monteagle?* That's what you're saying?' She shook her head. 'Oh, I don't believe it. It's impossible, besides being ridiculous—ludicrous. You *can't*...'

His brows lifted. '*Pourquoi pas?* Why not? Along with my lack of humanity, do you also claim that I have no feeling for history—or appreciation of beauty?'

'How do I know,' she said stormily, 'what you think—what you feel about anything? You're a complete stranger, and as far as I'm concerned you always will be.' She looked at him, her eyes flashing. 'But you're talking about *my home*. Mine.'

'At the moment, yes.' He shrugged. 'But for how much longer without serious investment? You say you will not consider the offer of Monsieur Newson, so I offer an alternative. One of its advantages is that you will be able to go on living in the house you prize so highly.'

'Except,' she said, quietly and clearly, 'I'd be obliged to live with you.'

'It's an uncertain world, *cherie*,' he said mockingly. 'And I travel to dangerous places. Think of this—I could be dead within the year, and you would be a wealthy widow.' He added sardonically, 'I might even die on our wedding night—of ecstasy.'

He saw her flinch, and laughed softly.

Helen sat in silence, her teeth doing yet more damage to her ill-used lower lip, as a waiter arrived with a pot of coffee and a bottle of cognac.

When they were once again alone, she said, 'Please reconsider lending me the money. I swear I'll work night and day, and repay you in full.'

'Yes, *ma belle*, you will,' he said softly. 'But in coin of my choosing.' He paused to allow her to absorb that. 'And my offer remains a gift, not a loan.' He smiled at her. 'A wedding present, perhaps, from the groom to his bride.'

Helen stared down at her hands, clenched painfully in her lap. 'Why are you doing this?' she asked in a low voice. 'You're forcing me to sell myself to you for Monteagle. What kind of man does something like that?'

'A rich one.' He sounded appallingly casual—even amused. 'If something I want is for sale, *cherie*, then I buy it.'

'No matter what the consequences?'

He shrugged. 'For me, they are good. I am gaining a house I want and a woman I desire. And maybe I have reached a time in my life when a home and children have become important to me.'

Her lips parted in a gasp. 'You think for one minute—you really expect me to have your baby?'

'Another consequence of marriage,' Marc drawled unsmilingly. 'If you still believe in the stork, *ma mie*, you have been misinformed.' He paused. 'But I am forcing you to do nothing, Hélène. Understand that. I merely offer you a solution to your most pressing problem. It is for you to decide whether you accept my proposal or deny me.'

He gave her a measuring look. 'And you have twenty-four hours in which to make up your mind,' he added coolly.

She picked up her glass and took a mouthful of cognac, feeling it crackle in her throat. At the same time she was conscious of a faint dizziness. It might be caused by the shocks of the past hour, but could also be ascribed to the amount of alcohol she'd unwittingly taken on board, she realised.

Well, there would be no more of that, at least. She wasn't accustomed to it, and she needed to keep her wits about her now as never before, she thought grimly.

She looked back at him defiantly. 'Is this how you usually propose marriage—by ultimatum?'

The hardness of his mouth relaxed into a swift, unexpected grin. 'Until this moment, *cherie*, I have never proposed marriage at all. Other things, yes,' he added shamelessly. 'But not marriage.'

She gave him a fulminating look. 'I suppose I should feel flattered,' she said icily. 'But I don't.' She reached for her bag. 'May we go now, please?'

He was still amused. *'D'accord.'* He signalled for the bill while Helen braced herself for the walk to the door, which would involve passing Nigel and his new fiancée.

But when she turned to leave she saw only an empty table, in the process of being cleared by the staff, and checked in surprise.

'They left about ten minutes ago,' Marc informed her quietly. 'They did not seem to be enjoying their evening.' He paused. 'Or perhaps your Nigel feared another dousing—from an ice bucket.'

Helen ignored that. 'Will you ask Reception to get me a taxi, please?' she requested with dignity.

She realised uneasily that she was having to choose her words, and her steps, with care, so the sooner she was rid of her companion, the better.

His brows lifted. 'My car and driver will be waiting,' he pointed out.

'But I really need to be alone,' she said. 'Surely even you can understand that?'

'"Even you,"' he repeated pensively. 'I see I shall have to change your low opinion of me, *cherie*.'

'By forcing me into marriage?' She shook her head. 'I don't think so.' She paused, lifting her chin. 'And now I'd really like to go home.'

He said lightly, 'As you wish,' and went to the reception desk.

'Your cab will be ten minutes,' he told her on his return. 'Shall I wait with you until it arrives?'

'No,' Helen said hastily, then added a belated, 'Thank you.'

She'd half expected a protest, but all he said was a casual, '*A bientôt,*' and went.

There was no avoiding the fact that she would be seeing him again—and soon, she thought wearily. After all, he'd given her only twenty-four hours in which to make up her mind—or rack her brains for a way out.

She still felt faintly giddy, so she made her way over to a high-backed chair in the shelter of an enormous parlour palm and sat down, leaning back and closing her eyes.

When she heard the main door open she assumed her cab had arrived early, but instead she heard Nigel's voice peremptorily addressing the receptionist.

'My mother seems to have mislaid her scarf. Could someone look in the cloakroom for me? See if it's there?'

Helen, transfixed, had a fleeting impulse to climb into the palm and vanish.

But it was too late. Nigel had seen her and was crossing the foyer. She got to her feet, her fingers tightening defensively round the strap of her bag.

'All alone?' he asked unpleasantly. 'Dumped you already, has he?'

She flushed. 'No, he hasn't,' she said, adding recklessly, 'On the contrary, I'll be seeing him again tomorrow.'

'Well, you're certainly full of surprises, Helen. I'll grant you that.' He scanned her insolently from head to foot. 'You do know who you're dealing with, I suppose?'

'Yes,' she said. 'I know.'

'So, what the hell's a high-flyer like him doing in this backwater?' Nigel demanded.

She shrugged. 'Perhaps you should ask him that yourself.'

'Oh, I don't know him that well,' he said. 'It's Amanda. She's met him at parties in London and she could hardly believe her eyes when she saw you together. You're hardly his usual kind of totty.'

Helen steadied her voice. 'I'm sorry if she's disappointed.'

'She's not interested one way or the other,' Nigel said rather stiffly. 'He's certainly not her type. Nor does he believe in long-term relationships,' he added waspishly. 'Just in case you were hoping. Apparently he has a very low boredom threshold where women are concerned. Two months is the top limit for his involvements. None of his girls are kept around for longer. He's notorious for it.' He grinned nastily. 'And you haven't even lasted the night, sweetie.' He paused. 'So how *did* you meet him—as a matter of interest?'

'I can't imagine why it should be any of your concern,' she said, 'but he happened to be on the committee that turned me down the other day and he was curious about the house. It's as simple as that.'

Oh, God, she thought with a pang. *If only it were…*

'Oh, the *house*,' he said disparagingly. 'That explains it.'

'Thank you.' Helen said coldly, wishing desperately that her cab would arrive—or that she would be abducted by aliens.

He flushed slightly. 'Believe it or not, I'm trying to warn you for your own good. Although why I should bother after the trick you played on me this morning, God only knows,' he added sulkily. 'Do you know how long it took me to come up with an excuse for being soaked to the skin?'

'Am I supposed to care?' Helen threw back at him.

He shrugged, giving her a faintly injured look. 'We've known each other for a long time. I assumed it might be possible to remain friends.'

'Difficult,' she said, 'when we don't even occupy the same planet. And here's my taxi.' She offered him a small polite smile. 'Goodbye, Nigel, and—good luck.'

'And you,' he said venomously, 'deserve everything that's coming to you. When your house has gone, and your French millionaire has used you up and spat you out, don't come to me for a handout.'

There wasn't even a fountain to push him into this time, Helen thought, let alone the preferred swamp. And that was her sole regret as she walked away from him and out into the night.

Nor was it because of this brief confrontation that she found herself trembling as she sat huddled in the back of the taxi taking her home through the darkness.

It was Marc Delaroche who occupied her mind, imprinting himself indelibly on her inner vision.

My first real proposal of marriage, she thought, fighting back the bubble of hysteria rising within her. And it's from him.

She looked down at the hand he'd caressed and found she was clenching it into a fist.

As they headed through the village towards Monteagle her driver slowed as a car approached them, travelling smoothly and swiftly in the opposite direction.

Helen recognised it instantly. Oh, God, she thought, as she shrank further into her corner. *His car.* On its way back to the Monteagle Arms, no doubt.

But where on earth could he have been up till then? she asked herself in bewilderment. He should have returned long before her. Had his chauffeur become lost in the twisting lanes?

Whatever, he was far too close for her comfort. But perfectly poised for tomorrow, just an hour or so away, when he would come for his answer.

His package deal, she thought bitterly, for which he was apparently offering a blank cheque. Her house and herself—not necessarily in that order—and no expense spared. Or so he wanted her to believe…

It was—almost flattering. But she wasn't fooled, Helen told herself with sudden, desperate decision. It wasn't a genuine offer—not in a civilised society. It couldn't be…

He was merely testing her resolve, and of course he expected her to refuse. He probably relied on it.

After all, why should he want to spend a fortune on a place he'd seen briefly a couple of times?

And, besides, even a marriage that was only a business arrangement had too permanent a sound for someone who counted his relationships in days rather than years.

It's a wind-up, she thought with an inward sigh of relief, as the cab turned into Monteagle's gates. It has to be, and unfortunately I fell for it. Let him see I was rattled. Big mistake.

But at least she had a whole day to decide how to deal with it.

She considered, and immediately discarded, the idea of trying to rattle him in turn. Of letting him think she was actually tempted by his proposition and allowing him to talk her out of it. It might be amusing, but it was also dangerous.

He was too unpredictable, and—which annoyed her even more—invariably several steps ahead of her.

The sensible plan would be to tell him unsmilingly that the joke was over and request him to leave her in peace—seriously and permanently.

Except that might not be as simple as it sounded. Marriage might not be in the equation, but Marc Delaroche still wanted her. Inexperienced as she was, Helen was unable to deny that. If she was honest, she'd recognised it from their first encounter, with a stark female instinct she'd never known she possessed until that moment. And he was determined for his desire to be satisfied, however fleetingly.

It was that knowledge which dried her mouth and set up that deep inner trembling when he was near, invaded her thoughts when he was far away.

Nigel had never looked at her with such hungry intensity, she admitted painfully. Had never touched her skin as if he was caressing the petals of a flower. Had never stirred her senses to the edge of fear.

That alone should have warned her, she thought, as she paid off the driver and turned to go into the house.

There was no sign of Daisy, but the kitchen was filled with the aroma of coffee and the percolator bubbled away cheerfully.

She still felt fuzzy round the edges. Daisy's rich brew would clear her head and hopefully remove the shakiness in her legs too. Because she needed to be in total control, able to think positively. To plan tomorrow's response to Marc. Convince him once and for all, and with some force, that both she and Monteagle would remain forever beyond his reach.

She locked the back door, then took a mug from the big dresser and carried it, with the percolator, along to the library. She had some heavy decisions to make, so why not in comfort?

The lamps were lit, and a small fire was burning briskly in the hearth. God bless Daisy, she thought gratefully, and took one step forward into the room, only to halt in startled disbelief as she realised suddenly that she was not alone.

As she saw, with stomach-lurching shock, who was rising from the sofa to greet her.

'So, you are here at last,' Marc said softly. And his smile touched her in cool possession.

CHAPTER SIX

HER heart was beating like a stone being thrown against a wall. She stared back at him, her eyes widening endlessly in dismay. His jacket and tie had been discarded, tossed over the arm of the sofa, and his shirt was unbuttoned almost to the waist, the sleeves rolled back over his forearms.

He could not, she thought numbly, have announced his intentions any more clearly.

Her voice, when she finally found it, was hoarse. 'We—we said goodnight earlier. I saw your car on the way to the village—the hotel. So, what are you doing here?'

'You have a short memory, *ma belle*. It was my unfortunate chauffeur you saw going to the hotel.' The dark eyes glinted at her. 'I told you that on my next visit I intended to spend the night here in this house.'

'Yes, but I never thought…' She stopped, biting her lip, struggling for dignity. For some kind of rationality. Most of all, for some way of keeping him at arm's length—or an even greater distance. 'I prefer my guests to wait for an invitation.'

'I feared I might be made to wait for ever.' His mouth curled sardonically. He walked across and took the percolator from her wavering hand. 'Before you damage yourself, Hélène,' he added drily. 'Or me. Now, come and sit down.'

If she turned and ran he would only follow her, she knew, and she didn't want to demonstrate that kind of weakness—let him see that she was scared in any way.

So she moved on legs that did not seem to belong to her to the sofa, and sank down, grateful for its sagging support. A small table had been drawn up, holding a tray with cups, a cream jug and sugar bowl, plus a decanter of brandy and two glasses.

She said shakily, 'You certainly believe in making yourself at home—in every way.'

He shrugged. 'Perhaps because I believe that very soon this will be my home.' He sat down at the other end of the sofa and began to pour out the coffee.

She gave him a swift, wary glance. 'Isn't that a premature assumption?' She tried to keep her voice toneless. 'After all, you said you'd give me twenty-four hours to answer you.' She paused. 'And I also thought you'd have the decency to allow me to consider your proposition in private,' she added, with a touch of hauteur.

'But I decided I would pay court to you instead, *cherie*,' he drawled. 'Decency has always seemed to me such a dull virtue.'

His words, and the amused glance which accompanied them, were like an icy finger on her spine. Her hands were clamped round each other in an attempt to conceal the fact that they were trembling.

But she lifted her chin. 'Virtue?' she echoed cuttingly. 'I'm surprised you even know what the word means.'

'What a low opinion you have of me, *ma chère*,' Marc drawled, pouring measures of brandy into the glasses. 'But at least it releases me from any obligation to behave well.'

He leaned towards her and Helen flinched instinctively, realising too late that he was simply putting her coffee and brandy within her reach on the table. She saw his mouth tighten with sudden harshness, but when he spoke his voice was casual.

'And I made you a proposal, not a proposition. Perhaps you would like me to demonstrate the difference?'

'No,' Helen said too hastily. 'I wouldn't.'

'To hear you,' he said softly, 'one would think that your namesake in the portrait had been a Vestal Virgin and that you were following her example.' His gaze rested fleetingly on her mouth. 'Yet all the evidence denies this.'

'I dislike being railroaded,' Helen told him, flushing. She was searingly aware of the lean body lounging so casually beside her—and alarmed by her awareness. 'That does not, however, make me a prig.'

'I am glad of the assurance.' His tone was faintly mocking. 'So,' he went on after a pause, 'what did Nigel say to you that has put you so much on edge?'

Avoiding his gaze, she picked up her glass and drank some brandy. 'I don't know what you mean.'

'But you don't deny that there was another *rencontre*, I hope.' He spoke pleasantly enough, but she was aware of a faint, harsh edge in his voice. 'You are not the only one to take note of passing traffic, *ma mie*. I saw his car returning to the restaurant. You must still have been there. Also,' he added judiciously, 'you are paler than before, and your eyes look bruised. Was he angry, perhaps, at your attempt to drown him?'

Helen took another restorative gulp of brandy. 'It was mentioned,' she said shortly. 'But he seemed more interested in bad-mouthing you.'

His brows lifted. 'I was not aware I had the pleasure of his acquaintance.'

'But you know—his new lady.' She had to struggle to say the words. 'Apparently you've met—at parties in London.'

'Ah,' Marc said softly. 'But I meet a great many people at a great many parties, *cherie*. She made no particular impression on me at the time.'

'Well, she remembers you very well,' she said, adding recklessly, 'And your reputation.'

He laughed. 'Do I have one? I was not aware.'

'You're said to be anti-commitment.' Helen stared down into her glass. 'You never continue any of your love affairs longer than two months.' She paused. 'Can you deny it?'

'*Certainement.*' He was still amused. 'I can assure you, *ma mie*, that love has never entered into any of my *affaires*.'

She bit her lip. 'Now you're playing with words. But then you like to do that, don't you, Mr Delaroche? Proposal versus proposition, for example. Not that it matters,' she added, 'because we both know that it's just some private game for your own amusement, and that you haven't the slightest intention of getting married to me—or to anyone.'

She drew a breath. 'So, can it stop right now, please? I'm getting bored with the joke.'

He reached for his jacket, extracted something from the pocket, and put it on the table. Helen saw it was a jeweller's velvet covered box, and nearly choked on the brandy she was swallowing.

'This is not the moment I would have chosen,' he said quietly. 'But perhaps this will finally convince you that I have indeed asked you to be my wife. And that I am quite serious.'

The diamonds in the ring were a circle of fire surrounding the deeper flame of an exquisite ruby. Helen's lips parted in a silent gasp that was part wonder, part horror.

'So, do you believe at last?' His smile was grim. 'Now all you need do, *ma belle*, is make your decision.'

She said huskily, 'You—make it sound so easy.'

'Yes, or no,' he said. 'What could be simpler?'

She shook back her hair in a defiant gesture. 'You seem to forget that I'm being asked to choose between freedom and a life sentence—with a stranger.'

'And what does this freedom allow you, *ma mie*?' His voice was hard. 'The right to struggle, to work endlessly while the house you adore crumbles around you? Never to be able to indulge your beauty—your joy in life?'

He paused. 'Besides,' he added cynically. 'If your informants are correct, the maximum term for you to serve would be only two months. Is that really such a hardship?'

Helen stared at him, aware of a strange icy feeling in the pit of her stomach. Yes, she realised, with sudden paralysing shock. Yes, it would be—if, somehow, I started to care. If, however incredible it may seem, you taught me to want you— to love you—and then you walked away.

Because that would be more than hardship. It would be agony. And it could break my heart for ever...

She said in a small taut voice, 'I suspect, *monsieur*, that even one month of your intimate company might be more than I could bear.' She took a steadying breath. 'Is there really nothing else you would agree to—for Monteagle?'

'You are brutally frank.' His mouth twisted. 'So let me be the same. My answer to that is nothing. I take the house and you with it, Hélène. Or you will be left to your—freedom. The choice is yours.'

Her fingers played with a fold of her dress. 'I—I'll give you an answer tomorrow.'

He glanced at his watch. 'It is already tomorrow. You are running out of time, *ma belle*.'

She said with sudden heat, 'I wish—I really wish you'd stop saying that. Stop pretending that I'm beautiful.'

He studied her for a moment with half-closed eyes. 'Why do you do this?' he asked quietly eventually. 'Why do you so undervalue yourself?'

'Because I'm a realist.' She finished the brandy in her glass. 'I loved Nigel and he chose someone else. Someone beautiful.' She paused. 'I didn't get a chance to look at her at the restaurant, so I assume she is—beautiful.' Her glance challenged him. 'You're supposed to be a connoisseur, Monsieur Delaroche. What do you think—now that you've seen her again?'

He was silent for a moment, then he shrugged. 'She has her charms. Dark hair, a sexy mouth and a good body. And a tigress in bed, I imagine,' he added sardonically. 'Is that what you wanted to hear?'

Colour flared in her face, and her own completely unsexy mouth didn't seem to be working properly.

She said thickly, 'That's rather—too much information.'

'You hoped I would say she was plain and undesirable and that her only attraction is her father's money?' He spoke more gently. 'I wish it was so.'

'Don't pity me,' she said raggedly. 'Just don't—bloody pity me.'

He watched her for a moment, his expression wry. 'I think, Hélène, that you have had enough brandy.'

'Well, I don't agree.' She held out her glass defiantly. 'In fact I'd like some more—lots more—if you don't mind.'

Marc lifted the decanter. 'As you wish. But it is really too good to be used as an anaesthetic, *ma mie*.'

Helen tilted her chin. 'Maybe I want to be…' She tried the word 'anaesthetised' under her breath, but decided not to risk it. The room seemed very warm suddenly, and her head was swimming. 'Drunk,' seemed a safer alternative, and she said it twice just to make sure.

'I think you will achieve your ambition,' he told her drily. 'And sooner than you believe.'

She hoisted the refilled glass in his direction, aware that he seemed to have receded to some remote distance. Which was all to the good, of course. Perhaps, in time, if she went on drinking, he might disappear altogether.

'Cheers, *monsieur*,' she articulated with great care, and giggled at her success. Fine, she told herself defiantly, swallowing some more brandy. I'm—perfectly fine.

'*Salut, petite.*' His voice sounded very close. She felt the glass being removed from her hand, gently but firmly. Felt herself drawn nearer so that she was leaning against him, her cheek against his shoulder.

She knew she should resist, and swiftly, but her senses were filled with the warm male scent of him, and she was breathing the musky fragrance of the cologne he used. An odd weakness seemed to have invaded her body, and she wasn't sure she could get to her feet even if she tried, or stand upright if she did.

She was suddenly aware, too, that his hand was stroking her hair, softly, rhythmically, and she was shocked by this unexpected tenderness from Marc of all men. Because it seemed as if he had, in some strange way, become her sole rock in an ocean of desolation.

But that, she knew, was impossible. The complete opposite of the truth. Because he was danger, not comfort. Her enemy, not her friend. The predator, with herself as prey.

She moved suddenly, restlessly, trying to free herself, but the arm that held her was too strong, and the caressing hand almost hypnotic as it moved down to smooth the taut nape of her neck and the curve of her shoulder.

'*Sois tranquille.*' His voice was gentle. 'Be still, Hélène, and close your eyes. There is nothing to fear, I swear it.'

And somehow it was much simpler—almost imperative, in fact—to believe him and obey. To allow herself to drift endlessly as her weighted eyelids descended. And to surrender her own body's rhythms to the strong, insistent beat of his heart against hers.

She was never sure what woke her, but suddenly she was back to total consciousness, in spite of her aching head and her eyes, which some unfeeling person had filled with sand.

She took a cautious look round, then froze, all self-inflicted wounds forgotten. She was still on the sofa, but stretched out full-length in the arms of Marc, who was lying asleep beside her, his cheek resting on her hair.

She was so close to him, she realised, alarmed, that she could feel the warmth of his bare, hair-roughened chest through the thin fabric of her dress.

One arm was round her shoulders and the other lay across her body, his hand curving round her hipbone, and her movement was further restricted by the weight of his long leg, which was lying slightly bent over both of hers, imprisoning her in an intimacy as disturbing as it was casual.

Dear God, she moaned silently. How did I let this happen?

Her only small comfort was that apart from their shoes, which were on the floor, they were both dressed. But she could hardly have felt more humiliated if she'd woken up naked.

And just how long had this been going on anyway? she wondered miserably.

The lamp was still burning, but the fire was a pile of grey ash covering just one or two glowing embers.

Moving her arm carefully, she glanced at her watch and saw that it was nearly four a.m.

She took a steadying breath. I have to get out of here, she thought. Right now.

It didn't appear as if anything untoward had happened—in fact, she knew it hadn't—but she felt totally vulnerable like this, in his embrace. She certainly couldn't risk his waking and finding her there with him, in case he decided, after all, to—take advantage of the situation.

With the utmost caution she pushed his leg away, then slid,

inch by wary inch, from beneath his arm, putting down a hand to balance herself before lowering herself slowly to the floor.

She sat motionless for a moment, listening intently, but he did not stir and there was no change in his even breathing.

In spite of the pounding in her head, she managed to get to her feet. Then, sandals in hand, she tiptoed to the door and let herself out into the dark house. She knew every step of the way, every creaking floorboard to avoid as she fled to her bedroom. Once safely inside, out of breath and feeling slightly sick, she turned the key in the lock, and for good measure pushed a small wooden chair under the handle.

Then she stripped, letting her clothes lie where they fell, and crept into bed, pulling the covers over her head.

All that damned brandy. She groaned, fighting her nausea and praying for the bed to keep still. I must have been insane. Why, anything could have happened while I was unconscious.

Only to her own bewilderment it was apparent that nothing had. Instead, Marc had let her sleep, peacefully and comfortably.

So he can't have wanted me that much, after all, she thought, turning over and burying her face in the pillow. It's the house—just the house. And found herself wondering why that particular realisation should sting so much?

She certainly didn't need to be desired by a serial womaniser, she reminded herself forcefully.

She had to think, clearly and rationally, she told herself. Find a watertight reason for turning him down and dismissing him from her life, whatever the consequences for Monteagle's future.

But her mind was still teeming with images and sensations, and it was difficult to focus somehow. To stop wondering what form his promised wooing of her might have taken. And to forget, as she must, the way he'd looked at her, the things he'd said, and—his touch. That, dear God, above all else.

Once he'd gone she'd be able to put him out of her mind, and devote herself to the on-going struggle to make Monteagle financially viable. She wouldn't have time to think about anything else—especially ludicrous might-have-beens.

She stayed awake, her brain going in weary circles, until sunlight penetrated the curtains, then dressed and went downstairs to go for a walk round the lake. Every movement was a penance, but the fresh air might help to clear her head, she told herself optimistically.

The door of the sitting room remained closed, and to her relief she had the kitchen to herself too, as she made some strong black coffee and drank it, wincing.

She stood by the water, looking across at the grey mass of Monteagle's half-ruined keep, wondering how much longer she could keep it standing without a substantial cash windfall.

Football pools, she thought. The Lottery. Quiz shows paying out thousands. What hadn't she considered in her efforts, however forlorn the hope? And now no other avenues suggested themselves.

However, she looked at it, Helen thought wretchedly, she was between a rock and a hard place.

Time was running out, and she still couldn't figure how to frame her refusal to Marc Delaroche.

With most men a simple 'I don't love you' would be enough. But he didn't want her love anyway. He wants Monteagle, she thought, her throat tightening, and maybe a son to inherit it. And a wife who'll pretend not to notice when he becomes bored and starts to stray. Or when he stops coming back altogether.

And, if I'm truly honest with myself, that's what really scares me—that I'll begin to love him because I can't help myself. That last night I felt safe and secure, for the first time in months, with his arms round me. And that in the end I'll be left alone and lonely, because that's what he does.

And I know now I couldn't bear that. It would kill me.

And that's something I can never let him guess—which is why I have to say no, once and finally.

She walked slowly back to the house. She would bathe, she thought as she went upstairs, and change. Put on a brave face.

She gave herself a little heartening nod, then flung open the bathroom door and marched in.

'*Bonjour,*' Marc said softly from the depths of the tub. He picked up the sponge and squeezed water over his head, letting it run in rivulets down his face and chest. 'Have you come to say that you will marry me? If so, you could begin your wifely duties by washing my back.'

'Oh, God,' Helen said, appalled, and backed out into the passage, slamming the door behind her to shut off the sound of his laughter.

Daisy was at the sink in the kitchen, dealing with the cups and glasses from the previous night, when Helen arrived, flushed and breathless from her headlong dash downstairs.

'Why,' she demanded, 'is Marc Delaroche still here? And what is he doing in my bathroom?'

'My guess would be—having a bath.' Daisy gave her a disapproving look. 'I dare say he could do with a bit of pampering—after last night.'

'And what's that supposed to mean?'

Daisy turned, hands on her hips, her gaze deepening into real severity. 'The very idea, Miss Helen—making the poor young man sleep on that wretched sofa when there was a perfectly good bedroom all ready for him upstairs. And Sir Henry always was such a hospitable man too. He must be turning in his grave.'

Helen took a deep breath. 'It's not a question of hospitality—' she began, but Daisy was firm.

'He told me when I saw him this morning that you were expecting him, Miss Helen. Isn't that so?'

Helen abandoned the struggle. 'Yes,' she acknowledged wearily. 'I suppose it is. I—I just wasn't sure when it would be.'

'Ah, well,' Daisy said comfortably. 'That's all right, then.' She hesitated, giving Helen a shrewd glance. 'I get the idea we'll be seeing more of Mr Marc in future.'

Helen murmured something non-committal.

I saw more than I needed just now in the bathroom, she thought, filling the kettle and placing it on the stove.

She was just making coffee when the bell at the front entrance jangled with two imperative bursts.

'Now, who on earth's calling at this time on a Sunday?' Daisy wiped her hands and moved towards the door. 'Have you invited anyone else, Miss Helen?'

'Not that I know of.' Helen attempted lightness. 'But maybe we'd better make up another room, just to be on the safe side.'

Of course it could be Lottie, curious to know how the previous evening had gone, so she turned, beaker in hand, prepared to be welcoming when Daisy returned. But the housekeeper was alone, her face set and stony. 'It's that Mr Newson,' she said shortly. 'He insists on having a word with you, so I've put him in the library.'

'Oh.' Helen abandoned her coffee and went reluctantly to join him, wishing that she looked tidier, more like the lady of the house instead of the hired help.

The room looked neat and cheerful in the sunlight pouring through the window, and her unwanted visitor was standing with his back to the empty fireplace, looking round him with his usual narrow-eyed appraisal.

She said icily, 'Is there something I can do for you, Mr Newson?'

'Yes,' he said. 'You can tell me that you've seen sense at last over this house and are prepared to sell to me. My team are all ready to go. I only need to say the word.'

'But I've already said the word.' Helen lifted her chin. 'And it's no. I thought I'd made that clear.'

'But that was when you thought you could get your hands on some money.' The fleshy face gloated at her. 'It's all round the village that you've been turned down for that grant you pinned your hopes on. You've nowhere else to turn, and you know it. So if you've got any sense you'll reconsider my offer, minus a small discount for the inconvenience you've put me to, and be quick about it. I'm planning to open next Easter.'

'Well, I hope you haven't spent too much on preliminaries,' Helen returned, with total insincerity. 'Because Monteagle is still not for sale.'

'I'm a tolerant man, Miss Frayne. Anyone will tell you that. But you're beginning to try my patience. Get it into your head, my dear. You've fought well, but you've lost. I hold all the cards, and I'm about to collect.'

Except, Helen thought, she held a final ace—if she chose to

play it. And what real choice did she have—if Monteagle was to be saved?

She heard the creak of a floorboard behind her. Knew without turning who had entered the room—and what he was waiting to hear. Her fight was over at last, and her choice made for her—whatever the consequences.

She took a deep breath, aware that she was shivering, her stomach churning as she faced Trevor Newson.

She said huskily, 'I'm afraid not. You see, I'm going to be married—very soon—and my future husband plans to restore the house completely—as our family home.' She paused. 'Isn't that right—darling?'

Marc's hands descended on her shoulders. His skin smelled cool and damp, but the lips that touched the side of her throat in a lingering kiss were warmer than the blaze of the sun.

He said softly into her ear, 'It will be one of my many pleasures, *mon amour*.'

He came to stand beside her, his arm circling her body, his hand on her hip in a gesture of possession as casual as it was disturbing. He was barefoot, bare-chested, a pair of shabby jeans his only covering.

'When I woke you were gone, *cherie*.' He clicked his tongue in a kind of amused reproach. 'And here you are, entertaining another man.'

'I don't think Mr Newson is particularly entertained,' Helen said coolly. 'Besides, he's just leaving.'

The older man's face was unpleasantly flushed. 'So this is your saviour?' He nearly spat the word. 'He doesn't look to me as if he's got two pennies to rub together, but I'm sure you've had him checked out.' He glared at Marc. 'She's a fast worker. I'll give her that. Up to yesterday she was supposed to be engaged to someone else, only he's dumped her. Now here she is with you.' Trevor Newson gave Helen a smile that made her skin crawl. 'So, where did you find this one, love?'

'She did not,' Marc said curtly. 'I found her. And you are offending my fiancée, *monsieur*. Perhaps you would like to go, before I throw you out.'

'You and whose army?' Trevor Newson blustered. He was

more heavily built than his opponent, but he was flabby and out of condition when compared with Marc's toned muscularity. 'But I'm leaving anyway.' At the door, he turned. 'This is going to cost you a fortune, my friend. I just hope you find she's worth the expense. Not many women are.'

As soon as he had gone Helen eased herself from Marc's arm and walked over to the window.

She said, 'Do you usually come downstairs half-dressed?'

'I had just finished shaving. You have some objection?' He sounded amused again.

She shrugged. 'It's—not very dignified.' She paused. 'And it made that awful man think…'

'That we had slept together?' Marc supplied cordially, as she hesitated again. 'But you can hardly deny that you spent most of the night in my arms, *ma mie*.'

'No,' Helen said between gritted teeth. 'I—can't.'

'But you wish so much that it were otherwise, *hein*?' He walked over to her. Turned her to face him, a hand under her chin, so he could look down into her eyes. 'So,' he said softly, 'you have agreed, after all, to make the ultimate sacrifice to save this house. For a while I thought your aversion to me might prove too strong.'

She bit her lip and stared down at the floor. 'So did I.' Her voice was bitter.

'I think I owe Monsieur Newson some thanks,' he said reflectively. 'If he had not come here this morning, your answer to me might have been different.'

'Yes,' she said. 'It would.' She took a deep breath. 'Don't you have any compunction about what you're doing—what you're forcing me to do? And all for a whim.' She shook her head. 'If you really want a house, there are so many others you could buy. So many women probably falling over each other to marry you.'

'But you are unique, *cherie*,' he said lightly. 'You do not profess undying love. You make it clear that you want only my money. I find that—refreshing.'

'And I,' she said in a low voice, 'find it degrading.'

He tucked an errant strand of hair behind her ear. 'Nevertheless, Hélène,' he said quietly, 'the bargain is made between us, and it will not be broken.' He dug a hand into the pocket of his jeans and produced the little velvet box. 'Now, give me your hand.'

She watched numbly as the ruby slid over her knuckle into its symbolic resting place. So beautiful, she thought, watching the slow fire that burned in its depths, and yet so totally meaningless.

He said, 'Will you give me a kiss, or do I have to take it from you?'

Swallowing nervously, she raised her mouth to his with reluctant obedience. But instead of the passionate onslaught she'd expected—and feared—Marc was gentle with her, his lips moving on hers with a strange, almost mesmerising sweetness, the tip of his tongue probing her defences softly and sensuously. Coaxing her, she thought, her mind reeling, to a response that she dared not risk—even if she wished...

She stood rigid in the circle of his arms, shakily aware of the heat of his naked skin through her clothes. Willing the kiss to end. Praying that she would escape unscathed.

At last, with a rueful sigh, he lifted his head, watching her through half-closed eyes.

'You lack warmth, *cherie*,' he told her wryly. 'But that will change once you have learned a little about pleasure.'

She stepped back from him, wrapping defensive arms round her body. 'Is that really what you think?' She invested her tone with scorn.

He laughed then, running the back of his hand teasingly down the curve of her stormy face. 'Yes, *petite innocente*, I do.' He paused, glancing at his watch. 'And now, *hélas*, I must dress and tear myself away from you back to London.'

'You're leaving?' She was genuinely astonished. 'Now?'

'*Pourquoi pas?*' He shrugged. 'After all, I have what I came for—and I have to prepare for an early meeting tomorrow.' He took the hand that wore his ring and kissed it. 'But I shall return next week. In the meantime my architect will be here, with his team, to begin restoration work on the house.'

His tone was brisk and businesslike, making her see the dynamism that drove him. See it, and resent it.

Monteagle, she thought, doesn't belong to you yet, *monsieur*. She bristled defiantly. 'I have my own local people, thank you.'

'And now you will also have Alain.' He grinned at her. 'So, don't give him a hard time, *cherie*. He might wound more easily than I do.' He paused. 'One more thing,' he added casually. 'The number of your bank account, if you please.'

She gasped. 'Why should I give you that?'

'So that I can transfer some money for you.'

She said coldly, 'I have funds of my own, thanks. I don't need any charity.'

'And I am not offering it. But there will be incidental expenses once the work starts that you cannot be expected to meet.' He smiled at her. 'Also you have your trousseau to buy. I intend to begin the arrangements for our wedding tomorrow. I suggest a civil ceremony before witnesses at the end of next month.'

Helen's heart was thudding again. 'But you said there was no hurry,' she protested. 'That—that you'd wait…'

'I think,' he told her softly, 'that I have been patient enough already. And last night has kindled my appetite, *ma mie*.' His smile widened as he looked down into her outraged, apprehensive eyes. 'So, be good enough to write down your account number for me, and I will go and leave you in peace.'

Quivering with anger, she obeyed, handing over the slip of paper with open resentment.

Marc walked to the door, then turned slowly, letting his eyes travel down her body.

'On the other hand,' he said softly, 'I still have the memory of how you felt in my arms last night. And I could even now be persuaded to stay.'

He watched her eyes widen in sudden shock, and went on silkily, 'But it is a matter entirely for you to decide, *mon amour*. Although I promise you would find the bed in my room more comfortable than that penance of a sofa.'

The words were thick in her throat. 'I'll have to take your word for that, *monsieur*. Goodbye.'

She turned back to the window, hardly daring to breathe until she heard the door close quietly behind him.

Monteagle is safe, she whispered to herself. And that's all that matters. All that I can allow to matter, anyway.

The cost to herself—well, that was different, and she would have to find some way to endure it.

God, but he was so sure of her, she thought, digging her nails painfully into the palms of her clenched fists. So convinced he could seduce her into passionate surrender. But he would have to think again.

'You may own Monteagle, *monsieur*,' she whispered under her breath, resolution like a stone in her heart. 'But you'll never possess me—and that I swear, by everything I hold dear.'

CHAPTER SEVEN

LOTTIE looked silently at the ruby lying on the table between them.

She said, 'That's costume jewellery, and this whole thing is a wind-up—right?'

Helen shook her head. 'Wrong.' Her voice was husky. 'I really am engaged to Marc Delaroche. He—proposed last night. I accepted this morning.'

Lottie stared at her open-mouthed. She said, half to herself, 'This can't be happening. Twenty-four hours ago you considered yourself engaged to Nigel.' Her voice rose. 'And now you're going to be married to someone you've known a matter of days?'

'You made me have dinner with him,' Helen defended. 'You practically twisted my arm.'

'Yes,' said Lottie. 'Because I thought it would do you good to go out with someone lethally attractive who clearly fancied you. But that was when I thought you were both sane.'

She sat back in her chair, her worried gaze resting on Helen's pale face. 'Are we talking serious rebound from Nigel, here? Or are you telling me that love at first sight actually exists?'

'Love has nothing to do with it.' Helen drew a deep breath. 'The truth is that he's absolutely crazy about Monteagle and is willing to spend whatever it takes to restore the place to its old glory. Only it can't be completely his—unless, of course, I'm part of the package.' She shrugged. 'And that's it.'

'Oh, my God,' Lottie said helplessly, and relapsed into frowning silence. At last she said, 'Helen—just sell him the place, and save yourself a lot of heartache.'

'I'll never sell Monteagle, and he knows it. I made it clear enough at that damned committee meeting. He also knows I'm desperate.' Helen shrugged again, aiming for insouciance. 'I—

can't afford to refuse.' She hesitated. 'It's a business arrangement. What they call a marriage of convenience, I suppose.'

'Ah,' Lottie said blandly. 'Then presumably, as you're still virtual strangers, the deal does not include sex.' Her gaze drilled into Helen's. 'Or does it?'

Helen looked down at the table. 'We—we haven't settled the final details yet.'

'Now I know you're kidding,' said Lottie derisively. 'I saw him look at you, remember? And, while Simon and I may have been apart for a while, I still recognise old-fashioned lust when I see it. And, as you're not in love with him, how will you deal with that when payback time arrives? Are you really that sophisticated?'

Helen stared at the burn of the ruby lying between them. She said, half to herself, 'I—I'll cope somehow. Because I have to.' She forced a smile. 'What would you do in my place?'

'Sell,' said Lottie. 'And run.' She paused. 'Or you could try closing your eyes and doing exactly what you are told. That could be interesting.'

'You mean lie back and think of England?' Helen's laugh had a hollow ring. 'Or Monteagle?'

'I doubt whether Marc Delaroche will let you think about anything but him,' Lottie said drily. 'Don't say you weren't warned.'

After Lottie had gone, Helen lingered in the kitchen, washing the cups and glasses they'd used, and recorking the barely touched bottle of wine.

Daisy can use it to cheer up tomorrow's chicken casserole, she thought.

The housekeeper had taken Helen's halting news in her stride. 'So, Mr Marc, is it?' she'd said thoughtfully. 'Well, I wish you happiness, my dear. Things often turn out for the best.'

Mrs Lowell was the only other one on Helen's need-to-know list, because she'd have to explain why there'd be no more guided tours.

I'll go round to the Vicarage tomorrow, she told herself.

As she walked through the hall the telephone rang, and in spite of the lateness of the hour she found herself reaching for it.

'Hélène?' His voice reached her huskily across the miles, making her start.

She steadied herself, trying to ignore the frantic drum of her heart. 'Marc? What do you want?'

'All the things I cannot have, because you are so far from me.'

She could hear the smile in his voice and stiffened, loading her tone with frostiness. 'I mean why are you calling so late.'

'To wish you *bonne nuit*,' he said. 'And sweet dreams.'

'Oh,' she said, nonplussed. 'Well—thank you.'

'And to tell you that, to my sorrow, I will not be with you next week after all. I have to fly to New York.'

'I see.' She knew she should feel relieved at the news, if not be dancing in the streets. Instead, suddenly, there was an odd flatness. 'It was—good of you to let me know.'

There was a pause, then he said softly, 'You could go with me.'

'To New York?' An unbidden quiver of excitement stirred inside her, and was instantly quelled. She said stonily, 'Of course I can't. It's quite impossible.'

'Why? You have a passport?'

'Somewhere, yes.'

'Then I suggest you look for it, *ma mie*,' he told her drily. 'You will certainly need it for our honeymoon.'

'Honeymoon?' She was beginning to sound like an echo, she told herself with exasperation. 'But surely there's no need for that,' she protested. 'It—it's not as if it is a real marriage…'

'You will find it real enough when the time comes, *cherie*.' His words were light, but she thought she detected a note of warning. 'And we are certainly having a honeymoon—although it can only be brief because of my work commitments.'

He paused. 'An old friend has offered us his villa in the South of France. It stands on a headland above St Benoit Plage, and all the bedrooms have views of the Mediterranean. What do you think?'

'You seem to have made up your mind already,' Helen said. 'So what does it matter?'

She thought she heard him sigh. 'Then consider again about New York, Hélène. After all, how long is it since you had a holiday?'

'I went skiing with the school in my last spring term,' she said. 'That's what the passport was for.' She paused. 'But I can't just leave here. I have things to do—responsibilities. Besides...' She halted awkwardly.

'Besides, spending time alone with me in America, or anywhere, is not your idea of a vacation?' His voice was faintly caustic. 'Is that what you were about to say?'

'Something of the kind, perhaps,' Helen agreed woodenly.

'I suppose I should find your candour admirable, *ma mie*,' he said, after a pause. 'However, one day soon—or one night— we shall have to discuss your ideas in more detail.'

His tone sharpened, became businesslike. 'In the meantime, I suggest you use some of the money I shall deposit in your account to begin recruiting extra staff for the house and grounds.'

'But there's no need,' Helen protested. 'We can manage quite well as we are.'

'It is not a question of managing, *ma chère*,' Marc told her crisply. 'Monsieur and Madame Marland are no longer young, *bien sûr*, and at some point will wish to retire. In the meantime they will be glad of help, especially when there is entertaining to be done or when you are away.'

'But I'm never away,' she protested.

'Until now, perhaps,' he said. 'But that will change. You will be my wife, Hélène, not merely my housekeeper. Perhaps I have not made that sufficiently clear. When my work takes me abroad there will be times when I shall require you to go with me.'

Her voice rose slightly. 'You expect me to be your—travelling companion?'

'My companion,' he told her softly, 'and my lover. Sleeping with you in my arms was so sweet, *cherie*, that I cannot wait to repeat the experience.'

'Thank you.' She kept her voice stony, telling herself that the faint quiver she felt inside was anger. Hating the fact that she was blushing.

She took a steadying breath. 'Have you any more orders for me, or may I go now?'

He laughed. 'If I gave orders, Hélène, you would be coming with me to New York.' He gave her a second to consider that, then added more gently, 'Sleep well, *mon ange*—but think of me as you close your eyes, *hein*?'

She murmured something incoherent, and replaced the handset.

His unexpected call had shaken her, and raised issues she'd not wanted to contemplate. Questions of autonomy, among others.

It was disturbing that he seemed to want her to share his life at all kinds of levels she hadn't imagined. Starting with this—this honeymoon in the South of France. Exercising his power by taking her from her own familiar environment to his own domain, she thought, and shivered.

Slowly, she went up to her room. She took off his ring and placed it in the box which also housed her grandmother's pearls—bestowed on her for her eighteenth birthday, and the only other real valuable that she possessed.

Jewellery like the ruby didn't go with her lifestyle, and its non-stop cleaning and gardening. Nor would she take on extra staff, as he'd decreed. The arrival of his tame architect and his work crew was quite enough of an invasion of privacy, making her feel as if her personal hold on Monteagle was being slowly eroded.

But that wasn't all of it, she thought, looking down at her bare hand. There was still part of her in rebellion against the decision that had been forced on her. And she didn't want to admit to anyone, least of all herself, that both she and Monteagle would soon belong to Marc completely. Or display the symbol of that possession.

Think of me. His words came back to haunt her as she slid into bed and pulled the covers over her.

Oh, but he'd made sure of that, she thought bitterly. Turned it into an essential instead of a choice. Placed himself at the forefront of her mind each time she tried to sleep, making himself impossible to dismiss.

And when sheer fatigue overcame her, her sleep was restless and patchy, scarred by dreams that she burned with shame to remember in the morning. Dreams so real that when she woke she found herself reaching for him again across her narrow bed, before shocked realisation dawned.

She turned over, furious and humiliated, burying her heated face in the pillow.

'Damn him,' she whispered feverishly. 'Oh, damn him to hell.'

She got up, late and listless, and searched for distraction. With Daisy's assistance she finally removed the fragile bed and window hangings from the State Bedroom, folded them carefully into plastic sacks, and took them down to the village to deliver to Mrs Stevens at the post office.

The post mistress accepted them with a workmanlike glint in her eye. 'Now, this will be a real pleasure,' she said. 'We'll start on the cutting-out at once, while you decide on the new fabric.' She gave Helen a kind smile. 'So you're courting, then, Miss Frayne—that French gentleman who stayed at the Arms a while back, I hear. Met him then, did you?'

The village grapevine, Helen realised, was in full operation already.

'Oh, no,' she said with perfect truth, aware at the same time that she was blushing. 'It was before that—at a meeting in London.' *Just don't ask how long before, that's all.*

Mrs Stevens nodded with satisfaction. 'I knew it must be so,' she said.

And I wish it had been. The thought came to Helen, unbidden and shocking in its implication, as she made the short trip to the Vicarage.

'Oh, my dear girl.' Marion Lowell hugged her ebulliently. 'How amazing—a whirlwind romance. And such a gorgeous man.' She turned to her husband. 'Jeff, darling, now we have an excuse to drink that champagne we won in the Christmas tombola. I'm so glad we didn't give it back.'

'I hope none of the parishioners call,' Jeff Lowell said, grinning as he passed round the fizzing glasses. 'They'll probably have me defrocked.'

'Will you be getting married here in the church?' Mrs Lowell asked, after they'd drunk to her happiness, and Helen shook her head, flushing.

'I'm afraid not. It will be at the registry office in Aldenford.'

The Vicar looked at her quietly. 'I'd be delighted to hold a short service of blessing afterwards, if you'd like that. Perhaps you'd mention it to your fiancé.'

'Yes, of course,' said Helen, hating herself for lying.

She felt sombre as she walked home. They were so kind, so pleased for her, as if she and Marc had really fallen headlong in love.

Thank goodness they had no idea of the soulless—and temporary—bargain she'd struck with him. His words still echoed in her mind. *You do not profess undying love... I find that— refreshing.*

And that, she thought wearily, seemed to say it all.

As she rounded the bend in the road a lorry carrying scaffolding poles went past her, and carefully negotiated its way between Monteagle's tall wrought-iron gates.

She watched it bewilderedly, then began to run after it up the drive.

In front of the main entrance chaos confronted her. There seemed to be vans and trucks everywhere, with ladders and building supplies being briskly unloaded.

As she paused, staring round uncertainly, a man came striding towards her. He was of medium height, with brown hair and rimless glasses, and his face was unsmiling.

He said, 'I'm sorry, but the house is no longer open for visitors.'

'Where did you get that idea?' Helen demanded coldly.

'From Monsieur Marc Delaroche,' he said. 'The owner of the property.'

'Not yet,' Helen said with a snap. 'I'm Helen Frayne, and

the house still belongs to me.' She paused. 'I presume you're the architect?'

'Yes,' he acknowledged slowly. Behind the glasses his eyes had narrowed, as if he was puzzled about something. 'I'm Alan Graham. It's a pleasure to meet you, Miss Frayne,' he added, with no particular conviction.

'Marc mentioned you'd be coming—but not all this.' She gestured almost wildly around her. 'What's going on?'

He shrugged. 'He wants work to start as soon as possible.'

She said, 'I can see that. But how? You can't have arranged all this in twenty-four hours—it simply isn't feasible.' She stopped, dry-mouthed. 'Unless this was all planned some time ago, of course,' she added slowly. 'And you were just waiting for his word to—swing into action. Is that it?'

Alan Graham fidgeted slightly. 'Is it important? The house needs restoring, and we're here to do it. And time is of the essence,' he added with emphasis.

His tone implied that there was no more to be said. 'Is there a room I could use as an office, Miss Frayne?' He paused. 'Marc suggested that your late grandfather's study might be suitable, but any decision must be yours, naturally.'

Helen bit back the angry words seething inside her. Marc must have made his decision and given his orders almost as soon as they'd met, she realised with incredulity. As if he'd never had any doubt that she would ultimately accede to his demands.

How dare he take her for granted like this? she thought stormily, grinding her foot into the gravel in sheer humiliation. Oh, God, how dare he?

But it was done now, and she could see no way to undo it.

She took a deep breath. 'My grandfather's study has been unoccupied and unfurnished for some time,' she said expressionlessly. 'But you may use it if you wish.' She hesitated, still faintly stunned by all the activity around her. 'May I ask where all these people are going to stay?'

'That's not a problem. Accommodation has been arranged for them in Aldenford, and I've got a room at the Monteagle Arms.'

'Oh.' Helen digested this. She gave the architect a small cold smile. 'I'm afraid you won't be very comfortable there.'

'So Marc has told me.' For the first time Alan Graham's face relaxed a little. 'But it won't be for long. My wife is joining me today to look for a cottage to rent for the duration.'

'I see,' Helen said woodenly. 'And meals?' She had a horrified vision of cauldrons of soup and platters of sandwiches to be prepared daily.

'Packed lunches will be delivered.' He paused. 'Perhaps you'd direct me to the study, so that I can unpack my papers and drawings?'

'Of course,' Helen said, turning and leading the way to the house.

It seemed that Mr Graham shared Lottie's disapproval of this lightning marriage, she brooded over a mug of coffee a little later, having left the architect sorting out his workspace with chilling efficiency.

'Well!' Daisy exclaimed, bustling into the kitchen. 'You could have knocked me down with a feather when all those men started arriving. Mr Marc certainly doesn't waste any time.'

'No,' Helen agreed through gritted teeth. 'None at all.'

'They're starting on the State Bedroom,' Daisy informed her with excitement. 'The Helen Frayne portrait is being sent to London to be cleaned, and they're turning the little dressing room and the room next door as well into a lovely bathroom, with a wardrobe area.' She gave Helen a knowing look. 'Seems as if Mr Marc intends to use the room when you're married.'

'Does he, indeed?' was all Helen could find to say.

The master bedroom, she thought, her stomach twisting into nervous knots, being lavishly created for the master—and his bought bride.

When Marc telephoned that night, she was ready for him.

'You had this planned all along,' she stormed across his polite enquiries about her welfare. 'Even before you came here and saw the place you knew you were going to take on Monteagle's restoration. Why?'

'I found your application for help—intriguing. Then I saw you, *ma belle*, and my fascination was complete.' He had the gall to sound amused. 'But it seemed I had a rival, so I decided to offer you an interest-free loan in the hope that my generosity might ultimately be rewarded.'

'Then why didn't you?' Her voice was ragged.

'Because I realised that Nigel was betraying you and soon there would be nothing to prevent me claiming you for myself. It seemed unlikely that you would become my mistress, so I offered the money as a wedding gift to you instead. Do you blame me?'

'Blame you? Damned right I do,' she flung at him. 'I asked you to loan me that money—you know that. I begged you...'

'But we are both getting what we want, *mon coeur*,' he said softly. 'And that is all that matters. Why question the means?'

'Because you've deceived me,' Helen said hotly. 'You've behaved with a total lack of scruples. Doesn't that trouble you at all?'

'It is not of major concern to me, I confess,' he drawled. 'Particularly when it involves something—or someone—I desire. But if you wish it I will practise feeling ashamed for five minutes each day.'

Helen struggled to speak, failed utterly, and slammed down the phone.

He did not call her the following night, or the one after it. Gradually a week passed, and there was still silence.

And, Helen realised, she had no idea how to contact him. How ridiculous was that?

She presumed he was still in New York, and found herself wondering how he was spending his time, once work was over for the day. But that was a forbidden area, she reminded herself stonily. How Marc passed his evenings, or his nights, was none of her business. Or not until he spent them with her, of course.

Her only concern was, and always would be, Monteagle—not this ludicrously small, lost feeling that had lodged within her over the past days. There was no place for that.

All around her was a welter of dust, woodchips and falling plaster, as damp was eradicated and diseased timber ripped out amid the thud of hammers and the screech of saws and drills. Her dream was coming true at last, and Monteagle was coming slowly and gloriously back to life.

Alan Graham might still be aloof, but he knew his job, and his labour force were craftsmen who loved their work. No expense was being spared, either. Marc was clearly pouring a fortune into the project.

And that, as she kept reminding herself, was all that really mattered. She would deal with everything else when she had to.

She watched almost with disbelief as the State Bedroom was beautifully restored to its seventeenth-century origins, and, discreetly hidden behind a door, a dressing room and a glamorous twenty-first-century bathroom were created out of the adjoining room, all white and silver tiles, with a state-of-the-art shower stall and a deep sunken bathtub. Big enough for two, she noted, swallowing.

Members of the village embroidery group were already stitching the designs from the original hangings on to the pale gold fabric she'd chosen for the bed and windows, and had also promised a fitted bedcover to match.

Without the dark and tatty wallpaper, and with the lovely ceiling mouldings repaired and cleaned, and the walls painted, the huge bedroom looked incredibly light and airy, she thought. Under other circumstances it could even have been a room for happiness…

She stopped, biting her lip. Don't even go there, she told herself tersely. Happiness is a non-word.

Particularly when there had still been no contact from Marc. Clearly he was enjoying himself too much in America to bother about a reluctant bride-to-be in England.

But on the following Wednesday, while she was standing outside watching, fascinated, as the new roof went on, she heard the sound of an approaching vehicle.

She didn't look round because there always seemed to be cars and vans coming and going, until she suddenly heard Marc's voice behind her, quietly calling her name.

She turned sharply, incredulously, and saw him a few feet

away, casual in pale grey pants and a dark shirt. He held out his arms in silent command and she went to him, slowly and uncertainly, her eyes searching the enigmatic dark face, joltingly aware of the scorch of hunger in his gaze.

As she reached him he lifted her clear off the ground, and held her tightly against him in his embrace. She felt her body tremble at the pressure of his—at the pang of unwilling yearning that pierced her. Her throat was tightening too, in swift, uncontrollable excitement.

All those lonely nights, she thought suddenly, shakily, when she'd been able to think of nothing else but his touch—and, dear God, his kisses… All those restless, disturbing dreams that she was ashamed to remember.

Suddenly she wanted to wind herself around him, her arms twined about his neck, her slim legs gripping his lean hips. And realised, swiftly and starkly, the danger she was in.

As Marc's mouth sought hers she turned her head swiftly, so that his lips grazed only her cheek.

'Marc.' She tried to free herself, forcing a laugh. 'People are watching.'

He looked down into her face, his mouth hardening. 'Then that is easily remedied,' he told her softly. He lifted her effortlessly into his arms and began to carry her towards the house.

Colour stormed her face as she heard faint whistles and laughing applause from the workmen, but common sense warned her that to struggle would only make her look even more ridiculous.

Once inside, she expected to be put on her feet, but Marc carried her straight up the main staircase and along to the State Bedroom.

She said breathlessly, 'What the hell are you doing? Let me down at once.'

À votre service, mademoiselle.' His voice was cold, almost grim, as he strode across the room to the bed. Gasping, Helen found herself carelessly dropped in the middle of the wide bare mattress.

She fought herself into a sitting position, glaring at him as he stood over her, hands on hips. 'How dare you treat me like this? If you imagine I'm impressed by these—caveman tactics—then think again.'

'I should not say too much,' he told her with ominous quietness. 'It is nothing to what I would like to do to you. And will,' he added harshly, 'if you refuse my kisses again, in public or in private, no matter what grudge you may be harbouring.'

She bit her lip, avoiding the starkness of his dark gaze. 'You—you took me by surprise. I wasn't expecting to see you.'

'*Évidemment,*' he said caustically. 'Is that why you are not wearing my ring?'

Of course he would have to notice that!

'I'm living on a building site,' Helen returned a touch defensively. 'I didn't want it to get lost or damaged.'

He gave her a sceptical glance. 'Or did it remind you too much of how soon you will be my wife?'

She bit her lip. 'What do you expect—eager anticipation?'

'No,' he said softly. 'But if not a welcome—a little co-operation, perhaps?'

Before she could move she felt his hands on her shoulders, pushing her back on to the mattress again. Then, lifting himself lithely on to the bed beside her, he pulled her close, and his lips began to explore her mouth with cool, almost languorous pleasure.

Taking, she realised, all the time in the world.

Her hands came up against his chest, trying to maintain at least some distance between them, but that was all the resistance she dared attempt. His warning still rang in her mind, and she knew she could not afford to provoke him again. She would have been wiser to offer him her lips in front of everyone just now rather than risk this.

She was too vulnerable, she thought, shut away with him here in this room they'd soon be sharing. And, because they were known to be together, no one would be tactless enough to come looking for them. No one…

The midday sun was pouring in through the high windows, lapping them in heated gold.

She seemed to be sinking helplessly, endlessly, down into the softness of the bed, her lips parting in spite of herself to answer the sensuous pressure of his mouth, to yield to the silken invasion of his tongue.

Inside her thin shirt, her breasts were suddenly blossoming in greedy delight as his kiss deepened in intensity. Her hardening nipples seemed tormented by the graze of the lacy fabric that enclosed them, aching to be free of its constriction.

As if she'd moaned her yearning aloud, she felt his hand begin gently to unfasten the buttons on her shirt.

She lay still, scarcely breathing, the sunlight beating on her closed eyelids, her pulses frantic, waiting—waiting…

Marc was kissing her forehead, brushing the soft hair away from her temples with his lips, discovering the delicate cavity of her ear with his tongue, then feathering caresses down her arched throat to the scented hollow at its base, where he lingered.

His fingers slid inside the open neck of her shirt, pushing it and the thin strap beneath away from her shoulder.

Then he bent his head, and she experienced for the first time the delicious shock of a man's lips brushing the naked swell of her breast above the concealing lace of her bra, and knew that she wanted more—so much more that it scared her.

She made a small sound, half-gasp, half-sob. For a moment he was very still, then suddenly, unbelievably, she felt him lift himself away from her.

When she had the power to open her dazed eyes she saw that he was standing beside the bed, almost briskly tucking his own shirt back into the waistband of his pants.

'Je suis désolé,' he said. 'But I have arranged to see Alain for his progress report, and I am already late.'

Helen felt as if she'd been hit by a jet of freezing water. She scrambled up on to her knees, feverishly cramming her shirt buttons back into their loops. Restoring herself to decency with a belated attempt at dignity.

Her voice shook a little. 'I apologise if I've caused you any inconvenience.'

'Au contraire,' he said, his smile glinting at her. *'Tu es toute ravissante.'*

Anger began to mingle with shock inside her as she met his gaze. The victor, she thought stormily, with his spoils. And she'd nearly—nearly—let him…

She should have been the one to draw back, not him, she realised with shame. Oh, God, how could she have been such a fool?

He paused, glancing at his watch. 'But the report should not take long,' he went on softly, outrageously. 'Perhaps you would like to wait here for my return?'

'No,' Helen said between her teeth. 'I would not.'

One of her shoes had fallen off, and she began to search for it with her bare foot.

'Quel dommage,' he commented. 'I hoped you would show me round the rest of the house. Let me know what you think of the work that has been done so far and of any changes you would like to make.'

'I'm sorry,' Helen said icily, 'but we no longer provide guided tours. And the only change I want is never to see you again.'

He had the gall to grin at her. 'How fickle you are, *cherie.* When only a moment ago…' He shrugged and gave an exaggerated sigh.

'But your mention of tours has reminded me,' he added more slowly. 'As I drove here I met Madame Lowell in the village. She asked if you had told me of her husband's offer to bless our marriage. I said you had not been able to contact me, but that it was a great kindness of Révérend Lowell, which we would be delighted to accept.'

'You said *what*?' Helen abandoned the hunt for her shoe and stared at him, bright spots of colour flaring in her pale face. 'How could you do that? How could you? The Lowells are a sweet couple, and they really believe in marriage. Genuine marriage, that is,' she added, her voice stinging. 'It's sheer hypocrisy to involve them in our—sordid little bargain.'

His mouth tightened. He said harshly, all trace of amusement fled, 'Perhaps, *ma mie*, I feel that in spite of what has taken place between us here our—bargain needs all the help it can get.'

He took her by the shoulders, jerking her off the edge of the bed towards him, and his mouth was hard on hers in a kiss which bore no relation to his earlier tenderness.

It was, Helen thought, her mind reeling, almost a punishment.

When he released her, his eyes were glittering as they studied her startled face. Her hand went up mechanically to cover her tingling lips.

He said, 'So, understand this, Hélène: our marriage will be as genuine as anyone could wish—in all the ways that matter.' His voice was ice. 'On that, *ma belle*, you have my solemn word.'

He walked away from her across the big room, opening a space like an abyss between them. And left, slamming the door behind him.

CHAPTER EIGHT

HELEN stood, her hand still pressed to her mouth, as she tried to calm her flurried breathing.

She heard herself whisper raggedly, 'I—should not have said that.'

But she could not deny she'd wanted to make him angry—even to hurt him. She'd wanted revenge for his staying away in silence—for her dreams and her loneliness—and most of all for the way his hands and mouth had made her feel. Only revenge hadn't been so sweet after all.

Nor had he been angry enough to call off the marriage. And for Monteagle's sake she should be thankful for that.

She pushed her tangled hair back from her face and walked slowly to the door.

It might be politic to make some kind of amends, however. Not go to the lengths of an apology, of course. But perhaps if she prepared his room herself—put flowers in it?

She got sheets and pillowcases from the linen cupboard and carried them to the room he'd used briefly before. She opened a window to let in the sunlight and the faint breeze, wrinkling her nose at the sound of the building work, then quickly made up the bed, the pillows plumped and the sheets immaculately smooth.

She was coming back from the garden, her hands full of roses, when as she rounded the house she heard Alan Graham say, 'What are you going to do about Angeline Vallon?'

Helen halted, puzzled, then realised his voice was coming from the open window of her grandfather's study, just above her head.

Marc, she thought, shrinking against the cover of the wall. He must be talking to Marc. And felt her whole body tense.

She strained her ears, but couldn't catch the quietly spoken reply.

Then the other man spoke again. 'Marc—she's not a problem that will simply vanish. And she's bound to have heard by now that you're to be married. There could be trouble.' He paused. 'And your *fiancée* might find out.'

'Then I shall take care she does not.' Marc must have come to the window too, because, for her sins, she could hear him clearly now. And regretted it with all her heart.

'You worry too much, *mon ami*,' he went on. 'I will deal with Angeline—and that jealous fool she is married to if I have to. And Hélène need know nothing.'

Helen felt frozen. She was terrified in case Marc glanced down and saw her there below—eavesdropping—and knew she could not risk staying where she was a moment longer. Besides, she couldn't stand to hear any more.

I ought to be glad that there's another woman in his life. Relieved that our marriage is of such little importance to him, she told herself brokenly. But I'm not—*I'm not*...

Slowly and carefully, she tiptoed back to the house, pausing only to thrust the roses into one of the bins by the back door.

Some of the thorns, she saw, had drawn blood from her hands. But what she'd just overheard seemed to be draining the blood from her heart.

Because she realised she could never let him see how much this painfully acquired secret knowledge was hurting her. Nor dared she ask herself why this should be so. Her instinct told her that the answer she sought might be beyond all bearing.

The dress wasn't white, Helen told herself defensively. It was ivory. A major difference when it came to symbolism. But it was still her wedding dress, and in little more than an hour she would wear it as she stood in Aldenford registry office and became Marc Delaroche's wife.

Time had run out at last, and she was frightened.

Her hair, which had been skilfully layered and highlighted, framed a face that looked pale and strained in spite of the best efforts of the beautician who'd just left.

Also reflected in her mirror was the set of elegant matching luggage on the bed, containing the trousseau that Lottie, once she'd become convinced that Helen would not turn back from her chosen course, had relentlessly forced her into buying.

Including, of course, this slim-fitting dress in heavy silk. The skirt reached just below her knees, and the bodice was cut square across her breasts with slender shoestring straps, now hidden discreetly under the matching jacket, waist-length, mandarin-collared, and fastened with a dozen or more tiny silk-covered buttons.

It was beautiful, thought Helen, and in truth she hadn't needed much persuading to buy it.

Lottie had approved of the evening and cocktail dresses, the casual day clothes and beachwear that Helen had reluctantly selected.

'Don't be such a Puritan,' she'd urged. 'You're marrying a multimillionaire and going on honeymoon to one of the smartest resorts on the Riviera. Marc will expect you to dress—and undress—accordingly.'

'Why are you on his side all of a sudden?' Helen had asked, flushing.

'I'm on your side.' Lottie had given her a swift hug. 'Which is why I'm determined that you'll do yourself credit.'

She'd pulled a face at Helen's choice of lingerie, in crisp white cotton and broderie anglais, and raised her eyebrows at the nightgowns too, demurely simple in pale silk, and cut severely on the bias.

'Expecting fire to break out?' she'd teased, probably puzzled that there was no lace, no chiffon. Nothing sheer or overtly sexy.

But for that, thought Helen, wincing, Marc had someone else.

Even if she hadn't heard that betraying snatch of conversation she would have guessed as much by now. Because since those brief delirious moments she'd spent in his arms, and their angry aftermath, Marc had not made the slightest attempt to be alone with her, or to touch her—apart from a formal brush of his lips across her cheek on greeting or leavetaking. And sometimes not even that.

Nor had he spent a single night at Monteagle in the room

she'd made ready for him, choosing instead, on his flying visits, to stay with Alan and Susan Graham at Lapwing Cottage.

But that would end tonight. In a matter of hours they would be alone together in a starlit room overlooking the Mediterranean. And she supposed that in spite of the coldness between them he'd expect her to share his bed, submit to whatever demands he made of her.

Although that same chill might spare her the seductive persuasion he'd used the last time she was in his arms. There had been little defence she'd been able to summon against that, she thought, her throat tightening as she recalled her body's naïve response—and his almost amused rejection.

But tonight she would be on her guard, fighting ice with ice.

For the sake of her emotional sanity she had to try, anyway. Because this was the price she had to pay for Monteagle, and there was no escaping it.

Unless Marc himself let her go. And she could always hope—couldn't she?

Helen was shocked to find the parish church full as she walked up the aisle, her hand reluctantly in Marc's.

A lot of people were there, she knew, because they were simply curious to take a look at the French millionaire who'd swept young Helen Frayne off her feet. Probably quite a few were disappointed because she wasn't wearing a white crinoline with a veil. But the majority had just come to wish her well. She could feel the waves of goodwill rolling towards her as she stood at the altar with her bridegroom, and she felt the colour deepen in her face.

Oh, God, she thought. The blushing bride. What a cliché.

She wanted to turn and tell them, Don't be fooled. I'm a total fraud and this marriage is strictly business.

Up to that moment things had passed almost in a blur. The formal phrases uttered by the registrar in Aldenford a short while before had hardly impinged on her consciousness. But now the gleam of Marc's wedding ring on her hand was a cogent reminder that the deed was done.

She was aware that Marc had turned slightly to look at her,

and kept her own gaze trained on Jeff Lowell's kind face. She didn't want to see what might or might not be in her new husband's eyes.

When they'd met at the registrar's office, he had told her quietly that she looked very beautiful. He looked amazing too, she thought with a pang, the elegant dark suit doing more than justice to his tall, lean body. But naturally she hadn't said so. Instead she'd thanked him with equal politeness for the cream and yellow roses he'd sent her.

She'd been aware of Lottie looking anxious, and of Alan Graham's tight smile as they stepped forward to act as witnesses for the brief ceremony.

Now she stood taut as wire, the Vicar's serious words on God's gift of love reaching her from some far distance. She found herself wondering what he meant—questioning what relevance his words bore to her confused and panic-stricken situation.

This is wrong, she thought, her throat tightening. What we're doing is so wrong...

She knelt at Marc's side to receive the blessing, and realised with surprise that he had made the sign of the cross as it was pronounced.

As they rose, Marc took her hand and turned her towards him. He said quietly, *'Ma femme.'*

She knew he was going to kiss her, and that this time there could be no protest or evasion. Silently she raised her mouth to his, allowing his lips to possess hers with a warm and lingering tenderness she had not expected. And if she did not respond he was the only one who knew it.

At the same time Helen was aware of a faint stir in the congregation. No doubt they were pleased to see the romantic myth fulfilled, she thought, torn between irony and bleakness.

Still clasping her hand, Marc led her down the aisle, courteously acknowledging the congratulations and good wishes from all sides.

And then Helen, halfway to the sunlit doorway, understood the reason for that sudden restlessness behind them. Because

Nigel was there, leaning against the wall at the back, smiling thinly as he watched them approach.

For a moment she thought she was having a hallucination—a waking nightmare. Because he was the last person she wanted to see—and what was he doing there, anyway? What could he possibly want?

She cast a fleeting glance up at Marc and saw his face become a coolly smiling mask just as his fingers tightened round hers.

Their car was waiting at the lych gate to take them to the airport, and suddenly she wanted to run to it. To be inside it and away without any further leavetaking or good wishes from anyone.

But there was no chance of that. People were pouring out of the church around them, and a lot had cards and lucky silver horseshoes to bestow, while even more seemed to have cameras.

Helen stood, smiling composedly until her facial muscles felt stiff. At some moment Marc must have relinquished her hand, because they'd become separated. Looking round for him, she saw he was standing a few yards away with Alan, enigmatically receiving rowdy advice from some of the local men.

'Do I get to kiss the bride?' Nigel's voice beside her was soft and insinuating, but the arms that pulled her into his embrace held no gentleness. Nor was there any kiss. Instead, his cheek pressed against hers in a parody of a caress as he whispered into her ear, 'If the conversation flags tonight, sweetie, why not ask him about Angeline Vallon? And see if he tells you.'

She pulled herself free, pain slashing at her. I don't need to ask, she wanted to scream at him. I already know.

But Nigel had already gone, melting into the laughing crowd.

Instead, she saw Marc coming towards her, his face granite-hard.

He said curtly, 'I think it is time we left, Hélène. *Allons.*'

And silently, shakily, she obeyed.

Their silence during the ride to the airport had continued during the flight to the South of France.

Marc had apologised briefly for having work to do. 'But once it is completed I shall be able to devote myself to you,' he'd added, slanting a coolly sardonic smile at her before becoming immersed in papers from his briefcase.

Helen's heart had lurched uneasily, but she'd made no reply. Instead she sipped the champagne she was offered, and stared out of the window.

The flight should have provided some kind of respite from the stress of the day, but not when the name Angeline Vallon was buzzing in her brain.

The fact that she was Marc's current mistress must be common knowledge if Nigel was aware of it. Common sense suggested that she should confront her husband on the subject, letting him know she was not the innocent dupe he clearly imagined.

Yet some instinct told her that she had reached a threshold she should not cross. After all, Marc had never promised to be faithful, she reminded herself painfully. And it might even make her life easier if his physical demands were being satisfied elsewhere and she became simply his official wife, to be produced in public when required and left to her own devices in the country at all other times.

All she really needed was—somehow—to make her life bearable again.

Although her immediate concern, she realised, dry-mouthed, was to get through the week ahead of her—and particularly the next twelve hours of it.

She sat tensely beside Marc in the back of the chauffeur-driven car which had met them at the airport. It was already sunset, and lights were coming on all along the Promenade des Sables at St Benoit Plage, illuminating the marina, with its plethora of expensive yachts, and the up-market boutiques, bars and cafés that lined the other side of the thoroughfare.

Behind the promenade terraces of houses rose steeply to be crowned by a floodlit pale pink building with a dome, which Helen thought was a church until Marc informed her with faint amusement that it was the town's casino.

'Would you care to go there one evening?' he asked. 'There is an excellent restaurant, and you could try your luck at the tables.'

'Thank you, but, no,' she refused curtly. 'My father was the gambler of the family. I don't want to follow in his footsteps.'

He shrugged slightly. 'As you wish,' he returned. 'Then I shall go alone.'

The Villa Mirage occupied its headland in splendid isolation and was reached by a narrow snaking road. It was large and rambling, built on two storeys, and surrounded by a broad terrace at ground level. The first floor rooms were served by communal balconies, each with a flight of steps that led down to the luxuriant gardens, and bougainvillaea tumbled over the white walls.

In other circumstances she'd have been entranced. Now she was just scared.

The owners, Thierry and Nicole Lamande, were abroad on an extended business trip, Marc had told her, and they would be looked after by the staff, Gaston and Elise.

'I hope,' he'd added ironically, 'that you will not find it too secluded.'

Gaston turned out to be a taciturn man with a grave smile—in direct contrast to his wife, who was small and ebullient with a mass of greying hair. Chattering volubly, she conducted Helen upstairs to a large room at the back of the house, overlooking the swimming pool, with its own dressing room and elegantly appointed bathroom.

Gaston followed with her luggage, but, to her surprise, Helen realized that Marc's bags, brought up by the chauffeur, were being placed in an identical room just across the passage. And presumably by Marc's own order.

So the immediate pressure seemed to be off, she thought, suppressing a gasp of relief.

All the same, she tried to ignore the wide bed, with its immaculate white-embroidered linen, as she walked across to the long windows that led to the balcony and opened the shutters. The air was warm and still, carrying a faint fragrance of lavender from one of the local flower farms, while the rasp of cicadas filled the gathering dusk.

She took a long, luxurious breath, trying to calm herself. 'It's going to be all right,' she whispered. 'Everything's going to be fine.'

She turned to re-enter the bedroom, and halted with a stifled cry. Because Marc was there, leaning in the doorway, arms folded as he watched her.

She said unevenly, 'You—you startled me.'

'You seem easily alarmed, *ma mie*.' His mouth twisting derisively, he came forward into the room. 'I have only been asked to say that our dinner will be ready in twenty minutes.'

'Oh,' she said, trying to sound pleased when she'd never felt less hungry in her life. 'Then I'll come down.' She turned away, beginning to fumble with the little satin-covered buttons on her jacket, trying to drag them free from their loops.

'Be careful,' he said. 'Or they will tear.' He walked over to her and removed her shaking hands from their task, dealing with the fastenings himself, deftly and impersonally.

She'd planned to take the jacket off, of course, but she felt absurdly self-conscious as she slipped it from her shoulders—as if, she thought, she was suddenly naked under his inscrutable dark gaze.

'Your dress is charming,' he said, after a pause that seemed to Helen's overwrought senses to have lasted fractionally too long. 'Perhaps we should give a party when we return to England, so that all your friends in the village can admire its true glory. What do you think?'

She shrugged as she walked past him towards the door. 'I'm sure people will want to see how the house is progressing, anyway,' she returned quietly. 'But won't you find a village party rather boring?'

His brows lifted. 'With you beside me, *cherie*?' he asked mockingly. 'Impossible. Now, let us go and eat our wedding supper.'

A table had been set for them under an awning on the terrace, bright with tiny bowls of scented flowers and candles in little glass shades. Gaston brought Helen the dry white wine she'd asked for, while Marc drank Ricard.

The food was wonderful, even though Helen was fully aware she was not doing it justice. A delicately flavoured vegetable

terrine was followed by poached sole, then tiny chickens sim-
mered in wine and grapes. After the cheese came *milles-feuilles*,
thick with liqueur-flavoured cream.

Helen was sparing with the excellent Chablis offered with the
meal, and, to Marc's open amusement, resolutely refused the
brandy that arrived with the tall silver coffeepot.

'Afraid that it will send you to sleep again, *ma chère*?' His
brows lifted. 'I promise it will not.'

Her heart lurched. 'Did Elise do all of this?' she asked, keen
to change the subject. 'She's a miraculous cook.'

'A lot of people would agree.' He smiled faintly. 'And many
attempts have been made to lure her away, but she remains faithful to Thierry and Nicole.'

She said stiltedly, 'It was kind of them to lend you this beautiful house.'

'And I am sorry we have only a week, instead of the month
they offered,' he returned. 'But it may be that we can go on a
longer trip later in the year—to the Caribbean, perhaps, or the
Pacific islands.' He paused. 'Would you like that?'

She didn't look at him. 'It—it sounds wonderful.'

Oh, stop pretending, she begged silently. *Please, stop pretending.*

It was growing very late, she realised. The deep indigo of the
sky was sparked with stars, and a slight breeze had risen, carrying with it the murmur of the sea.

She suddenly realised she was going to yawn, and tried desperately to mask it with her hand. But he noticed.

'Tu es fatiguée?'

'No—not at all.' Her denial was too swift—too emphatic. 'It's
so lovely here,' she added, forcing a smile. 'I'm trying to take
it all in.'

'That may be easier in daylight. And I am glad that you are
not tired.' Marc finished his brandy and rose. He came round to
her and extended his hand. 'It is time for bed, *ma femme*,' he
said softly. *'Viens.'*

Shakily, Helen got to her feet and let him lead her into the
house, across the shadows of the *salon* and up the stairs beyond.

At her door, Marc paused, running a rueful hand over his chin. 'I need to shave,' he told her. 'So I will join you presently.'

Swallowing, Helen backed into her room and closed the door. The lamps had been lit on either side of the bed, and the covers were turned down. One of her nightgowns—the white one—was waiting for her, fanned out over the foot of the bed.

So she was not to be spared after all, she thought numbly. Even though there was another woman in his life, Marc was still not prepared to forego the novelty of possessing his virgin bride.

It had been bad enough when she'd only had the danger of her own responses to fight, she thought. But now she had the added humiliation of knowing that she would be sharing him. That even on their wedding night she'd be denied the small comfort of knowing that, for a brief time, he'd been hers alone.

A laugh like a sob escaped her. 'My God,' she whispered. 'And I thought I could fight him.'

She went over to the dressing table and sank down on the padded stool. In the lamplight she looked pale, her eyes wide and almost bruised.

She thought, How can I bear this? What shall I do? And sat motionless, her face buried in her hands.

She did not hear the door open, but some deep instinct warned her when she was no longer alone. She raised her head and met his gaze in the mirror. He was standing behind her, wearing a robe of dark silk which she knew would be his only covering.

He had showered as well, she realised. The clean damp scent of his skin filled her senses, and she took a swift breath of helpless longing.

He said quietly, 'I thought you would be in bed, *ma belle*.'

'My dress,' she said, snatching at an excuse. 'I—I couldn't reach…'

'You could have come to me, Hélène. Asked me to help you.' His hands closed on her shoulders, urging her gently to her feet. 'Like this,' he whispered.

Helen felt the tiny hook on her bodice give way, and the faint rasp of the zip as he lowered it. She felt his mouth touch the nape of her neck, then move with sure gentleness to her shoulder, pushing away the thin strap, baring the soft skin for his lips.

She felt the dress begin to slip down her body, and clutched it with both hands as the first dangerous and uncontrollable tremor of need quivered through her body.

He turned her slowly to face him, his mouth seeking hers. He said softly, *'Mon ange.'*

Angel, she thought dazedly, her pulses swimming. My angel. My—Angeline… Was that what he called her too—*mon ange*? Were these the caresses he used to seduce his mistress—and countless others?

Marc's women—so easily interchangeable. So soon forgotten.

But only if she allowed it, she told herself, anger building on wretchedness.

As he kissed her she turned her face away sharply, so that his mouth grazed only her cheek. In a voice she didn't recognise, she said, 'No—no, Marc, please.'

He paused, frowning, but more in surprise than annoyance. His hands cupped her face, making her look at him. *'Qu'as tu?'* His tone was still gentle. 'What is the matter?'

'I can't do this.' She swallowed. 'I thought I—could. But it's impossible.'

He put his arms round her, his hands slipping inside the loosened dress, gently stroking the naked vulnerability of her back, making her shiver and burn.

'Mon amour,' he murmured, as if he sensed her body's confusion. 'There is nothing to fear. Do you think I would hurt you? I promise I shall not.'

But she was in pain already. She screamed at him soundlessly. She occupied an agonising wasteland where need fought with reason and heartbreak and humiliation waited to devour her like hungry tigers. And if she turned to him now, she would be lost.

'Please—you have to let me go.' Her voice cracked. 'I—I can't be what you want—do what you want. You—you said you'd be patient…'

'Patient,' he repeated, almost incredulously. 'You dare to say that to me? *Mon Dieu!* When have I not been patient? Even when your body was mine for the taking, I held back. Waited for the moment when you would be my wife in honour.'

'There is no honour,' Helen said, her voice a shaken breath. 'We—made a deal. That's all.'

Grim-faced, he stepped back from her. *'Mais, oui,'* he said. 'We had a deal—that sordid little bargain of ours, to which you agreed, *ma chère*, however much you may regret it at this moment.'

She faced him, her arms wrapped round her body. 'You threw me a lifeline,' she said. 'And I was grateful. I didn't let myself consider—the personal implications. At least, not until now.'

'Not even when you were in my arms, *ma belle*?' His laugh was harsh. His words seared her to the core. 'I think you are lying.' He paused. 'But here is something else for you to consider. Why should I continue to keep to the terms of our agreement if you do not?'

There was a silence. At last she said hoarsely, 'You mean you'd—abandon Monteagle? Stop all the work because I—I won't…'

She stared at him pleadingly, but found she was looking into the narrowed angry eyes of a stranger.

She said, stammering slightly, 'But you couldn't do that, surely? You—you love it too much. Besides, you promised…'

'And you,' he said, 'made a vow also. Just today. And, whatever I feel about the house, I hate being cheated far more, *ma petite trompeuse*. And if you can break your word so easily, then so can I.'

He paused. 'Or maybe you would prefer to—reconsider, my beautiful wife. After all, we still have the rest of the night. And surely for the sake of your beloved Monteagle you can endure this—minor inconvenience. But do not make me wait too long for your decision,' he added coldly, turning away. 'And this time, *madame*, you will come to me.'

Helen stood motionless, hardly breathing as she watched the door close behind him.

After a while she unclasped her arms and let the dress slide to the ground. She stepped out of it and went into the bathroom, running water into the tub as she took off her underwear and put it in the linen basket.

Then she climbed into the bath and lay back, closing her eyes, trying to be calm—rational.

All over the world, she thought, women were having sex when they didn't want to. That was nothing new. She couldn't, of course, fake an orgasm. Even if she knew how she guessed Marc would not be deceived for a moment. Instead, she would have to feign the frigidity that Nigel had once accused her of. Maintain some kind of integrity by her indifference, no matter what the cost—and instinct told her it would be high.

This minor inconvenience, he'd said, his mouth twisting cynically.

Oh, God, she whispered wretchedly. How little he knew.

She could only hope he would soon become bored by her passive resistance. But until then...

She dried herself, cleaned her teeth and brushed her hair. Calming herself with the usual routine of bedtime.

She went over to the bed, picked up the pretty, fragile thing that lay there, and slipped it on over her head. She supposed he would want her to take it off. Supposed, but did not know. Not for certain. Nothing for certain.

It's ludicrous, she thought, swallowing a small, fierce sob. My first time with a man and I haven't a bloody clue.

Except, of course, the remembrance of his hands weaving their dark magic on her skin only a short time before. The magic she'd always known could be her downfall.

The white silk rustled faintly above her bare feet as she went slowly out of the room and across the passage. The door of his room was ajar, and she pushed it open and stepped into the lamplit silence.

CHAPTER NINE

MARC was lying propped up on an elbow, facing the door. Waiting, she realised, without one solitary doubt for her to appear. Savouring his victory in advance. The enjoyment he so confidently expected.

Yet there was no triumph in the brief, bleak smile he accorded her.

He pulled back the cover, indicating without words that she should join him. Helen obeyed, lying rigid and awkward beside him, aware of the painful thud of her heart, but even more conscious of his naked warmth and the grave dark eyes studying her face.

Still propped on his elbow, Marc lifted his other hand, stroking the hair back from her temples with his fingertips, then moving down to trace the arch of her eyebrows. His touch was as light as the brush of a butterfly's wing as it followed the hollows of her cheekbones, then hovered at the corner of her mouth.

'Hélène.' His voice was oddly gentle too. 'Do you know how I have longed for this moment—and for you?'

He bent his head and kissed her, his lips moving coaxingly on her unresponsive mouth while his hand slid down to the demure neckline of her nightdress, brushing its straps off her shoulders.

'*C'est très jolie, ça,*' he whispered. 'But I think you would be even lovelier without it.'

She was shaking inside as the silk slipped down her body, and she heard his soft murmur of satisfaction as his fingers cupped her bare breast. No matter how determined she might be to withstand him, she found with dismay that she could not prevent her nipple hardening in excitement at his caress, or deny the sudden languorous melting between her thighs.

132

Marc bent towards her again, his mouth closing on the rounded softness he'd uncovered, his tongue laving its engorged peak with passionate finesse.

He was lying beside her now, his arm round her shoulders, holding her against him, leaving her in no doubt that he was fiercely aroused. His hand drifted slowly downwards over her body, exploring each curve and contour through the thin fabric of her nightdress, creating a delicate, enticing friction against her skin.

She felt his fingers linger on her hipbone, then move inwards across the flat plane of her stomach with unmistakable purpose while his mouth sought hers with renewed intensity.

She moved then, swiftly, frantically, both hands capturing his and dragging it away from her body. 'Don't,' she said hoarsely. 'Don't touch me.'

He was still for a moment, then she heard him sigh.

'Ah, mon amour.' He took her hand and raised it to his lips, caressing her palm softly. 'Don't fight me, *je t'en supplié*. Relax. Let me make this beautiful for you.'

'Beautiful?' She echoed the word with bitter incredulity. 'You bought me for sex, *monsieur*, so how can it possibly be beautiful? Not that it matters. I—just want it to be over.'

He was suddenly tense, his fingers gripping hers almost painfully. At last he said quietly, 'Hélène, you do not know what you are saying.'

'Yes—yes, I do.' The words tumbled out of her, heartsick and wounded. 'I'm sick of this hypocrisy—this pretence that I'm anything more to you than just another girl in another bed, marriage or no marriage. And I can't bear to be touched—kissed,' she added quickly. 'So just—do it and let me go. Because I don't want you and I never will.'

His sudden harsh laugh made her flinch. He released her and sat up, the sheet falling away from his body, his mouth grim. 'And what now, *madame*? I am expected, perhaps, to admit defeat and send you back to the virgin sanctity of your room. Is that it? To be followed by a swift, discreet annulment back in England?'

He shook his head. 'Well, you may dream on, *mon coeur*.

Because you will go nowhere until I have made our marriage a reality.'

Before she even realised what was happening he had lifted himself over her, his hand pushing back her nightgown and parting her thighs with ruthless determination.

She felt his fingers discover the moist silken heat that he'd created, in spite of herself, heard him laugh softly, and could have died of shame.

'You'll make me hate you,' she stormed, trying to twist away from him and failing totally.

'That is your privilege,' he said. 'This—is mine.' And, poised above her, slowly, skilfully, he guided himself into her.

She lay beneath him unmoving, hardly able to breathe, her eyes closed and one fist pressed against her mouth, waiting for the pain but determined that she would not cry out.

Yet there was no need. She had not expected consideration. Probably did not deserve gentleness. But he offered them to her just the same. In spite of the unyielding tautness of her body, his possession of her was deliberately leisured and totally complete. Also utterly determined.

Yet at the same time it was a curiously sterile performance. Sexually naïve as she was, Helen could still recognise that. And although she'd stipulated no kisses or caresses she'd not expected him to listen. But it seemed that he had, because apart from that one supreme intimacy of his body joined to hers there was no other physical contact between them. His weight was supported by his arms, clamped either side of her on the bed.

When he began to move, it was also without haste. The drive of his body was controlled and clinical, expressing an almost steely resolve, and when Helen risked a scared, fleeting glance upwards at his face she saw that it was set and expressionless, his gaze fixed on the wall above the bed. As if he had withdrawn behind some silent, private barricade.

And even as she realised with anguish, This is not—*not* how it should be…she felt, deep within her, at that moment, a small stirring, as if the petals of a flower were slowly unfurling in the sunlight. But as her shocked mind acknowledged it, tried with a kind of desperation to focus there, it was gone.

At the same time she heard his breathing change suddenly, and felt his body convulse violently inside hers as he reached his climax.

She heard him cry out something that might almost have been her name, his voice hoarse and ragged, as if that unyielding wall of reserve had suddenly crumbled, and for an instant she felt his weight slump against her, pressing her down into the bed.

But he released himself almost at once and rolled away from her, burying his face in his folded arms so that she was free.

For a while she lay still, adjusting to the slight soreness between her thighs and knowing at the same time that it did not compare with the vast ache of loneliness and frustration that now filled her bewildered body, making her want to moan aloud.

She moved away a little, towards the edge of the bed. She said, dry-mouthed, 'May I go now—back to my own room?'

For a long moment there was silence, then slowly he raised his head and looked at her, his face wearily sardonic. '*Pourquoi pas?* Why not? I assume you do not wish to sleep in my arms and have me kiss you awake in the morning. So go back to your sanctuary, my little cheat.'

His words stung, especially when she knew that even now, if he reached for her—held her—she would not be able to resist him.

She lifted her chin. 'I hardly cheated. I did what you expected.'

'Did you?' His mouth twisted. 'How little you know, *cherie*.' He shrugged a sweat-slicked shoulder. 'And I still say you are a cheat. Because your victim is now yourself. You have defrauded your own body of the warmth and passion of being a woman. And you did it deliberately. Or did you think I would not know?' he added with contempt. 'So sleep with that, *hein*?'

Somehow Helen got back to her own room. Somehow she stripped off her crumpled nightdress, kicking it away, and turned on the shower, letting the warm water rain down on her in a torrent, mingling with the sudden tears on her face.

She whispered brokenly, 'It could have been worse. It could have been so much worse...'

And knew that she was lying.

It was late when Helen came back to full consciousness the next morning. She'd eventually fallen into an uneasy sleep around dawn, but now the sunlight was burning through the shutters, she realised, shading dull eyes with her hand as she peered at the window.

And somehow she had to shower, dress, and go downstairs to face Marc, she thought, uttering a soft groan at the prospect.

Yet at least she'd woken alone, and not been roused by his kisses, she told herself, remembering with a pang his soft-voiced taunt of the night before, as she pushed away the tangled sheet and swung her feet to the floor.

His accusation that she'd cheated herself of fulfilment still rankled bitterly, however, and her body was haunted by a feeling of numb emptiness that almost amounted to desolation.

Inexperienced as she was, her inner desolation was not helped by the recognition that her husband had subjected her to a possession without passion—a disciplined and calculated exercise for his own satisfaction. Nor was it alleviated by the knowledge that she'd deliberately instigated this bleak and un-tender consummation.

Was this a foretaste of what she could expect each night of this caricature of a honeymoon? she wondered. If so, at least it would make it marginally easier to withhold herself, as she knew she must.

She had to be careful too, she thought, remembering that brief instant when simply the stark rhythm of his body inside hers had been enough to provoke that strange flicker of desire, as unwelcome as it was unexpected, but no less potent for that.

She could only hope that, caught between boredom and an-ger in this war of attrition between them, Marc would be keen to put the whole wretched episode behind him and return to his former way of life—and the women who shared it. Once this painful pretence of a marriage was finished in any signif-icant way, she might be able to attain some peace.

After all, she thought, swallowing, Marc still had the house, which was and always had been his main concern in all this. She'd only ever been intended as a bonus in the transaction. His personal perquisite. He would simply be forced to write her off as a loss. Well—he was a businessman. He would understand that, and shrug.

And although she would be freed from any kind of sexual partnership with him, and ultimate and inevitable heartbreak, she would make sure she was nothing less than the perfect chatelaine for Monteagle. He would have no complaints about the way his home was run, or her behaviour as his hostess.

She sighed, and trailed across to the dressing room. In the meantime she'd have to pretend that this was the first day of a normal marriage and find something appropriate to wear.

Much as she might wish it, she could hardly go for the full covered-up blouse and skirt look when the temperature was clearly in the high eighties. Besides, Marc might even regard that as some kind of challenge, and that was the last thing she wanted.

It was probably better to attempt the role of radiant bride, she thought. And her pride demanded that she should behave as if the previous night had never happened, even if she was still weeping inside.

Eventually, as a concession to the climate, she picked out a black bikini that wasn't too indecently brief, topping it with its own filmy mid-thigh shirt.

But, in spite of her fears, it was only Elise who was waiting for her as she apprehensively descended the stairs half an hour later.

'*Bonjour, madame.*' Her eyes were twinkling. 'You 'ave sleep well, I think? Your 'usband say to let you rest as long as you desire. But now you like *un petit dejeuner*?'

'Just coffee, please,' Helen said, self-consciously aware that her watch was saying it was long past breakfast-time. She glanced around her. 'Er—where is *monsieur*?' she ventured.

''E 'as go for drive into the 'ills,' Elise informed her. 'But 'e will come back soon. For the lunch. It is my fish soup, which 'e does not miss.' She nodded with satisfaction, then bustled off to get the coffee.

Well, she was being allowed a brief respite at least, Helen thought. Given a breathing space to decide how she should behave and what she should actually say when she encountered him at last.

Elise's coffee was a dark and vibrant brew, and it managed to rid Helen's head of the last unhappy wisps of mental fog and enable her to think clearly.

It was vitally important not to give Marc the idea that she cared too much about the bleak conclusion to their wedding night.

Perhaps she should give the impression that it was no more than she'd expected. Or maybe she should wait, she thought. Judge his mood when he returned. Leave it to him to dictate the scenario.

In the meantime, this was a wonderful house, with beautiful grounds and the luxury of a swimming pool. At least she could allow herself a little enjoyment.

She finished her coffee, then set off. The pool was sited in a sunken area of the garden, surrounded by flower-filled shallow terraces. At the deep end of the azure water was a diving board, while a small hexagonal pavilion had been built at the opposite end for changing purposes, and to house a comprehensively equipped refrigerator.

Cushioned loungers, each with its own parasol, had been set round the surrounding tiled area.

Helen applied some high-factor sun lotion and lay down, sighing gratefully. There was a paperback book in her canvas bag,' but, for a while anyway, she preferred to close her eyes and drift, blocking out the dark fears and uncertainties that plagued her, her head full, instead, of the distant wash of the sea and the busy hum of insects among the flowers.

She almost slept.

The sudden instinctive awareness that she was no longer alone brought her back to full consciousness, her eyes flying open to see Marc standing at the foot of the flight of shallow steps. He was wearing black swimming briefs, and, apart from the thin cotton shirt flung over one shoulder, the rest of him was tanned skin.

For one shocked, unguarded moment, she was pierced by a shaft of yearning so strong it seemed to penetrate her bones.

And he was looking at her too, his mouth unsmiling, his eyes masked by his sunglasses.

He said laconically, '*Ça va?*'

'Fine,' she said, jack-knifing herself into a sitting position too swiftly and defensively. It had suddenly occurred to her that apart from last night, this was the nearest to naked Marc had ever seen her, and the realisation made her feel disquieted and uncomfortable.

'I regret this intrusion,' he went on. 'But Elise was insistent that I needed a swim before lunch.' He tossed the shirt on to another lounger. 'She feels, I think, that I am neglecting my bride,' he added, his mouth twisting. 'I could hardly tell her that I am merely obeying your wishes.' He paused. 'Unless, of course, you would like to join me in the pool?'

Helen swallowed. 'Another time—perhaps.'

'Why pretend?' Marc asked derisively. 'Why not say no?'

She turned away. She said in a stifled voice, 'Isn't it a little late for that?'

'Perhaps that is something we should discuss.' He walked across and sat down on the end of her lounger. He'd discarded his sunglasses and his expression was searching—sombre. She watched him, her own eyes wary, her body tensing instinctively at his proximity.

She said, 'You mean to apologise—for last night?'

'Apologise?' His brows lifted. 'No. Let us say instead, *ma mie*, that neither of us was very kind—or very wise—in our treatment of each other, and put last night far behind us.'

'How can we do that?' Helen asked stiffly.

'By agreeing that it is the present—and our future together— that should concern us more.'

Her small workmanlike hands were gripped tightly together. 'What future is that?'

He sighed, his mouth tightening. 'I have taken you as my wife, Hélène. How can we live as strangers?'

She lifted her chin. 'Because that's what we are—as last night proved.'

'It proved nothing,' Marc said shortly. 'Except that you had decided for some reason that you no longer wanted me.'

'No longer?' Helen echoed indignantly. 'When did I ever?'

His brows rose sardonically. 'You wish me to list the times, perhaps?' There was a pause then he added, 'I regret that I did not seduce you when I had the chance, *ma belle*, instead of waiting to offer you the security of marriage first.'

'Perhaps,' Helen said stonily, hating the colour that had flared in her face at the unforgivable truth of his words, 'perhaps even then you wouldn't have found me as easy as you seem to believe.'

'I never expected to find you easy, Hélène,' he returned softly. 'Merely—infinitely rewarding.' He smiled faintly. 'As your beautiful mouth promises, *mon coeur*. The mouth you would not allow me to kiss last night in case you melted for me as your ancestress once did for the King,' he added quietly.

The breath seemed to catch in her throat. 'You—flatter yourself, *monsieur*,' she said. 'And you're quite wrong, too. They were different people in a different age. No comparison.'

He shrugged, his mouth wry, '*Bien sûr*, I am not a king, but a good republican—and I am your husband as well as your lover. But are we really so far apart? She fled him and he followed, just as I am here with you now, in spite of all that has happened.'

'We're a world away.' Her voice sounded thick and strained. 'And you are *not* my lover.'

For a moment his head went back as if she'd struck him, and he was silent.

'Then may we not begin again?' he asked at last, his voice deepening huskily. 'You are my wife, Hélène, and I want you—I long to show you how it should be between us. How it can be. If only…'

He reached for her hand, but she snatched it away.

'*Ah, Dieu.*' Marc shook his head. He was silent for a long moment, then said gently, 'Don't fight me any more, *cherie*. Let me come to you tonight and make love to you, as I wish to do. If you would only allow it, I know I could make you happy.'

'I think you're more concerned with your own satisfaction,' Helen flung at him. 'And the fact that your masculine pride's been damaged. In spite of your fantasies, last night can't have been particularly *rewarding* for you.'

'Or for you,' he said with sudden harshness.

It was her turn to shrug. 'Nevertheless,' she said, 'that's as good as it gets. Come to me—stay away—it makes no difference.'

She saw the dark eyes flare and his mouth harden.

He got to his feet in one lithe movement and stood over her, reminding her suddenly of the previous night, his body poised above hers. Forcing her to remember that piercing instant of need...

She went rigid, her eyes almost blank with fright, and saw his mouth move in a faint smile that was almost a sneer.

'*Sois tranquille,*' he said coldly. 'I shall not ask again.'

He turned away and walked to the edge of the pool. His body cut the water in a clean dive.

Heart hammering, she scrambled off the lounger, cramming on her shirt and picking up her pretty embroidered beach bag.

She went hurriedly up the steps, not looking behind her. Back to the house, she thought shakily. Out of harm's way.

Yet she knew at the same time that it was not that simple. *She fled him and he followed.* That was what Marc had said. And, in spite of that icy parting assurance from him, Helen knew she would never feel completely safe again while they were under the same roof.

She made herself go down to lunch when Elise came, clearly puzzled, to call her. For one thing she needed to repair the damage done by that moment of recoil at the pool. She'd shown Marc too clearly that he had the power to disturb her, and then, even more stupidly, she'd run away.

Also, more prosaically, she was hungry.

He was already waiting at the table that had been set for them in the shade of the terrace, and rose formally as she approached, his eyes skimming over the pale green sundress with its halter strap that she'd changed into, although he refrained from the comment she'd expected as she seated herself opposite him and unfolded her napkin.

He had changed too, she realised, into dark blue linen trousers and a matching polo shirt, and his still-damp hair was combed back from his face. As Elise arrived with the tureen he smiled up at her, said something teasing in his own language, and the force of his attraction made Helen catch her breath.

Concentrate on the food, she adjured herself silently. It's safer that way.

The fish soup was delicious, aromatic and filling, forcing her to eat sparingly of the platter of cold meats and salad that followed, and choose just a peach from the bowl of fresh fruit that ended the meal.

She declined any coffee, and was rising to her feet when he said crisply, '*Un moment, madame.*'

Helen halted, startled and reluctant.

'We need to reach a certain level of agreement.' Marc did not look at her as he filled his own cup. 'Whatever our private arrangements, we should try to behave in front of others as if we were truly *les nouveaux mariés. Par chance*, we do not have to stay here for very long, but we need to spend some time together each day—and in public.'

Helen bit her lip. 'Is that really necessary?'

'By now the news of our marriage will have reached the newspapers, and the gossip columnists will know we are here.' He shrugged. 'They will wish to take photographs of us together—being happy. We should indulge them. What happens at night is the business of no one but ourselves,' he added coldly.

Helen bit her lip. She said, 'I suppose—if we must. What—what do you suggest?'

'You overwhelm me.' His tone was barbed. 'To begin with, I propose we go down to St Benoit. The car and driver have been placed at our service, so I have ordered him to come round in half an hour. With Louis at the wheel, you do not even have to be alone with me.' He paused, allowing that to strike home. 'Also I intend to work for part of each day,' he went on. 'There are matters that require my attention even on honeymoon, so I recommend you use the pool area during those times, in case the sight of you in a bikini arouses me beyond bearing.'

Unhappy colour rose in her face. 'Please—don't talk like that.'

'Tes conditions sont trop rigoureuses, ma mie,' he told her mockingly. 'I cannot sleep with you—I may not even swim with you—and it is obvious you would prefer to eat alone. These I accept. But I refuse to censor my words—or my thoughts. *D'accord?'*

There was a silence, then Helen nodded jerkily. 'As you wish.'

'I recommend you treat your time with me like medicine, *cherie.'* Marc swallowed the remainder of his coffee and re-placed the cup on its saucer. His eyes were hard. 'To be taken quickly and as soon forgotten.' He rose to his feet. 'Half an hour, then. And try, if you can, to smile for the cameras as if you were happy. This week will soon pass.'

By the time they came back to the villa that evening Helen had already reached at least one conclusion.

In the sunlit hours, she thought, she could—just—play the role assigned to her. But it would be an entirely different matter when the velvety darkness descended. That was altogether too intimate an ambience, and if she was to survive, as she must, her evenings had to be her own.

So when Marc turned to her after dinner and invited her to go with him to the Yacht Club, for coffee and brandies, she refused, saying mendaciously she had a headache.

'Pauvre petite.' His mouth curled with faint irony. 'Do you wish me to remain here and cherish you?'

'No, thank you,' she returned coolly. 'I'm not chained to your wrist. You're free to go out alone whenever you want.'

'How sweet you are,' he drawled mockingly. 'And how un-derstanding.' He paused. 'I shall try not to disturb you on my return.'

Elise, who was clearing the table, sent them a look that said louder than words that such a new wife should *expect* to be disturbed by her husband, and should, *en effet*, actively welcome it, headache or not.

Marc walked over to Helen, dark and devastating in his tuxedo, and bent, his lips swiftly brushing her hair.

He said quietly, 'Sleep well,' and went.

There was a silence, then Elise said dourly, 'I will fetch you a powder, *madame*, for ze 'eadache.'

She not only fetched it, she stood over Helen while she swallowed the foul-tasting thing. 'Now you will be restored for the return of *monsieur*,' she said with a firm nod.

But Helen wasn't so sure. The tension of walking round St Benoit Plage all afternoon, hand in hand with Marc, was threatening her with a genuine headache. It had been quite an ordeal for her, however impersonal his touch.

The villa was equipped with a state-of-the-art audio system and an eclectic mix of music. Helen curled up on one of the giant hide sofas in the *salon* and put on some slow sweet jazz. But the music alone couldn't stop her thinking, her mind replaying all the events of the past twenty-four hours. Above all she found herself wondering what Marc was doing—and who he might be with.

She'd been aware all afternoon of the predatory glances being aimed at him by tanned and sexy women keen to get closer regardless of her presence. And now she'd turned him out on the town alone…

But then what choice did she have? she argued defensively with herself. She certainly had no right to expect physical fidelity from him.

Sighing, she picked up one of the glossy magazines arranged on the low table in front of her and began to flick over the pages. She paused to glance at a double-page spread showing people attending a charity performance at the opera. The name 'Angeline Vallon' seemed to leap out at her.

She looked at the accompanying picture, her heart beating slowly and unevenly.

She saw a tall, beautiful woman, with a mane of dark auburn hair tumbling down her back, standing beside a much smaller man with a beard and a faintly peevish expression, described as 'her industrialist husband Hercule'.

Madame Vallon was wearing a very low-cut evening gown that set off her frankly voluptuous body, and a magnificent diamond necklace circled her throat.

She didn't look like someone who had to ask more than once for what she wanted, thought Helen, trying not to wince. Nor someone who would be easily persuaded to let go.

And you're quite right to opt for self-preservation, she told herself stoically. Because you're no competition for her. No competition at all.

She closed the magazine, replacing it with meticulous exactitude on the table, and made her solitary way up to bed.

But not to sleep. Not until much later, when she eventually heard quiet footsteps passing her room, without breaking stride even for a moment, and then the sound of Marc's door closing.

Helen turned on to her stomach, pressing her burning face into the pillow.

I shall not ask again. That, after all, was what he'd told her. And apparently he'd meant every word.

Somehow she had to be grateful for this one mercy at least.

But, dear God, how painfully, grindingly difficult that was going to be for her. And she found herself stifling a sob.

CHAPTER TEN

MARC had told her the time would pass quickly, but to Helen the days that followed seemed more like an eternity. Yet under other circumstances she knew they could have been wonderful.

From that first afternoon in St Benoit Plage she seemed to have stepped through the looking glass into a different and totally unreal world, peopled only by the beautiful and the seriously affluent.

To her astonishment, Marc had been right about the photographers, and Helen had been chagrined to find herself described in the local news sheet as 'charming but shy', under a picture of her with her mouth open, clinging to her husband's hand as if he was her last hope of salvation.

Not shy, she'd thought wryly. Just shocked witless at all this unwonted attention.

'Relax, *ma mie*,' Marc had advised, clearly amused. 'They will soon focus on someone else.'

In the days that followed he took her to Cannes, Nice and Monte Carlo, until her mind was a blur of smart restaurants and glamorous shops. She had learned early on not to linger outside the windows of boutiques, or admire anything too openly, otherwise the next moment Marc would have bought it for her. It was heady stuff for someone who'd existed up to now on a skeleton wardrobe, but she found his casual generosity disturbing.

No doubt he treated his mistresses equally lavishly, she thought unhappily, but at least they deserved it. Whereas she, patently, did not.

Not that he cared, she told herself defensively. After all, when this pathetic honeymoon had stumbled to its close he had Angeline Vallon waiting for him. And life would return to normal for them both.

She had to admit that Marc had kept his word about their own relationship. He'd made sure from the first that they were rarely alone together. In the car, with Louis as unwitting chaperone, they exchanged polite but stilted conversation, and at the villa, as he'd suggested, they pursued a policy of positive avoidance, under the frankly disapproving gaze of Gaston and Elise, who were clearly baffled by these strange newlyweds.

She had no idea where or how Marc spent his evenings, although she was always courteously invited to accompany him and had to struggle to invent excuses. She only knew that she lay sleepless, listening for his return, however late it happened to be. And how sad was that?

There were times when she longed to confront him—tell him to his face that she knew he had a mistress. But that would only betray to him how much it mattered to her, and she couldn't risk that. Couldn't admit that he had the power to hurt her.

Also, he might ask how she knew. And she could hardly confess that she'd been eavesdropping.

It was far less humiliating to simply keep quiet and count her blessings that she still had Monteagle, if nothing else.

She halted, startled, aware that she'd never regarded the situation in that light before. Always her home had been paramount in her thoughts. She'd said openly that she would do anything to save it, yet now, for the first time, she was counting the cost and finding it oddly bitter.

It will be easier when I go home, she promised herself. When I get back to the real world again.

And yet, as she at last began packing for the return journey, she found herself feeling oddly wistful—even empty. And for once she had a genuine headache. The sky had become overcast towards the end of the afternoon, and she wasn't surprised to hear a faint rumble of thunder from the hills.

When she arrived downstairs for dinner, she found that Gaston had prudently laid the table in the *salle à manger* instead of the terrace. 'It makes to rain, *madame*,' he told her lugubriously.

Elise came bustling in with a dish of home-made duck pâté.

'*Monsieur* begs you will commence,' she announced. ''E is engaged with the telephone.'

It was over ten minutes later when Marc eventually made his unsmiling appearance. 'I regret that I have kept you waiting.' The apology sounded cursory, and he ate his meal almost in silence, his thoughts quite evidently elsewhere.

Eventually, when coffee was served and they were alone, he said abruptly, 'We will be leaving for the airport in the morning, *à dix heures*. Can you be ready?'

Helen put down her cup. 'Has the flight been changed?'

'We are not catching the London plane,' he said. 'We shall be spending a short time in Paris instead.'

'Paris?' she echoed. 'But where will we stay?'

'I once told you that I have an *appartement* there,' he said.

'Yes,' she said. 'And a hotel suite in London.'

His faint smile was twisted. 'The *appartement* is larger, *je t'assure*. To begin with, there is more than one bedroom,' he added pointedly.

She flushed dully, annoyed that he should read her so accurately. 'All the same,' she said stiffly, 'I'd prefer to go straight home.'

He glanced at her meditatively. 'You are my wife, Hélène,' he said quietly. 'It might be thought that wherever I am your home is with me.'

'We don't have that kind of marriage.' She didn't look at him. 'And, anyway, I need to be at Monteagle. I want to see what progress has been made there. Besides, what would I do in Paris—apart from cramp your style?' she added recklessly.

Marc's brows lifted. 'Cramp my style?' he queried, as if he'd never heard the phrase before. 'In what way, may I ask?'

Helen bit her lip. 'Well—you have things to do—people to see,' she offered nervously, backing away from his challenge. 'And I'd be in the way.' She poured herself some more coffee. 'Anyway, I think we both need—breathing space—from each other.'

'You think so?' His tone was mocking. 'Shall I calculate for you, *cherie*, exactly how many hours we have spent together this week? Not that it matters, of course. Monteagle calls, and you obey.' He paused. 'So, I will go to Paris alone, and arrange to have you met at the airport in England.'

He swallowed the rest of his coffee and rose. 'And now you will excuse me. I intend to try my luck at the casino again tonight.'

'Is that where you've been spending your evenings?' Helen asked the question before she could stop herself. 'I didn't realise you were such a gambler.'

'And nor did I, *ma belle*,' Marc said softly, 'until I met you. And I find the turn of a wheel or the fall of a card infinitely kinder, believe me.' He kissed the tips of his fingers to her. *'Au revoir.'*

Helen hated thunderstorms. But she was almost grateful to this one for giving her something more to worry about than her immediate problems. After all, she'd won a victory over her return to Monteagle, she thought defensively. So why did it feel so much like a defeat? And Marc's absence so soon after the honeymoon would excite the kind of local comment she most wished to avoid.

But anything was better than accompanying him to Paris, like a piece of extra luggage.

And he certainly hadn't tried too hard to persuade her, either, Helen told herself defiantly.

She spent a restless evening trying to read, while lightning played around the hills, making the villa's electricity flicker. Eventually she gave it up as a bad job and went to bed.

Perhaps it was the prospect of going home that made her feel more relaxed, but tonight she found herself drifting into a doze almost at once.

When she awoke, everything was pitch-black and completely silent. The storm, it seemed, had rolled away at last, leaving the room like an oven and the bedclothes twisted round her. Clearly she hadn't been sleeping as peacefully as she'd thought. She struggled out of the shrouding covers and got out of bed, treading across to the window and opening it wide to step out on to the balcony, planning to cool off a little.

But the air outside was just as stifling. Helen leaned on the balustrade and inhaled, but the garden smelled raw and thirsty, and possessed by a strange stillness, as if it was waiting in anticipation of—what?

A moment later she found out. As if some cosmic tap had been turned, the rain began to fall in huge, soaking drops, and by the time Helen made it back into her room she was already wet through, her nightgown sticking in clammy dampness to her skin.

Grimacing, she peeled it off and dropped it to the floor. She discarded the coverlet from the bed, too, and slid back under the single sheet, listening to the heavy splash of rain on the balcony tiles, hoping it would have a soporific effect.

She had to train herself not to lie awake listening for Marc, she told herself wearily, because there would be so many nights when he would not be there. Starting with tomorrow.

She turned on to her side, facing the window, and stiffened as a tall shadow walked in from the balcony and moved soundlessly towards her. She wanted to scream, but her throat muscles didn't seem to be working.

Then the heavily shaded lamp at the side of the bed clicked on, and she realised it was Marc, his hair hanging in damp tendrils, water glistening on his dinner jacket.

She said hoarsely, 'What are you doing here?'

'I came to tell you that I won tonight.' He reached into his pocket and took out a packet of high denomination euros. 'Every table I sat at yielded gold.'

'I'm very pleased for you,' Helen said tautly. 'But the morning would have done for your news.'

He smiled down at her. His black tie was hanging loose, and several of the buttons on his dress shirt were unfastened. 'But it is the morning, *ma mie*. And besides, I have something else I wish to share with you.'

'Can't it wait?' She tried unobtrusively to raise the sheet to chin level. 'I—I'm very tired.'

'And I,' he said, 'have waited long enough. On our wedding night you accused me of buying you for sex. If so, Hélène, I made a poor bargain. And it occurred to me, as I came back tonight, that perhaps I had not yet paid enough for the privilege of enjoying your charming body. So—'

He scattered some of the banknotes across the bed. 'How much will this buy me, *mon coeur*? A smile—a kiss, *peut-être*? Or even—this.'

He reached down and took the edge of the sheet from her, stripping it back to the foot of the bed, leaving her naked.

'Oh, God,' Helen said, with a little wail of shock. She tried to curl into the foetal position, covering what she could of herself with her shaking hands. 'You said—' she accused breathlessly. 'You told me you wouldn't ask again.'

'But I am not asking,' he said gently. 'This time I am taking.'

'But why?' There was a sob in her voice. 'Weren't there any women at the casino you could have chosen—with all that money?'

'Dozens,' Marc told her pleasantly. 'And all of them more eager and welcoming than you, *ma chère*. But I decided I preferred a little—domestic entertainment.' He paused. 'And you can always close your eyes—pretend that I am someone else.'

Quietly ruthless, he unpeeled her arms from her body, one hand closing on both her slender wrists and lifting them above her head. Holding them there. Helen cried out in startled protest as his other hand grasped her ankles, straightening her body and drawing it gently but inexorably down the bed, leaving her with nowhere to hide from the insolent hunger in his dark gaze.

'Marc,' she whispered imploringly. 'I beg you—please don't do this.'

Marc lifted himself on to the bed and knelt over her, trapping her legs between his knees while he studied her.

He said quietly, '*Tu es vraiment exquise, Hélène*. And this is what your body was made for.' Then he bent his head and began to kiss her, his lips cool as the rain as they touched her.

Helen tried to resist, her mouth clamped shut, her head twisting frantically on the pillow. But he was not to be denied.

His tongue was like a flame against hers, teasing her slowly and sensuously, demanding that her lips yield him their innermost secrets. At the same time his hand found one small, pointed breast, his fingertips delicately stroking its soft curve, wringing a response that urged the nipple to bloom sweetly and helplessly into his caressing palm.

Helen found herself almost unable to breathe—to think. He was still clasping her wrists—but so loosely that she could have pulled free at any time, at least tried to fight him off. Instead, she realised she was sighing into his mouth, her body gradually slackening under the sensuous insistence of his lips and fingers.

When he had finished with her she would die of shame at her own weakness, she told herself dazedly. But for now…

His mouth moved down to her throat, making the pulse there leap and flutter. He explored the soft hollows at its base, then trailed kisses down to her breasts, his lips suckling each excited peak in turn, piercing them with sensations she'd never dreamed of.

When at last he raised his head she stared up at him, her eyes wide with bewilderment, her lips slightly parted.

He touched them lightly with his own, then released her wrists, turning her slightly so that the long, supple line of her back was at the mercy of his mouth instead, while his hands still stroked and pleasured her tumescent breasts.

He brushed the soft strands of hair away from the nape of her neck with his mouth, and she felt her whole body quiver in helpless response to the caress.

His lips and tongue travelled slowly, almost languidly, between her shoulderblades and down her spine, as if he was counting each delicate bone with kisses, while his fingers pursued their own erotic path across her ribcage to the flat plane of her stomach, coming to rest on the slender curves of her hipbones.

As he caressed the sensitive area at the base of her spine she gave a muffled moan and her body arched involuntarily, vulnerably. He drew her back against him, his arm across her breasts. At the same moment his other hand moved, cupping the soft mound at the parting of her slackened thighs with terrifying intimacy.

'No—please.' Helen's voice splintered as his fingertips be-

gan their first silken journey of discovery into the moist, scalding heat of her most secret self.

Marc kissed the side of her throat and she felt him smile
against her skin. 'No?'

His hand moved, delicately, subtly, and she cried out, her
body writhing helplessly against his enfolding arm.

Suddenly, unexpectedly, he turned her on to her back, and
she caught a dazed glimpse of the heated glitter in his eyes.
But she had no idea of his real purpose as he bent to her, his
hands sliding under her flanks, lifting her towards him. The
next instant, before she could move to prevent him, his mouth
had taken possession of her, and the powerful glide of his
tongue had sought and found the tiny hidden bud, continuing
its exquisite arousal.

Helen's entire being tensed in shock, followed immediately
by an agony of guilty, terrified delight. She tried once more to
say no. To find the strength, somehow, to push him away and
stop this shameful, delicious pleasure before it carried her away
beyond all the barriers she'd tried to build against him.

But the only sound that came from her throat was a small
sob. She closed her eyes in a desperate attempt to distance
herself—to hang on to some kind of self-control. But it was
already too late.

Her awareness had shrunk to the distant splash of the rain,
her own jagged, fevered breathing, and the hot, beautiful semi-
darkness that surrounded her—invaded her. She knew nothing
but the response that Marc was forcing from her trembling
body, the alchemy of his experienced caresses, seducing her
bewildered senses and sweeping away her innocence for ever.

The pleasure began slowly, at first little more than a breeze
rippling across still water, then building with irresistible, quivering urgency into a great wave, gathering force and speed as
it lifted her, all control gone, to some unimagined peak of rapture and held her there.

Then the wave broke, and she crashed with it, helpless,
whimpering, torn apart by the spasms of ecstasy that possessed
her.

She lay dazed and trembling, unable to speak or move, or

even to comprehend what had just happened to her. She was no longer certain where she was, or even who she was.

A strange euphoria was spreading throughout her body. Every bone, muscle and skin cell was utterly relaxed, tingling with this new delight, as if she was floating in some beatific dream, drained and weightless.

She was dimly aware that Marc had moved away from her, and found herself reaching out a bereft hand, searching for him blindly across the empty bed.

'*Sois tranquille, mon amour.* I am here.' His voice was a whisper. He'd used his brief absence to strip, she realised, as he drew her to him, and she gasped silently as she felt the warmth of his aroused and powerful nakedness against her body.

Instinctively, she arched towards him, thrilling again at his touch, her arms circling his neck, the tips of her breasts grazing his hair-roughened chest, and heard him groan softly. His hands took her gently, positioning her, then he entered her with one strong, fluid thrust.

Her yielding was total, immediate. Almost languidly she lifted her legs, locking them round his hips, her own movements mirroring the smooth, almost voluptuous drive of his loins, drawing him deeper still into her body.

'Tell me.' His voice was a hoarse whisper. 'Tell me if I hurt you.'

'I want you.' Her reply was hardly more than a breath. 'I want—everything…'

She'd thought after that previous implosion of ecstasy that still lingered, suffusing her with its joy, she would find herself exhausted, emptied of sensation, incapable of anything but compliance. But she was wrong.

The controlled force of his possession was evoking a response that went far beyond mere surrender. Suddenly her body was coming unexpectedly, ardently to life again, and as his rhythm increased, became fiercer, she found she was being carried away with him, striving with him on some long, sweet spiral of such intensity that it frightened her.

Pleasure hovered on the verge of pain, and she heard herself crying out, crushing her mouth against his shoulder as the long, shuddering convulsions of her climax pulled her over the edge into Paradise. Seconds later he followed her, wildly groaning her name as he reached the white heat of fulfilment in his turn.

Afterwards they lay quietly in a tangle of sweat-soaked limbs, his arms holding her as she pillowed her head on his chest, both waiting for the storm of their breathing to subside.

But for Helen the descent to earth was swift, and soon unhappy.

Because now she knew there was no more room for pretence. She had taken as completely as she had given. And by so doing she'd sacrificed her self-respect, and any forlorn hope of feigning her indifference.

However it might have begun, Marc had given her a night she would remember always. But soon he would be lying with his lips against someone else's hair, his long fingers drowsily caressing another woman's breast. And she'd allowed herself to forget that for the sake of a few hours of total ravishment.

A little domestic entertainment. The coolly jeering words came back to haunt her. Because that was all he wanted—to ensure that when he came to Monteagle she'd be waiting for him with passionate eagerness, ready to give him anything he wanted. A perpetual honeymoon, Helen thought, biting her lower lip, still swollen from his kisses. Until, of course, her sexual education was complete, by which time her novelty for him would probably have worn off.

And all this pain—this heartbreak—she had brought upon herself.

I shall have to learn not to think, she told herself, as Marc's soft, regular breathing informed her that he'd fallen asleep. Not to wonder what he's doing when he's away, or who he might be with. No scenes and no accusations.

If I can manage to turn a perpetually blind eye, and he is reasonably discreet, then maybe our separate lives can be made to work.

She leaned across and switched off the lamp.

And now, she thought, she would try to sleep.

*   *   *

She opened her eyes to sunshine and birdsong, and Marc bending over her, clearly about to kiss her—and not for the first time, she thought, blushing, assailed by a vivid memory of him kissing her awake in the early dawn, and making love to her with such tenderness and grace that afterwards she'd found herself weeping in his arms.

'*Bonjour.*' He propped himself on an elbow and smiled at her. 'You awaken very beautifully.'

Her blush deepened. At some point during the night he must have retrieved the sheet, she realised, and covered her with it, because she now had a shield against the over-bright light of day. And, more importantly, against his eyes.

'Good morning,' she said, a touch awkwardly. 'Has—has the rain stopped?'

'You are a true Englishwoman, *cherie.*' He was laughing. 'You wish to discuss the weather even when you are in bed with your lover.'

But you're not my lover, she thought with sudden pain, even as her body clenched once more in unwilling yearning. Last night had nothing to do with love. It was simply a vindication of your own prowess in bed, because I rejected you. You needed to prove that you could make me want you against my own will and judgement. And against all reason—because I'm not the only woman in your life, and we both know it.

'I'm sorry,' she said stiffly.

'No, you must not be. It is charming.' He leaned down and kissed her mouth softly. 'And I wish very much that we could stay here for ever, but we have a plane to catch. Besides,' he added, stroking her cheek, 'there will be tonight.'

'Two planes,' Helen corrected, remembering the resolution she'd made last night and how badly she needed to keep it. He only had to look at her, she thought. Or smile. Or touch her lightly with a fingertip, and she was dying to melt in his arms. But she could not allow him to do this to her. Could not—would not—live this lie with him. 'We—we're on different flights.' She took a steadying breath. 'And yours, if you remember, is the earliest.'

'Different flights?' Marc repeated slowly. 'What are you

talking about? We will be travelling together. You are coming with me to Paris, *naturellement*.'

'No,' she said. 'I'm going back to England and Monteagle, as we agreed.'

Marc sat up abruptly, the sheet falling away from his body, and she looked away swiftly. Oh, God, she needed no reminders…

He said, 'But that was yesterday—before…'

'Before we had sex, you mean? You feel that should make some difference?' She kept her voice light. 'I don't see why.'

'I had hoped,' he said very quietly, 'that perhaps you would want to be with me. Now that we have found each other at last.'

But not in Paris, she wanted to scream at him. Never in Paris—at this famous apartment of yours, in the bed where you make love to your mistress. Don't you see that I *can't* go there? And that I won't—ever?

'But I shall be with you,' she returned instead. 'That is whenever you choose to come back to Monteagle.'

'Which may not be for some time,' he said. He looked at her steadily. 'That does not concern you?'

'You may come and go as you please. It's not up to me to interfere in your life—your decisions.' The rawness in her heart gave her voice an edge.

'I believed,' he said with sudden bleakness, 'that I had given you that right. So why do you refuse me?' He paused, and his voice hardened. 'Is it because there is some other one involved in our relationship? Has that come between us? Answer me.'

'You seem to know already.' She felt her heart give a sudden jolt. She hadn't intended this, she thought wretchedly. She hadn't thought he'd want to discuss Angeline Vallon or any of his women with her. She'd assumed he'd prefer her to ignore the rumours which would no doubt reach her. That he'd expect gratitude for Monteagle to keep her silent.

Why, she asked herself desperately, wasn't he playing according to the rules? But then, when had Marc ever done so?

'*Ah, Mon Dieu.*' He almost groaned the words, then was silent for a moment. At last, he said unevenly, 'Hélène—you

are being a fool. Yet in spite of all this we can make our
marriage work—I know it. This—other thing—it will not last.
It cannot. And you cannot allow it to matter. To damage what
we might have together.

'*Cherie.*' His voice deepened. 'You must not do this to yourself—to us.'

Us, Helen thought. There is no 'us' and never can be.
Because even when Angeline Vallon is history, as you suggest,
there'll be someone else in her place. There'll always be someone else—for a month or two…

'But I can't pretend it doesn't exist either,' she said raggedly.
'That wasn't part of the deal. So I shan't be going with you to
Paris.' She took a deep breath. 'But Monteagle is yours too, of
course, and when you choose to be there I'm prepared to reach
some—compromise with you.'

'As you did last night?' The words slammed at her.

'Yes,' she said defiantly. 'Exactly like that.'

He said something under his breath—something harsh and
ugly—then threw himself off the bed, grabbing for his discarded clothing. But he made no attempt to dress himself.

Instead, he reached into the pocket of his dinner jacket.
'Then allow me to congratulate you on your performance, *madame.*' His voice seared her like acid. 'You learn quickly—
and, as I explained, I would not wish you to go unrewarded
for your efforts.'

He tossed the roll of money into the air, and watched the
banknotes flutter down on to the bed around her.

'Consider yourself paid in full, *ma femme,*' he added. 'Until
the next time—wherever and whenever that may be.'

And he left her, white-faced and stricken, staring after him,
as he strode to the door and vanished.

CHAPTER ELEVEN

'YOU mean it?' Lottie's face lit up. 'You'll let me have my wedding reception in the Long Gallery? Oh, Helen, that's wonderful.'

Helen returned her hug. 'Well, you can't squeeze everyone into your cottage—not without appalling casualties and structural damage anyway,' she added drily. 'And the Gallery looks terrific now it's finished. It really needs to be used for something special.'

Lottie hesitated. 'And you're sure Marc won't mind?'

'Why should he?' Helen asked with a light shrug. *As he's so rarely here...* She thought it, but did not say it aloud.

'I only wanted a tiny wedding,' Lottie said mournfully. 'A few close friends and family.' She sighed. 'But that was before our respective mothers presented us with their final guest lists, and a string of other instructions as well. I've had to rethink all my catering plans, for one thing, as well as dashing off to the wedding hire place in Aldenford for some ghastly meringue and veil.'

Helen patted her consolingly. 'You'll look wonderful,' she said. 'And I guarantee Simon will be secretly thrilled.' She paused. 'Shall we get some music laid on for dancing? Really test the Gallery's new floor?'

'Why not?' Her friend shrugged lavishly. 'In for a penny, in for a pound. The whole nine yards.' She gave Helen a speculative glance. 'Does Marc like dancing? I mean, he will make it to the wedding, I hope? Or will he be in Bolivia or Uzbekistan?'

'I—really don't know,' Helen admitted uncomfortably. 'But, wherever he is, I'm sure he'll do his best. I'll ask Alan to remind him. After all, he seems to see much more of him than I do,' she added, with attempted nonchalance.

159

There was another silence, then Lottie said fiercely, 'Oh, this is all so wrong—such a mess. Simon and I are so happy—so crazy about each other—and you're so damned miserable. And don't argue with me,' she warned, as Helen's lips parted in protest. 'Even a blind person could see it.'

'I have what I asked for,' Helen said quietly. 'And so has Marc.' She tried to smile. 'He seems quite content—and you have to admit the house is looking terrific.'

'I don't have to admit anything.' Lottie picked up her bag and prepared for departure. 'In fact there are times when I wish you'd sold Monteagle lock, stock and barrel to bloody Trevor Newson. So there.'

And there are times when I wish that too, Helen thought with sudden wry bitterness. The shocked breath caught in her throat as she realised what she had just admitted to herself.

She managed to keep a smile in place as she waved her friend off, but her stomach was churning and her legs felt oddly weak.

How can I suddenly feel like this? she asked herself as she made herself turn, walk back into the house she loved. The home she'd always considered worth any sacrifice.

Monteagle's been my life all this time. My lodestar. And so it should be still—because I have nothing else. Nothing…

She found she was making her way up the stairs, breathing the smell of paint, plaster and wood as she'd done for so many weeks. But, as usual, she encountered no one. The restoration team were busy at the other end of the house, and she was able to enter the State Bedroom once again unnoticed. Where she paused, staring round her, drinking in the room's completed beauty. And its strange emptiness.

The embroidery from the old bed curtains had been transferred exquisitely to its rich new fabric, and it gleamed in the mellow sunlight that poured in through the mullioned windows. While above the fireplace the other Helen Frayne looked enigmatically down on her descendant.

And, dominating the room, that enormous bed—made up each week with fresh linen, yet still unused.

Helen had stood in this room grieving after her grandfather's funeral, knowing that she was entirely alone. She'd tried with a kind of desperation to convince herself that it wasn't true. That she would spend her future with Nigel and find happiness and fulfilment—but only if she could save her beloved home and live there. That had always been the proviso.

No guy stands a chance against a no-win obsession like that. She found herself remembering Nigel's petulant accusation.

But it wasn't an obsession, she cried inwardly. It was a dream—wasn't it? Only now the dream was dead, and she didn't know why.

Except that she was lying to herself. Because it had begun to fade six weeks ago, when she came back from France.

Without Marc. Without even saying goodbye to Marc. Because he'd already left for the airport when she arrived downstairs that last morning at the Villa Mirage.

Later, on her own homeward journey, she'd asked Louis to stop at a little church she'd seen on the way out of St Benoit Plage, and she had filled the poor box to bursting with the euro notes that Marc had scattered so scornfully across her shocked body, hoping that by doing so she could somehow exorcise the stunned misery that was choking her.

All the way back to Monteagle she'd told herself over and over again that it would all be worth it once she was home. That somehow she'd even be able to survive this agony of bewildered loneliness once she could see her beautiful house coming back to life.

Only it hadn't been like that. Not when she'd realised that she was actually expected to move into this room—that bed—alone, and had known that she couldn't do it. That it was impossible. Unthinkable.

An unbearable solitude—worse than any imagining.

So she'd informed Daisy quietly that she'd prefer to sleep in her own bedroom for the time being, and the housekeeper, noting her pale face and tearless eyes, had tactfully not argued with her.

And there the matter rested. In distance and estrangement.

She'd explained, charmingly and ruefully, to anyone who asked that Marc was in serial business meetings and would join her as soon as he was free. But it was an excuse that sounded increasingly thin as a week had passed and edged into a fortnight without a word from him.

She'd found this lack of communication unnerving, and eventually swallowed her pride and approached Alan Graham.

'I was expecting Marc here this weekend,' she had fibbed, fingers crossed in the pockets of her skirt. 'But I've heard nothing—and I've stupidly mislaid his contact number in Paris. Do you know what's happening?'

'I certainly know that he's not in Paris,' Alan returned with a touch of dryness. 'He left for Botswana several days ago, and is going on to Senegal. He's unlikely to be back in Europe until next week, but even then I don't think he has any immediate plans to visit the UK.'

'I see.' Another lie. She forced a smile, but the architect's face remained impassive. 'Well, perhaps his secretary could supply me with a copy of his itinerary—or let me know if there's an opening in his schedule.'

She expected him to offer an address, a telephone extension and a name, but he did none of those things.

He hesitated perceptibly. 'Marc is incredibly busy, Mrs Delaroche. It might be better to leave it to him to get in touch—don't you think?'

In other words, if Marc had wanted her to make the first contact he'd have supplied her with the means, she realised, mortified. And Alan Graham—not just her husband's friend, but also his employee—had been instructed to block her, to keep her at a safe distance where she could not interfere with the way he lived his life.

'Yes,' she said, her voice stumbling over the word. 'Of course.'

As she turned to leave she saw an odd expression flicker in his eyes—something, she thought, which might have been pity. And her humiliation was complete.

Even now she could remember how she'd gone out of the house and walked round the lake, struggling to come to terms with the fact that her marriage was already virtually over.

Yes, she'd made him angry that last morning. But she'd been

upset, and desperately hurt. So how could he behave as if he
was the only injured party in all this? If he cared for her at all,
wouldn't he have been concerned more for her feelings and
less for his own convenience?

Suggesting she should accompany him to Paris had been an
act of brutal cynicism. Surely he must have realised that admitting there was another woman in his life had robbed her of
any chance of peace and happiness whenever he was away
from her?

Even now, when they were miles apart, she was still racked
by jealousy and wretchedness. That last passionate, overwhelming night in France had done its work too well, creating
a hunger that only he could assuage. But she was no longer a
priority on his agenda.

She'd turned and stared at the bulk of the house through
eyes blurred with tears. Her kingdom, she'd thought, where she
ruled alone, just as she'd wanted. Her kingdom and her prison.

But even if Marc didn't want her, his plans for the house
were clearly still foremost in his mind.

His team of craftsmen were still working flat out, over long
hours, and she could only guess at the size of the wage bill
being incurred. Also, the extra staff he'd insisted on were now
in place—pleasant, efficient, and taking the pressure from
George and Daisy. Far from feeling resentful, they were now
talking cheerfully about the prospect of retirement on the pen-
sion that Marc had also set up for them.

'But what would I do without you?' Helen had asked, startled and distressed. 'I rely on you both totally. You're my family.'

Daisy had patted her gently. 'Everything changes, my dear.
And you'll be having a new family soon—a proper one, with
Monsieur Marc.'

Which, thought Helen, was almost a sick joke—under the
circumstances.

She'd tried to keep busy, to stop herself from thinking, but
apart from arranging the flowers and deciding what food to eat,
there was little to occupy her at Monteagle, she had to admit.
The place seemed to run like clockwork. Instead, she spent two

days a week helping in a charity shop in Aldenford, and another afternoon pushing round the library trolley at the local cottage hospital.

So she'd been out when the longed-for telephone call had come to say Marc would be arriving the next day.

But her initial relief and elation had been dealt an immediate blow when Alan had informed her with faint awkwardness that this was simply a flying visit, to check on the progress of the house, and that Marc would be leaving again after lunch.

She'd managed a word of quiet assent, then taken herself up to her room, where she'd collapsed across the bed, weeping uncontrollably.

The next day she had departed early for a ceramics auction in a town twenty miles away. It had been purely a face-saving move. She had no particular interest in porcelain and pottery, and no intention of bidding on any of the lots.

She'd arrived back at Monteagle just before lunch was served, and returned Marc's cold greeting with equal reserve before eating her way through salmon mayonnaise and summer pudding as if she had an appetite, while Marc and Alan chatted together in French.

The meal over, she had been about to excuse herself when Marc detained her with an imperative gesture. Alan quietly left them alone together, standing on opposite sides of the dining table.

'The new staff? You find them acceptable?' he'd asked abruptly.

'Perfectly, thank you.' She hesitated. 'Of course it helps that they're local people.'

'And the house? The work continues to your satisfaction?'

'It all looks wonderful,' she said quietly. 'But naturally I shall be glad when it's over.'

There was an odd silence before he said, 'Then I hope for your sake, Hélène, that they continue to make the same progress and you are soon left in peace from all of this.' His brief smile did not reach his eyes. *'Au revoir,'* he added, and was gone.

And that, Helen thought unhappily, had set the pattern for

his two subsequent visits—except that Alan's wife had been invited to join them for lunch. But, as Susan treated her with the same polite aloofness as her husband, it couldn't be described as the most successful social experiment of the year.

There had never been any hint that he wished to spend the night here. In fact he didn't even want to touch her, she admitted, swallowing a desolate lump in her throat. It seemed that the beautiful Angeline was supplying all his needs, and that she herself was excluded from any intimate role in his life, however temporary.

Why did he do it? she asked herself. Why did he take me and make me want him so desperately that every day and night without him makes me feel as if I'm slowly bleeding to death?

But she already knew the answer. Because he could, she thought. And how cruel was that?

As unkind as the way he'd suddenly ended that brief interlude on the bed over there, she reminded herself. Her whole body had been singing to the touch of his mouth and hands when he'd stepped back, apparently unaffected by her response—except to be amused by it.

How silly and futile all her subsequent protests must have seemed to him—and how easily they'd been overcome, she thought bitterly. And she knew still that, in spite of everything, if he so much as beckoned to her she would go to him.

Her body was aching—starving for him. Demanding the surcease that only he could give, but which he chose to deny her.

Making it clear that there was no place for her even on the margins of his life.

Perhaps, she thought, wincing painfully, Angeline Vallon doesn't like sharing either, and has enough power to issue an ultimatum.

Sighing, she walked over to the portrait and stood staring up at it.

'How did you cope?' she asked softly. 'When your royal victor became tired of his spoils and moved on? How many days before you stopped hoping? How many long nights before he ceased to feature in your dreams? And what else must I endure before my sentence is served and I can get out of jail?'

On the other hand, if she did escape somehow, then where would she go?

Her mouth twisted wrily. Bolivia, she thought. Uzbekistan— or any of the places that Marc had been flying between over these long weeks. She'd always secretly yearned to travel, to get to the heart of cities and countries that were only names in an atlas, but she'd given up all hope of that for the sake of Monteagle.

If she could turn back time, she knew now she would have followed Marc downstairs that last morning, held out her hand and said, Take me with you. Because half a life at his side would have been better than no life at all.

A fly had appeared from nowhere, and was grumbling vainly against one of the windows. Helen walked across the room and opened the casement to allow it to escape, and stood suddenly transfixed, staring across the lawns below.

A woman was standing, a hand shading her eyes as she looked up at the house, her long red hair gleaming in the late summer sunlight.

No, Helen thought with disbelief. And, as the anger began to build in her, *No.*

Has Marc allowed this? she asked herself. Has he dared to let her invade my territory? And is she going to spend time here—with him—forcing me to move out for the duration? Why else would she be here, spying out the land?

Oh, God, she thought. How could he hurt me—insult me— like this?

She closed the casement with a bang and ran from the room, and down the stairs, almost flinging herself out into the open air.

As she reached the grass she saw the other woman walking rapidly towards the side gate.

She is not getting away with this, Helen told herself grimly. She'll stand her ground and hear what I have to say.

'Wait!' she called, cupping her hands round her mouth. *'Attendez, madame!'*

The other woman paused, turning as if surprised, then waited awkwardly, hands thrust into the pockets of her cream linen trousers, as Helen came running towards her.

She only stopped, breathless and shocked, when she realised that, apart from hair colour, her quarry bore no resemblance at all to the woman whose magazine picture still haunted her mercilessly.

She was considerably older, and thinner, and her face was pleasant rather than beautiful—although at the moment she looked embarrassed and wary.

'I'm sorry,' she said. 'The house isn't open to the public any more, is it? And I'm trespassing.'

'Yes, I'm afraid so.' Helen struggled to control her breathing. 'Did you want anything in particular?'

'Not really.' The other woman shrugged. 'Just a final glimpse, really. I went round with the guided tour a few times before the restoration work started, and I was curious to see if much had changed.'

Helen stared at her. 'You're quite a devotee.'

'I feel I've known the place all my life. You see, my great-grandmother was in service here years ago, and my grandmother too, and they loved it. I grew up with all these stories about Monteagle—felt as if I was part of them. Daft, I know, but we all have our dreams.'

She paused. 'You're Helen Frayne, aren't you? But you confused me when you called out in French. I thought that was your husband's nationality.'

'It is. I—I thought you were someone completely different. I'm sorry.' Helen hesitated. 'May I know who you really are?'

'Why not?' Another almost fatalistic shrug. 'My name's Shirley—Shirley Newson. You know my husband, I think?'

Helen said slowly, 'Yes—yes, I do.'

'And wish you didn't, I dare say.' Shirley Newson's smile was affectionate, but wan. 'Trevor's a good man, but when his heart's set on something he turns into a bull in a china shop. I know full well he ruined any chance we had of buying the place. All those stupid ideas about theme parks and the like.' Her eyes flashed. 'As if I'd have allowed that.'

She sighed. 'But I suppose he thought he could make my

dream come true, bless him, and turn a profit at the same time. It's what he's always done, so I can hardly blame him. But all I wanted was to live here quietly, doing the repairs bit by bit. Making it just like it was years ago, when my family worked here. Loving it, I suppose.'

She looked at Helen, biting her lip. 'Now I guess you'll call your security and have me thrown out.'

'Actually,' Helen said gently, 'I was going to offer you a cup of tea, Mrs Newson. And another guided tour—if you'd like that.'

It had been an oddly agreeable couple of hours, Helen decided when her unexpected guest had left. Shirley Newson had spoken no more than the truth when she'd said she knew the house. She was as accurate about its history as Marion Lowell, but she was also a fund of stories—amusing, scandalous and poignant—about the Fraynes and their guests, which her relations had handed down to her, and which Helen, thoroughly intrigued, had never heard before.

Perhaps, she thought wryly, if the wife had come to conduct negotiations a year ago instead of the husband there might have been a different outcome. Perhaps…

Anyway, she thought, it was all too late now. And she sighed.

'You did give Marc my message—about Lottie's wedding?' Helen tried to hide her bitter disappointment as she spoke. 'Because it starts in just over an hour, and he's cutting it incredibly fine if he intends to be here.'

'Mrs Delaroche.' Alan Graham's voice had an edge to it. 'Does it occur to you that there could be—circumstances which might make it difficult for Marc to leave Paris right now?'

Helen bit her lip. 'Meaning Madame Angeline Vallon, I suppose?' she challenged, too hurt and angry to be discreet.

Alan stared at her in open bewilderment. 'You know about that?' he asked incredulously.

'Yes,' she acknowledged curtly. 'After all, it's hardly a secret.'

'You know?' he repeated slowly. 'And yet you carry on with your life as if it didn't matter?' He'd never been friendly, but now he sounded positively hostile.

Riled, Helen lifted her chin. 'Marc makes his own choices,' she said. 'They have nothing to do with me. My world is here.'

His laugh was derisive. 'And so as long as it's looked after you don't give a damn about anything else. I'd hoped that, all appearances to the contrary, you might actually care.'

Care? she thought. *Care?* Can't you see I'm in agony here—falling apart?

She said freezingly, 'You may be my husband's friend, but that gives you no right to criticise me like this.'

'Mrs Delaroche,' he said, 'you are perfectly correct about that, and you can have me removed from this project any time you like. I have other more worthwhile proposals in the pipeline.' He paused. 'I'm sure Marc will be at this wedding if it's humanly possible. No matter what it may cost him. Because you've asked him to do it. Is that what you want to hear?'

And with a final scornful glance at her, he walked away.

Helen wasn't sure if she had the power to fire him, but she knew she shouldn't let the matter rest. That she should go after him—demand an explanation for his extraordinary behaviour.

Except she had a wedding to dress for, she thought, pushing her hair back from her face with an angry, restless hand. And if she had to attend it alone, she would do so looking like a million dollars.

Because no one was going to accuse her of wearing a broken heart on her sleeve.

She'd decided, after a lot of consideration, to wear her own wedding outfit again. After all, Marc had once suggested that she should do so at a party of their own, she remembered unhappily, and under the circumstances Lottie's wedding reception was probably as good as it was going to get.

But once today was over, she told herself grimly, she would develop some attitude of her own—and deal with Alan Graham.

*   *   *

The service had already begun when she was aware of whispering behind her, and at the same moment Marc slipped into the pew beside her. She turned to look at him, lips parted, delight churning inside her—along with an almost savage yearning.

'I—I didn't think you'd be here,' she breathed.

'I had an invitation.' His whispered reply was cool and unsmiling.

Helen sank back into her seat, her heart thumping painfully. What had she been hoping? That he'd kiss her, murmuring that he could not keep away when all the evidence was to the contrary?

She hadn't been to many traditional weddings, and she'd almost forgotten the timeless resonances of the Prayer Book ceremony. Now they came flooding back with a kind of desperate poignancy, making her hands clench together in her lap and her throat tighten.

She watched Simon and Lottie with painful intensity—his unhidden tenderness, her glorious serenity—knowing that was how it should be when you were safe and loved.

If only Marc had looked at her like that, adoring her with his eyes, when they'd stood together to receive the same blessing the Vicar was pronouncing now, she thought passionately. And if only she'd been free to whisper the oldest vow of all— *I love you* as he bent to kiss her.

Because she knew now with terrible certainty that this was the truth she'd been fighting since she met him. That it wasn't simply the beguilement of sexual union that she'd feared, but the deeper spiritual and emotional commitment that she'd tried to reject. The recognition that in this man—this stranger— she'd somehow met the other half of herself.

Everything else had been a blind—the bargain they'd made, even Monteagle itself.

But only for me, she thought, pain lancing her. Not for Marc. To him it was never more than a deal, and now he has what he wants he's moved on.

She sent him a swift sideways glance from under her lashes,

silently begging him to turn towards her—take her hand. But
Marc sat unmoving, his profile like granite, his expression as
remote as some frozen wasteland.

And she knew that if there'd been a moment when she might
have captured his heart it was long gone. All she was left with
was loneliness, stretching out into eternity.

CHAPTER TWELVE

NOT long now, Helen promised herself wearily. The bride and groom had departed for their honeymoon in an aura of radiance, and the usual sense of anticlimax had immediately set in, so the party would soon be breaking up. And just as well, because she was almost at the end of her tether.

She could admit it now. She hadn't felt well all day—tired and vaguely sick. And it had been the same for the past week or more, if she was honest. Stress, she supposed. And sheer uncertainty about the future.

Not that the reception hadn't been a great success. The Long Gallery had looked wonderful, its mellow panelling gleaming in the late sunlight while Lottie's delicious food had been eaten and the toasts drunk, then later assuming an atmosphere of total romance once the candles were lit and the music began.

And Helen couldn't fault Marc. Wherever else he might wish himself to be, he'd behaved like a perfect host. He had danced with practically every woman in the room—bar one. He'd even stood beside her, his hand barely touching her uncovered shoulder, as Simon and Lottie thanked them lavishly for their hospitality and called for their health to be drunk.

'Marc and Helen—who saved our lives.'

And Helen had stood mutely, smiling until her face ached, determined to overcome the churning inside her and trying also to ignore the fact that Marc had not danced with her. Other people had, of course. She'd hardly been a wallflower. But she and her husband had been on parallel lines all evening—never meeting, never touching until that moment. Hardly speaking. And that was clearly the way he wanted it.

Wearing her wedding outfit had been a mistake too. As she'd removed the jacket, her nervous hands struggling once again with those tiny slippery buttons, she'd sensed him near her, and glanced up, wondering if he remembered—if he would come to her rescue this time too. But Marc's dark gaze had swept over her in total indifference, and then he'd turned away, his mouth hardening. And deliberately kept his distance ever after, she realised forlornly.

But when the guests had finally departed and they were left alone—what then?

She'd learned from Daisy that he'd brought a travel bag, which had been put in the State Bedroom. So it seemed he was planning to stay the night at least. But Helen had no idea whether or not he intended to sleep alone, or if, in spite of everything, he would expect her to join him in that vast bed.

The warmth of Lottie's farewell hug and her fierce whisper, 'Be happy', still lingered, taunting her with its sheer impossibility.

Because even if she went to Marc tonight, and he took her, it would mean nothing. Just a transient usage of his marital rights, which she knew she would not have the power to resist. Because she wanted him too badly.

His arms around me, she thought sadly, on any terms. Any terms at all. No pretence. No defence.

And above all she needed to talk to him—to ask him to give their ill-conceived disaster of a marriage another chance. Even if she had to resort to the self-exposure of confessing how much his infidelity was hurting her.

But when she returned from saying goodbye to the bride and groom's parents, and the other departing guests, awash with gratitude and good wishes, the Long Gallery was empty and dark. Daisy and the staff were not scheduled to begin the big clear-up until the morning. But there was no sign of Marc either.

He hadn't even waited to wish her goodnight, let alone offered the chance of the private conversation she needed.

So I'll have to go to him instead, she told herself, taking a deep breath.

The door to the State Bedroom stood slightly ajar, and Helen paused before tapping lightly at its massive panels.

'*Entrez.*' His voice was brusque, and not particularly welcoming.

When she went in she saw that he'd changed into jeans and a sweatshirt, and was packing the elegant dark suit he'd worn for the wedding into a clothes carrier, his movements swift and economical.

She halted, the breath catching in her throat. 'You're leaving already? You're not staying the night?'

'As you see,' he returned unsmilingly. 'I am expected elsewhere.'

'Where this time?' She tried to speak lightly. 'Kabul? Rio de Janeiro? I can hardly keep pace with your travels.'

'I have to return to Paris.'

'Of course.' Helen lifted her chin. 'Another place that occupies much of your time and attention. But couldn't you delay your trip just a little—please? Go back tomorrow, perhaps, or the next day? I think we need to spend some time together—and talk. Don't you think so?'

'Yes,' he said slowly. 'That will probably be necessary very soon. But not quite yet.' For a long moment he looked at her, the dark eyes scanning her slender body in the pale silk dress, but he took no step towards her.

He added quietly, 'It is essential that I go tonight. Accept my regrets.'

But she was not quite beaten. Not yet. She braced herself for a last throw of the dice.

She said huskily, 'Marc, you—once asked me to go to Paris with you, and I refused. But I could pack very quickly—if you'd consider asking me again.' She stared at him across the space that divided them, her eyes shining with sudden tears. She whispered, 'Please don't leave me again. Take me with you. Keep me with you.' She paused, swallowing. 'Or couldn't you just—forget Paris altogether and stay here?'

She saw a flash of something like pain cross the dark face.

'I am sorry.' His voice was harsh. 'But that is not possible. Please do not ask me to explain.'

But no explanations were necessary, she thought, knifed by desolation. She already knew why there would be no second chance for them. For her. Why he'd decided to shut her out of his life. Angeline Vallon had won, and she was no longer wanted.

Her marriage was over almost before it had begun.

She said quietly, 'I—I'm sorry to have embarrassed you.' And turned to go, praying that she would not break down completely in front of him.

He caught her before she reached the door. 'Hélène.' His voice was low and urgent. 'Ah, *Dieu*. I did not mean it should be like this. Forgive me, if you can.'

Then his mouth was on hers, and he was kissing her with a kind of stark desperation, his lips plundering—bruising—as if he intended to leave his mark on her for ever.

His hands were in the small of her back, pulling her against him, and she was gasping, trembling, her body grinding against his hardness in open longing as desire scalded her. Her arms wound round his neck as her lips parted in trembling, passionate response.

Stay with me…

But he was already detaching himself, putting her away from him. He said hoarsely, 'I cannot do this. I have to go.' There was a kind of agony in his eyes. 'One day, perhaps, you will understand.'

She leaned against the massive frame of the door, listening to the sound of his retreating footsteps.

What was there to understand? she wondered drearily. Only that she'd humbled herself totally to try to win him and been rejected. And now she had to live with the shame of it, she thought. And began to weep very softly.

Helen came out of the doctor's surgery and stood for a moment, as if she wasn't sure which direction to take. She was shivering a little, but whether it was because of the autumnal feeling in the air or the news she'd just received she couldn't be certain.

Why didn't I realise? she asked herself numbly. How could I not have known?

At first she'd attributed her feeling of malaise and the disruption of her monthly routine to the strain imposed by the last turbulent weeks. But this morning she'd been swiftly and comprehensively sick as soon as she'd got up. And her immediate shocked suspicion had just been cheerfully confirmed by the doctor who'd known her all her life.

'Another page in Monteagle's dynasty,' he'd congratulated her. 'Your husband must be thrilled.'

'I—I haven't mentioned anything to him.' Helen had looked at her hands, twisted together in her lap. 'Not yet. I wanted to be sure.'

He'd said once, in a distant past that was somehow only a few weeks ago, that he wanted children. But since then everything had changed, and she could be certain of nothing.

She had received a keen look. 'I gather this wasn't planned?'

Her lips had formed themselves into a soundless 'no'.

'Then it will be a marvellous surprise for him,' Dr Roscoe had said confidently, and dismissed her with sensible advice about the morning sickness and instructions to make another appointment.

Now, somehow, she found herself outside again, taking great gulps of air and wondering when exactly this had happened. She could only hope it had not been during the brief nightmare of her wedding night, but on that other never-to-be-forgotten time, when Marc had ravished her body and her senses, unaware or uncaring that her heart was already reluctantly his.

But how would he react when he learned she was pregnant? she asked herself wretchedly. He had not wanted to stay with her for her own sake. Would he come back for the baby she was carrying?

Slowly, she turned and began to head back to Monteagle, her mind treading wearily round the same questions and coming up with uncomfortable answers.

She was so deep in her own thoughts that she hardly realised where she was, until a familiar voice said, 'You're looking glum, darling. Trying to figure out where you'll find your next millionaire?'

Her head came up instantly, defensively, and she met Nigel's derisive grin. His car was parked on the other side of the road, outside his parents' empty house with the 'Sold' board in the garden. And he was here, standing in front of her, the last person she wanted to see.

Strange, she thought, that worrying about Mrs Hartley's good opinion had once been her major problem.

She said, 'What are you doing here?'

He shrugged. 'Mother thought she might have left some things in the roof space, and asked me to check.' He paused. 'I saw you walking past and thought I'd say a last goodbye.'

'Thank you,' she said. 'And—goodbye.'

'I also wanted to say—hard lines.' Nigel detained her, his hand on her arm. 'It looks as if you'll have to sell that expensive heap of yours after all,' he added with a sympathetic whistle.

'I'm sorry,' Helen said coldly, 'but you're not making any sense.'

'No?' He started artistically. 'Then maybe Monsieur Delaroche hasn't told you the bad news. There's been a boardroom revolt in his company—too much going wrong, drop in profits, et cetera—and he's going to be out of a job very soon. Out of money too. He's wasted any fighting fund he might have had pouring money into Monteagle. And there'll be no golden handshake either—not if Hercule Vallon has anything to do with it.'

She said scornfully, 'I don't believe you.'

'Maybe you should take more interest in your husband's affairs,' Nigel drawled. 'His business ones, that is. The board's voting to replace your Marc some time this week, and as his company's his only asset, you're going to need another backer to keep Monteagle. Because he can't afford to.'

He grinned insolently into her shocked face. 'The beautiful Madame Vallon will have her revenge at last. But then you know all about that,' he added insinuatingly. 'You told me so at your wedding.' His smile widened. 'Maybe you should have considered the implications more carefully. You wouldn't have rushed into marriage with such indecent haste if you'd known your millionaire would soon be broke.'

Her heart was hammering and her mouth was dry, but she

managed to say with icy pride, 'I'd have married Marc if he'd been penniless.'

'You married him for Monteagle,' Nigel sneered. 'We all knew that. And once he loses everything do you really think you'll be able to afford to keep the place on? I don't.'

'No,' Helen said quietly. 'Nor do I.' She paused, lifting her chin. 'But I know a woman who will.'

As the taxi took her into the centre of Paris the following day Helen felt strangely relaxed. The calm after the storm this time, she thought.

She had wrung Marc's private address and the whereabouts of his company's head office out of a patently unwilling Alan Graham.

'This is Marc's battle,' he'd kept saying as she had confronted him. 'He didn't want you to know—to be involved.' He gave her a bitter look. 'After all, you only cared about this great white elephant of a house. You never displayed the slightest interest in his work—or his life, for that matter. Why start now?'

'Because I am involved,' she told him. 'I'm his wife, and I'm going to be the mother of his child.' She paused, allowing him to digest that. 'If he's fighting for our lives, then I should be with him.' She paused again. 'Especially as you seem to hold me entirely to blame,' she added drily.

'You came into his life at just the wrong time,' he said bluntly. 'Marc owed his success very much to instinct. He could almost smell political instability—knew when there was trouble brewing. But when he met you he took his eye off the ball. Even when things started to go wrong he thought the company's problems could wait a little while he made sure of you.'

He shrugged. 'But like most successful men he had enemies, and they were soon circling, smelling blood in the water. Given the chance, he could pull things around, and that's what he's been trying to do for the past weeks. But the odds are stacked against him.'

She said, 'And Angeline Vallon? Wasn't she—his mistress? I—I heard—rumours.'

'Angeline Vallon,' Alan said carefully, 'is a self-obsessed bitch, married to a man who's mega-rich and mega-stupid, who lets her do pretty much as she wants. A couple of years back what she wanted most was Marc, but he wasn't interested, and he made the mistake of letting her see it. So she started stalking him—letters—gifts—phone calls. She rented an apartment near his, boasted that they were lovers, tipped off the gossip columns. Turned up at any social event he was attending.

'In the end, he had to take legal action. She was turning his life into a nightmare. And for a while, admittedly, it went quiet. But that was just while she was thinking what to do next. And, of course, she came up with the alternative idea of taking his company away from him. He'd turned her down, so he had to be punished in a way that would hurt him most.

'She made her husband believe—God knows how—that she was the injured party—that Marc had been pursuing her, frightening her with his sexual demands. And, urged on by Angeline, Hercule got together with some of the board who thought they could make a better job of running the company than Marc. All they needed was a window of opportunity.'

He shook his head. 'And when Marc saw you, he left that window wide open.'

She said fiercely, 'Why didn't he tell me any of this?'

His mouth twisted ruefully. 'Because he thought that you only cared about the money—and saving this house. That if he lost the company he'd also lose what little he seemed to have of you.'

His voice deepened harshly. 'We've been friends for years. He always seemed—invincible. Until he met you. You made him vulnerable. And you didn't seem to give a damn about him either.'

He shook his head. 'When I saw him after the honeymoon he was like a stranger—so withdrawn, so wretched. Naturally he wouldn't talk about it, and I couldn't ask. But he no longer seemed to have the will to watch his back, just when he needed to most. And now it's probably too late.'

'No,' Helen said, swiftly and clearly. 'I don't accept that. Oh, why didn't he tell me what was happening?'

Alan was silent for a moment. 'Perhaps because he didn't want you to see him lose?' He hesitated. 'It might be better to wait until he sends for you.'

'But if he loses he may never send for me,' she said. 'And I'm not risking that. Because if he has to start all over again, I intend to be with him.'

It was late afternoon when she reached the Paris offices of Fabrication Roche, only to find the main entrance locked. She rang the bell and a security guard appeared.

She said in her schoolgirl French, 'Where is everyone?'

'They have been sent home, *madame*, following the meeting today.'

Her heart sank like a stone. 'And Monsieur Delaroche?'

'He is still here, *madame*,' the man admitted. 'In the boardroom. But he has given orders not to be disturbed.'

She said briskly, 'I am his wife—Madame Delaroche. Please take me to him at once.'

He gestured helplessly. 'But I have my orders, *madame*, to admit no one.'

Helen stared at him tragically, allowing her lip to tremble convincingly. 'But I have travelled all the way from England, *monsieur*. And I am *enceinte*. These rules cannot apply to me.'

She could never be sure whether it was her announcement that she was pregnant or the threat of tears that did it, but next minute she was in a high-powered lift, travelling to the top floor.

At the end of the short passage a pair of double doors confronted her. She opened them and slipped inside.

Marc was standing by the huge picture window at the end of the room, silhouetted against the fading afternoon light. His bent head and his arms folded tautly across his body spoke of a weariness and tension almost too great to be borne. And of a loneliness that tore at her heart.

She put down her travel bag. 'Marc,' she said softly. 'Marc, darling.'

He turned abruptly, his eyes narrowing in disbelief. 'Hélène—what are you doing here?'

She walked towards him. 'I made myself homeless this morning,' she said. 'I was hoping you might offer me a bed for the night. Or for quite a lot of nights. The rest of our lives, even.'

His mouth tightened. He said, 'Is this some game?'

'No,' she said. 'I'm deadly serious. You see—I've sold Monteagle.'

'Sold it?' His hands gripped her arms. He stared down into her face. 'But that is not possible. It is your home, the centre of your life.'

She said steadily, 'Marc, you're the centre of my life. Nothing else matters. So Monteagle now belongs to Trevor Newson—every brick, every beam, every blade of grass. All except the portrait of Helen Frayne,' she added. 'And Alan's taking care of that for us.'

He let her go, stepping backwards, his face a mask of consternation. 'You sold to Trevor Newson—to that man? But you loathe him—and his plans for Monteagle. You have always said so.'

'Yes,' she agreed. 'But I don't think his schemes will be as bad as I thought. He's buying the house primarily for his wife, and I suspect she won't let him go too far. Besides,' she added, shrugging, 'I won't be there to see what happens. I'll be with you, if you want me. And if you don't hate me too much for selling the place you loved so much.'

'I loved it for your sake, Hélène,' he said quietly. 'Because I adored you, *mon amour*, and I wanted only to make you happy.'

'And now perhaps I can make it up to you in turn, for losing Fabrications Roche.' She took an envelope from her jacket pocket. 'Marc, darling, this is for you. It's in your name.'

'*Comment?*' He was frowning as he tore open the envelope, then he stopped, his lips parting in a gasp of sheer astonishment as he saw the amount on the bank draft it contained. '*Mon Dieu!* He paid you this much?'

'Without a murmur,' she said. 'Egged on by the wonderful

Shirley. Alan and the bank manager advised me what to ask, and I think I could have got more.' She paused. 'But it's enough, isn't it?' she asked almost diffidently. 'Enough for us to start again—together? Begin a life—a real marriage? Because I love you, and I don't think I can live without you.'

He stared at her in silence and she tried to laugh, the memory of his last rejection burning in her. 'Marc—please. Haven't you got anything to say?'

He said unsteadily, 'I think I am afraid to speak in case I awake and find that I have been dreaming.'

Helen moved to him, sliding her arms round his waist under his jacket, pressing herself close to him. She whispered, 'Do I feel like a dream?' His body quickened and hardened against hers. 'Because you feel incredibly real.'

'Ah, mon ange.' He sank down to the floor, pulling her with him to the thick carpet. Their hands tugged and tore at each other's clothing, made clumsy by haste and need. She returned his kisses eagerly, moaning faintly as his hands uncovered and caressed her naked breasts, then lifted herself towards him, sobbing with acceptance as he entered her.

He said thickly, *'Hélène—je t'aime—je t'adore.'*

'Yes,' she whispered, her voice shaking as she began to move with him, their bodies blending hungrily. 'Oh, my love— my love…'

It was not a prolonged mating. Their mutual desire was too fierce, too greedy for its satisfaction. As the soft, trembling pulsations deep within her reached their culmination she cried out, and heard him groan his pleasure in turn.

When she could speak again, Helen said faintly, 'Thank heaven I packed some stuff. You've wrecked this dress completely.'

'I hope you do not want me to apologise.' He wrapped her closely in his arms, his lips against her hair. 'Perhaps you should stop wearing clothes altogether.'

'With winter coming?' Helen pretended to shiver. 'Besides,' she added, trying to sound casual, 'the baby might catch a chill.'

His caressing hand abruptly stopped its ministrations. 'Baby? What are you saying?'

'Yes, darling,' she told him softly. 'That's the other thing I came to tell you. It seems you're going to be a father.'

'*Ah, Dieu.*' He lifted himself on to an elbow, staring at her in a kind of anguish. 'What have I done?'

She looked back at him, her throat tightening in shock. 'You—don't want our baby? I admit the timing isn't ideal, but—'

'Want it?' He seized her hands, covering them in kisses. '*Mon coeur*, I cannot believe such happiness. But we should not have made love,' he added grimly. 'It could be dangerous when you are only just *enceinte*.'

'Well, the baby will just have to cope.' She smiled up at him. 'We have to make up for lost time, my love.'

'Then I shall have to learn to be gentle. You have to be kept safe, even if I have to wrap you in silk,' Marc told her softly.

'Safe.' She sighed the word. 'The first time you made me feel safe was when I'd had too much to drink and you slept with me on the sofa.' Her eyes widened. 'I think that was when I realised I was falling in love with you.'

He framed her face between his hands. 'And yet you ran away,' he reminded her teasingly. 'Why didn't you awaken me, Hélène, and tell me how you felt—what you wanted me to do?' he added, kissing her mouth softly and sensuously.

'Because Nigel had told me you exercised a two-month limit on your affairs, and I was frightened,' she said frankly. 'Scared to love you, or let you make love to me, in case you broke my heart.'

'But with you, it was never to be an *affaire*,' he said quietly. 'It was to be a lifetime. Because you were the one I had been waiting for, *cherie*. The girl of my heart. With the others before you—' he shrugged '—I can say only in my defence that I tried to be honest—to make no promises I would not keep, nor offer commitment I would not fulfil. When they knew there was no future in the relationship, most of my girlfriends walked away.'

She said in a low voice, 'But with me, you always said it was the house you wanted. And I was just part of the deal.'

'I said that to protect myself. And to stop you running away from me. You see, *mon amour*, at that time I thought you still cared for Nigel.'

'Nigel!' Helen sat up indignantly. 'Oh, you couldn't have done.'

'I saw you together at the wedding,' he said, his mouth twisting. 'You seemed quite happy in his arms.'

She said flatly, 'I think I was temporarily paralysed. He was telling me to ask you about Angeline Vallon. He—he implied she was your mistress.'

'And you believed him?' His voice was incredulous. 'But why did you not ask me?'

'Because I couldn't guarantee what your answer might be,' she said. She took a deep breath. 'I'm afraid I'd heard you talking to Alan about her, and I'm not proud of that. Nigel appeared to confirm what you'd said. So heartbreak seemed to be right there, waiting for me.' She paused. 'Anyway, why didn't you ask me about Nigel?'

'Because I told myself that once we were married, and in bed together, I could make you forget him,' he said huskily. 'That I could persuade you to fall in love with me. I was that arrogant—that stupid. I should have known that with you it could never be that simple.'

'I fought you for my own sake,' she said quietly. 'No one else's. But I still could not stop myself wanting you.' She was silent for a moment. 'That money—I gave it to the poor in St Benoit.'

His smile was crooked as he drew her back into his arms and lay down again, her head pillowed on his chest. 'How estimable of you, *cherie*.'

'I wish I hadn't now,' she said regretfully. 'After all, we need every penny we can get.'

He laughed. 'Things are not that bad, *ma petite*.'

'Marc—don't pretend. Alan told me you stood to lose everything.' She stirred uneasily. 'I don't suppose we should even be here—especially, my goodness, like this,' she added, recognising their joint state of *dishabille*. 'The security men might come to escort you from the building. Isn't that what happens? And don't you have a desk to clear? Because I could help…'

'Hélène,' he said gently. 'Do not upset yourself. There is no need, I promise.'

'I'm bound to be upset,' she protested. 'You've lost Fabrication Roche, and I know what it meant to you. How difficult it must be…'

'*Mon coeur,*' he said patiently, 'I did not lose. It was close, but I won. I still have the company.'

She stared up at him, open-mouthed. 'But Alan said—'

'Alan is a realist. He knew the odds were against me. But I had suspected a long time ago that someone might be planning a boardroom *coup*. We were suddenly encountering problems where there had been none before.' Wryly, he counted them on his fingers. 'Sabotage, strikes, accusations of racism, key workers abducted and held to ransom.'

He shook his head. 'Someone wished to acquire Fabrication Roche, and cheaply, but I did not at once see that Angeline Vallon might be involved. I thought that difficulty was behind me—that she had seen the error of her ways. But I was wrong.

'However, I knew that I had not been her only target. Not all of them had resisted, *naturellement*, but they had all found it was not easy to escape her talons, even when the relationship had palled and they wished it to end. She had a capacity for revenge, that one.'

Helen's eyes were like saucers. 'But her husband…'

'He worshipped her,' Marc said briefly. 'And she dominated him. He decided that her beauty made her the prey of other men's lusts, but that she was always innocent. I had insulted her, therefore I must be punished. He has a simplistic mind, *le pauvre* Hercule.'

His mouth twisted. 'And, as Alan saw, I had allowed my attention to wander a little. But what could I do, once I had seen the woman I had been waiting for all my life? I had to make you mine.'

She nestled closer. 'You were certainly persistent.'

He kissed her again. 'I was in love. So much so that I could almost understand poor foolish Hercule. That day when I sat beside you at Charlotte's wedding I knew I would give anything to have you look at me as she did at her husband, but it seemed hopeless. And I was afraid, too, that if I could not afford Monteagle I might lose you for ever.'

'But I came to you,' she said. 'I offered myself. You know that.'

'I did not know, however, what I could offer in return.' He stroked the curve of her cheek. 'I was scared that if it was a choice between Monteagle and myself, I would lose. So it seemed best to fight on alone, until I knew what kind of life I could lay at your feet.'

'And I thought you preferred Angeline Vallon and couldn't wait to get back to her,' she confessed.

'In a way, you were right. My legal advisers had contacted me to say that they had finally drawn up a dossier of her affairs, with testimony from her other victims. So I was able to present it to Hercule before the final meeting today and watch him collapse. It was not pleasant, and I felt,' he added quietly, 'like a murderer.

'But his bid for Fabrication Roche collapsed with him, along with his allies on the board.' His smile was grim. 'They were the ones who found themselves being escorted from the building. Now there will be some restructuring and—*voilà*—life goes on.'

'So you didn't actually need the money I brought you.' There was a touch of wistfulness in her voice.

'Ah, but I needed the love that came with it.' His arms tightened round her. 'And the look in your eyes I had prayed for. A far more precious gift, *mon amour*.' He paused, his hand caressing the curve of her body that sheltered his child.

'Although,' he added. 'We could use the money, if you wish, to try and repurchase Monteagle.'

She shook her head slowly. 'No, that's all in the past, and I'd rather let it go—invest in our future. Find a new home for us both, and our children.' She hesitated. 'Marc—when I came in, you didn't look like someone who'd just won a famous victory. You looked—sad.'

'I was thinking of you,' he said quietly. 'And all the mistakes I had made. Wondering how soon I could go to you—to explain and ask you to forgive me. To try once more to persuade you to let me share your life—to love me. It seemed at that moment my real battle was still to come. Until you spoke, and smiled at me, and I realised that, little as I deserved it, I had been offered a miracle.'

He bent and took her mouth, gently and reverently.

'And now,' he told her, 'I must get you dressed and fed, my wife. But the only bed I can offer is in my apartment,' he added ruefully. 'And you have never wished to go there.'

'I thought I had my reasons,' she said. 'But I was wrong. About so many things.' She allowed him to lift her to her feet, and slid her arms round his neck, her eyes shining into his with joy and trust. 'Please, Marc—take me home.'

BLACKMAILED
INTO MARRIAGE

by

Lucy Monroe

Lucy Monroe started reading at age four. After she'd gone through the children's books at home, her mother caught her reading adult novels pilfered from the higher shelves on the book case...alas, it was nine years before she got her hands on a Mills & Boon® romance her older sister had brought home. She loves to create the strong alpha males and independent women that people Mills & Boon® books. When she's not immersed in a romance novel (whether reading or writing it) she enjoys travel with her family, having tea with the neighbours, gardening and visits from her numerous nieces and nephews. Lucy loves to hear from readers: e-mail Lucymonroe@Lucymonroe.com or visit www. LucyMonroe.com.

In memory of my dear friend and fellow writer,
Paulette Jerrells,
and with much love for the rest of our chapter,
Olympia RWA. Many thanks for taking this
amazing journey with me.

CHAPTER ONE

"YOU are Rosalia Chavez-Torres."

Lia turned at the deep, masculine voice and found her line of vision blocked by a well-honed male torso clothed in formal black and white. He was standing much too close. She could smell his expensive cologne and powerful energy radiated off him in imposing waves. She took a quick, jerky step backward only to run into a small table that prevented further retreat.

She tilted her head back so her gaze could travel up to the man's face and the breath rushed from her chest.

This man did not belong in a room filled with civilized businessmen.

Oh, he was dressed as the others in a hand-tailored tuxedo that fit his tall, muscular body perfectly. However his eyes burned with a vibrant intensity lacking in the other men in the room. Even her grandfather's presence paled beside this man.

She was absolutely certain he was not old money, nor did she recognize him as a member of the Spanish nobility her grandfather counted among his cronies. She was pretty sure she had met all the eligible men of her age in that circle six years ago…before she'd turned her back on a world she hadn't wanted to belong to. She didn't know *who* he was, but he'd been watching her all evening and it did strange things to her equilibrium. Impossible things she had long ago decided she was not destined to feel.

All of this ran through her mind in the short silent moments after she turned around. Still, his eyes asked why she had not yet responded.

Giving herself a mental shake, she stuck her hand out and said, "Lia Kennedy, actually. And you are?"

"Damian Marquez. You are Benedicto's granddaughter, are you not?" His fingers closed around hers, the heat in them warming hers.

"Yes."

His hands weren't those of a man who had never labored. They were rougher, like Toby's hands had been. Only her husband had been a classic laid-back beta male. Damian exuded an aura of power and hardness that made her already chilled body shiver convulsively.

"You are cold?"

"The air-conditioning…" She let her voice trail off, knowing the AC had nothing to do with it.

Neither did he really. She'd been cold from the inside out since the doctor told her about the hole in her daughter's heart. Returning to Spain and a grandfather who disapproved of all her life's choices had done nothing to warm her.

"We could step onto the terrace. It is still quite warm outside."

She shrugged. Why not? Her grandfather wasn't going to listen to her plea about Kaylee with all these other people around and the prospect of escape was too good to pass up. She hadn't been to his villa on the eastern coast of Spain since Christmas and hadn't been expected until the holiday rolled around next year.

The curiosity of the other dinner guests had been pressing in on her since she walked into the drawing room just as dinner was announced an hour and a half ago. Once dinner had ended and the guests started to mingle, it had become almost unbearable in her current fragile state. If the other guests weren't asking subtly worded questions trying to draw out the reason for her unexpected visit, they were watching her and whispering behind their hands about the too independent granddaughter who was such a disappointment to the old man.

Taking her acquiescence for granted, Damian took her arm and led her through a set of French doors at one end of the long drawing room.

He had been right. The night air was warmer than the chilled interior of the house.

She breathed deeply, enjoying the sensation of heated air caressing her body and filling her lungs. She'd been cold for so long. "This is much better, thank you."

"Most Americans prefer the air-conditioning, but then you grew up here."

"Actually I was raised in the States until I was fifteen." The year her father had died.

The Conde Benedicto Chavez-Torres had insisted Maria-Amelia return to Spain to live with her teenage daughter and Lia's mother had moved across the ocean without a single protest. Sunk in grief over the loss of her husband, she had not noticed how miserable her daughter was in their new home.

She had rejected every concern Lia had voiced, telling her daughter she needed to learn to live with the Spanish side of her nature. Lia hadn't wanted to live in the rarified atmosphere of the wealthy Spanish nobility. She had simply wanted to go home, a request denied time and again by her grandfather.

It should have been no surprise to anyone when she'd eloped with her high school sweetheart at the age of eighteen. Despite the fact their relationship had been long distance for the better part of three years, Toby had expressed more loving understanding toward Lia than either her mother or her grandfather had over those same three years. Yet, both Maria and Benedicto had been furiously shocked by Lia's marriage.

Her grandfather had immediately disinherited her and then been appalled when his action had done nothing to bring her crawling back to Spain. Nothing had done that, not his disapproval, nor her mother's tears and not even Toby's death. Kaylee's illness was another matter.

Lia would do anything for her daughter. Anything at all.

Ignoring the pain her thoughts caused, she added, "I make my home in New Mexico now. It's hot and I like it."

"I see." His dark gaze fixed on her meditatively. "I live in New York. It is hot in the summers, but the winters are very cold."

"Poor you. I would hate to live anywhere with a real winter."

"Perhaps you could learn to like it."

"I don't think so."

He didn't reply immediately and she got the distinct impression he was sizing her up. "Your grandfather said you do not visit Spain very often. I doubt it is the air-conditioning keeping you away."

"My daughter and I come at Christmas every year," she said defensively, not knowing why she should feel the need to defend herself, but feeling it all the same.

"Surely you could come more frequently?"

"Frequent travel doesn't fit into my budget."

"Benedicto would pay for you to come."

She shrugged. No doubt, but then she would have to spend yet more time listening to his lectures about moving to Spain and her mother's more subtle guilt trips. No thank you.

"Perhaps you are so dismissive of your family because you have never had to live without them." Damian's tone was disapproving. Not only did that surprise her—why should he care how close she was to her family—but it also got her back up.

"Tell me something, do you live with *your* parents?"

"My parents are both dead."

"I'm sorry. Losing a parent is devastating, losing both must have been an incredible blow."

"Yes."

His ready agreement surprised her. She had expected him to do the macho, nothing hurts me routine.

"What about your grandparents?" she asked, not willing to concede the point so quickly.

"Neither set recognizes my existence."

All her irritation at his high-handed questioning drained away. "Idiots."

She'd seen that kind of obtuse behavior among her

mother and grandfather's friends and it always made her angry. Her own family had done a fair job of snubbing Toby for the three brief years of her marriage. Her grandfather hadn't even warmed up to Kaylee completely until after Toby had died. Even so he had never tried to completely ignore her existence.

Lia's mother hadn't been so hard, but neither had she made the smallest attempt to make Toby feel like a welcome member of the Chavez-Torres family.

Damian's lips tilted in a half smile. "That is one way to look at it." Benedicto's granddaughter was not shy about speaking her mind. He approved.

He had no desire to marry a doormat, or breed such a character trait into his children.

"It's the only way to look at it. You asked me if family was important to me."

"*Sí*, and you told me that it was." Though clearly not as important as it was to Benedicto.

"*It is,*" she stressed, her amber eyes dark with sincerity. "I could never dismiss my daughter's choice of a husband as a person not worthy of respect and affection just because he wasn't the one I'd chosen for her and no way will I ever reject Kaylee's children because I don't agree with her choices."

His own mother's parents had not felt the same and his father's parents had never once acknowledged the familial connection. He had spent too many years on the outside of a world that should have been his by right of birth. Benedicto Chavez-Torres had helped Damian change that. The help he had given the older man since then had been a small enough price to pay for the vindication of his pride.

"That is not the usual attitude among the people in our world," he said to Lia.

"This world…" She swung her hand out to indicate her grandfather's villa and what it represented. "Is not *my* world. This is my mother and my grandfather's world and I only share it with them because I love them. I prefer the world my daughter and I inhabit in New Mexico."

"Do you?" Or was she making the best of things because her grandfather had disinherited her when she'd married against his advice?

Yet she had made no move to ingratiate herself again, at least not one that had not been of her own choosing. She did not even call herself by her grandfather's name now that both her father and husband were dead. She had to know it would have pleased Benedicto a great deal if she had changed her name back.

Independent. Rosalia Kennedy was very independent, but was she really as uninterested in her grandfather's world and the life of luxury inherent in it as she implied? The terms of the deal Benedicto had proposed said not.

Something of his doubts must have shown on his face because she frowned. "You're very cynical, aren't you?"

A bark of laughter surprised him. Not only independent, but refreshingly frank, not to mention discerning. He was cynical. Life had ensured he became that way. "And you are very forthright."

"More than I should be, probably."

He moved closer to her, invading her space and watching with interest as the pulse at the base of her throat began to beat more rapidly. "I like it."

"Grandfather doesn't." Her breathless voice caressed him like the hand of a very skilled lover.

How much had she learned in three years married to a man who was little more than a boy? Remembering his own sexual knowledge at the age of eighteen, he conceded she might be less innocent than she appeared. However, she was blushing like a virgin and he was not even touching her.

"You are nervous."

"Most women would be around you."

Again he laughed, delighted by her honesty. "Do you know, Rosalia, I believe I like you?"

She tipped her head back so their eyes met squarely. "You sound like that really surprises you."

"It does." He took another step forward, wanting to taste the lips she bit in her agitation.

She retreated, almost stumbling in her haste to get away, but the terrace railing stopped her and he made no effort to allay her obvious discomfort by backing up. Her reaction fascinated him. Women did not usually retreat when he moved forward. They met him with open arms, but hers were crossed defensively over her generous curves.

He wanted to know why. Was she playing a deep game, or was she genuinely nervous around him? He was, after all, still a stranger to her.

She clearly didn't remember the two occasions they had met six years ago, and if she did, he doubted she would have been reassured. He'd made her nervous then, too. She'd been so beautiful she had made him ache with desire, but she'd been too young for what he had wanted from her. Not quite eighteen, she had been strictly off-limits to a man of twenty-three and he had done his best to forget his mentor's granddaughter.

But he had not forgotten.

He wanted her and her current situation dictated that he would have her.

"Rosalia, are you out here?"

Damian moved away, not willing to openly acknowledge his desire for Lia. It would be leverage for Benedicto. While Damian trusted the older man more than anyone else in his life, he had not made tycoon status at such a young age by revealing his weaknesses to anyone. Besides, there was more to this deal than passion and he had a week to decide whether or not he would agree to Benedicto's proposition.

Benedicto's leverage was sadly lacking in this game.

"She is indeed here, Benedicto. We have been getting to know one another."

The older man surveyed Lia and Damian keenly. "And have you learned much of her?"

"Not as much as I would like," he said honestly.

"Ah, this is good." Benedicto smiled.

Lia blushed again and averted her face.

"And you, Rosalia, do you enjoy the company of my friend?"

Lia's head came up and she searched her grandfather's eyes, her own starkly vulnerable. "I thought he was a business associate."

"That, too. We have known each other many years."

"I see. Grandfather, I need to speak to you. Kaylee—"

"Not now, Rosalia." The harshness of Benedicto's tone shocked Damian.

Even more unexpected…anger welled up at the way

the words made Lia flinch. "I am happy to leave you two in privacy," he said in a tone he knew Benedicto would not mistake.

Indeed the old man's face tightened and his eyes said he recognized the warning. However, he shook his head. "Nonsense. The terrace during a dinner party is hardly the place for the conversation my granddaughter wishes to have. Is that not true, Rosalia?"

She looked like she wanted to argue, but she nodded instead. Then she sighed as if acceding with more than mere words. "Yes, Grandfather. You are right." She stepped away from the terrace railing. "That being the case, however, I think I'll say goodnight. I'm still adjusting to the time change."

She stopped speaking, her body held in tension as if she was waiting for Benedicto to react.

He smiled again, the warmth in his eyes unmistakable to Damian, but he got the impression Lia did not see it. "Sleep well, Rosalia."

"I will see you tomorrow," Damian promised.

"Tomorrow?" she asked uncertainly.

"Damian is staying with us."

"Oh. Goodnight then." She turned and fled. There was no other description for her hasty exit.

"Your granddaughter is shy," Damian remarked as the silence stretched between him and the first person to believe in him enough to invest in a Marquez, Ltd. venture.

"She will make an admirable wife. You will not find her flirting with the waitstaff in the kitchen during one of your parties."

The reminder of one of the less than pleasant memories he shared with Benedicto routed the softened feelings he had allowed to creep in while talking to Lia. It was exactly memories like that one that had made him listen to Benedicto in the first place when the old man had come to Damian with his proposal.

Marry Lia and be guaranteed at least half of the Chavez-Torres business holdings. While the collapse of the world's stock market had dictated that Benedicto's fortune was not what it once was, his holdings had more value than mere money. They represented a foothold in business interests usually reserved for the Spanish nobility. Damian's pride demanded more than undeniable wealth, he wanted what the illegitimacy of his birth had denied him.

Acceptance. Even if it was forced. He would sit on the boards of several companies with his younger brother, the only legitimate son to their father and their sister as well, the holder of the title that should have been his.

Another reason Benedicto's proposal had been so palatable. Under a special dispensation from the king, the Conde was prepared to cede one of his lesser titles to Damian once he became a member by marriage of the Chavez-Torres family. All of his other titles would pass eventually to his granddaughter and ultimately to Damian's own children.

It would require Lia and her grandfather signing documents to the effect that Kaylee Kennedy, an American citizen, would not inherit the titles from her Spanish family. According to Benedicto, Lia would be more than willing for such a passage of events. And if her earlier words were to be believed at all, Damian suspected the old man was right.

The next morning, Lia saw Damian at breakfast, just as he had promised the night before, but her grandfather was nowhere in sight.

"He had a business meeting," Maria-Amelia said from the other side of the table. "He told Rosa not to expect him back in time for dinner."

Dinner? "What about lunch?"

"We are meeting associates in Alicante," Damian said, his demeanor that of the hard-bitten businessman again.

She had thought last night he had relaxed with her, but she must have been mistaken. She certainly hadn't been thinking straight, or she would not have let him get so close. She was almost positive he would have kissed her if Grandfather had not interrupted. For once, she was grateful for his interference.

"Perhaps you would like to join me on a shopping trip?" Lia's mother asked.

Lia smiled, knowing it was her mother's way of getting her mind off of her problems. She accepted, more for the chance to distance herself from Damian's disturbing presence, than any hope shopping could keep her from worrying about Kaylee's future.

That night, as she tucked her daughter into bed, Lia found it very difficult to believe the small, blond pixie-faced girl looking up at her had something as serious as a hole in her heart. Her blue eyes clear with child-like innocence and her skin a soft, healthy pink, she didn't look in the least bit sick.

But looks could be deceiving when it came to a genetic defect like the one Kaylee carried, as the heart specialist had taken pains to point out to her.

"Mama, are you sad?"

Lia smiled, concentrating on projecting the love that had filled her soul since the moment she'd learned she carried her daughter. "I'm fine, sweetheart. How about you? All recovered from the plane ride?"

Kaylee grinned, but then covered her mouth with a small hand as she yawned. "I love flying, silly."

"It's a good thing since your grandmother and great-grandfather live so far away."

"Abuela Maria-Amelia must not like to fly because she never comes to see us."

Lia leaned down and kissed her daughter's cheek. Her mother's lack of visits had a lot more to do with the humble way Lia and Kaylee lived than discomfort on a plane. She didn't say that however. Her daughter would not understand and Lia never wanted Kaylee to feel rejected by her family. Not as she had been.

"That must be it. I can't imagine anyone not wanting to see lots and lots of a sweet girl like you otherwise."

Kaylee giggled. "I love you, Mama."

"I love you, too, butterfly." Lia finished tucking her daughter in, making sure the blanket was snug around her small body.

Grandfather really did keep the house rather chilly.

She stood up to go. Stopping at the door, she turned off the light and then looked back over her shoulder to say goodnight one last time. Kaylee's eyelids were already drooping.

"Mama?"

"Yes, sweetheart?"

"I met a nice man today."

"You did? When?"

"You were gone with *Abuela* and he came outside to watch me skip rope." The doctor had said that mild exercise should not be a problem for Kaylee…not yet. "He counted skips with me."

"Who was it?"

"Damian. He said he was your friend."

Damian had watched her daughter play? The concept shocked her, but she found herself smiling. "A *new* friend."

"He's my new friend, too."

"And I am a very lucky man to have made two such lovely friends in less than two days." Damian's voice from directly behind her shocked Lia into whirling around.

"What are you doing here?"

"I hoped to be early enough to say goodnight to Kaylee."

"Oh." Nonplussed, she didn't know what else to say, but her daughter was not so reticent.

"Damian!" She sat straight up in bed, her tiredness disappearing as if it had never been. "I want a hug."

Lia knew there was nothing for it but to turn the light back on and allow the big man to say goodnight to her small daughter. He did so, easily cajoled into reading Kaylee a second bedtime story. Lia had read her the first one. It was all so unreal that Lia spent the next fifteen minutes in a complete daze. This was simply not a side of the powerful executive she had expected to see.

Even more shocking was the effect his proximity
had on *her. She was attracted to him.* For a woman with
her past, that was more than amazing, it was unbelievable and yet even she could not misread the way her
heart raced and breath went short when he was near. She
wanted to touch him and that scared her to death.

While her grandfather seemed intent on avoiding her
over the next couple of days, Damian was always there.
He drew her like an irresistible force and he didn't seem
to mind at all. No doubt he was staying with her grandfather for business purposes, but he spent more time
with her and Kaylee. Neither Benedicto nor Maria
seemed taken aback by this state of affairs.

Despite her growing concern on her daughter's behalf—why had her grandfather refused to make time to
talk to her—Lia enjoyed her time in Damian's company.
They had a lot in common and merely being in the
same room with him sent a sensual charge zinging
straight to the core of her. The feeling was so remarkable that even if he hadn't returned the attraction, she
would have found it impossible to stay away.

However, he made it clear in one subtle way after another that he saw her as a desirable woman and his desire fanned her own in ways she found both confusing
and frightening.

Damian Marquez was a master tactician and true to
the nature she had first sensed in him, he entered a battle to win it. She had the distinct impression he saw her
as the spoils of victory. Toby could have told him that
when it came to sex, she was more likely to spoil the
victory than enhance it. And yet, despite her past and

what she knew of her own body, Damian succeeded in seducing her latent sensuality to life.

It had been so long since she felt anything like it, she'd forgotten what it meant to be a woman and the reminder added to her already charged emotions. Something had to give soon, or she was going to fly apart at the seams from everything tearing at her.

She needed to know her daughter was going to be okay. Every passing day increased her fear for Kaylee's future. As inconceivable as she found it, she could not shake the worry her grandfather was avoiding her because he was going to refuse help.

Desperation clawed at her insides with growing ferocity until she felt like her emotions were the powder inside a stick of dynamite with a short fuse.

And Damian was the fire that would light it, blowing apart her world and her ability to deal with everything happening to her. She urgently needed to get away from him before she did something unutterably stupid, like try to act on the feelings he aroused in her.

CHAPTER TWO

LIA was once again outside, hoping the warm summer evening would dispel some of the chill her grandfather's latest refusal to speak to her had left inside her chest. He hadn't actually come out and said he would not speak to her, but he'd made it clear he and Damian had business to discuss after dinner. Lia wanted to tell him to stuff his business, but what good would that do?

And it could do a great deal of harm for Kaylee. No matter what it took, she had to get the money for Kaylee's surgery, even if it meant swallowing her anger along with her pride. She would beg if that was what it took, but she *needed* her grandfather's help. She'd run out of other options before ever coming to Spain.

The insurance company had denied her claim based on the "preexisting condition" clause. Lia still fumed when she thought of that stupid doctor who had said Kaylee's abnormal test results were nothing to worry about when she was a baby. This was the same doctor who had told her to drink a glass of wine before sex and everything would be fine.

He'd been wrong about that, too.

The test results had indicated a hole in Kaylee's heart that would only get worse as she got older. While the risk of heart attack or stroke was extremely low, *it was there* and if the condition wasn't fixed...that risk would increase with each passing year.

Toby's parents would have given the money if they could, but they had had their son late in life and were living on a small, fixed retirement income. They'd offered to sell their two-bedroom house in the New Mexico desert, but the truth was, even if they gave her all the proceeds, it still wouldn't have been enough. And Lia's income as a nursery school teacher barely covered the necessities of life. It certainly left nothing over to save for a possible disaster, medical or otherwise.

Lia sighed, curling her legs onto the bench. Even with the cushion, the stone surface wasn't exactly comfortable, but she didn't mind. At least she was alone with her thoughts. A soft breeze on the warm evening air-brushed her skin, reminding her that she was still capable of enjoying physical sensations. Strange how that could be true after all she had been through.

"Are you avoiding the air-conditioning again?"

Startled at the now familiar voice when she thought she was alone, her head jerked up. "Damian."

He stood over her with one eyebrow tilted quizzically. "You appear pensive."

"I am. I need to talk to my grandfather, but he's made himself scarce for three days now. I'm getting desperate." In spite of her disturbing thoughts, Damian's proximity sent frissons of sensation rushing along her nerve endings.

"I am sure he will discuss all the details with you when the time is right."

"You know why I'm here?" she asked, shocked her grandfather would have shared the information.

After all, family business was just that. *Family business* and while it was obvious Damian and her grandfather shared a special rapport, Señor Marquez was not family.

"*Sí*. Benedicto and I have talked a great deal." He sat down beside her, laying his hand across the back of the bench and his fingertips brushed the bare skin of her shoulder.

The small touch sent more tremors through her nervous system and she wished she'd worn a dress that had more to it than her simple black sheath with spaghetti straps. It left her all too vulnerable to such casual caresses.

"Your skin is so soft." His rich, masculine voice did impossible things to her insides while he ran a single fingertip along her collarbone. *"Bonita."*

He thought her beautiful? She almost laughed. She'd gotten so used to seeing herself as a sexless being, incapable of a woman's pleasure that she'd forgotten men could still find her attractive.

"We shouldn't—"

"Shh…" His fingertips moved to cover her mouth, stopping her protest before it could form. "This is something we must know."

She couldn't form a coherent thought to wonder what he was talking about. It was as if a sorcerer's spell had been cast and she was paralyzed by its enchantment. The still lucid part of her knew she should pull away, but she couldn't make herself do it. The small touch was too intoxicating.

For just this moment in time, she felt connected to another person and she desperately needed that.

She'd been alone so long.

He moved closer until his hard thigh brushed up against hers, his arm coming down to close around her shoulders. "Your grandfather and I were discussing details and I realized there was one thing I had to be sure of before making a final decision. No doubt you are curious, too."

"Curious?"

She wasn't sure he heard her barely whispered question because his mouth was already descending. Had she even spoken it aloud?

"Your voice is very breathy," he said, answering her thoughts. His lips hovered above hers. "Why is that I wonder?"

Warmth unfurled inside her at his teasing tone.

"I find you very attractive," she admitted, knowing even as she said the words, she shouldn't.

He would think she was inviting intimacy and she could not do that, no matter how much she wanted it... but oh how she wanted it.

His nostrils flared. "I am attracted to you too, Lia. This is a good thing."

"I—" She never knew what she would have said because his mouth closed over hers at that moment.

Time stopped.

Sensations she'd never known buffeted her and the world and everything in it ceased to exist...except Damian and what he made her feel.

His mouth moved over hers with expert seduction, drawing her lips into parting slightly so he could barely penetrate her with his tongue. He tasted like the wine they'd had with dinner and something else, something she found far more powerful of an aphrodisiac…himself.

She moaned and grabbed his pristine white shirt with both fists, terrified he would pull away and end the amazing sensations pouring through her. But his lips remained warm and insistent, coaxing her to a response she had not known she was capable of giving.

Her lips parted further of their own accord and Damian's tongue slipped completely inside, laying claim to her mouth with total possession. His mouth said, *You belong to me.*

Her lips responded silently but with unmistakable intent. *Yes, I do.*

And for this moment out of time she did.

Strong, but gentle fingers cupped her breast, jolting her with the intimacy of the action, but even then she could not force herself to pull away, to tell him they had to stop. Even though part of her waited with trepidation for him to grab her roughly and squeeze, she loved the feel of his fingers against her sensitive flesh. Only he didn't grab. His thumb brushed over her nipple, making her groan as the peak tightened with unexpected pleasure.

He pulled her closer against him and she let her hands flatten against the hard muscles of his chest. She shuddered at the contact, unable to believe she was this way with him. Exploring with her fingertips, she traced the bulge of his muscles and the shape of his torso.

Being so close to another person, having the freedom to touch was such a heady sensation, she lost what little remained of her common sense.

His mouth moved to her cheek and down her neck, wreaking havoc with her nerve endings. "Lia, you are driving me crazy."

"I don't mean to," she moaned.

His husky laughter shivered through her like an internal caress. "I do not mind."

"I'm gla…" He bit her earlobe and she lost the ability to speak.

A very tiny voice in the back of her mind told her she had to stop, that she couldn't let this go on. But it was drowned out by the clamoring voice of passion, a voice she had not heard since her wedding night seven years ago. His fingers did something to her nipple that sent her coherent thoughts rocketing to the heavens. She pressed herself into his hand while her own fingers scrabbled with the buttons on his shirt.

She wanted to feel the heat of his skin, just once.

She found the light dusting of hair across his chest unbearably exciting as she brushed through it until she found the hard points of his nipples. She caressed them and his big body shuddered.

"Yes, touch me, *querida*."

She did, lightly pinching them as he had done to her, and he groaned, long and low.

His grip on her waist tightened until she had no hope of movement, but she didn't mind because his lips were slanting over hers again.

When she felt warm air on her breasts, it only vaguely registered. Even the feel of his rough fingers against her bare flesh only filled her with searing desire, none of the fear she'd experienced during sex in her marriage.

His mouth broke away from hers to move to her bourgeoning peak and she dug her fingernails into his chest. When he started suckling, she cried out, and then bit her own hand to keep the moans from coming out.

"You are so responsive. It is amazing."

She wasn't. Not with anyone but him. Her head moved from side to side in a mixture of sexual frenzy and denial, but then his hand slid up inside her thigh. Nerve endings that had gone without stimulus for years flared into life with the power of a flash-fire in a bone-dry forest. The heat between her legs crackled and blazed, searing her with its intensity.

His touch skimmed closer to the heart of her need and a tendril of sanity reached out to wrap around her mind. Memories of her numerous failed attempts at intimacy pressed for recognition, but she refused to give in to them.

Surely it would be all right. She was so excited, her body would admit him. It had to.

But it didn't. He touched her between her legs with just his fingertip and she could feel the spasms, knew her vaginal walls were closing. Soon, he would know, too. He would discover her complete lack of femininity and she could not stand it.

Toby's love had turned to anger and finally pity, but her husband had made one thing very clear. No man wanted a woman incapable of having sex.

She broke away from Damian and surged off the bench, shocking him with her violent rejection.

His body was shaking, the unmistakable bulge of his arousal a testament to what he wanted to do with her.

"Lia. What is it?"

"We can't."

He looked around him, as if he could not believe what he saw. "You are right. Not here. Come to my room."

She shook her head, incapable of vocalizing her rejection, her hands coming up to hide her nudity that now made her feel vulnerable.

Comprehension followed by an expression of pure cynicism washed over his features. "You wish to wait."

"No...you don't understand."

"Ah, but I do." He smiled, though no humor or warmth entered his eyes. "At least my question has been answered. I will finish negotiations with your grandfather."

"You think I did that—" she flailed her hand toward the bench where they had come so close to making love "—so you would negotiate something with my grandfather?"

She felt sick and it wasn't just because her body had once again failed her.

His expression unreadable, Damian looked at her for several seconds and then he shook his head. "No. I believe the passion, it is real. You want me and that is enough. Who am I to complain if you want the deal closed before you are willing to consummate it? It is, after all, how I do business all the time."

She didn't know what he was talking about, but she wasn't hanging around to figure it out. Her emotions were all over the place and it was because of the man who stood there looking and talking as if what had just occurred had been nothing more than a particularly physical form of business negotiations.

She turned and fled without another word.

The sound of her name on his lips only made her walk faster until she was almost running up the stairs to the safety of her bedroom.

Benedicto Chavez-Torres kept his study only slightly warmer than the rest of the house and Lia shivered as she waited for her grandfather to finish his phone call so they could talk.

He hung up the phone and fixed his steely gaze on her across the expanse of his huge mahogany executive desk. "Your mother said you have something you wish to ask me."

There was no point in hedging, so she didn't even try. "I need money, a lot of it."

"For?"

Her heart sank to the pit of her stomach. "Please, let's not play these games, Grandfather. Mother told you about Kaylee and her heart condition. I know she did. And now I need to know whether you will help."

"*Sí.* Your daughter needs surgery, I gather."

"She's your great-granddaughter, too." How could he play this cold game again?

She thought he'd finally accepted Kaylee after Toby died. True, Lia's grandfather hadn't made any extra efforts to get to know his great-granddaughter in the last three years, but he hadn't made any over-tures toward Lia, either. It was just his way. He was not a demonstrative man, or so she had always told herself.

"I do not deny the Chavez-Torres blood in her veins. Surely it is you who do that."

"Choosing to live in America is not a denial of my Spanish family."

"That is a matter of interpretation."

She'd been prepared for this. She knew the money would not come without a cost and she was willing to pay it, whatever it was. His first sally was expected and one she actually welcomed.

Moving to Spain to live for the next few months would be the best alternative for Kaylee. Lia could not afford to maintain a separate dwelling without working and she needed to stay home full-time with her daughter to care for her after the surgery.

"Will our moving back to Spain change your attitude?"

"How much money do you need?" her grandfather asked, without answering her question.

She named a sum that covered the surgery, Kaylee's stay in the hospital and basic living expenses for her and Kaylee during the time that Lia would not be able to work. It was an astronomical figure as far as she was concerned, but she knew her grandfather could easily afford it.

"You will receive twice that on two conditions."

"What conditions?" she asked warily.

Her grandfather was a shrewd negotiator and he had long since made it clear he did not approve of Lia's life choices.

"I am an old man now, Rosalia. I have no son to leave my company to. I feel this more deeply as each year passes."

"You have a daughter," she reminded him.

"Your mother has no interest in business."

Lia could not argue that truth. "What has this got to do with Kaylee?"

"Nothing."

"But…"

"It has to do with the conditions I have for gifting you the money you require."

She remained silent, waiting for him to list the conditions.

"I want an heir, someone to leave my company to."

"You want to raise Kaylee here as your heir?" The thought horrified her. Lia's daughter would have no chance to pursue her own dreams in life if she were locked into her grandfather's will.

"You mistake me." He leaned back in his chair and smiled. "It is time you remarried."

Lia gasped, the blood leaching from her face, leaving her skin frigid with cold and her lips stiff. She was never marrying again. She couldn't! *"No."*

"Yes." Her grandfather stood and towered over the desk, all pretense of pleasant affability gone. "You mourn your first husband like he was a god. He was but a man and not a great man at that."

She would have stood, too, but she doubted her legs would have supported. "Toby was good to me." In every way but one and that one hadn't been his fault. It was hers.

"He was a boy playing at being a man." Benedicto's lips curled in derision. "He took you from your family, forcing you to live with less than even my servants live with."

"Millions of people the world over live under much worse financial restrictions."

"These millions are not my granddaughter." He was every inch the Spanish nobleman in that moment, his expectation that she would always live as a Chavez-Torres stronger than ever, even if technically she was a Kennedy.

"I'll move back to Spain. I'll even do my best to fit into your and my mother's world, but I will never re-marry."

He looked down his patrician nose at her and she thought, not for the first time, that she knew how peasants had felt in the face of her ancestors hundreds of years ago. "You are in no position to dictate terms. The insurance company has refused to pay for Kaylee's surgery and convalescence and your *other* relatives are in no position to help you."

"Are you sure about that?" She hadn't told her mother about her insurance policy, hoping not to let her grandfather know how desperate she really was.

"Quite sure. A few phone calls after your mother told me of Kaylee's condition and I knew all. Your financial situation is as dire as it can get."

"I'm not exactly living in my car."

"Neither do you own your own home and the small house you rent is a hovel."

"It isn't, but that is not the issue."

"No. The issue is what you are willing to do to guarantee your daughter's future."

She blanched at the cruel ruthlessness of his words. "Are you saying Kaylee's life means nothing to you?"

"You both mean a great deal to me, but I will not pay

to have her heart fixed only to stand by and watch you destroy both yours and her life out of misguided pride and stubbornness."

"You think me remarrying will not do that?"

"I'm sure of it."

"You can't be serious." But he could, his implacable expression said so. "I'm not even dating."

"I do not expect you to find your next husband, in fact, it would no doubt be another disaster if I allowed you to do so. I have selected him for you."

"You've picked out a husband for me?"

"Yes."

"Impossible. Even you aren't such a dinosaur that you believe in arranged marriages."

He shook his head and sat down again, his tanned aristocratic features set in grim lines. "But I do, *niña.* In certain circumstances, they are the only way."

"And you believe this is one of those circumstances?"

"Yes."

"How can you use a child's life as a bargaining chip to get what you want?" She swallowed the bile that filled her throat at his machinations. "I always knew you were hard, but I never thought you were without a conscience."

He shook his head almost wearily, for a moment looking every one of his sixty-eight years. "You have never understood me, *niña,* nor do you truly know me. I do not expect you to begin now. Believe only that if you do not fulfill my conditions, you will not receive the money you have asked for."

"Please, Grandfather. Don't do this."

His expression turned as impassive as a rock, all softness gone as if it had never been. "I have no choice."

"But you do…" Her voice trailed off at the implacable glint in his dark eyes.

They stared at one another, her weighing his resolve, him simply waiting for her to come to terms with it. Or so it seemed to her.

But then he spoke and his voice was laced with unexpected desperation. "Believe me when I tell you, I truly have no choice."

The cracks in the front of his Spanish pride convinced her as no words could do.

"Who have you chosen to fill the exalted role of husband to the granddaughter of Benedicto Chavez-Torres?" she finally asked, unwilling to beg for information he had not offered.

Like why he had no choice and what that meant for her and Kaylee.

"Damian Marquez."

She'd known the man was staying with her grandfather for business, only she *hadn't* known *she* was the business. "You're assuming he will be agreeable?"

"We've already settled on terms."

"Impossible," she said, her voice scratchy with tension.

"No, it is not. Your marriage will be the final contract in a merger that will benefit us both, but I must be honest, myself more than Damian."

He saw marriage between her and his business associate as nothing more than a financial merger? "That is sick."

This sort of thing simply did not happen in this day and age. *Of course it did,* her practical mind contradicted her outraged heart, *just not in the circles you've been living in the last seven years.* Her grandfather would see nothing out of the ordinary in directing her life like this, but it was still so medieval, it should be a historical movie script, not her life.

He merely shrugged as if to say her emotions had no place in his business dealings. "I admire Damian much as I would a son. It is more than good business."

"He's hardly from your class," she broke in bitterly.

"That is a foolish remark and it is not true. His father was a *don,* but his mother was the man's mistress, not his wife. Neither family acknowledges him and that is their loss. Damian is very intelligent, ruthless when he needs to be and he knows how to run a business and make a profit."

He sounded like a carbon copy of her grandfather, especially the *ruthless when he needed to be* part.

"Lia, you need a great deal of money. Due to a reversal of fortune, I am in no place to give you that money. Damian is. I suggested the marriage as a personal seal on a merger between the two of us, a way for him to receive some compensation for the financial help he has given me over the past few years and the help you need now. It is little enough to ask."

"You think marriage is a small price to pay for his help?" she asked, unable to hide her horror at the idea.

Her grandfather ignored it. "He came to stay this week to see if he would be amenable to the marriage and I am happy to say he is."

"You mean he was here to check out the merchandise?" she demanded, knowing she was being crude and not caring.

"Do not speak of yourself this way. It is beneath you." Her grandfather's words of angry disapproval barely registered as a wave of hurt broke over her with drowning force.

She'd liked Damian. How could she have been so stupid? No man in her grandfather's world would have spent the kind of time Damian had with her and Kaylee without an ulterior motive. His had been a business deal.

Funny, she would have thought the man she'd gotten to know over the past few days incapable of blackmailing a woman into marriage, but then he probably didn't see it that way. To him it was no doubt a matter of getting adequate return on his investment. A cold and calculated motive, but not one entirely foreign to her grandfather's world.

Still, she had thought Damian was different. More the fool her. Clearly she was a lousy judge of character.

"He would give you the money if you asked without marriage to me a stipulated condition." She said it in desperation, not at all sure it was true.

Her grandfather shook his head, dashing not even fully formed hopes. "He is a shrewd businessman. He will not give something for nothing. What besides yourself do you have to offer this man for his money?"

"You make me sound like a whore."

"*No.* A whore would become the man's mistress."

A job she was even less qualified for than being a wife.

"You are not selling your body," her grandfather continued in her silence, "you are agreeing to share his life in exchange for your daughter's well-being. And I am not merely discussing her heart condition here, *niña*."

"You could *try* asking."

"I have no desire to do so. I want you to marry him, Rosalia. Accept that."

"I can't accept that you are willing to use Kaylee's health as blackmail leverage."

"I want more than one granddaughter."

Suddenly she understood. This wasn't just about business, this was about propagating the Chavez-Torres line. "You expect me to give you a grandson with Damian," she whispered in appalled tones Benedicto would not begin to understand.

"Damian is ready to have children. Only God may determine whether one of them is a boy."

"But you'll take the chance so you can get your heir…"

The old man had the temerity to shrug. "Your mother had only you and you have but one child, an American citizen at that…it is not enough to see the continuation of a family line, nor will you raise Kaylee to accept the responsibilities due the title."

He was right, but what difference did that make?

She shook her head, punch-drunk from what he was saying. If only he knew it, he asked the one thing she was totally incapable of giving, even if she'd wanted to.

CHAPTER THREE

"I NEVER want to marry again. *I can't.*"

"Nonsense." His will washed over her like an incoming tide. "You are young. You are fertile."

"Did you make calls regarding that as well?" she asked scathingly.

"I did not have to. Kaylee is proof of your ability to conceive. She was born within a year of your marriage to Tobias Kennedy. While I approve your choice to prevent conception soon after, sufficient time has passed for you to safely become pregnant again."

"Do you even hear yourself? You're not God, Grandfather. You can't dictate life."

"I am a mere man, but one that has what you want more than your freedom I think. You *can* marry and you will."

"What does Damian get out of this?"

"A title. Entrée into a society that has spurned him. The legitimacy he craves."

"I wouldn't think that would matter with a man like him."

"His pride demands recognition where it has been denied."

"He doesn't need an old man arranging his marriage."

"I can give him what few others can."

"What?"

"I will cede a lesser title to him. Your oldest child will inherit a legacy denied him as well *and* he approves of you as a bride."

"Why?"

"He finds you pleasing." When she snorted at that, he went on. "You are a Chavez-Torres. You will not marry him only to divorce him a year hence and take a large settlement with you."

"What's stopping me?"

"Your promise."

"You expect me to promise to stay married to him indefinitely?"

"Yes."

"Absolutely not. That leaves me open to abuse and humiliation because all the power is on his side," she said, a desperate plan forming in her mind. "My promise is only binding as long as he maintains the sanctity of his marriage vows."

"This is to be expected."

"I want it in writing and it must be understood that I will not stay with him if he mistreats me or Kaylee in any way."

"Granted." His tone rang with satisfaction. "However, you will give me your word you will do nothing to undermine the marriage."

"What do you mean?" Her word meant a great deal to her, but not as much as her daughter's life.

"You will respect your vows and you will not attempt

to embarrass or infuriate Damian into ending the marriage."

Relieved, she smiled. "I promise."

She wouldn't have to. When he discovered she was incapable of performing as a woman, he wouldn't be able to get out of the marriage fast enough. Toby had loved her, but even he could not continue with a marriage that included no physical intimacy.

"I want the money transferred into my account the day of my marriage, before I leave the reception."

"That can be arranged, but you realize once you marry Damian, you will have access to more than sufficient funds to care for Kaylee's health concerns."

"That is not part of the bargain. You promised me a certain sum and I don't care who's paying it. I want it in my account that day."

"Very well."

The rest of the negotiations were completed in a matter of minutes.

Damian sipped at his club soda while he and Benedicto waited for Lia to join them. "You know, when you first suggested this arrangement, I was skeptical, Benedicto."

"I could see that you were."

"But your granddaughter is everything you said she would be. Lovely. Charming." Passionate, but that wasn't one of the things the old man had listed when he'd extolled Lia's virtues. Damian had been forced to discover it on his own and the test had been no hardship. He looked forward to his wedding night with a sense of anticipation he had felt for nothing else in a very long time.

"She is a good mother." As his own had been.

Lia was also like his mother in that she was willing to do whatever necessary to make sure Kaylee's life was the best it could be. Benedicto had made no bones about the fact that Lia was willing to agree to the marriage because she wanted to guarantee Kaylee's future.

Damian could respect that.

"She loves her daughter and she will make a fine mother to the children she will give you."

"Your great-grandchildren."

"*Sí.*" Benedicto's eyes warmed. "Kaylee is a treasure, but I want to leave behind a legacy, not a single child I hope will pass the blood of my ancestors on to the next generation."

Damian did not scoff at the older man's desires. They matched his own after all. He had worked hard to build a business from nothing, but had realized on his thirtieth birthday that he had no one who truly appreciated his efforts, no children to pass on a birthright that was infinitely better than the one his parents had passed on to him.

Benedicto had suggested marriage to his granddaughter as the solution to both their problems.

It did not bother Damian that Lia proposed to marry him for the security he could give her. It was at least an honest business proposition, not avarice masquerading as love. He'd been down that road, not once, but twice and both times Benedicto had been there not only to point out the truth of the situation, but to support him afterward.

Marriage to the man's granddaughter felt right in a way Damian wasn't sure he understood. It had something to do with feeling like he belonged to a family again, but such considerations were not inner issues he would willingly examine.

The lawyer arrived with his assistant and all personal talk ceased.

"I see everyone is here and I am the last to arrive." The sound of Lia's soft voice had the men surging to their feet.

Damian smiled. "Surely that is a woman's prerogative."

She shrugged gracefully and took the empty chair nearest him. "I suppose, but I'm sorry if I've made you all wait."

"It is nothing," Benedicto dismissed while Damian studied Lia closely.

Her eyes lacked the warmth they had held on the previous occasions they had met and her tone was almost brittle.

"Lia," he said, using the name she'd told him she preferred.

"Yes?"

"Are you certain you want to go through with this?"

Her golden eyes widened and for just a second he saw vulnerability there that kicked at his gut, but then she masked it and smiled. "Yes."

"Do not worry, Damian. My granddaughter would not have given her word if she did not intend to keep it."

"Perhaps she has changed her mind." He did not want a reluctant wife.

Either she was okay with this business proposition, or she wasn't. There was no in-between.

"Have you changed your mind, Rosalia?" Benedicto asked, the words coming out like a challenge.

Her shoulders squared and her kissable mouth firmed in a determined line. "No. I assume *you* are still willing to go through with this merger?" she asked Damian.

"A marriage is much more personal than a merger."

"Yes, it is." The husky softness of her voice impacted his libido like a sledgehammer against a crumbling brick wall.

His usual defenses tumbled in a heartbeat, leaving him aching with a desire he had to wait four weeks to slake.

The lawyer cleared his throat and placed a set of documents on the large desk Benedicto had ceded to him for use during this meeting. "Ms. Kennedy, these papers are for your signature."

She did not move. "I was under the impression we all had papers to sign today."

"Yes, of course, Ms. Kennedy. Your grandfather will sign some of these documents and Señor Marquez as well."

"I see. Ladies first, is that it?"

"It was the *Conde's* wish to sign in this order."

Without another word, Lia leaned forward and began reading the papers. She flipped through the prenuptial agreement with no more than a cursory glance and set it aside. She barely skimmed the agreement ceding any and all rights Kaylee had to the Chavez-Torres titles. She spent a little more time reading the two-page document agreement between the two of them stipulating grounds for the end of their marriage, but she set it aside as well without signing it.

The final document detailed the financial sum that Damian had agreed to settle on her the day of their marriage. He would have been worried if it had been a million dollars, but the few hundred thousand she asked for was hardly enough to justify her reneging on their marriage and taking Kaylee to live on their own on his largesse.

She read the document carefully and then lifted her head. "I want you to sign this before I put my signature on anything else here."

Damian frowned, offended at the lack of trust she appeared to have in his integrity. "I have given my word to sign it as well as the others."

"Then you won't mind signing this one first."

"I mind your implication of mistrust."

She bit her lip and then squared her shoulders. "I'm sorry. Is it really such a big deal, or is this a male pride thing?"

He found his lips twitching in a smile. "You don't think much of the male pride thing?"

"No."

He shook his head and thought marriage to her might be less serene than he had at first anticipated, but he didn't mind. In fact, his blood heated in his veins at the prospect. "Very well." He signed the papers.

Once he was done, Lia put her signature to all three documents without reading them again. Damian had already read the papers, having hammered out the terms with Benedicto earlier in the week. So, he quickly added his signature to hers.

Lia stood up. "I'll leave you gentlemen to your business. I need to pack for my return to New Mexico."

"There is no need," Benedicto said.

"I don't like others packing for me."

"I mean, you have no need to return. We can arrange for your belongings, such as they are, to be shipped to Spain. You are needed here to help your mother with the wedding preparations."

"She doesn't need my help. She has you. I'm sure you've already got the entire event planned down to the last detail." She turned to go, but stopped in the doorway and looked back at Damian, the expression in her amber eyes unreadable. "I will be back in time for the wedding. If you need to contact me, Grandfather has my phone number."

"Lia, this is rid—" Benedicto stopped mid-word because his granddaughter was already gone.

"She's an independent woman, is she not?" Damian asked.

"*Sí.*" Benedicto sighed. "Too independent."

"Does she really intend to leave the entire wedding planning to you and Maria-Amelia?"

"I'm afraid so."

"Well, Lia may not have any ideas for our wedding, but I do. I do not want any plans made without my approval."

Benedicto laughed. "This, I expected. You are a man much like myself."

Damian was coming to the conclusion that might not be a good thing where his future wife was concerned.

Lia sipped her champagne, feeling numb as the noise of the wedding reception ebbed and flowed around her. She'd married again. Even knowing her reasons for doing so, she was having a hard time accepting that she had stood before a priest and five hundred guests to recite wedding vows two hours before.

She was now Rosalia Marquez…for a while anyway. Damian's years living in America showed themselves in different ways. His desire for her to take his last name was one of them.

His hand against her waist burned into her like a brand. It spoke of possession and feelings she had not anticipated plagued her.

She had thought that knowing he was a blackmailing bastard like her grandfather would have inured her to feelings of guilt, but she'd been wrong. It was so obviously apparent that he was pleased with their marriage, she hated thinking what her revelations later would mean to him.

He would be embarrassed, maybe not as much as if she was the one who did the walking out, but it would still be a source of public speculation. While she did not care what the dozens of people filling the luxury hotel's ballroom thought, she got the impression he did.

He had kept her by his side almost constantly since the wedding ceremony and already several people had commented teasingly on his besotted behavior. She knew he wasn't besotted. He was keeping a close eye on his newest acquisition and that knowledge should diminish her guilt as well.

It didn't. She wasn't like her grandfather and Damian. She had a very difficult time being ruthless when she needed to be and if it weren't for Kaylee's illness, she would never have had the temerity to embark on her current plan.

It would have been so much easier if he'd done as she expected. He had not used the reception as an opportunity to cement business contacts in a social setting and he had vetoed her grandfather's suggestion that Kaylee be excluded from the reception. Lia had learned that from her mother.

Damian had made it clear he wanted children to attend with their parents and for Kaylee to feel welcome. Lia's daughter was already half in-love with the man she believed was to be her father from now on.

Lia had hoped to avoid that kind of bonding by staying in the States until the last minute, but Kaylee and Damian had grown very close, very fast. It had only been a small step apparently for the little girl to make the transition in her mind from new friend to stepfather for Damian. She was already calling him Papa and every time she did, it tore at Lia's heart.

At this point, she might very well have stayed married to him if she could, if only for her daughter's sake.

Only the choice wasn't hers. If it had been, all her high-minded ideals to make Kaylee's life a happy one with her own Papa would probably go flying out the window anyway…the next time Damian showed his ruthless side. There was no telling what a man who would use a child's illness for blackmail was capable of doing, she reminded herself.

Nevertheless, she was glad he had insisted on Kaylee's attendance at the reception. Whatever emotional aftermath Lia would have to face because of it, she was happy to have her daughter nearby. While Kaylee's condition was far from critical, just knowing the little girl had a hole in her heart made Lia feel over-protective and nervous about having Kaylee out of her sight.

She scampered among the guests now, playing a low-key game of tag with several other children under the age of six. They didn't run, but scooted around adult bodies they used as barriers to tag one another. No one seemed to mind and Lia wasn't about to curb the innocent play otherwise.

Seeing her daughter happy was one of the main joys in Lia's life. She often thanked God that while she'd been forced to give up the intimacy of marriage, she had been given the gift of motherhood.

"Señora Marquez?"

Lia turned from watching her daughter to look into the face of her grandfather's extremely efficient accountant. She had learned only that morning, he was also Damian's accountant. Normally he would not have been invited to an occasion of such familial importance, but he had a job to do here today.

"Yes?"

"The funds have been transferred. If you would like to come with me, you can verify the deposit into your account."

She nodded and set her glass of champagne on a table behind her before moving away from Damian.

He grabbed her wrist, stopping midspate in a somewhat heated discussion about the latest Spanish football loss with one of her distant cousins. "Where are you going?"

"To verify the funds transfer."

His mouth tightened in obvious disapproval. "Does that have to happen now?"

Mindful of her cousin's undisguised interest, she merely nodded instead of telling him that if he wanted her to leave the building with him later, it did. "I won't be long."

"When you return, we will make our exit."

"Fine." The sooner she got the big revelations over with the better.

It was weighing more and more heavily on her mind.

"I will tell your mother."

Maria-Amelia planned to keep Kaylee while Damian and Lia went on their honeymoon. Lia had agreed to the two-week separation without argument because she knew it would only actually last one night. Maybe not even a full night.

"Thank you."

When Lia pulled up her online banking page, the uncertainty and fear she had been feeling for the six weeks since learning of her daughter's condition finally began to dissolve. There was enough money in her account to not only cover the surgery, but to pay for all living expenses for the six months following so Lia could stay home full-time with Kaylee. Happy tears washed into her eyes and she had to bite down hard to keep a sob of relief from escaping.

Her baby would be safe now.

No matter what happened in her marriage to Damian, Kaylee would be all right.

The accountant cleared his throat and turned away. She kept staring at the bank balance, unable to look away from the number that represented a new lease on life for her daughter.

"Kaylee is safely with your mother."

Damian.

She didn't want him to see her blubbering like an idiot and she wiped hastily at her tear wet cheeks before turning to face him.

Damian put his hand out, his expression blank but for the fires burning in his dark eyes. "It is time to go."

They were in the back of the long black stretch limo, pulling out of Alicante, before he spoke directly to her again. "We should be at the villa in a little more than an hour."

They were headed north. She wondered if it were near Calpe, or maybe Benidormo. "Is the house yours?"

"Yes. It has singular significance to me." He smiled. "Soon it will be the place of more very special memories."

"What's its significance?"

His eyes laughed at her for the sidestepping, but he answered. "It is the first property I bought after making enough money to do so."

"I thought you lived most of the year in New York."

"I do, but Spain is the land of my birth. I wanted a piece of property to call my own here. I have a caretaker, though, because I only make it over two, or maybe three times a year."

"That must be why we've never met."

He opened the minifridge and pulled out two bottles of sparkling water which he poured into glasses. "You are mistaken."

"I would have remembered meeting you." This man with his glossy black hair and sculpted features was unforgettable.

"You were only a girl at the time, not even eighteen."

Thinking back to that time, when she had been so desperate to get out of her grandfather's house, she realized she could have met King Kong and not noticed. Still, it surprised her she hadn't remembered him. She would never forget him again, no matter how much she might want to.

He was smiling again, watching her with that hungry jaguar expression she'd noticed the first night they met. "Even then, I thought you were beautiful."

She took a sip of the fizzy water he'd handed her.

His expression altered subtly, taking on a truly feral cast. "I wanted you."

She choked. Water sprayed across the seat and onto the pristine white of his tuxedo jacket.

He leaned forward and pounded her back while she tried to breathe again. "Surely this is not such a shock to you?"

She took a trembling breath and then another. "I…" She started wiping at the water with some paper serviettes and her voice faded as she realized she had no idea what she wanted to say.

He took the napkins from her hand and set them aside along with her glass, his gaze hot enough to singe even *her* nerve endings.

She sucked in more air and tried to calm her galloping pulse, but it didn't do any good.

Her gaze was snared by mahogany rich eyes. "You are a beautiful, desirable woman and now you are mine."

She wasn't expecting his next move, or she would have tried to get away, but she landed in his lap in the same moment she realized his intention to put her there. By then it was too late for evasive action.

He cupped her face and that quickly, she was back to the way she'd been on the terrace that night four weeks ago. Immobile in the face of sensations she had never experienced and did not understand.

Once again, she could not make her mouth form the words of protest she knew had to be said. All she could manage was a much too husky, "Damian."

"I have spent twenty-nine nights fantasizing about this moment. I wake remembering the taste of your lips under mine and while I understood your desire to wait, I have not enjoyed the sacrifice. No more sacrifice, Lia," he said as his mouth covered hers with uncompromising passion.

She fell into the kiss like a climber standing on the edge of the cliff with the ground giving way beneath her. No safety rope stopped her freefall to a place she could not see. Her thoughts became a swirling vortex of color and sensation while her lips learned the contours, depth and warmth of Damian's mouth.

Damian tasted the passion and need on Lia's lips and it was all he could do not to strip her and take her right then, but this was their wedding night and he would make it one for his bride to remember.

She felt so perfect in his arms. She fit him exactly, her breasts pressed against his chest, her bottom caressing his sex with little wiggles he doubted she was even aware of. She didn't seem to be aware of anything but his lips and he liked that—more than he would have thought possible.

This woman who had just become his wife was truly his.

His woman. His wife. His family.

He curled his hand around her rib cage, loving the soft feminine curve of her under the silk jacket she wore. He caressed her, brushing his thumb up to tease the underswell of her breast and then down again to press against her hipbone in a statement of sexual possession.

There were many spots on a woman's body only her lover would touch, only a few of which most women, or men for that matter, ever gave serious thought to. A woman's hipbone, the inside of her thigh, behind her knee, the portion of her rib cage just below her breast, her tailbone, the indentation of her waist—they were all spots on Lia that now belonged to Damian and no other man would touch them again.

He laid claim to each one with contact he knew would arouse, concentrating on drawing forth her pleasure bit by bit until she was panting and squirming in a mindless frenzy of passion on his lap. The touching had impacted them both and his erection was so hard, it ached and jumped with every movement of her perfectly shaped derriere.

He broke his mouth from hers and she made a mewing sound that turned his need up one more notch. "It is all right, *querida*. I will give you what you want, but first I must taste your soft skin."

She stared up at him, her amber eyes dazed in a face flushed with desire. "T-taste me?"

"*Sí.*" Did she think he meant that he would put his mouth on the essence of her here in the back of the limousine and did the idea offend her?

It excited him, but was not what he had meant. He

showed her what he wanted, sipping at the smooth skin of her neck and laving the hollow of her collarbone before lifting her hand to suckle at the pulsepoint on her wrist.

She moaned and her head dropped back against his shoulder as if she had not the strength to keep it up one second longer.

"You are sweet and just a tiny bit salty, *mi mujer.*"

"Damian, oh, please…"

He kissed her palm with his teeth and tongue while he peeled her jacket off. She let him do whatever he wanted and her trusting abandon drove his need to please her to a fever pitch.

He sucked her thumb into his mouth and she arched against him. Biting the pad he began to unbutton her blouse. He loosened one slow button at a time, the whole time sucking on one small, feminine finger after another. He was on her final pinky when the last button came undone and the sheer blouse parted to reveal the perfection of her skin beneath. Her bra fastened in the front and he undid it with one deft flick of his fingers. Firm, tip tilted, generous curves spilled out of their restraints and he twitched in his trousers, a small convulsion wetting the tip of his sex.

"Exquisito," he said on a sigh as raspberries and cream perfection filled his vision.

He dipped his head and tasted the valley between her breasts, knowing that the brush of his hair against her sensitive skin would excite her and the way he avoided her tender points would drive her mad.

He was right. She grabbed his head, her own thrashing from side to side against his shoulder. "Damian, what are you doing to me?"

He would have laughed if he wasn't so busy trying not to climax right then and there.

He kissed his way up her chest, to the graceful column of her throat and finally to her lips. They were parted on a moan and he penetrated her mouth with a deep, possessive thrust of his tongue. She stiffened against him and pressed her ripe curves against the wall of his chest while sucking on his tongue as if he offered her the ambrosia of the gods.

He played with her breasts, kneading them, caressing them lightly and then more firmly, but always avoiding the nipples now puckered to pebble-hard points. She moved against him as if she didn't know how to get what she needed.

CHAPTER FOUR

DAMIAN had never made love to a virgin, but if he had, he was sure this is what it would have been like.

Lia had been married three years, but she started at every new pleasure. She moaned like a woman possessed from an admittedly carnal kiss, but only a kiss nonetheless, and squirmed against his sex as if she had no idea what effect her movements were having on him.

She might not know what it was she wanted—though he found that difficult to believe, but he had no doubts about it. He once again broke the lock of their lips to lower his head and take one rosy ripe nipple into his mouth. He started suckling and she screamed. It was the sound of a woman shocked by pleasure, in thrall with her own pleasure and aching for more. He gave it to her. She called his name, then screamed again and started thrusting her hips in an ancient gesture of wanton invitation.

He took the invitation, sliding his hand up the inside of her thigh and then cupping her mound in another moment of possession so primitive he could barely admit it to himself.

She came apart in his arms with a long, keening moan and quivering convulsions that shook her body with their force. He gently rubbed her through the thin silk of her panties and seconds later, she came again, this time bowing toward his hand, her hips lifting off his lap.

He would have consummated their marriage right then if she had not started sobbing in great agonizing shudders. Her reaction so surprised him that he went completely still.

"Oh, Damian…" She said his name over and over again while tears streamed down her face and her body curled into his in a defensive posture he could not mistake.

She was shattered by her reaction and totally incapable of coping with it.

"Shh…*querida.* You must not cry. It is all right." He said other such things, not knowing if they were the right things. He had very little experience with weeping women and her tears unmanned him as a room full of executive sharks did not.

Damian's calming words and soothing caresses finally penetrated the emotional cataclysm roaring through Lia. Her crying diminished to a few hiccupping sobs and she took the snowy-white handkerchief he offered and mopped herself up.

She couldn't look at him, though. She didn't know what had happened. One second she was going to tell him to stop and the next her body was on a journey it had never taken, one more exhilarating than the fastest roller coaster ride in the world and more terrifying as well.

Silence had reigned for several minutes when he tilted her head back and looked into her eyes, his own dark with concern. "Are you all right, *mi esposa bonita?*"

His beautiful wife? Tears washed into her eyes again and she choked on the yes she was trying to get out. She wasn't his wife, not really and never could be.

"You must tell me what is wrong. Are you upset I touched you so freely in the car? The privacy window is shut. No one knows of our intimacy."

Intimacy. She had never known it. Not like this. And after she told him her truth, she would never know it again.

"I'm not worried about that," she forced herself to say.

"Then what has upset you so much?"

She pulled the edges of her shirt together in a defensive gesture not lost on him and his expression plainly told her so. It also questioned her sanity. He wasn't alone in that. She was wondering about her mental stamina right now herself.

"I don't understand what just happened to me," she admitted.

He stared at her as if she had spoken a language he did not understand, not English, which he was as fluent in as his native Spanish.

"I went crazy," she tried to explain. Maybe he was used to kissing women and causing that sort of reaction, but she'd never had it before. "My body, it… Well, I felt things. Amazing things… Like everything inside me contracted and exploded at once. It's frightening."

So was the look of fascinated disbelief on his face. "You climaxed."

No, that was impossible. "You weren't inside me."

"You only climaxed with your husband inside you before?"

She almost laughed at the ridiculous question, but was afraid if she started, she wouldn't stop. "No."

"Then…"

"I never…um…did that at all." She could hardly accept she'd done so now in a car on the road to her new husband's villa.

Did nice girls do that? She'd be afraid she was a closet sex maniac if she didn't know the vicious truth.

Still, this was incredibly embarrassing. Her mother's idea of a sex talk had been to suggest Lia read a few of the racier romance novels. She *had* read a couple before getting married, but her experience with Toby had been so different than the one the authors wrote about that she had never picked up another. Reading about whole women capable of responding sexually only made her feel like more of a failure.

"You have never climaxed?" Damian asked with obvious shock and absolutely no tact.

She felt heat pouring into her face like someone had turned on an oven inside her head. "No."

"You mean with a man, right?" At that moment, he sounded much more American than Spanish and she almost wished he had a little of her grandfather's fixation with polite behavior.

Grandfather would die before asking a woman if she'd engaged in self-pleasuring.

"No."

"Not at all?"

"Stop sounding so shocked. Some women don't you know."

"You were married for three years."

"So?"

He shook his head, his expression dazed. "I have a feeling being married to me is going to be very different for you."

No kidding.

"And there is nothing to be ashamed about if you've given yourself pleasure before."

If the floor of the car opened up right then and she disappeared through it, she would thank God six times a day and seven on Sundays. "Can we not talk about this please?"

"We are married."

"I'm aware of that."

"There should be no secrets between us in this regard."

Where did he get his marital advice? A tacky talk show? Of course women kept secrets. "Some things are private."

"But—"

"I've never done that, all right?" she said with total exasperation and then wanted to hide her face in her hands.

How could he have pushed her so far she'd blurted something that private out loud?

"You've been a widow longer than you were married."

More than three years. "I know that."

"I suppose your mother told you it was wrong?"

"No, I just never wanted to." She had learned to almost hate her femininity. No way was she going to try touching herself to bring pleasure. Besides, being touched down there hurt, or at least it had before.

Damian's hand against her most secret flesh had brought indescribable pleasure. She'd barely even noticed when her vaginal walls started spasming in the contractions that would prevent intercourse. For once her body's inadequacy simply hadn't mattered.

A long drawn out yawn surprised her and she hastily covered her mouth with her hand.

"You are tired now."

"Is that normal?"

"*Sí.* You are sated and your body therefore is ready to relax into sleep."

"Doesn't seem fair to you," she mumbled as she let him press her head against his chest, more than ready to abandon the embarrassing conversation.

"I will have my pleasure later."

He wouldn't, but wild horses would not have dragged that confession out of her at that moment. She was too busy wallowing in the aftermath of the only truly pleasurable intimacy she had ever known.

Lia woke to the sensation of being carried. She savored the feel of Damian's warm, strong arms around her, knowing it would be the last time and wishing it could be different.

She let her eyes slide open and saw that he was carrying her up a flight of stairs. The villa was bathed in late-afternoon light, the peach colored walls warm with the burnished glow from the sun. The staircase was stone with a wrought-iron balustrade and his shoes made a clicking sound on each stair.

"Where are you taking me?" she asked in a still drowsy whisper.

"To bed."

That woke her up fast and she tried to sit up in his arms. "We can't!"

"I assure you, we can."

"Damian, there is something I have to tell you."

"It can wait, but I cannot, *querida.*"

"You have to. Please, let me tell you."

They were in a large bedroom at the front of the house now and he set her carefully down on the bed. "Speak, but be quick. I have little patience left."

Her gaze dropped to the front of his tuxedo trousers and she gulped down air. He wasn't kidding. If this was his normal state of arousal, she doubted they would have fit even if she didn't have her problem.

"I…"

He looked at her expectantly, waiting for her to continue.

She had spent the last four weeks relishing the thought of telling Damian Marquez how her body would thwart both him and her grandfather's wishes.

Only now that the moment of truth had come, the righteous anger that had fueled her since agreeing to her grandfather's blackmail had deserted her. Several emotions fought for supremacy in her battered heart, but not one of them was satisfaction at outwitting the two blackmailing men.

She had hated her inadequacy too long to be sanguine about revealing it, even to thwart the despicable attempt at blackmail.

Though she had vowed never to put herself in such a circumstance again, once more, she felt like a failure as a woman. "You cannot make love to me, Damian."

He looked down at himself and then back at her

where she lay on the bed, her blouse buttoned, but the bra still unfastened and her nipples showing through. "Are you sure about that?"

"I'm positive." Tears clogged her throat and she had to swallow twice before continuing. "We can't. You have to believe me."

His eyes registered comprehension. "Is it that time of month?"

She wished she could take the easy out, but a face-saving lie would only put off for later what was better faced now.

"No."

"Then what is the problem?"

"I've never had another lover besides my husband. I mean, I haven't even dated since Toby's death."

"Your grandfather told me this."

"I bet he didn't tell you that you were the first man I've even kissed in more than three years."

His brows drew together. "I do not understand the problem here. To be truthful, knowing the only other man who has shared your body is no longer in this world satisfies the throwback in me."

"There's a reason I stayed away from other men."

"You were mourning your husband. Your grandfather told me. Do you still love him? Is that the problem?" He didn't sound nearly so complacent now. In fact, extremely irritated would be a much better description. "You feel you are betraying him by taking me to your bed?"

The compassionate question asked with such obvious male impatience made her want to smile, but the truth made her want to cry even more. "No. I *can't* take any man to my bed. I can't make love, Damian. My body won't let me. I freeze up." Which was not the whole truth, but enough of it for him to get the picture.

"You were raped?" he asked, looking ready to kill someone.

"What?"

"You speak as if you have been traumatized in a sexual way. You say your body will not allow you to make love, that you freeze up. These are classic reactions for a woman who has been hurt sexually."

Did she have to tell him everything? Wasn't it bad enough that her body had let her down in this way for so long? Why did she have to humiliate herself by spelling her flaw out to him? "I was never raped."

His eyes said he didn't believe her.

"I wasn't. I promise, Damian. That is not the problem."

"Then what is? You are too passionate to live like a nun, Lia."

That made her laugh, though the sound was not a pleasant one. Passionate? Not likely. "I'm about as sexual as an amoeba."

"You are kidding, right?"

She just stared at him.

"You responded to me both that night on the terrace and on the way here. You are not sexless. You came twice today with little more touching than what is usual for foreplay."

Really? *That was foreplay?* Not like any she'd ever experienced before. "But that's *all* I can do, Damian. The truth is, I didn't even know I could do that much."

And she wouldn't have been able to if she wasn't

feeling something more for him than mere physical attraction, she was sure of it. Her emotions hit overload on that admission. It was the final blow to defenses sieged for weeks on end.

How many nights had she lain awake wondering how she would pay for Kaylee's surgery and if surgery was even the right choice for her daughter? She'd come to Spain with the intention of swallowing her pride and asking her grandfather for money. But her pride had taken a lot more abasement than a family size serving of humble pie. She had been blackmailed into bartering her body in marriage to the first man she'd responded to sexually since shortly after her disastrous wedding night.

Realizing that she might actually be starting to care for him on an emotional level, no matter how shallow, took what was left of her peace of mind and destroyed it.

Her body started shaking with reaction, like she was in shock and if she didn't concentrate very hard, she was going to hyperventilate. Weak tears she hated because they revealed a vulnerability she didn't want exposed rushed into her eyes and tightened her throat.

As they spilled over, she surged to her feet. "P-please believe me, Damian. I c-can't make l-love with you." She was shaking so badly, she was stuttering. "Let me sleep somewhere else. I c-can't…I can't share that bed with you."

She stumbled past him, but he reached out as if to stop her and she reeled backward, bumping into the wall. "P-please… Don't touch me!"

"I will not allow you to go off on your own in this state." He moved inexorably forward and swung her into his arms before she could argue further. "You will sleep here. I will find another bed if you insist, but first you must calm down."

"I can't. I can't handle it any m-more. *Not any of it.*" She sobbed into his shirtfront, not bothering to question how she could find comfort in the arms of the enemy.

He sat down with her on the end of the bed and held her while she cried for the second time that day, but this time it was grief not gratitude and shock that sent her emotions careening out of control. He soothed her, much as he would a child and she let him, her tears finally subsiding after she'd thoroughly soaked his shirt.

She pressed against his chest and he allowed her to move off his lap.

He stood up, his expression grim. "Get into your nightgown. I will be back shortly."

Then he was gone. She didn't know where and didn't really care. She only wished he wasn't coming back. She felt like such an idiot crying all over him. She was certainly giving him some kind of a wedding night. From her response in the car, he had to have been looking forward to making love and she'd shut him down and then lost her emotional control all over him.

Even blackmailers deserved better treatment.

Realizing she didn't know how long he would be gone and terrified he might return while she was still undressing, she started fumbling the buttons open on her shirt. She ended up ripping the blouse trying to get it off, but by the time she'd stripped, she was sufficiently composed to contemplate a shower. Hot water and the privacy of a shower stall seemed incredibly alluring in that moment.

When she came out, Damian sat on a chair beside the bed, his tie and jacket gone. His shirt was unbuttoned several buttons, revealing a slice of bronzed chest lightly covered in black curling hair. While his clothes and posture were relaxed, his expression was forbidding.

She swallowed a sigh and tamped down the urge to turn around and spend the rest of the night hiding in the bathroom. "I'm sorry."

"Tomorrow we will talk, when you have rested. For now, I want you to drink this." He held up a brandy snifter half-filled with the dark amber liquid.

She wasn't particularly fond of the stuff, but she did not demur. It had been a tumultuous day and her insides felt shredded.

She took the glass and sipped at it.

"Are you afraid of me?" He lounged back in the chair, his feet crossed at the ankles and she realized they were bare.

"No."

"You are my wife. You belong to me."

"Yes." At least she agreed with the wife part, she wasn't so sure about belonging to him, but she'd had enough confrontation for one day.

"I would like to sleep with you in my arms tonight."

All the tension that the hot water from the shower had drained out of her came back. "I can't…"

"Make love. *Sí.* You have made this patently clear, but you can allow your husband to hold you, can you not?"

"Toby moved to another bed three months after Kaylee was born. He said it was too hard to sleep next to me and not be able to make love to me."

"I am not your former husband. If I make a request, be assured I know the limitations of what I ask. I think that tonight, you do not need to be alone."

The offer was such a generous one, after what she had told him that she didn't know what to say.

"Say you will allow me to hold you through the night," he said, letting her know she'd voiced her disconcertion aloud.

"Yes." It was selfish of her, but she hadn't been held in such a long time, and tonight he was right…the last thing she wanted was to be left with the loneliness her failures had forced on her.

She finished her brandy and climbed into the bed. Damian removed his clothes down to his boxers and then joined her, pulling her into his arms and curving his body around hers. She felt cosseted and protected.

"Thank you," she whispered as he pressed a button above the headboard that cut the lights.

"It is both my right and my pleasure. Be assured this is where I meant to be this night."

She could feel the resurgence of his arousal and doubted his words, knowing he would get nothing but frustration from sleeping with her. However, he did not complain and she had to wonder if his assertion of rights indicated his male pride was involved in some way.

Too weary to think about it, she allowed the steady beat of his heart to lull her into a dreamless sleep that lasted until morning.

She woke alone, but the smell of coffee alerted her that Damian was close by. She turned over and found him in the chair he had occupied the night before. A mug of steaming coffee rested in one hand while the newspaper rustled in the other.

She scooted into a sitting position, letting the covers slip to her waist. Her cotton pajamas were anything but revealing.

"Good morning."

The newspaper came down and chocolate-dark eyes gave her a serious appraisal. "Good morning. You slept well."

It was not a question, but she answered it anyway. "Yes, thank you. Did you?" she asked, not without some trepidation.

"After I reasoned many things out, I slept." He laid the paper and his cup of coffee aside. Then he picked up a carafe she had not noticed before. "Would you like some?"

"Yes, please."

He poured it, his expression meditative. "You did not intend our marriage to last, did you?"

"No." There was no point in prevaricating; besides he was smart enough to know the truth. "I did not believe you would want to stay married once you knew the truth."

He nodded and handed the cup to her, nothing of his reaction to her words revealed in his face. However, his demeanor was every bit as forbidding as it had been the night before.

She took a sip, savoring the rich chicory taste while wishing life could be even half so pleasant. "I'm sorry. I realize now that no matter how angry I was with you and my grandfather, what I have done is just as wrong."

"Marrying me with no intention of keeping your promise?" he asked.

"I didn't intend to break my promise."

That seemed to interest him and he studied her in silence for several seconds. "You thought that I would back out of the marriage and you would therefore have kept your end of the bargain. Your sense of integrity would remain inviolate?"

"Yes." But she'd been wrong. She felt like a cheat even if she had been forced into her circumstances.

"You did not consider refusing to make love to me an action that would undermine our marriage?"

"It isn't something I have a choice about."

"You are sure of this?"

"Yes."

"How? If you have had no intimate relationships since the death of your husband?"

"It didn't work with him, either."

Damian tensed. "Did he hurt you?"

"Not intentionally."

"But unintentionally?"

"Yes, just as I unintentionally hurt him."

Damian weighed her words while she finished her coffee. "Explain why you believed I deserved to be married under false pretenses."

He was so calm, she could hardly believe it. Any other man would be yelling by now, but Damian acted like he was on a fact-finding mission for a new business venture.

She wasn't so sanguine. Just thinking about what he and her grandfather had done to her, the pain and fear they had put her through made her see red. "Only a monster would use the life of a child to blackmail a woman into marriage."

That startled him and his dark eyes narrowed. "Explain."

"Don't feign ignorance."

"And yet, I sit here before you…ignorant. Do you wish me to call Benedicto and ask him? I assume he knows the details of this *blackmail*."

Not wanting her grandfather brought into this, Lia explained, even though Damian had to know already. She played his distorted game, but let him know in every way possible what she thought of the threats used to coerce her.

When she was done, he stood up and walked to the window. It overlooked the ocean, but she doubted the view of the beautiful waters of the Costa Blanca was what drew him there at the moment. In point of fact, it was the place in the room farthest from her and she felt his withdrawal as if it were a physical line being reeled in, pulling all his life energy away from her.

"Did it never occur to you that I might be unaware of Benedicto's methods of persuasion?"

"No. How could Grandfather believe he could get away with it otherwise? I was under no obligation to keep it from you."

"And yet you did."

"Only because I knew you knew." That hadn't made a lot of sense, but he didn't ask her to clarify.

"Did I? Your grandfather is a master tactician and he outmaneuvered both of us."

"No." A sick feeling started growing in the pit of her stomach and she put her almost empty cup down, knowing she would be unable to drink any more. "What do you mean?"

"I believed you married me because you wanted to assure your future and that of your daughter, perhaps even to please your grandfather. I was unaware Kaylee faced such a serious health complication."

"And if you had been?"

He turned back toward her, but stayed by the window. "I am not sure it would have changed the outcome, but I would have better understood your reaction to me yesterday."

"Grandfather said you are a shrewd businessman and would expect something for the money you gave to me."

"This is true. However, you are not."

"Not what?"

"Shrewd when it comes to business. You should have asked for a great deal more in an up-front settlement. It surprised me that Benedicto did not insist upon it, but I assumed he saw himself in debt to me."

"In debt to you? He said you'd helped him out financially over the past few years." She hadn't really understood what that had meant and hadn't cared beyond the fact Benedicto could not pay for Kaylee's surgery.

"His fortune was severely reduced by poor investments. Not the ones he made in my company, I might add."

"Naturally."

"In order to continue living at his current standard, he sold his villa to me."

"But…"

"The agreement included him living there for his lifetime and me providing a home for your mother upon his death."

"But the villa belongs to you?"

"Yes, among other things. In this way, he was able to maintain many of his business holdings and keep your mother in comfort."

"But—"

"That is unimportant. We have more pressing matters to discuss right now."

"Our marriage."

"And its future." The way he said *future* sent shivers down her spine.

"We don't have a future."

"I disagree." He held up his hand when she opened her mouth to argue. "*Silence.* You took vows before God and many people yesterday, as did I."

"But…" He was right she had, only she hadn't been thinking of them as binding vows, knowing as she did she could not maintain a true marriage.

His dark eyes narrowed and she thought she would not like to be this man's business adversary. "The question I want answered now is: are you prepared to honor those vows?"

"Why should I be when my daughter's life was used to coerce me into saying them?" she asked with a belligerence that was only surface deep. Underneath she was scared to death.

He caught her gaze with his own and for the first time she saw the emotion he was tamping down. It was pure, unadulterated fury. "And yet, I kept my side of the bargain, did I not?"

In the face of that fury she could only nod dumbly.

"Kaylee can be taken care of now because I will see she is taken care of. Both her and your future are assured so long as you stay as my wife."

"But you want children."

"*Sí.*"

"I can't give them to you."

"That remains to be seen."

"You expect me to try?"

"You owe it to me. It is a promise you made to both myself and your grandfather."

CHAPTER FIVE

BUT it was a promise she had thought she would not have to keep. She let her head fall back against the headboard, her eyes shut tightly against a truth she did not want to acknowledge, but one that refused to be ignored. Her grandfather had ruthlessly manipulated her fear for her daughter to get his way, but she had also ruthlessly used Damian to get the money she needed.

"I'm no better than he is," she whispered.

"You take after him more than he realizes, but I like Benedicto. I do not think this is a bad thing."

Her eyes flew open. "I tricked you into marriage and you don't think that's a bad thing?"

"That depends."

"On what, for Heaven's sake?"

"Whether or not you intend to keep the promises you made and honor the vows you spoke."

She sighed. "I'll keep them," she said dully, "but it won't make any difference. No amount of *trying* will make intimacy possible between us."

She'd learned that with Toby and the prospect of

going through more of the same with Damian made her heart go cold.

"I want you, Lia. I mean to have you."

"But you can't." Wasn't he listening? She hit the bed with both fists. "Don't you understand? *I can't do it.* If I could, I would." And she would if only to maintain her own sense of integrity.

He smiled, all masculine complacency where before fury had reigned. "That is good to know. Now, tell me why you believe you cannot make love to me."

The words fell like stones between them, sending out ripple after ripple of waves through the murky waters surrounding them.

"I don't just *believe* it, I *know* it."

"So tell me why."

"What difference does it make?"

"I want to know."

"Why?" She was going to break apart into itty-bitty pieces if she had to expose her defectiveness to him. "Knowing the cause won't make any difference to the outcome."

"Perhaps, but I believe you owe this explanation to me."

"Apparently you believe I owe you a lot of things."

"Don't you?"

"Maybe." But that didn't make answering any easier. "It hurts to talk about it, can you understand that at least?"

But he wouldn't…couldn't understand. He didn't know what it felt like to be broken and defective.

"I don't want to hurt you," he said.

"But you will if it means learning what you want to know."

"Sometimes you must experience pain before you can get to the pleasure."

"Toby said a similar thing on our wedding night, only the pleasure never came."

"Are you afraid to make love to me because you do not trust me not to physically harm you?"

"Of course not." Though if he tried to make love to her, he wouldn't be able to help hurting her.

"I do not believe it is because you do not want me. You respond too readily and beautifully to my touch."

"I do want you," she admitted with aching honesty, even though right now she would also cheerfully have strangled him.

And she might want him, but no way was she going to care for him. That thought last night had to have been a result of an over stimulated brain.

"Then tell my why you cannot have me." He sounded angry again, and frustrated. She knew that tone. She'd heard it enough in her first marriage.

He said he wanted the truth. She'd give it to him. "I have vaginismus."

He stared back at her with no recognition sparking in his intense, chocolate-brown gaze.

"It's a condition that causes my vaginal muscles to contract involuntarily when I try to make love." She tried to talk about it as clinically as possible, distancing the physical reality of the condition from her, the woman she was inside. "My body will not allow you to penetrate me."

She could not tell if she disappointed him, or disgusted him, or even if he pitied her. "What causes it?"

"I don't know." She had her suspicions. She'd read

a little on the sexual dysfunction, but she didn't really want to know that much about the condition that had robbed her of her femininity.

For six years, the part of a woman's body that was supposed to give her the most pleasure had been Lia's own personal enemy. There had been times during her brief marriage that she hadn't just hated that part of her body, she'd hated herself.

Her doctor had been very clear. He believed the muscular spasms began in her head and she would have to will them to stop. She'd never been able to.

"It happened when you kissed me on the terrace, when you tried to touch me."

Understanding flared in his eyes. "That's why you pulled away from me. I thought you wanted to wait for our wedding night."

He'd thought she wanted to consummate the deal. Right now, she could wish it had been that simple, no matter how cold-blooded.

"At the time I didn't know we were supposed to have a wedding night."

"You thought I expected you to let me make love to you to sweeten a deal for your grandfather." He sounded like he'd just worked that out.

She shrugged. "Frankly I preferred the righteous indignation angle over having to tell you the truth."

"You had this problem with your first husband?"

"Yes. My marriage ended the night he died, but not *from* his death like everyone thinks. He told me he was leaving me and then got in the car and was hit by a drunk driver on his way to a hotel. Toby needed sex like other men, but unlike other women, I couldn't give it to him."

"Lia…" Pity shimmered in the brown depths of Damian's eyes and she wanted to scream.

Toby had looked at her just that way when he asked for the divorce. Seeing it in Damian's expression made her furious.

"Are you satisfied now?" She felt wild with grief and frustration.

Damian winced at the volume of her voice, or was it the look in her eyes?

Unexpectedly he moved and reached toward her, but she jerked away. "Don't! I don't need or want your pity, Damian."

It devastated her to have to reveal her shattered sexuality to him and she wondered how she'd ever thought she could be complacent about it.

"Lia, I did not mean to hurt you, but for us to face the future together, I have to know the facts."

"We don't have a future, or haven't you figured that out yet? All the pity in the world can't change that." She surged off the bed and spun away. "I'm going to take a shower."

She didn't hear him move, but all of a sudden two hands clamped down on her shoulders and spun her around. She didn't even have time to yell at him again before his mouth came down on hers.

It should have been a kiss full of aggression.

His body was fairly vibrating with it, but his lips were gentle and coaxing. She remained stiff against him for as long as she could, but he was offering comfort when she desperately needed comfort and human connection when she was grieving that lack in her life.

Her mouth softened under his lips.

He rubbed his hands up and down her back, soothing her, gentling her. His tongue tasted her, sharing the ambrosia of his mouth with her, but without overt sexual implications.

It was as if he was using his kiss to appease her emotional pain. Then he pulled her melting body into his and she felt the press of his erection against her. Proof that he wanted her, but she could not give him what he wanted and no amount of tears or pain could change that.

Tears nevertheless seeped out of her eyelids and she turned her face away, pushing against him until he let her go.

"I need to get dressed."

"Yes. And then we will talk."

"Haven't we talked enough?"

"No, but it is best left for the moment." He propelled her away from him, a possessive hand caressing her backside. "Go. Take your shower."

Damian wanted to curse in six languages.

He had blackmailed her into marriage. Perhaps he had not known at the time what his money was going for, but the results were the same. She had been forced and his money had been the weapon.

A less hardened man might let her go but he had no intention of taking that route. He wanted her, more than he had ever wanted another woman. He would have her. Somehow. Some way. Damian Marquez did not give up and he had learned how to get the things he wanted in life.

More to the point, Lia was now his wife and that made her his responsibility. She needed someone to rely on, someone on her side, helping her to fight her battles and those of Kaylee.

He had every intention of being that someone.

He would take care of her.

He let out a low curse as he thought of the first husband who had done such a poor job of that very thing.

What kind of man divorced a woman he supposedly loved because she could not give him sex? Not a man...Tobias Kennedy had been an eighteen-year-old boy when he married Lia and not much older when he asked for the divorce. A teenager wouldn't know how to handle the kind of difficulty they'd faced in the marriage bed.

Infierno, the boy had probably thought it was his fault and been too devastated to say so. He had finally given up on trying to make it better and ripped Lia's sexual identity to shreds in the process.

However, Damian was not an inexperienced child with sexual stars in his eyes. He did not believe there was nothing that could be done. There had to be treatment for, what had she called it? *Vaginismus.*

Maybe there was no treatment. He would find out, but even if he could not penetrate her, there were other ways of making love. Ways his body ached to try. He had spent four weeks in a constant state of sexual anticipation and no other woman could relieve his need.

He did not let that bother him. She was his wife. It was only right he wanted her alone. It certainly didn't mean he had feelings for her that could make him vulnerable.

Perhaps their lovemaking could not result in the children he craved, but the potential for pleasure between the two of them was limitless. Did she not realize that?

He suspected she did not. After the experience in the limo the day before, he could conclude only that she knew less about her own sexuality than most teenagers. And this should not surprise him. He knew Maria-Amelia and Benedicto very well. They would not have spoken openly about sexual matters to Lia.

She would have expected Tobias Kennedy to know something, but clearly the young man had not and Lia's perception of herself as a woman had been damaged in the process. Was it really such a surprise that in the three years since the man's death she had ignored the passionate side of her nature completely?

Which left Damian with one burning question.

How soon could he give her another lesson in the pleasure her body was capable of?

Lia found Damian on the upper terrace that overlooked both his private pool and the bright blue sea beyond. The villa was on the side of one of the many hills that lined the Costa Blanca. Surrounded by trees and rock cliffs, it had more privacy than many of the houses she had seen along the way.

She was grateful for that solitude. After their discussion that morning, it would have been torment to be surrounded by other people.

He stood and pulled a chair out for her. "Feeling better?"

Did one feel better after an emotional holocaust? "I'm in control of myself, if that's what is worrying you." She wasn't about to start shouting at him or crying again.

"You are my wife. I am concerned for your emotional well-being. Is that such a shock?"

She determinedly buttered a slice of toast, refusing to let his words instill hope in a heart that had long ago learned the cost of that emotion. "How long do you want me to remain your wife?"

More than likely, for his pride's sake, he would prefer to wait to reveal their separated status for a year, or so.

He poured her a glass of juice. "I recall making lifelong vows yesterday and you assured me of your plans to honor those vows earlier this morning."

"And then you learned that I cannot be the wife you need."

"Look at me, Lia."

She'd avoided doing so since sitting down. As her gaze clashed with his, she felt the world around her distort with a sense of unreality. He did not look condemning, or angry, or disappointed, or even pitying.

His expression was filled with masculine stubbornness. She ought to know, she'd seen it often enough on her grandfather's face.

"You told me you would keep your promises."

"You can't want me to."

"You are wrong. In fact, I demand it."

"But it's impossible."

He relaxed back in the oversize wrought-iron outdoor chair. "Climbing a mountain seems impossible until taken one step at a time."

She didn't buy the old-wise-man attitude one bit. This man got what he wanted and right now he wanted value for his money. She couldn't give it to him in the heirs he expected to have from her. What else did he think he could get out of marriage to her?

An awful, heart destroying thought formed. "Do you think I'll make an *understanding* wife? That I will turn a blind eye to you getting from another woman what I can't give you?"

"Would you?"

"No."

"Que bueno. I would not ask you to. I would not be flattered by a wife who does not care if he visits another woman's bed. Now, eat your breakfast before we continue this discussion. You did not take enough sustenance yesterday."

"Has anyone ever mentioned your domineering side to you before?"

"I am a self-made multimillionaire. It is no shocking revelation. Now eat."

She harrumphed, but did as he suggested simply because he was right. She hadn't eaten enough yesterday and she was hungry.

When she was done eating, he called for a woman to take the food away. Lia learned the woman's name was Juana and she was the wife to the man who watched over the property while Damian was away. They acted as housekeeper and gardener/maintenance man while he was in residence.

He stood and put his hand out. "Come, we will hike down to the beach."

Exercise sounded good and she was dressed for it in a pair of casual jeans, T-shirt and tennis shoes. "Let me get my jacket." The spring air was chillier than usual for this time of year.

He was waiting for her outside, his own arms bare in short sleeves and his long legs encased in a pair of black jeans. He had a black backpack slung over one shoulder. "Ready to go?"

She nodded and followed him onto the rocky trail to the beach. He put his hand out to steady her in several places and each time it happened, her body shivered with feelings that had nothing to do with the salt-laden wind blowing her hair around her face.

His nearness impacted her more every time they were together. She'd never felt this way, not in her marriage, not since. It was as if her body was a piano and his nearness pressed keys that resulted in a sonata played along every nerve ending she possessed.

When they reached the beach, the sudden stoppage of the wind surprised her and she looked around. They were in an alcove in the rock face of the cliff she hadn't been able to see from the top of the path. A private paradise of white sand, palm trees and beautiful jagged cliffs surrounded them. There was even a small inlet of water that looked deep enough to swim in near the alcove's opening. The break in the rock face afforded a narrow view of the blue sea, but no one on the beach outside would realize she and Damian were there.

He pulled a brightly colored throw blanket from the backpack and laid it out. "Sit down."

She did, ready for a rest after their trek down the trail. It hadn't been all that tiring, but keeping control of rampaging hormones was another story altogether.

Enjoying the warmth the protected spot afforded, she pulled off her jacket and tossed it aside, then stretched her legs out in front of her. She crossed them at the ankles before leaning back on her elbows and turning her face up to the sun. "It's nice here."

"I like it, but I must admit the beauty today is even more eye-catching than usual." There was an odd note in his voice.

She opened her eyes to see why and found his gaze riveted to the way her posture thrust her full breasts into prominence.

She quickly sat up and crossed her arms over her drawn up knees. "Uh, it's very private."

"Yes." He sat beside her, his dark gaze probing. "Does it bother you that I look at you? You are my wife. You should expect it."

"Being blackmailed into marriage isn't exactly a recipe for trust and togetherness. Besides, I'm not such a witch that I want to tease you with my body when I can't follow through."

Damian frowned. "Let us get one thing straight between us, *mi esposa,* before I lose all patience with you."

"What?"

"You married me to provide a way to take care of Kaylee. It was not a matter of blackmail, but necessity."

"I wouldn't have married you otherwise."

"Perhaps."

"You're too arrogant to be believed."

"No, merely aware of how strongly attracted we are to each other. Ignoring the attraction would have been the challenge, not giving into it."

"I wouldn't have given into it. I knew it couldn't go anywhere."

"You gave a very convincing performance to the contrary on the terrace a month ago and then in the car yesterday."

She was floundering like a fish out of water trying to think of a proper set down, when he asked, "Did your first husband accuse you of teasing him?"

"Sometimes." Even talk of her disastrous marriage was a welcome change of topic from her weakness in controlling her response to Damian. "We were young. He wanted things I couldn't give him. It was hard on us both."

"It is as I thought. You were both too young to handle the challenges your body faced."

"I can't make love, Damian. Age isn't going to change that and as mature and worldly as you might be, you'll quickly grow tired of a wife who can't give you what you want."

"Penetration is not the only form of lovemaking that can give pleasure."

Blood rushed into her cheeks. "You're so blunt."

"What use is there in attempting subtlety when bluntness is what is needed?"

"We don't have to discuss things in their nitty-grittiest detail to know a lifetime commitment between the two of us won't work."

"I do not agree. It is the detail that interests me and will dictate what level of intimacy we can enjoy in our marriage."

"I told you…none."

"Are you saying you cannot bear any touch at all?"

She sighed and then huffed out a frustrated, "No."

"Then intimacy of one form or another is possible, but perhaps you are not aware of this."

"I am aware of it. I'm not stupid."

A small smiled curved his lips. "Not stupid, but naïve, I think."

"I'm not."

He shook his head. "Your innocence showed itself startlingly well in the limousine yesterday."

She felt oh yet another blush coming on and grimaced. Her hot cheeks would be taken as proof of his assertions about her naïveté. And what was the point in pretending otherwise? She was more awkward than a virgin raised by nuns when it came to talking about sex.

"Well, I'm not *that* innocent anyway," she muttered.

"Ah, so you are aware of the many ways a body can give and receive pleasure?" he asked, his eyes mocking.

"Uh, yeah…of course. Who isn't?"

Speaking of bodies, his was awfully close and it was wreaking havoc on her nervous system again. Although she'd never been into self-torment, she couldn't make herself move away from his disturbing nearness.

"And still you think we can have *no* intimacy at all?" His tone questioned her veracity, or her sanity, she wasn't sure which and maybe neither was he.

"It didn't work for me and Toby," she blurted out, frustrated by the growing desire she could do nothing about and the fact he was forcing her to reveal her every failure in the femininity stakes. "Neither of us liked it."

They'd both been extremely embarrassed by the whole thing, even when she tried touching him with the lights off. Using her mouth had been even worse. She just couldn't relax. Nothing fit right and it made her gag, which had really irritated Toby. Needless to say, she'd had very little success giving him any kind of sexual release.

Which had been really demoralizing. Not only had she been incapable of opening her body to her husband, she had not been able to give him pleasure in other ways, either.

"You tried what exactly?"

He wanted her to be blunt, so she'd be blunt. "Touching him with my hand and mouth." Saying it intensified the heat in her face until she felt hot enough to fry an egg, but she forced herself to meet his eyes. "You think I can give you something that will make up for my lack, but *I know* that whatever I can do won't be enough."

"You are wrong." She watched the sensual lips that had given her so much pleasure the day before form the words and wished with everything in her that he was right.

But he wasn't. "No, I'm not. I know, Damian."

He shook his head, his expression rueful. "*Querida,* if you stroked *me* with your hand, it would be *enough.*" It was his turn to shudder, but the sensual cast to his features said it had not been in revulsion. "The mere *idea* of your small, pink tongue touching me *anywhere* on my body excites me to the point of pain."

"But, Toby—"

"Was an eighteen-year-old boy who did not know some very basic things about sex or he would have found a way for both of you to be satisfied. I think also that he was not confident enough to allow you to pleasure him. I have no such inhibitions."

She could imagine. The man didn't have any reticence in what he talked about, he was probably totally abandoned when it came to making love. Maybe it *could* be better with him, but it couldn't be complete and that still posed a problem.

"Toby wasn't the one with a defective body. I was… am. You want children. It was part of our bargain. I can't give them to you."

"That is a matter we will leave for a later date. Let us deal with one issue at a time."

"It's the same issue."

"No, it is not."

She wanted to scream at his deliberate obtuseness.

His eyes told her he knew how frustrated she was, but he wasn't backing down. "Neither you nor Tobias Kennedy had enough experience or maturity to make sex work between you. That will not be a problem between us."

"My body doesn't work! There's no way around that, no matter how *experienced* you are."

"It is not merely a matter of experience. It is also a matter of desire. I want you, Lia, any way I can get you."

"That's what Toby said too, but it wasn't true…not in the long run." Why was he making this so hard for her? Pushing at her until she felt like she would break. Making her think maybe this time things could be different. Hope was an insidious emotion and she'd had her share of it shattered.

It was killing her that he kept trying to make her deficiency sound like it was less of a problem than she knew it to be.

He leaned over her and cupped her nape. His thumb pressed against her chin, gently preventing her from opening her mouth when she tried to say something else. "Your vaginal walls spasm and that prevents intercourse. That does not mean your sexuality is dead or that your entire body does not work."

She jerked her head back so she could talk, even in the midst of her misery wishing she could stay connected to his touch. "You don't understand—"

"Lia, *mi mujer,* you are the one who does not understand." He tilted her chin up until her lips were a breath away from his. "There are infinite ways to make love."

He kissed her, a soft, slow melding of their mouths that sent tremors of awareness skating along unused nerve endings.

"It sounds to me—" another soft, slow kiss "—like you did not try—" a gentle nibble of her lips "—any of them—" he kissed her again, a longer, more evocative kiss "—with much effect."

By the time he lifted his head, she was trembling and could only stare at him, dazed.

"There is a lot you do not know, *mi querida inocente.*"

Remembering her very first orgasm, at his hand, her bemused brain conceded that maybe he was right and the tiniest flicker of hope began to smolder inside her. She'd never experienced anything like it. Perhaps the magician who could make her body do that could find a pleasure in her body she had not believed could be found there.

Still, she had to ask, "What if I don't please you?"

He ran his thumb over her kiss swollen lips. "It is not possible. But let us say for expedient's sake and so you will quit arguing with me—if there is a problem, I will fix it."

"Toby thought he could fix it, too…"

"Tobias Kennedy was the husband of your girlhood,

I am the husband of your womanhood. I can handle it."
Arrogant confidence stared her down and she found
herself believing.

CHAPTER SIX

"ARE you willing to try, Lia?"

"I don't really have a choice, do I? I gave my promise and if I can keep it, I will."

He didn't appear bothered by her bitter words. In fact, he smiled. "You will learn you do not have to hide behind this front of false anger."

He thought her anger was false? God help her if that was true because without it, she would be defenseless.

Before she could answer the ridiculous accusation, he kissed her again, this time letting his lips linger, coaxing hers to response. He cherished her mouth until her tension drained away and she was clinging to him, emotion swamping her in terrifying, but beautiful waves.

He withdrew his lips, his breathing irregular. "I'm shaking with the need to touch you and be touched by you." His big body trembled, giving credence to his words, no matter how hard she found them to believe. "Do not deny me."

She didn't intend to, but old fears rose to haunt her. "What if you want intercourse…after the touching? Toby always did."

The passion gave way to a sulfuric narrow-eyed gaze that went through her like shards of breaking glass. "*Infierno*, I am not a teenager with rampaging hormones. I am a thirty-year-old man who understands the limits you have laid before me. I will not pressure for what you cannot give."

"You've been pressuring me for the past half an hour."

"For what I know you can give and will be glad for doing so. Trust me to know what is best."

His angry demand had the peculiar effect of calming her fears. A man like Damian would not insist she trust him if he did not believe with absolute certainty he could deliver. His pride would not allow him to do anything else.

He took a visible rein on that Spanish temper that had blown up so unexpectedly. "If I say we can make love in a way that will leave us both satisfied, you need to believe me."

The promise in his voice and dark brown gaze went deep inside her, touching a place she'd kept locked tight for years. It left her with no alternative but to ride the wave of desire threatening to drown her.

She took a deep breath and plunged. "You'll have to show me what to do. I don't know how to please you."

Damian shook his head, finding it hard to believe she was so worried about that. Couldn't she see the effect she had on him? He had not been lying when he told her one touch would be enough. If she put her hand on him right now, he would explode.

"This is not about pleasing me," he said, wishing he could bury the words so deep in her mind, she would never again doubt them. "What we do together is about finding pleasure in one another. I guarantee you, we will do so."

Damian watched as one expression after another flitted across her face in response to his words. There was still some uncertainty and as much as he wanted to simply start touching her, she had to be sure this was what she wanted.

"Okay," she said softly.

"Are you certain?" He would have her, but not as the result of rape or coercion. She would come to him willingly, or not at all.

Her golden eyes misty, she nodded. "I trust you, Damian."

Something inside him contracted at that assurance. "I will not allow you to regret placing your trust in me." He cupped her cheek, the skin soft like silk. "You are so beautiful."

"Oh, Damian…"

He had to taste her lips. Really taste them, not just kiss them. He closed the slight distance between their mouths. She parted her lips on a soft sigh and he licked them, tracing the pretty pink contours before slipping his tongue inside her mouth and savoring the sweetness waiting for him there.

Her response was shy at first, but he gently teased her until her sexy little tongue followed his back into his mouth. He sucked on it and she moaned.

He concentrated on kissing her into a state where she would allow him to do whatever he pleased. It would require the lowering of her inhibitions completely for this time of intimacy to succeed in giving them both what they needed.

He pushed her backward and she let him lower her to the blanket, opening her body to him on the first level of sensual intimacy. When she began to move on the blanket, he knew it was time to take the touching to the next level.

He slid his hand down her rib cage and then back up again, this time under the hem of her short T-shirt. Once again, her bra had a front catch and he disposed of it easily without removing his lips from hers. He peeled back the silk and cupped the petal softness of her breast, brushing one thumb over her already straining nipple.

She whimpered against his lips and he knew she was remembering yesterday, like he was, when she'd come so close to climaxing from him merely touching her breasts.

She was so responsive, more than any woman he had ever known. How could she have this condition that prevented her from experiencing the full range of her sensuality?

He squeezed her generous breast, unexpected shivers going through him at the feel of her hard peak against his palm. It was tame loveplay, but it impacted him as he had never been impacted by a woman, no matter how experienced in the art of love.

Small, feminine fingers began exploring him, touching and testing him until he thought he would go mad with it. His own hand moved down to cup her through her jeans. Even the thick denim could not hide the level of her arousal and knowing she was excited heightened his own desires to a fever pitch.

Then he felt a touch as light as butterfly wings against the fly of his jeans and he jerked his mouth from hers, uttering a low growl from deep in his chest.

Her hand stilled, but her eyes glowed dark amber. "Do you like that?"

"Yes," he hissed as she grew bolder, cupping him much the same way he held her.

Her smile about took his breath away. "I want to touch you all over."

"There is nothing I would like more, but first will you grant me a favor?"

"What?" she asked, her breath hitching as his fingers pressed against the seam of her jeans.

"A woman has an infinite capacity for sensual enjoyment, but a man does not recover so quickly once he has spent his pleasure."

She blushed, something she did quite frequently when they discussed sexual matters and he kissed her to show his approval of her sweet innocence. He got sidetracked by her lips and it was several seconds before he again lifted his head.

"I want to watch you come apart, but if you continue to touch me, it will be me who loses control first."

"Why do you want to watch me?" she asked with genuine confusion and it was all he could do not to groan out loud.

"I cannot forget the way you shimmered like starlight in my arms yesterday. I want to see it again."

She still looked perplexed.

"It is a man thing," he said, in lieu of explaining why or how much sexual pleasure it gave him to watch her climax.

An impossible task.

"Okay." Her hand fell away from him and he bit back a groan of protest even while he shuddered with relief.

He kissed her and whispered against her lips, "Thank you."

She didn't say anything, her mouth opening on a silent scream as he kneaded her resilient flesh before pinching her swollen peak between his thumb and forefinger.

She arched off the blanket into his touch. "Damian, that feels *so good*."

"Yes, it does." He caressed her again, his fingers deriving incredible pleasure from touching her gorgeous body. "You have the softest skin."

"Oh…"

Changing the pressure of his fingers, he watched carefully for signs of what she liked, but if her panting little moans were any indication, she liked it all. He moved his hand to the other breast and did the same thing and she started to rock against him, driving him crazy.

He wanted to touch her between her legs without the barrier of denim, but he knew he had to take things slow. He wanted her so mindless with pleasure when he caressed her down there that she accepted the touch without worrying he was going to try to penetrate her.

But he could touch the rest of her and he did, lightly tracing each of her ribs and running his fingertips along her collarbone and down between her breasts.

Her fingers were digging into his shoulders and she was kissing his neck, his chest, inhaling against the skin of his throat.

He drew circle after circle on each soft mound of her breasts, this time purposefully keeping his fingers away from her distended nipples. He wanted to see them. Nibbling on her earlobe, he started pulling her top off.

She grabbed the hem and held it down. "What are you doing?"

The nervous shake in her voice turned him on. It probably shouldn't, but it was like taking a virgin to bed for the first time and he liked it.

She hadn't been this nervous the day before, but that was probably because she'd had no time to think about what was happening between them. Passion had flared out of nowhere and he had been intent on burning past every barrier.

He traced her stiff fingers. "I want to see you."

"I'm too big."

"You are perfect."

When she didn't reply, he said, "You promised to trust me."

Her eyes widened and her lips parted, but then she nodded. Taking a deep breath that pressed her curves against his chest, she dropped her hands. She let him remove both her bra and top, leaving her upper torso completely bare to his hot gaze. Her nipples were deep red and turgid against the pale, creamy smoothness of her breasts.

"You are a work of art, Lia."

She choked on a sound and averted her face, while he devoured the sight of her large, but perfectly proportioned, tip-tilted breasts with his eyes. Then she did something unexpected. She looked at him, her face flushed with excitement, and leaned up on her elbows. Then she arched her back, displaying herself for his benefit.

"Lia…" He couldn't get enough air into his lungs to say more.

"I like you looking at me," she said shyly.

"I like to look…" He reached out with one hand and rolled his fingertip over and around the tip of each breast. "And I like to touch."

"So good…" Her head fell back in abandon and he lowered his so he could take one of the hard peaks in his mouth.

He sucked and she cried out, collapsing against the blanket again. He followed her, keeping his mouth on the succulent little berry.

He looked up, greedy for further evidence of her response and saw that she was biting the back of her hand. Muffled sounds came from her mouth that caused his erection to grow to painful magnitude in his jeans. He cupped her other breast and began to tug at its nipple as well.

Her head thrashed from side to side on the blanket, her hand now covering his own. "It's incredible. Damian… Just like yesterday…"

Unlike yesterday, today he would have her completely naked when he brought her to completion. He began stripping her out of her jeans. This time, she didn't make a peep of protest, not until he had to stop touching her to get rid of his own shirt. And then it was to complain about him moving away from her.

He left his jeans on, thinking she didn't need to see the extent of his arousal just yet.

He reached down and touched between her legs, this time without barriers. His finger slid easily between the slick folds of her feminine flesh, but he was careful not to stray past her clitoris.

Lia couldn't believe he was touching her so intimately and she was not freaking out. Maybe it was because she was too busy trying not to faint from pleasure. The way he was touching her, sent wave after wave of it through her body.

Without warning, he picked her up and rolled on his back at the same time. She ended up on top of him, her legs sprawled to the side. A large bulge pressed against the exposed flesh of her core and she couldn't help pushing herself more firmly against him.

He groaned.

She stilled. "Did I do something wrong?"

"No, *querida*. Only do it again."

She did.

"Sí. Perfecto."

They weren't exactly touching, not with his jeans between them, but the friction it created felt fantastic. It still wasn't enough, though, and she didn't know what to do to make it better.

"Damian, I…" Her voice faded into a high-pitched moan as he did something extraordinary to her nipple.

"What?" he asked against her ear, the warmth of his breath making her whole body quiver.

"I want more, but I don't know what to do."

"I do." Pressing against her derriere with one strong hand, he surged upward in a caress that sent shards of pleasure splintering through her.

But it was more intimate than she'd been with a man in over three years and she went tense, even though she didn't want to.

He rubbed her back in a soothing motion. "Don't get worried. I am still dressed. I will not hurt you. Trust me."

That word again. Trust. If she withheld it, she would only make it harder for both of them. Nodding in acknowledgement to his demand and her inner musings, she forced herself to relax.

"Sit up."

She didn't think she could, but he gently pushed her torso upward until she was straddling him like a horseback rider.

He spread his big hand against her spine. "Lean back."

She obeyed, shocked when the position made her rub against him in an incredibly exciting way. He rocked his hips and she gasped. Loud.

"Don't stop!" *It felt so good.*

"I could not. I have wanted you too long and now I will have you. I will not stop until we are both so exhausted from pleasure, sleeping will seem like it takes too much energy."

Warmth gushed between her legs at that diabolical promise.

He pulled her down a little so he could suckle her again, but this time they were connected intimately, if not joined and she convulsed without warning.

She screamed as her body bowed and her insides clenched in one almost vicious spasm after another. The explosion of pleasure going on inside her was so cataclysmic that their surroundings went fuzzy around the edges and then blackness claimed her.

When she came to, she was lying on the blanket with Damian leaning over her.

Her body was so languorous from pleasure, it was as if reality had completely receded and what she and Damian were doing was all that existed in the world.

"I want to see you," he said, his voice strained from un-spent passion. "All of you. And then I want to taste you."

"But—"

"Do you trust me, *mi esposa?*"

He kept calling her his wife and she was beginning to believe the title could be real. "Yes."

"Then, relax."

Lia lay quiescent as Damian moved into a kneeling position between her legs, pushing her thighs apart and her knees up. She had never been this open to a man, but Damian wanted to see her and after all the pleasure he had given her, she could not deny him.

Watching him look at her was unbearably arousing. His expression was so intent, so filled with desire.

But as his gaze grew hotter, she felt a familiar tight-ening inside her. Not this time. It wasn't fair. He'd given her so much pleasure, but her body would not cooper-ate. She knew that within seconds, even a cotton swab would not be able to penetrate her shrinking opening.

Tears burned her eyes.

He came down over her so his face was right above hers. "What is the matter, Lia?"

She averted her face. "It's happening."

"You mean the muscle contractions? Your body is closing?"

"Yes." She tried to blink the tears away, but one slipped down her temple.

He brushed it away. "Does it hurt?"

"No." At least not physically. The sense she was not a complete woman devastated her emotions.

"Are you certain? You are not merely saying this to appease me?"

"Yes. It will only hurt if you try to go inside."

His smile was tinged with relief. "Then do not worry about it. We knew it was going to happen, *es verdad?*"

"Yes, but…"

He put his finger over her lips. "Shh…as long as you are not hurting, I do not want you even thinking about it, *comprendes?*"

He could not be for real. "But…"

"You promised me, Lia, your trust."

"I do trust you and I'll try not to think about it."

His eyes showered approval down on her, warming her insides as effectively as his touching did. Then he leaned down and kissed her until her body was involuntarily straining up toward his, seeking the contact of skin to skin.

She wrapped her arms around him, reveling in the feel of his hot strength beneath her fingers.

She moaned when he broke the kiss, but he moved down her body again, kissing and licking her *everywhere*. The things he did to her belly button made her cry out in both fear and pleasure. It was too much.

She tried to tell him, but he shook his head, his eyes filled with knowing. "I have barely begun."

Then he was kneeling between her legs. "I'm going to touch you, but that is all. I will not attempt penetration even with my fingertip, all right?"

She nodded, incapable of speech. It took more courage than he could ever know to let him touch her there, to believe he wouldn't hurt her, even accidentally. But she did believe him.

He traced her with his fingertip, but just as he promised, he made no attempt to press his finger into her tightly closed passage. "Were you aware that your outer tissue has more nerve endings and is therefore more sensitive than your inner tissue?"

"No." She could barely get the one word out past the tightness in her throat.

He continued touching her, building up a nameless need inside her until she was gyrating against his fingers.

She'd never known such wantonness, or such need. "Damian!"

He smiled, all sexy, primordial male. "What do you want? This?" And he brushed her sweet spot.

Just once, then again...and again.

The pleasure was more intense than anything she'd ever known. No one had touched her like he was touching her.

He knew exactly how much pressure to exert, how long to linger, what direction to move his fingers, what type of movement to use and when. It was mind-boggling, incredible, physically devastating.

He amazed her.

"Please..." He couldn't consummate, but he had to do something and she trusted him to do it.

He cupped her most secret place, like he was protecting her with his hand and what that did to her heart, she could not even bear to contemplate. Then he circled her clitoris with his thumb. Once. Twice. Three times and the tension coiling tight in her body threatened to spring.

"I must taste you."

That was all the warning she got before his head delved between her legs and his tongue took the place of his thumb.

She called his name, her voice thready with need and a fear she was desperately trying not to feel.

But his tongue did not trespass flesh too tight to accommodate it. He laved her most secret place tenderly and her legs closed of their own accord, trapping his head between them. He didn't seem to mind as he ministered to every millimeter of the soft, swollen flesh between her legs.

He even gently licked the seam of her stubbornly closed opening, but he didn't attempt to push his tongue inside. She shuddered with excitement. He'd been right. She was very sensitive there.

And he did exactly what he said he'd wanted to do.

He tasted her.

She arched her pelvis upward, pressing herself to his mouth. "Damian, I can't stand it! *It's too much*. You've got to do something…"

He slid his hands between her legs, pushing her thighs apart just as if she wasn't trying to push them together as hard as she could. His strength would have astonished her if she wasn't already so dazzled by his prowess at loving. Exerting pressure until her muscles were stretched just this side of pain, he relentlessly opened her body completely to his questing mouth.

He kissed her swollen, slick flesh with his tongue until she was straining against the hold of his hands on her thighs and her fingers were buried in his hair, pulling and pushing from one second to another. Then he took her highly sensitized, swollen nub between his teeth and sucked.

She shattered into a million bitty pieces, her scream echoing around them. Bucking against the tongue that would not still, mini tremors shook her body, keeping every muscle in her body tense. She began to sob. The pleasure was just too much.

"Damian, please!"

He lifted his mouth and she collapsed back onto the blanket covered sand. Her body trembled from head to foot.

He kissed the inside of both of her thighs and then her now damp curls with his lips. "*Querida,* you are amazing."

She had to touch him and brushed his temple with her fingers. "You're the incredible one. That was… There are no words for what you just gave me."

He turned his head and kissed the center of her palm. "I am glad."

Her body all of a sudden bowed again, her muscles going into momentary rigor before she fell back again. "Damian, what's happening to me?"

"Do not worry. You flew very high and your body needs to come down." Then he pressed another kiss to her thighs.

Moving up her body, gentling the volcanic vibrations of her body with his mouth, he let her calm down until her breathing was almost back to normal. She tried to sit up, but he pressed her back down. It didn't take much. Her muscles were still rubbery from exertion.

But she needed to touch him. "I want…"

He kissed the words from her mouth.

After several long moments of pure pleasure with his mouth molding hers, he lifted his head. "I want to lie on top of you and make love to your body, but I need you to trust me not to attempt intercourse."

By giving her pleasure with no thought to his own,

not once, but twice, he'd more than proven that she could trust him with her femininity and her limitations. "I trust you, Damian."

His jaw locked and he kissed her, hard.

Then he stood up and stripped out of his jeans, revealing his straining desire to her hungry and curious gaze. He let her look for several seconds before coming down on top of her. He aligned their flesh as it had been before when she was straddling him, but this time the barrier of his jeans was not there. She forced herself to remain relaxed as he moved against her.

And soon, it became easier as he made no move to attempt penetration and the pleasure and tension grew inside her once again. She locked her hands behind his neck and twisted her legs around his, opening herself to him as completely as it was possible for *her* to do. She pushed her pelvis upward to increase the friction, moving with Damian in an age-old rhythm that they made uniquely theirs.

Damian felt himself losing control. Her trusting acquiescence sent him straight into oblivion and he pistoned against her, not even caring that he could not be inside her.

He felt his body going rigid, the pressure building, and then he was exploding with nuclear proportions. Incredibly she was crying out with him, straining her body toward his. They both collapsed at the same time.

"That was miraculous," she whispered against his neck and then kissed him.

He moved his mouth over hers, savoring the sweet, softness of her lips for as long as he dared, but when he felt the renewal of arousal, he stopped. "I had better move before I crush you."

"But this feels good."

It did. Too good, but she was not up to another round of lovemaking. He got up, pulling her with him and then carried her down to the surf where he insisted on washing her. Even after their intimate touching, it embarrassed her and she blushed.

"Your innocence fascinates me, but this blush..." He ran his finger from her cheek down her throat and over her flushed breasts. "It is *very* interesting."

"Stop that," she said breathlessly, but she was smiling and he grinned back.

He felt lighthearted, full of hope. It was not a feeling he trusted, but he would enjoy it while it lasted. "I've never seen a woman blush with her whole body before," he teased.

She grimaced and averted her face. "You've probably never gone to bed with a twenty-four-year-old woman who has less sexual experience than most seniors in high school, either."

Her vulnerability was every bit as charming as her innocence. "I like knowing that for all intents and purposes, you were practically a virgin."

Her mouth opened, but nothing came out and then she swung around and faced him, her expression filled with shocked disbelief. *"I wasn't a virgin."*

"You had never found the ultimate pleasure with a man before yesterday. That is a type of virginity. I am unashamedly glad to have had the privilege of initiating you."

"Initiating me? You're a real Neanderthal in some ways, you know that?"

They were standing waist deep in water and he liked

how he could see the shadow of her feminine secrets below the crystal clear water. *"Sí."*

"You're not the least embarrassed to be so primitive?"

"Why should I be? Tobias Kennedy was probably more New Man than I will ever want to be, but he was not the one to teach you the secrets of your body."

He watched her temper flare with satisfaction. She was not nervous around him in her nakedness and he liked that.

"You are so arrogant." The words barely left her mouth before she splashed him right in the face.

The splashing fight that ensued left her panting and laughing and him feeling as if he'd touched something incredibly precious inside himself that he had forgotten was there.

CHAPTER SEVEN

LIA lounged on the blanket, dressed again, hair a wet tousle around her face. Damian had put his jeans back on, but left his bronze chest bare. They'd eaten the picnic he'd had in the backpack he brought down to the beach, but a companionable silence had fallen since they finished eating.

Which was a little surprising. Not only had he taken all her preconceived notions about her complete lack of sexuality and shredded them, but he threatened to do more. His demand she try to make love completely and give him the children her initial promise implied set her up for more heartbreak and failure down the road.

And yet right now, she was…happy. She had satisfied her husband and that felt very, very good, she realized.

"Grandfather said your family is from this area," she said, wanting to know more about him and wishing she didn't.

He was a dangerous threat to her emotional well-being.

His eyes turned cold and remote, shocking her with

the speed with which his mood could change. "They are."

"None of them were at the wedding."

"I told you, they do not acknowledge me."

Her grandfather had said the same thing, but she hadn't realized how total was her husband's status as persona non grata with his relatives. "None of them?"

"Not one. It is why I left Spain in the first place, but I did well going to New York to make my fortune."

"Was it hard leaving everything you knew behind?"

"No. After the courts denied my claim to my father's title, I wanted to get away from Spain and everything the country of my birth represented."

"How old were you when your father died?"

"Sixteen."

"I was fifteen when my daddy died. It was awful. I missed him so much."

"I cannot say the same. I'd never known Don Escoto, but I grew up knowing who he was, what I came from, what I should have been."

"Why did you sue for the title?"

"It was mine by right." It was hard to believe this remote stranger was the same man who had touched her so intimately earlier.

"But you are…."

"Illegitimate. *Sí.* I am this, however I was also the oldest child of my father."

"And titles are transferred by right of progenitor."

"Don Escoto's family denied his paternity to me. It was ridiculous. Everyone, including the judge who tried my case knew I was his son, but without proof, I had no case."

"Why didn't you have the DNA tests done, or something?"

"I was sixteen. I had no resources. Mama had no resources. The Escoto family had the money to drag the case out for years. I could not stand the thought of my mother losing everything to pursue what should have been mine without a fight. For years, I dreamed of accumulating enough wealth to challenge my younger sister for the title."

"Why didn't you?" He'd certainly gotten rich enough.

"My mother died and I realized that revenge would not give me what I wanted."

Such a stark statement, but so powerful.

"What *do* you want?"

"A sense of family."

"I can't give you a family, either."

"You already have. You and Kaylee belong to me now."

But she knew a stepdaughter and wife who was incapable of truly making love would not be enough for a man like Damian. She said nothing however, already regretting spoiling the rapport that had existed between them since their intimacy.

Instead she changed the subject. "Speaking of Kaylee... I didn't expect to spend the entire two weeks here and I'm not comfortable being apart from her right now."

Some of the tension drained out of him. "I anticipated this and had my car sent for her after our initial discussion this morning. She is no doubt already at the villa being acquainted with Juana and Carlos."

* * *

Which turned out to be exactly the case when Lia and Damian hiked back up to the house. They found Kaylee in the kitchen, helping Juana roll pastry for dinner.

She grinned up at her mother, her blue eyes dancing, her face flushed with enjoyment. "Mama, Señora Juana is letting me help her, see?" She pointed to her flour covered self and the misshapen pastry dough on the smooth wood tabletop in front of her.

Lia grinned, trying not to laugh. Kaylee was just so darn cute in Juana's apron, which had to be wrapped around twice to fit her. "I see. What are you two making?"

"*Empeñadas,* Mama. We get to put cherries in them."

Since her daughter's favorite food in the entire world was cherries in any shape or form, Juana couldn't have picked anything better to break the ice with the little girl.

"Sounds yummy."

"*Sí.*" Damian came up beside her and put his hand on her waist in a casual gesture of possessiveness.

Kaylee's smile stretched across her whole face. "You are my papa now, aren't you, Señor Damian?"

"*Sí.* You can call me Papa instead of Señor, do you not agree?"

"*Sí.*" Kaylee drew the word out in a long drawl and then hurled herself at Damian, who caught her in a bear hug, flour covered apron and all.

Lia wouldn't be the only one devastated when Damian decided to walk away. She wished she could change that, but she couldn't. She had bought Kaylee's life with a set of circumstances guaranteed to bring them both emotional pain, but Kaylee would survive that. She would not survive the hole in her heart. Their course had been set and it had to be run, no matter what the outcome.

Damian insisted on bringing in a leading heart surgeon to consult on Kaylee's case. The doctor was affiliated with a well-known institute in Seattle where researchers were on the forefront of treatment for heart disease.

Damian arranged for Kaylee and Lia to accompany him on his private jet to Seattle six days after the wedding.

Kaylee, who loved air travel anyway, adored the opportunity to go on a private plane and was ecstatic when the pilot allowed her up front to watch him fly the plane.

Damian sat down beside Lia, heaving a sigh. "Where does one tiny body come up with so much energy?"

"I don't know. I think it shows God's sense of humor. He matches exhausted parents with inexhaustible children."

Damian turned toward her, all sensual predatory male. "You did not feel exhaustible to me last night."

Remembering all they had done in the dark warmth of the night, she blushed. "You're the one who doesn't seem to have an off button."

He laughed, a low, tigerish chuckle and bent close to her, breathing in her scent, surrounding her with his. "And would you be happy if I did, *mi esposa?*"

"No, Damian. You are an amazing man, in and out of the bedroom." The words slipped out unbidden, but she would not take them back if she could.

He had shown himself to be two men. One a ruthless negotiator who demanded she keep her side of an unholy bargain. The other a charming companion who had stolen her daughter's heart and was making a major dent in her own. Perhaps Damian was as her grandfather had said, only ruthless when he needed to be.

She was doing what he wanted and he rewarded her and Kaylee with consideration and kindness. She liked it.

"*Sí*…the spa bath was fun, was it not?"

She choked on a laugh. "I didn't mean tha—"

He cut her off with his lips and then she lost all will to attempt to communicate on any level but this one.

Damian checked his new family into a corporate apartment style hotel with two bedrooms and an office. Lia would appreciate the privacy and homelike atmosphere, but it also had the benefit of daily maid service should he choose to pay for it. He, of course, paid.

He wanted everything as easy for Lia as possible and told her so when she questioned the maid service scheduled for the next morning after they had settled Kaylee in to sleep. His new daughter had wanted him to read her bedtime story and he had put off an international business call to do it. He'd made the call and now wanted to see his wife.

He went in search of her and found her in the kitchen. She was wearing a caramel colored satin robe that reached her toes. The soft lighting from the stove's overhead light cast the valleys and curves of her luscious body in shadow.

Desire, hot and urgent, swept through him with tidal wave force. That body belonged to him just as the woman belonged to him. Did she realize it yet? Did she understand that whatever the deal had been, now she was his?

She looked up from a pot she was stirring on the stove, her amber eyes warm with welcome. "I made some hot cocoa, do you want some?"

"Hot cocoa?"

She grinned and nodded. "You know that stuff you make with cocoa powder, cream, sugar and some other stuff that if I told you, I'd be in danger of losing my reputation as the Queen of Cocoa Making."

"Heaven forbid such a thing would happen."

She was so different from the other women he had had in his life. She did not act like a woman raised with privilege, the granddaughter of a wealthy *conde*.

"Kaylee would be devastated. I've promised to pass the recipe down to her on her sixteenth birthday."

He moved so he could look over her shoulder and take a whiff of the aroma coming from the pot. The decadent richness of the chocolate competed with the soft, feminine scent he knew to be hers and hers alone.

He nuzzled her neck. "It smells good."

"It, or me?" she asked with a catch in her voice that never failed to turn him on.

"Both, *querida,* both." He kissed her neck and she shivered. "I smell sensual, sweet woman, chocolate and cinnamon."

She tilted her head back, put her finger to her lips and widened her eyes in exaggerated concern. "Shhh… That's one of the secret ingredients."

"Is it?"

"Well, lots of people use cinnamon, but they use the

powder, not dried chips." She went back to stirring, letting her head rest back against his chest.

No longer did she respond to his nearness like a wary doe to the hunter and it pleased him.

She turned off the burner with a flick of her wrist. "Now you know one of my secrets."

"One day, I will know all your secrets, *querida,* then watch out."

"You already know the ones I've hidden from everyone else in the world." She sounded resigned to that reality rather than pleased by it.

She was still bothered by her sexual limitations and he did not know how to help her accept them. It had to be obvious he enjoyed their sensual intimacy as much, or more, than she did, but still she saw herself as defective.

She was not defective, but he was not convinced her condition was untreatable. Both she and her first husband had been naïve and embarrassed by the challenges her body presented; they would not have felt comfortable pursuing a medical remedy.

He hoped that reticence on her part was diminished because his initial research indicated he was right to believe there were treatments available. He had plans to consult with a specialist in sexual dysfunction while they were in Seattle as well as the cardiologist for Kaylee.

"Do you mind me knowing you so intimately?" he asked.

She didn't answer for a long time and when she did, her voice was thoughtful. "No. You took my secret and changed it. I thought I could not share any sort of sexual pleasure with you and you've taught me differently." She paused as if preparing herself to say something difficult. "I know I haven't said it, but thank you."

Her gratitude made him uncomfortable and he moved away. "You have no need to thank me. The passion is shared between us and giving you pleasure is my privilege."

She busied herself pouring the hot cocoa, but the slight downturn of her mouth indicated his withdrawal had bothered her.

He found himself wanting to explain, when explanations of any kind were usually an anathema to him. "I was almost married twice for the things I could give."

Her head lifted and serious amber eyes probed straight into his soul. "What happened?"

"I was twenty-two when I made my first million. I underwrote a start-up venture with capital I had amassed from other sources, convincing men like your grandfather to invest in the business. It took off and I'm still getting residual income on the investment, but success carried a price. Most of the people around me wanted something. I made the mistake of believing Crystal was different. Your grandfather revealed her duplicity to me, much to the devastation of my pride."

"Did you love her?"

"I thought so at the time, but I realized later I loved the woman she had pretended to be…the one I wanted her to be, not the woman she was. It was a sobering experience, but still I did not learn my lesson."

"You got suckered a second time?" Lia asked, sounding shocked.

And well she might be. He wasn't proud of the fact

he had been so stupid, not once, but twice in his life. "*Sí*. This time by a woman in the Spanish nobility."

"You were susceptible because you were still looking for acceptance."

"You are perceptive."

"I suppose Grandfather revealed this woman's duplicity to you as well."

"No, but he told me he suspected she wanted my money and not me. I had her background investigated and discovered her father faced bankruptcy. Had she been honest about her circumstances, I would not have cared. But that's not why I left her. She had something I wanted and I would have married her to get it."

"An entrée into the society your father's ignoring you denied you."

"As I said, you are perceptive, but she was also the oldest child and would inherit the title, a title that would pass on to my children."

"You know, you've spent years living in the States, I'm surprised you're still so impacted by what is essentially an empty name you get to sign on legal documents."

He shrugged and leaned against the counter beside where she stood. "I am still very much a Spaniard at heart."

In other words, it was a matter of his pride. "I guess you've got pretty much the same deal with me."

"*Sí*, but this time Benedicto sought approval of a special dispensation to assign one of his lesser titles to me during my lifetime. The king granted the dispensation the day before our wedding."

"So, what…you are now *Don* Marquez?"

"*Sí.*"

"And that makes you happy?"

He shrugged. Happy? "I am satisfied with it."

She nodded. "I see."

"The title of Papa given me by Kaylee gives me far more satisfaction," he said, admitting a surprising truth.

She scooped a fluffy white dollop of whipped cream onto each of the mugs of cocoa and then grated some chocolate on top. "You were born to be a father, Damian."

The flat tone of her voice bothered him. "Are you again worried about not being able to give me more children?"

"You can't pretend it doesn't matter." She handed him one of the warm mugs. "It's part of the package you thought you were getting. You want your child to have the title and place in Spanish society you were denied."

He couldn't deny her words, but if the worst happened and she could not conceive his child, he would not abandon her because of it. The knowledge did not surprise him. He was, after all a fair man. She was doing her best to keep her side of their bargain and he would keep his.

"So what happened with your second big romance?" she asked in an obvious bid to change the subject.

"Juliana was in love with another man, one she eloped with after I caught them together kissing in the kitchen."

"In the kitchen?"

"He was her father's chef."

"His chef? You've got to be kidding."

"No."

"I bet he didn't make hot cocoa as good as this stuff."

She touched his cup with hers in a universal toasting gesture, her amber gaze filled with an invitation to share the joke.

He tipped the cup to his lips, letting the smooth, rich chocolate slide across his tongue. "You are right. It is delicious."

She wiped her brow with the back of her hand, her expression teasing. "Whew. I was worried I might not impress you with my cocoa making skills."

No woman had ever teased him so much before.

"Do not worry, such skills are only one of the many things about you that impresses me."

She smiled and took a sip, leaving a swath of white cream on her upper lip when she put the cup down.

"You have a cream mustache."

"Do I?" she asked with batting eyelashes, all provocative innocence. "Maybe you'd like to clean me up?"

Although she responded beautifully in their bed, she rarely took the initiative. It did strange things to his heart to realize his feelings were important enough to her to step outside her comfort zone to make him feel better.

He leaned down until his mouth was only a breath from her own. "I believe I would like that very much."

She was everything he had thought she would be and more, but was that because she was coming to care for him? Her generous affection in and out of the bedroom could be the result of so many things…her gratitude over what he was doing for Kaylee, her guilt at tricking him into marriage under false pretenses or a simple physical reaction to the passionate pleasure he gave her.

His thoughts splintered as her tongue came out to mesh with his, licking the sweet cream from her sweeter lips.

Kaylee's appointment with the heart surgeon went extremely well. His kindness and warmth made the little girl comfortable and Lia was grateful. She didn't want her daughter terrified by what she was facing. Lia was scared enough for both of them and doing her best to hide it. It helped her so much that Damian had made time to attend the doctor's appointment with them.

The surgeon confirmed what the doctor in New Mexico had said regarding Kaylee's condition, but the procedure he suggested was not anywhere near as invasive or risky as open heart surgery.

When Lia asked why, the doctor explained that not all hospitals paid for the privilege of using surgical techniques other doctors had patented. This doctor had been performing a new procedure for the last two years with a great deal of success. It took about an hour and had one-sixth the recovery time of open heart surgery. It was only available for certain types of heart disease, but the hole in Kaylee's heart was one of them.

The surgeon had a nurse come in and take Kaylee for a dish of ice cream in the hospital cafeteria.

"We can schedule the procedure as early as next week," he said after the two had left.

"And she will only have to remain in the hospital for a couple of days?"

"Her activity will be limited for a certain time, but she will be quite safe going home."

"Can we fly her back to New York?" Damian asked.

"That should not pose a problem, but I would let her convalesce in Seattle for three or four days before taking any plane trips."

"No problem."

Lia smiled. That was Damian's approach to everything. No problem. He made things happen. She had gotten a lot more out of their marriage deal than money, she'd gotten a man she could rely on. The fact she wanted to worried her a little, but she was so tired of being independent.

He scheduled the surgery and hospital stay while she and Kaylee explored the cardiac center.

"Mama, am I gonna have surgery?"

"Yes, baby, but then you'll be all better."

"And you won't cry anymore when you think I'm sleeping?"

Lia dropped to her knees and took her daughter into her arms, trying hard to stop herself from hugging the breath right out of her, but not sure she succeeded when Kaylee squeaked. "I won't cry anymore. I'm sorry you heard me before, butterfly."

"It's okay, Mama. I love you."

"I love you, too."

They were back at their temporary apartment and Kaylee was watching a cartoon when Damian broached the subject of contacting Lia's grandfather.

"Call him if you like, but I have nothing to say to him." She hadn't forgiven or forgotten that he'd used her daughter's illness to manipulate her into marriage with Damian. She'd needed her grandfather and instead of being there for her, he used the situation to his own advantage. Maybe he hadn't had the money to help, but using that lack to push her in a direction he wanted her to go was unconscionable.

He had said it that day in his study. He hadn't *wanted* to look for alternatives. He had wanted her to marry Damian.

"Benedicto only wants what is best for you."

"Blackmailing me with my daughter's health is not best for me."

"But the results are not so bad, surely?"

She shook her head, knowing she didn't know how to explain to Damian that in this case, the ends, no matter how wonderful, did not justify the means. And she wasn't sure they would all be fantastic, was she? She had been happier in the last few days than she'd been in her whole life, but she was just waiting for the roof to cave in on that happiness.

When it did, Kaylee was going to be hurt, too, and she might have to accept that, but she didn't have to like it.

Every night Damian took her on a sensual journey that left her exhausted and sated with pleasure. However, she could never forget the fact that her condition made it impossible for her to give him the children he craved. It weighed on her mind, tingeing even the most incredible lovemaking with a sense of impermanency.

"Our marriage has been surprisingly good so far," she said, unable to lie or tell the complete truth—that she was just waiting for him to walk. It would offend him, especially if he had convinced himself he was in it for the long haul.

"So you still see yourself as a victim of your grand-father's scheming and my insistence you keep your word?" he asked, his expression unreadable.

His cell phone rang before she could answer, not that she was sure she knew what she would have said.

She was still angry with Grandfather, but that anger did not extend to her husband. Probably because she knew he thought he would stay married to her. He didn't know that years of incomplete sex would eventually take their toll. They had to.

She watched him walk away with a strange feeling in her heart. If she didn't know better, she might think she was falling in love with the impossible man.

He found her later in the living room watching a re-run of *I Love Lucy*. "Are you ready for bed, *mi mujer?*"

She looked up. "I really like being your woman." That at least was one truth she could openly admit.

He lifted her high in his arms and carried her to the bathroom where she found herself taking a very erotic shower. Then he swept her off to bed to make love to her all over again. She was in the throes of frenzied passion when she felt his finger gently press inside her. He slid it in to the first knuckle and exultation like nothing she'd ever known coursed through her.

However, even as the joy flashed into her wounded heart, her flesh betrayed her again, closing around his finger with vise-like intensity.

Tears filled her eyes and her entire body shook with a violent sob. "I can't do it!"

He gently withdrew, oh so careful not to hurt her and

she tried to turn on her side to curl into a fetal ball. She just wanted to give in and stop trying to be strong.

He wouldn't let her. One hand caught her shoulder and the other her hip, holding her in place. "I am not done with you."

"I'm defective, Damian! We both know it. What's the use?"

"I want you, Lia."

"How can you?"

He didn't bother to speak, didn't feed her the platitudes Toby had done right up until he asked for the divorce. Damian was too honest for that, but he was also determined. He started to kiss her again, stoking the fires of her passion with his hands until she forgot her defeat and could only think of the way he made her feel.

Which was incredible.

CHAPTER EIGHT

THE next few days flew by with Damian, Lia and Kaylee seeing the sights of Seattle while they waited for the day for her procedure to arrive. The day before it was scheduled, Damian had business that required him leaving Lia and Kaylee.

"I thought this was our honeymoon," Lia complained, pouting for maybe the first time in her life.

He smiled and kissed her mouth with its protruding lip until she melted against him in a boneless mass of feminine submission. "It is a small thing and I will not be gone very long, *querida*."

She sighed, soaking in the certainty that burned down at her from his dark eyes. He was a multimillionaire business tycoon, and sometimes that business was going to take precedence. "I guess I should be grateful you're here with me at all. I'm sure there's a lot of stuff in New York that could do with your personal attention."

Her grandfather would never have spent so many weeks away from the base of his business operations.

"I would never be so remiss as to leave you to face this ordeal with Kaylee alone, you must know this."

Remiss. A word connected to duty and responsibility. A cold chill swept down her spine and she stepped away. "Yes, of course."

She could not start believing he did any of this out of a newfound affection or caring. He was simply once again keeping up his end of the bargain. He did it so darn well, she almost fooled herself into believing he cared sometimes. Why she wanted to do such a foolish thing, she refused to even contemplate.

"Maybe I'll take Kaylee shopping."

His eyes searched hers. "That sounds like a good idea, and do not hesitate to buy something if you like it."

She'd spent so long on an economy budget that she had a hard time remembering she could now afford to splurge a little. Damian had noticed her tendency not to buy things for herself when they visited The Museum of Natural Science and she had found a hand soldered glass kaleidoscope she liked. She'd put it down after exclaiming over it and he had presented it to her as a gift when they reached the car.

She smiled wryly. "Don't worry. I think I can get the hang of spending money indiscriminately."

He laughed and shook his head. "I doubt it, but I would not mind."

And she knew he told the truth. Damian took his role as her husband very seriously. It was all part of fulfilling his side of the bargain completely.

They hit one of Seattle's bigger malls and did the toy stores first, delighting Kaylee when she found the doll to go with her favorite movie.

They were walking by Victoria's Secret when Lia stopped to stare at a very daring, very sexy basque in the window.

"Mama, that lady's underwear is really pretty," Kaylee said pointing at the mannequin.

Lia agreed. She'd never worn sexy underthings because Toby would have considered them a painful form of teasing. After her marriage ended, she hadn't felt like highlighting her sexuality in any way. Things were different with Damian, even if it was temporary and she was positive he would appreciate the effort. She took Kaylee's hand and led her into the lingerie store.

Damian waited impatiently for Lia and Kaylee to return from their shopping expedition. He'd called her cell phone a half an hour ago and been told they were on their way home. Lia had also said she'd bought a surprise for him. It was ridiculous, but he couldn't wait to see what it was. He could not remember the last time a woman had bought him anything, or anyone else for that matter. Not since his mother's death anyway.

He heard the snick of a lock and the click of a door latch a second before a small blond dynamo came rushing into the room.

Kaylee threw herself against Damian, hugging him and planting a baby-girl kiss right on his cheek. "We had the bestest time shopping. Mama got me a doll and she bought you something too, Papa."

He loved the sound of that name on the small child's lips. "She told me, *niña*. I look forward to seeing it."

"Do you want to see my new doll, too?"

"Of course."

Kaylee dropped to the floor and opened the bag she'd been carrying. She pulled out a doll dressed like a medieval princess with very long blond hair. "Isn't she pretty?"

"*Sí*, but not as lovely as my new daughter or her mama."

Kaylee giggled, her blue eyes twinkling with happiness Damian hoped would never be diminished.

"Flattery will get you your present before dinner instead of after." Lia came into the room and straight to him just as Kaylee had done.

However, instead of a peck on the cheek, she pressed her lips to his in a lingering salute that made him wish their daughter was not so full of energy and they did not have company meeting them for dinner.

When she pulled back, her amber eyes glowed with an unfamiliar mischievous sparkle. "Let me put the bags in the bedroom and I'll dig out your present."

He had a better idea and he tugged her into his lap. "You can 'dig it out' here, I think."

She smiled, her expression filled with a delight he could become addicted to. "All right."

She dropped all the bags but one onto the floor beside him. When he saw a familiar pink and white bag, his body reacted instantly as images of her wearing something from that store flitted through his mind.

"Is my present in there?" he asked, pointing to the bag.

"No, silly, that's stuff for Mommy. You can't wear it," Kaylee said before her mother could get a single word out.

"I wonder." He touched his wife's petal soft, pink-ened cheek. "If it is not for me, then why are you blushing?"

"Don't tease, or I won't give you your other present."

"Ah, so that one is for me."

"You know it is…in a way anyway."

He could no more resist kissing her than he could have prevented himself taking his next breath. She was fast becoming every bit as necessary to his well-being as well.

When he lifted his head, Lia was breathing in an irregular pattern and Kaylee was talking to her doll. "I guess they're gonna do that a lot, but they sure stay at it longer than you did in the movie."

Lia's laugh preceded his by only a nanosecond. Then she handed a small bag to him.

"My present?"

"Yes."

He opened the bag and pulled out a compact disc of one of his favorite artists. "It is the new album." He had not realized it had hit the stores yet.

"I saw his other ones in the stereo cabinet at the villa. It just came out in stores yesterday. I took a chance on you not having it preordered."

"I did not."

She sighed happily and relaxed against him as if it were the most natural thing in the world for her to do. "I'm glad." She rubbed her cheek against his chest. "I'm so tired, I could sleep for a week. Do you mind if we order dinner in tonight?"

"I am sorry, *querida,* but we have plans."

Her head came up. "Plans? You didn't say anything this morning."

For the simple reason that Benedicto had not seen fit to apprise Damian of his and Maria-Amelia's trip to Seattle until they were already checked into a downtown hotel. They wanted to be with Lia during Kaylee's procedure.

"I didn't know about them this morning."

"Oh. Is it business? There won't be any problem with Kaylee coming will there? I really hate the idea of putting on a dress and makeup. You're going to owe me big time."

"There is no problem with Kaylee coming because it is not business. You can stay in your current outfit and I will change our reservations to a more casual restaurant." He liked her in her jeans and lace patterned T-shirt that showed just the tiniest bit of her tummy above her waistband when she moved.

"If it's not business, what is it? If you're thinking to take us out to relax before tomorrow, I'd rather just stay here and I'm sure Kaylee would, too."

He had suspected that was the case, but he also believed she would be more comfortable entertaining her family at a restaurant than in the apartment.

A peremptory knock sounded on the door as he said, "Your mother and grandfather have flown over."

Lia jumped off his lap. "Grandfather is here?"

"*Sí.* If I am not mistaken, at our door as we speak."

She looked at the door like an evil genie resided on the other side. "You invited my grandfather here?" she asked, her voice laced with accusation.

"It was not exactly—"

Another series of knocks cut him off.

Damian answered the door when he realized Lia had no intention of letting her grandfather and mother in.

When he led them back to the living room, Kaylee was its only occupant. Lia and all the shopping bags were gone.

Kaylee got up from the carpet to hug her grandmother and great-grandfather and show them her new doll. She kept a steady flow of childish chatter up for several minutes, until Benedicto asked, "Where is Rosalia?"

"She and Kaylee just arrived from their shopping trip. She is putting things away in our bedroom."

"Surely it can wait."

Privately, Damian thought so, too, but Lia's unpleasant surprise at her grandfather's arrival probably had more to do with her longer than expected absence than anything else. He was just about to go and see if she ever planned to join them when she walked into the room.

She was wearing a black dress and the despised makeup. Her hair had been brushed to a glossy flip around her neatly composed face.

She walked directly up to her mother and hugged her. "Hello, Mama. This is a surprise. I did not realize you planned to come to Seattle."

Maria-Amelia hugged her daughter back warmly. "I wanted to be here tomorrow." She looked at Kaylee, her gaze which Damian had often thought vague, focused with intense emotion on her granddaughter.

"Of course, we are here. You should not have expected anything different." At the sound of Benedicto's voice, Lia tensed, but she pasted a social smile on her face and turned to face him.

"Grandfather, thank you for bringing Mama over." Her lack of overt welcome toward the older man was obvious to everyone in the room but Kaylee.

The little girl's smile went undimmed as she held her grandmother's hand.

"I wished to be here as well, Rosalia."

She shrugged and looked down at her daughter. "Are you ready for dinner? Maybe we should fuss you up a little."

"Okay, Mommy, but do I have to wear tights?" she asked in such a plaintive tone that it was all Damian could do not to laugh.

Like mother, like daughter.

"You may wear pants. How about your new purple outfit with the kitties on it?"

Benedicto's harrumph of disapproval was drowned out by Maria-Amelia's suggestion she help her grand-daughter dress.

Lia accepted the help, but went with them, making it very clear she had no desire to remain in the company of her grandfather...or her husband.

"You said the two of you were getting along."

"We are."

"Then why is she still so angry with me?"

Damian didn't have an answer for the other man. If Lia was happy married to him, why hold a grudge against her grandfather?

On the other hand, "You hurt her when you used Kaylee's illness as a weapon to get what you wanted."

"Does she think I could have manufactured the money out of thin air?" he asked in an aggrieved tone.

But Damian just looked at the other man and Benedicto had the grace to look uncomfortable. "All right, I could have made it happen without our bargain, but I wanted you two married damn it. And by all accounts it's working, so why hold a grudge? You didn't."

"You withheld information from me, you did not successfully manipulate me into doing something I did not want. Lia's pride is probably still smarting. She is your granddaughter after all."

"Harrumph."

Damian had no desire to dwell on a reaction that indicated his wife was not nearly as content with her circumstances as he had believed before their surprise visitors arrived. He asked Benedicto about something related to business and refused to allow the conversation to return to Lia again.

Lia kicked off her shoes and unzipped her dress while she headed for the shower. Kaylee had fallen asleep on the way home from the restaurant and Damian had offered to put her to bed. Lia had gratefully accepted, so exhausted by an evening putting on a front of peaceful happiness when her feelings were anything but, undressing herself was almost beyond her.

Despite her fatigue, her mind was still whirling a mile a minute. Hopefully, a long, soothing shower during which she did little more than stand under the hot streams of water would relax her enough to sleep.

The sheath slid from her shoulders and she let it fall to the floor, uncaring that the laundry hamper was only two feet away. The panty hose took more effort and she snagged them in her clumsy efforts to peel them off. She threw them away with relish, using the last spark of energy in her body and then sagged down onto the vanity chair.

Did she even have enough energy to stand under the shower?

Her feet hurt from squeezing them into pumps while they were still swollen from her and Kaylee's shopping marathon. Her face hurt from forcing smiles she did not feel and her heart hurt because Damian obviously believed that she should have had no problem with her grandfather and mother's arrival.

She *didn't* have a problem with Mama wanting to be there when Kaylee had her procedure, but she found her grandfather's evinced concern hypocritical in the extreme.

"She didn't even wake up when I put her pajamas on her."

Lia looked up at the sound of Damian's voice. She still had her panties on, but that was all. For the first time in days, she felt uncomfortable in her seminudity around him and she grabbed a towel to wrap around her torso.

The movement was not lost on him and his dark brown eyes narrowed. "You are angry with me."

"How do you expect me to feel? You invited my grandfather here against my wishes."

"I did not invite him, he came on his own inclinations. However, I do not recall you stating a desire to the contrary."

She wasn't buying it. No way was he putting this back on her. "You had to know I wouldn't want him here, especially right now."

"It is right now that *he* needs to be here. He cannot wait a half a world away while his great-granddaughter's life hangs in the balance."

"And his feelings matter more to you than mine." If Damian loved her, *her* feelings would be paramount for him.

Like that was some surprise. Of course he didn't love her. They hadn't married for love and even if her feelings were growing, there was no reason to believe his ever would.

"I understand his feelings. I do not understand yours."

She couldn't believe he was that dense. Was it all men, or just tycoons that thought any road to Damascus would do, even one they had to bulldoze a village to build? "What's there not to understand? My grandfather threatened me with my daughter's life and that isn't something I can dismiss."

Damian frowned, his dark eyes both concerned and impatient. "Do not be melodramatic. He did not threaten Kaylee's life."

"What do you call refusing to pay for necessary surgery?"

"He never refused."

"He simply required I earn the money," she said with a bitter cynicism that shocked her.

It shocked him, too, if the expression on his too handsome face was any indication. "Do you consider our life together a series of payments on a debt you owe me?"

"I…"

"Do you respond to my passion with your own out of a sense of duty?"

"No." Duty could not ring that kind of response from her once deadened sensuality.

Damian nodded. "Do not talk of earning money in our marriage again."

"Fine, but that won't change what my grandfather did."

"Benedicto hurt you and this was wrong, but would you make him pay by refusing him the right to stand by you in your time of need?"

"He's not standing by me. This is about him needing to be here, you said so yourself."

"And you will dismiss this need because of what he did?"

"I am not dismissing his needs. I'm just not happy about having to deal with them on top of everything else."

He opened his mouth to speak, but she put up her hand to silence him. "Please don't say *anything else.* I'm tired. Really tired. I don't want to discuss my grandfather or anything else. Not Kaylee, not how you think I should feel differently...nothing. Even if you can't understand me, can you understand *that*?" She sounded every bit as weary and disillusioned as she felt.

"*Sí.*" All impatience drained from his expression, leaving only concern, but she didn't trust it.

She now knew that when it came to his concern for her and his concern for her grandfather, she came in a poor second. But then the two men had a long-term relationship built on mutual respect and business interests. What did she have with Damian? Passion and a sex life he would eventually grow weary of.

"I need a shower and then I'm going to bed."

He looked like he wanted to say more, but after a

long silence, he merely turned and left. She pushed the bathroom door shut after him, closing herself into a lonely isolation, something she'd known a lot of since her father died when she was fifteen. When she stepped into the steaming enclosure, she refused to dwell on the fact that her face was wet before the water even touched it.

They had to be at the hospital at 7:00 a.m. the next morning for anesthesia. Kaylee was brave, but Damian could tell she was nervous. Just as he could see the nervousness in her mother. However, unlike Kaylee, who had clung to both his and Lia's hand in the car ride over, Lia was intent on avoiding him.

She'd allowed Kaylee to sit between them in the car. He would have thought that normal under the circumstances, but she had been careful to avoid his physical proximity since arriving at the hospital as well.

Things only got worse after Kaylee was anesthetized and they went to the waiting room. Benedicto and Maria-Amelia were already there, seated in two chairs near the door. Lia drew into herself until Damian felt like she was not even in the waiting room with them.

"How long is the procedure supposed to take?" Benedicto asked.

Lia ignored the question, staring blankly ahead and leaving it for Damian to answer. "It could be done in as quickly as an hour."

"This is no fast-food restaurant. These doctors do not need to hurry. They should take their time. That is my great-granddaughter they are operating on."

"It is not technically an operation, Papa." Maria-Amelia darted a worried glance at her daughter after correcting her father. She'd obviously noticed Lia's withdrawal, too.

"Whatever it is, are you sure these are the best doctors for the job?" he demanded of Damian.

"*Sí.*"

"Humph!" Benedicto stood up and paced the room. "Operation or procedure, it is still damn nerve-racking having to wait for the results."

Lia stood up, and looking at no one, left the room.

She could be going to the bathroom, but somehow, Damian doubted it. He followed her, leaving a grumbling Benedicto and clearly stressed Maria-Amelia in the waiting room.

Lia was turning a corner when he came into the hall and in an outside courtyard when he caught up with her. "Why did you leave?"

"I want to be alone." She didn't look at him and that bothered him.

So did her desire for solitude. "You shouldn't be by yourself right now."

"It beats sitting around listening to my hypocrite of a grandfather espouse concern for my daughter's welfare and question decisions he wanted no part of."

"I did not ask his opinion."

"I did…or at least, I asked for his help and he gave me an ultimatum instead. He turned my daughter's welfare into a business proposition. He owed you and he willingly sacrificed me to assuage his pride."

Finally Damian was beginning to understand. Once, Benedicto had told him that Lia did not know the old man very well, but what he had neglected to mention was that what she did know…she did not trust.

"He did not encourage our marriage to benefit himself."

"Do you deny you have helped him out financially?"

"No."

"He offered me and all I represented to you as payment, isn't that right?"

"Lia, he wanted what was best for you, too. You must see that."

"I only see that he's been sponging off you for years, he saw a way to salvage his pride and he took it."

"It was not like that." He shook his head in frustration, wishing he could see her face, but not wanting to push her too far in her fragile emotional state. "He loves you, but you do not trust him at all."

Her body tensed as if under an intolerable burden. "How can I? He took me away from everything I knew after Daddy died."

"Surely that was your mother's decision."

"One she reached after a lecture on duty and her moral obligation to raise me among my family in Spain. But it wasn't enough to get us living under his roof, he had to control everything. He wouldn't even let me go home for a visit."

"That was shortsighted of him."

"Very." She spun to face him. "Do you really think I would have eloped with a boy I hadn't even seen in three years if I hadn't been desperate?"

"You had not seen Tobias Kennedy in three years?"

"No. The kiss we shared to seal our wedding vows was only the second one we'd ever had."

"I assumed you married in a passionate desire to be with the one your grandfather and mother denied you."

"They didn't even know about Toby. We kept in touch via e-mail and a handful of phone calls. I thought I loved him when I was fifteen. I was furious about having to move to Spain. I'd already lost the most important man in my life; I needed my best friend."

So many things became clear. "And yet the love of a friend is not necessarily the love needed to make a marriage work."

"According to you and my grandfather, love isn't a necessary ingredient at all."

He *had* believed that, but he was no longer so sure. He would like very much to believe she loved him.

"Hadn't you better get back to my grandfather? I'm sure he would appreciate your company." Her voice lacked any animation, but the accusation was there all the same and one thing became clear that he had not considered before.

She believed his relationship with Benedicto was more important to him than she was.

Damian cupped her shoulders, trying to impart some of his strength to the woman who had become intrinsically linked to his happiness. "The day after Kaylee joined us at the villa, I called Benedicto. I told him that what he had done was wrong and that I was furious with him for manipulating you with your daughter's health."

She shrugged, her shoulders moving jerkily under his hands. "So? It wasn't like you were willing to let me renege on my side of the deal."

"And would you be pleased now if I had done so?"

"That's not the point."

"In regard to me demanding you keep your word, that is exactly the point."

"Well, you and my grandfather have certainly made up now, so I'm not sure what point you were trying to make with that, either."

"He now understands that if he ever attempts to manipulate you or Kaylee in any way again, I will sever our relationship and dissolve the partnership. No matter how it happened, I am now married to the woman I want for my wife and I will protect you and our daughter always."

She seemed to stop breathing for a second.

"Lia?"

"Did you mean it?" she asked with a crack in her voice, her head bowed.

"*Sí.* Your grandfather knows me well. I do not bluff."

"And you really want me to be your wife?"

He carefully tilted her chin up and felt like he'd been kicked in the gut when he saw the tears on her face and wrenching uncertainty in her beautiful amber eyes. "*Sí.*"

"You can't." She shook her head, her eyes closing in distress.

Now was not the time for the conversation, but he could cement her trust in him…show her that she came before her grandfather in his priorities. He pulled Lia close, kissing her temple and then her lips in a tender salute that held no hint of sexual need or desire.

She sighed and melted against him, wrapping her arms around his waist. "I'm so scared, Damian."

"Kaylee will be well. You will see."

She nodded against his chest, but she did not let go

and that is how the surgeon found them forty-five minutes later.

"Your daughter is in recovery, Mrs. Marquez."

Lia pulled away from Damian, but he kept one arm over her shoulders. "The procedure…"

"Was a complete success. In a very short while, your daughter will be recovered and as healthy as any other child her age."

Lia sagged against Damian. "I'm so glad." Her voice was a bare whisper. "How can I ever thank you?"

"Kaylee's health is all the thanks I need, Mrs. Marquez. She's a wonderful little girl."

"Yes, she is."

CHAPTER NINE

Lᴵᴬ walked into Kaylee's hospital room with her hand in Damian's.

He hadn't allowed her out of touching distance since coming out to her in the courtyard.

She sucked in a breath and blinked back tears. "Her body looks so small in that bed."

Kaylee's eyes slid open and a wan smile curled her tiny bow lips. "Hi, Mama. Hi, Papa."

They walked over to her and took turns hugging her carefully and kissing her baby soft cheeks.

"I'm sleepy," she said as they both straightened to stand beside her bed.

"It is the anesthesia, *niña.*"

"It will wear off soon and then you'll feel better," Lia promised.

A sound from the doorway alerted her to the arrival of her mother and grandfather.

Lia's mom came rushing over to the bed, talking so fast and crying that Lia could not begin to understand what she said, but the words made Kaylee smile as she was touched with reverent affection by her grandmother.

Lia's grandfather still stood in the doorway, an expression on his face that Lia had never seen before. His stark angles were lined with grief and his eyes filled with it. He turned to her and she could see a sheen of tears.

"Rosalia, I…" He stopped, his voice choking to a halt. "I am sorry."

"Grandfather would you like to hug me before I go to sleep?" Kaylee asked from the bed in a voice faint with drug induced sleepiness.

He literally stumbled across the room and bent over the hospital bed with none of his usual elegant grace. He hugged Kaylee for a very long time telling her how much he loved her and how glad he was that she was all right.

When he was done, the nurse came in and suggested the visitors leave so Kaylee could sleep off the effects of the anesthesia. Lia wanted to sit with her daughter, but her grandfather asked her if he could speak to her.

She followed the others out of the room, feeling like she could face her grandfather and a roomful of more like him now that she *knew* her daughter was going to be okay.

"Rosalia, if we could have a moment of privacy?"

She'd never heard her grandfather sound diffident before and she didn't know how to respond to it.

"Anything you need to say to my wife you can say in front of me." Damian's instant defense and protective posture shouldn't have surprised her after what he had said in the courtyard, but it did.

The old man sighed heavily, but nodded. *"Eh, bien."* He put his hand out beseechingly toward her. "I am sorry, more sorry than I can say that I threatened you with your daughter's safety. In my mind it was all a power game. Like chess, where strategy was all that mattered. Our little Kaylee did not look sick. I could not think of her as sick. It was not until I saw her in that bed that I realized what I had truly done."

The passionately repentant speech shocked her into absolute silence.

A tear trickled down one weathered cheek. "I will understand if you can never find it in your heart to forgive me, but please believe. I never would have let her go without treatment. If you had refused to marry Damian, I would have found a way to provide it."

She wanted to believe that, if only because she loved the old man and couldn't stand the thought her daughter meant so little to him.

"I wanted you to be happy, *niña,* and for my sins, forcing you into the bargain with Damian was the only way I believed I could ensure your happiness."

"You're so sure I'll be happy with Damian?"

"I know it." A little of her grandfather's arrogance returned, but it was muted by the grief still mantling him like a dark and heavy cloak. "I groomed him for you from the day we met. I knew he would make you a good husband. I refused to let you go home to see that Tobias Kennedy."

"You didn't know about him."

"Of course, I did. You spent all your time with him the week after the funeral. Your mother was lost in her grief and she didn't see it, but I knew you had to be gotten away from the young man."

"He was a good man."

"Yes, but he was not the right man for you. He was too weak to care for you properly."

"Are you saying that you insisted we move to Spain and held me there as a virtual prisoner because you planned to marry me off to your protégé when I reached age?" It was so Machiavellian, it was unbelievable.

"*Sí.* And if I had not messed up somewhere along the way, all would have been well. Damian was attracted to you from the start, but you did not notice him. I thought you were still grieving your father. I did not realize you had been staying in contact with the American boy until after you eloped."

"What is this, what are you talking about?" Lia's mother demanded, her body tensed with distress.

Lia looked from her mother to her grandfather, who seemed to have aged twenty years over the past few minutes. Several things settled inside of her. She loved them both despite her mother's tendency to go through life in a fog that blunted her awareness of her family's needs and her grandfather's attempts toward manipulation.

"You pushed me right into his arms."

"I realized this. When it was too late."

"Using my fear for Kaylee to fix what *you* thought was a problem was wrong."

"I know and I am sorry." She'd never heard her grandfather use those words in all her life and now he'd said it three times in only a few minutes.

The genuineness of his repentance was unquestionable, but it did not erase all the pain from Lia's heart. "You hurt me."

"I have done little else since you were fifteen, but never once have I wanted that outcome. I see now that what you needed, I did not give. If I had, perhaps many things would have been different."

"Maybe," she conceded, though she didn't see the use in dwelling on that now.

Nothing could undo what had been done. She could not go back and undo her marriage to Toby even if she wanted to. And she didn't. Kaylee was worth all the pain Lia had experienced during and after her marriage.

But any relationship she had with her grandfather from this point forward had to be based on *mutual* respect. "If you want us in your life, you have to stop trying to orchestrate ours."

Grandfather nodded, frowning. "Damian has already made that very clear."

"I want to understand," her mother demanded again.

"I'll leave the telling to Grandfather, but it's going to be okay, Mama." She wasn't sure that was true, but Lia could not burden her mother with knowledge of her failure.

If her and Damian's marriage didn't work, it wouldn't be Grandfather's fault. And it wasn't his fault that marriage to Toby had brought so much pain to her. Maybe it was time she stopped blaming him for things that could not have been changed.

"I love you, Mama." She turned toward her grandfather. "I love you, too."

"Even after all this?"

"Even after. Love is like that." And only love could make the marriage between her and Damian work.

She saw that now, but that was a problem the two of them would have to work out.

Three days later, Damian and Lia returned to their apartment after leaving a quietly sleeping Kaylee at the hospital for her last overnight there. Damian suggested sharing the spa bath and she willingly agreed. They had been married for almost three weeks and the intimacy they shared continued to get better and better, making her believe maybe, just maybe, her marriage could work after all.

Damian settled her against him in the hot, bubbling water.

"You told me you were willing to try to achieve full intercourse on the day we agreed our marriage vows were binding. Did you mean that?" he asked, shattering the peace surrounding her like a pane of glass hit with a wrecking ball.

She gasped and tried to talk, but only unintelligible sounds came out of her mouth.

"I ask because there is a treatment."

She stared at him, still incapable of speech.

"For vaginismus," he clarified in her silence.

Memories she would rather forget surfaced. She wouldn't exactly call it a treatment. "My doctor told me."

"Then why have you not tried it?"

"Don't you think I did?" She'd tried so hard, but she'd never been able to overcome her body's reaction to the threat of intercourse. "It didn't work, I couldn't make my body relax."

"Maybe the doctor started with dilators that were too big."

"Dilators?"

"The treatment."

"What are you talking about?"

"You said your doctor told you about the treatment."

"My doctor said that vaginismus was the result of a subliminal desire on my part to withhold myself from Toby, that I was afraid of intimacy."

"He said what?"

"That if I loved Toby enough, my body would relax and let him enter me."

"That is ridiculous."

"It's what both the doctor and Toby believed, but I *did* love Toby. Maybe it wasn't the passionate and over-whelming feeling I...um, well anyway, it was real and I could still never control the spasms."

"Of course not. They are involuntary contractions of your vaginal muscles. No voluntary contraction could be nearly as complete. *It was not and is not your fault, do you hear me, querida?*"

He sounded fierce enough she'd have to be deaf not to have. "Yes, but the doctor said—"

"This doctor was an idiot."

He had been the same one to dismiss the hole in Kaylee's heart as an unimportant anomaly in test re-sults, so she had to agree with Damian.

"Um...what are dilators?"

"The most widely accepted treatment for the spasms."

She felt embarrassed now that she had never even looked into treatment, but then until Damian, she'd had no reason to want to reclaim that aspect of her feminin-ity. "You shouldn't know more about this than I do."

"Why do I?"

"I believed my doctor."

"Didn't you ever go for a second opinion, visit a specialist?"

"No."

"But the information I found is readily available on the Internet, and the one book I picked up was at the local bookstore. I did not even have to order it."

"What did the book say?"

"That the involuntary contraction is usually linked to sexual trauma in your past, but not necessarily rape."

"My wedding night…" she breathed. His brows rose in question, but she shook her head. She could tell him later. "You think residual fear from the trauma causes my spasms."

"It is possible. Your grandfather told me that you almost died giving birth to Kaylee. This too could have contributed."

After a long, painful labor, the placenta had torn and she still did her best to block the memory of the frantic pain-filled minutes that followed. She had no problem believing the experience impacted her ability to make love, but that didn't change her circumstances.

"Whether my doctor was right and I didn't want intimacy with Toby, or you are right about some subconscious fear causing the spasms, the problem is still inside my head and it's up to me to fix it."

"You are wrong, *mi mujer.*"

"But you just said—"

"That a trauma probably triggered it, but the treatment is not psychological. It is *physiological.* At least according to the vast majority of specialists in this area."

"You've done a lot of research."

"*Sí,* but you have not."

"After Toby died, I was sure I never wanted to be intimate with a man again."

He slid his hand across her breast, taunting her nipple with his fingers in the hot water. "And now?"

"I love intimacy with you," she said, stifling a groan of pleasure at the contact.

He turned her until they were looking at each other and her thighs were straddling his. "Tell me about your wedding night."

It was hard to concentrate on anything but Damian when the feel of his thighs against hers dominated her senses and his perfectly shaped body filled her vision.

She traced the brown disk of his nipple. "I was…very *intact* on my wedding night." It was getting easier to talk about this kind of thing with Damian. He knew as much about her body as she did, maybe more in some areas. She'd certainly never known she was capable of the pleasure he gave her. "It felt like Toby was ripping my body in two when we made love the first time. The second time wasn't much better. It still hurt, only he didn't have to try so hard to…you know. The next morning when he wanted to make love again, I cried and begged him not to."

"Did he rape you?" Damian looked ready to kill.

"No. I told you I'd never been raped, but he was a virgin, too, and he didn't always know how to touch me without hurting me, but he would never have forced himself on me. I let him try again a couple of nights later, but that was the first time my body rejected him. Neither one of us knew what to do and we were both too embarrassed to ask anyone about it, but after six months without sex, he told me I had to ask my doctor."

"And your doctor told you it was all in your head."

"He suggested I drink a glass of wine before trying to make love. It didn't help, but Toby tried more frequently and managed penetration a few times."

Damian's frown was ferocious, but his voice was mild when he spoke. "Are you still afraid of being hurt?"

Remembering her reaction to his finger, she nodded. "I must be. I don't want to be. I *know* you wouldn't hurt me, but Toby and I never had what you would call a successful attempt at lovemaking. And after Kaylee was born, the spasms happened every time we tried to make love. I told him he could try to force it a few times, but it didn't work. We both ended up in tears and hurting."

Damian cupped her face with gentle, wet hands. "And even after that your doctor told you it was all your fault?"

"He thought I had some deep-seated need to have control in the relationship. Toby thought I didn't love him enough. He loved me, but he couldn't stay in a marriage without sex."

"He could have," Damian ground out, dropping his hands to her hips and pulling her more intimately against him. "He chose not to."

"It amounts to the same thing." She could feel his hard flesh right against the heart of her. She couldn't help squirming against him and increasing the friction.

The movement made them both groan.

"Perhaps, but his choice left you with a mistaken impression of what you had to offer in a marriage."

"I didn't know what it could offer me, either. I thought getting married again would end up putting me through the hell I knew with Toby. Until you touched me, I didn't know what it meant to really want someone."

He liked hearing that. The forgivably smug expression on his face said so. "Do you want to hear about the dilators?"

"Yes."

His dark gaze caught hers and held it captive. "Short, narrow cylinders are placed here." He touched her intimately. "They start smaller than a Q-tip and are replaced in graduated sizes until the muscles have been stretched enough to accept intercourse."

Thinking of the size of his erection, she frowned with chagrin and opened her eyes. "It would take a year to get me ready to receive you."

He laughed, the sound masculine and warm. "No, it will not. Once you reach a certain point of dilation, your body will stretch to accommodate me without pain."

She didn't know if she could stand having a doctor administer the treatment. She knew it would require such a thing for her to become whole, but it was something so intimate to have done in a doctor's office. Her memories of her visits to the doctor were not appreciably better than those of her times of intimacy with Toby.

"How many visits to the doctor would it take?" she asked, trying not to look as repelled by the idea as she felt.

His expression said he wasn't fooled. "You do not like the idea of having a doctor touching you so intimately?"

"You asked me if I was willing to try to achieve full intercourse, the answer is yes," she said instead of answering his most recent question.

He was not fooled by her evasion tactics and his dark, knowing eyes said so. "Nothing dictates only a doctor may administer the dilators."

"Who else could do it?" A nurse? She wasn't sure that would be any better.

"Me."

"*You?*" she squeaked, shock coursing through her at the idea.

"*Sí, querida.* Me."

"But…"

"I would not hurt you."

"*I know,* but…" Her voice trailed off because she wasn't sure what to say.

She wanted to try and not just because she'd made a promise. If she could have a complete sexual relationship with Damian, she wanted it. Another woman might feel differently, but the idea of her lover witnessing her body's refusal to function sexually was more palatable than a stranger doing so, even if he or she was a doctor.

"Let me do it, Lia." His voice compelled her as did the expression in his dark eyes.

"Do you really think it will work?" Hope burned hot and deep inside her.

"According to what I have read, the procedure is almost always successful in making sexual intimacy possible. Sometimes, muscle relaxers are necessary and it could take more than one time to achieve our goal, but that is hardly a problem. We have the rest of our lives together, *mi esposa.*"

"How will you go about it?" she asked, giving her tacit agreement to trying. "I mean do you just stick it in?"

"When it comes to touching you here…" His finger brushed along her feminine heart. "I will never *just stick* anything in. I will touch you until you are lubricated then slide the first one in. Some of the articles I read said you should leave each dilator in for ten minutes, others until you feel ready for the next size, but the author of the book thought five minutes for each graduation would be sufficient."

"What do you think?"

"That we should only do what feels right and good to you. We are not in a doctor's office. We can take as long as we want to and I have the advantage of knowing I can arouse you. I believe your body will adjust to the dilators faster if you are sexually excited."

That made sense, but it was all so unbelievable. Not only the procedure itself, but the fact he had made the effort to research it all and come up with a solution. "When do you want to do it?"

"I will get a set of dilators and then we will see. Kaylee's needs are paramount right now."

"You are an amazing man, did you know that?"

His slashing grin made her heart flip over. "I am glad you think so because I believe you are the bravest woman I have ever known."

She shook her head, but he kissed any denial from her lips and then showed her once again that the shades of intimacy in marriage were varied and beautiful.

They spent five days at the apartment, spending a good part of each one in the company of Lia's mother and grandfather. Once the doctor gave Kaylee the okay, they flew to New York in Damian's private plane. When they arrived, she was delighted to discover he owned a house upstate.

He told her it was only a ninety-minute train ride into the city.

"You're gone commuting three hours a day?" she asked, aghast.

"I have an apartment in the city as well. I used to stay there five days a week, but I am concentrating on doing more of my business from my office here now."

"I'm glad."

He smiled. "You do not want me gone five days a week?" he teased.

"Kaylee and I would just follow you," she teased right back, growing more confident with him daily. "I hope your office in New York is big."

"It is large and it has a very comfortable sofa."

"For sitting?"

"Among other things."

She grabbed his silk tie and pulled him toward her. "Has it had a lot of that kind of use?" she asked only half jokingly.

His dark eyes mocked her. "What *use* would that be, *querida*?"

"You know what I mean, Don Damian Marquez."

"Sleeping?" he asked innocently.

She dropped his tie and spun on her heel, but he grabbed her from behind and brought her back around to face him with an implacable hold.

All humor had drained from his expression. "No, *querida*. It has not. You need not concern yourself with such worries regarding my office or our home. Our bed here is untouched. Any exciting moments of an intimate nature that occur in my office will be with you and you alone. As my wife, you are the only woman that exists for me anymore."

She let her body melt against him and smiled. She thought she would like to be the only woman who existed for him because he couldn't imagine wanting anyone else, but his declaration had still been pretty special. "You know exactly the right thing to say."

Soon his warm, firm mouth sent all other thoughts to the very darkest recesses of her mind.

He made no move to try the dilators for the next week and she was hesitant to ask why. Maybe he hadn't gotten any yet, but then again maybe he wasn't looking forward to having to do what was basically a medical procedure on her. He hadn't sounded like he minded doing it, though. In fact, he'd sounded pretty eager and very understanding.

So, maybe he was waiting for her to say something. She vacillated over what to do for two more days before deciding the wait was worse than knowing, even if he said he would prefer she go to a doctor for the treatment.

Damian walked into the bedroom he shared with Lia, anticipating that moment when he would slide between the sheets and take his wife in his arms. It felt so right, this cuddling they did before and during sleep. Even on the rare occasions they went to sleep without arousing each other, it felt better than anything he had ever known.

He felt *intimate* with his wife and no way was he ever letting her walk out on their marriage.

"Damian…" Her voice called out softly in the darkness and he stopped undressing.

He turned toward the bed, his slacks undone and his shirt discarded. *"Que?"*

"I was wondering…" Her voice ended abruptly, as if she couldn't make the next words come out.

"What is it?"

The lamp on her nightstand clicked on, revealing her beautiful form covered in the sexiest bit of nothing he'd ever seen. His heart jump-started and he experienced an immediate reaction that left him ready for things she'd probably never even considered.

The lingerie purchase.

He had wondered when he would get to see it. His only complaint now was that half of her was covered by the sheet.

"You look beautiful."

"Thank you."

"Is this what you wanted to discuss? If so, we can both agree you have impeccable taste in nightwear."

She laughed softly, her amber eyes glinting with desire and something more. Nervousness. Then, she took a deep breath, as if preparing to plunge into deep waters. "Have you had a chance to get the dilators?"

"I had them the day after we discussed it."

"Then why…"

"Why have I done nothing about it?" he asked when it appeared she was not going to finish her question.

"Yes."

"The past days, you have been very concerned for Kaylee, no?"

"Yes, I have."

"And this has made you tense."

She grimaced. "Yes, it has."

"It is best for you to be relaxed and worry-free the first time we attempt dilation. I refuse to give you another negative sexual experience." In fact, he would do his utmost to stop her from having one ever again.

"How could you?" she asked, sounding genuinely puzzled. "There is nothing negative about the way you touch me. It's all so perfect."

She was the perfect one. Perfect for him. "I am glad you find it so."

"I'm not worried about Kaylee anymore," she said with quiet hesitation. "I mean…the surgeon said her heart beats like there was never a hole in it. And… um…she's sleeping peacefully in her bedroom *now*."

A bedroom that was only across the hall from theirs so the little girl could easily find them if she woke nervous in the night. However the walls in the house had been built almost soundproof and now he appreciated that feature very much. Once their bedroom door was shut, they would be isolated in their own private world.

"Are you saying you want to try tonight?" he asked.

Her cheeks turned rose red, but she nodded with absolute assurance. "Yes."

Want and need jolted through him at her acquiescence and he finished undressing in record time. She watched him with intent fascination, her attention never straying from him and what he was doing.

He walked to the bed, his eyes locked with hers, his already excited flesh tight and full with his need. Her gaze flicked down to it and then up again, her pupils dilated. When he reached her, he put one knee beside her on the bed. She flinched slightly, but did not pull away.

He cupped her cheek. "You are nervous."

"And excited."

Both were to be expected. However, he would have to show her that she had no reason to be nervous of him and every excuse for excitement. "Tonight we replace your first wedding night with a new one full of pleasure not pain."

CHAPTER TEN

"You already did that." She smiled tremulously at him. "On our wedding night. You held me after I refused you. That was really special to me. I hadn't been held in so long and had never felt so safe."

His eyes closed and he fought unfamiliar emotion. "Lia…"

Her lips met his, the kiss taking him by surprise, but not for long. He devoured her lips, demanding absolute surrender because it had to be so. She seemed to understand and gave him everything his kiss claimed of her.

They were both shaking when he pulled away.

She whimpered, her nipples rigid points against the sheer lace of her teddy and his sex throbbed in response to the evidence of her need.

"I will get the dilators."

She nodded, total trust burning at him from her golden eyes.

Before he came down beside her again, he pulled the blankets and top sheet off the bed, revealing her entire body to his heated gaze.

The basque was scandalous in its miniscule proportions, the lace v-ing between her legs barely covering the silky curls that hid her secrets and the cut on the hips so high, it was almost to her waist.

"Very nice," he rasped, shocked by how hard it was to get words out past his tight throat.

"Thank you," she practically purred, stretching with a wantonness she never would have shown before the many passionate sessions of lovemaking in their marriage.

He loved the show of confidence, and like everything else about her, it increased his primitive desire to connect at the most fundamental level.

She put her arms out to him, an invitation as old as time and as beautiful as eternity. "Make love to me, Damian."

That was all it took for him to move. He covered her in a rush of need, pressing his lips against hers which were parted invitingly and kissed her with every bit of seductive skill at his disposal. He wanted her aching for him, pulsing with a craving only he could fill. The hunger in her lips easily matched his own and she was writhing in restless abandon under him almost immediately.

The hard tips of her breasts pressed against his chest, instilling a hunger that demanded immediate fulfillment. He took precious seconds divesting her of her sexy nightwear. He then went on a tasting expedition down the delicate column of her throat, over the flushed skin of her chest, to the soft, resilient flesh of her generous curves. He usually made a feast of them, but right now he wanted…needed…had to have…a tasting of her distended peaks.

He closed his mouth over one and exerted an immediate, gentle suction. Her body jerked as if struck with an electric jolt and he increased the pull of his mouth until she arched toward him, panting out her need.

"Damian…" His name was a long, drawn-out moan of desire.

No music had ever sounded sweeter, or lovelier to his ears. He adored her instant response to his slightest touch. She was the most amazing lover he'd ever known. Other women might have been more knowledgeable about the practiced technique that stirred a man's senses, but none of them had made him tremble with need. Only Lia could do that.

He played with her creamy, soft flesh, kneading her with fingers that shook, tasting her with his mouth, and nipping at her with careful provocation. Soon, not only her back was arched toward him in a silent demand for more, but her pelvis was tilting up toward him with the same fierce abandon.

It was what he had been waiting for. He slipped his hand between her legs and slid the first dilator inside her.

She made a startled sound and went stiff.

"Are you all right, *querida?*"

Lia didn't know how to answer Damian. "It doesn't hurt." It just felt alien, but then so had his finger on the few occasions he had managed to caress her inner flesh before it closed up.

"Bueno." He put his mouth on her breast again, his suction erotically intense and even the feeling of her body tightening around the small cylinder could not mute the pure pleasure he gave her.

But she wasn't sure if she was supposed to react this way to the dilator, so she said, "I'm tightening up."

"Does it hurt?"

"No."

"Then do not worry about it." His voice was rich with passion and approval, making it easy to do as he said.

He came up over her, aligning their bodies in warm intimacy and kissed her, his scent and the textures of his skin dominating her senses. She moaned and touched him everywhere she could reach, wanting to torment him with as much pleasure as he gave her. It seemed to be working because he made dark sounds of masculine need deep in his throat and moved against her with primitive force.

She loved that he did not withhold his passion from her, but that she also knew beyond a doubt she could trust him not to press for more than her body could give. He'd proven it to her over and over again in their non-consummated lovemaking.

"I think I could handle the next one," she panted seconds later as she felt pulsing sensations in her feminine core that had nothing to do with pain or fear.

He didn't say anything, but his hand went between her thighs and with sensual, but gentle mastery, he made the change. He never stopped kissing and touching her so she was ready for the next graduation very soon thereafter.

This time her body resisted, but her need was greater than her fear of failure and she begged, "Please, don't stop. There's no pain. I promise."

It took all Damian's control not to explode right there. She was so beautiful in her passion. Her dark, silky hair was spread across the pillow, her eyes wild with desire, and her body flushed from his lovemaking.

"I will not stop, *mi esposa preciosa.*" This was too important to both of them.

But if he did not do something to assuage his primal need to claim her body, he was going to lose control and that was not something either of them could afford to risk.

He began kissing his way down her body, exploring the sexy indentation of her belly button in minute detail with his tongue. When he moved lower, he parted her with his fingers, opening her to the possession of his mouth. She moaned and writhed and pulled at his hair when he kissed her between the legs, arching toward his mouth.

He concentrated on her sweetest spot, hungry for the sounds she made when she convulsed with pleasure. She shuddered with release as he changed the dilators once again, her silky wetness sweet against his tongue.

The succession up to the finger size dilator went by more quickly than he had anticipated, the residual satiation from her completion relaxing her body for easy penetration. Her initial fear had melted away completely and she didn't even flinch when he put the larger cylinder inside her opening.

It was only a matter of seconds before she panted that she was ready for the next one.

He touched her tentatively, running his finger along the slick and swollen tissue. "Now we go to my finger, okay?"

She nodded, her eyes filled with a mixture of excitement and renewed fear, but it was obvious her desire was much bigger than her worry. He moved up to kiss her mouth while he carefully pulled the dilator out and then slipped his finger inside.

Wet silk closed around him with such enticement his

sex ached in response. He wanted her so much, but this had to be perfect for her.

She deserved it.

He pleasured her with his finger, making this dilation a much more active step.

She moaned and writhed some more and when he went to slide a second finger in with the first, she didn't tense up at all. "That feels so good, Damian. Ahhhh…" Her voice cracked and went silent as he touched her the way he had wanted to since their wedding night.

However, she was tight and it took several minutes of gentle coaxing before her body relaxed around his fingers. Once it did, he moved them in and out with the same rhythm he would use to join their bodies.

She loved it, pushing herself toward his hand, taking him in as far as he would go. She pulled her mouth from his and panted, her face flushed with uncontrolled desire. "I'm ready for you, Damian, I know I am."

He looked into her golden eyes, darkened with wanting, the emotion burning enough to send him over the edge even without the thought of being inside her.

"Are you certain?" he asked. "There is a big jump from my fingers to me."

"You said there would come a time when my body would stretch to accommodate you. I think that time is now." She spread her legs wider under him, bringing her knees up to make room for him in her secret place.

He had passed hot to incendiary two dilation levels ago and did not begin to have the willpower or even the desire to continue arguing with her.

She tilted her pelvis upward in blatant invitation. "Make me yours."

"You have always been mine. Make no mistake, but now I join our bodies as intimately as two bodies can be."

He pushed inside. It was tight and he couldn't get much more than the tip of his erect flesh in at first, but he rocked gently against her and she strained upward.

"It's working!" The elation in her voice made his eyes sting and he buried his face in the fragrant hair lying against her neck.

He'd never experienced anything so profound in all his life.

Lia could not believe the sensation of fullness without pain she was experiencing. She'd never known anything like it. It was *nothing* like her disastrous wedding night. Damian was gentle and coaxing, not taking her body like a marauding invader, but enticing her to accept him, all of him.

And she wanted to. She wanted to so much! It felt beyond good. It felt wonderful.

She strained upward, rocking her own pelvis until the muscles inside her body gave and Damian pushed forward to fill her completely, stretching her inside to pleasure a step away from pain. But it was not pain and she could have cried at the beauty of it.

He started to move on her with a cadence she knew well. Only before, when he'd used it, he had not been inside her body like he was now. It felt very, very different this time. She moved with him and experienced the shattering sensations in the very core of her being.

Soon his breathing was hard and so was hers.

"Yes, Damian. Darling, yes!"

"*Querida,* you feel so perfect. I want—" He bit off

his words and she guessed he wanted to be rougher, but he'd promised gentleness from the very beginning.

"Don't hold back, *please.* You aren't hurting me. *I want to feel everything with you inside me.*"

Her words seemed to drive him wild because he started to plunge into her with powerful thrusts. Each stroke hit some secret spot inside of her body that made her shudder with pleasure over and over again. The sensation grew more and more devastating until she splintered apart, explosions going off inside her with the power of a nuclear reactor in meltdown.

Her body contracted around his hardness and she bowed up against him with more strength than she knew she had, lifting them both off the bed.

"*Sí, querida.* Give yourself to the pleasure of our joined bodies." He kept loving her and incredibly, it happened again, stronger than the first time.

He had taught her that her body was capable of prolonged pleasure, but even in his arms, she had never known anything like this. It was indescribably sweet and devastatingly powerful, both too much and not enough. She wanted to beg him to stop, but she would die if he didn't continue. The only sounds she could force out of her tight throat were unintelligible groans anyway.

And he didn't stop, didn't even slow down. How could any person maintain such powerful action for so long? More tension built low in her belly and this time she was determined not to go through the cataclysmic explosion alone. She wrapped her legs around his hips, her arms around his neck, and then stretched up so she could take his nipple into her mouth.

She bit him gently and caressed him with her tongue. When she started sucking, he went rigid and then flooded her with pulsing heat while his shout rang in her ears.

Her body convulsed again, this time sharing the experience so completely with him that she felt like they were one person, their bodies joined on a much more profound level than the mere physical. She didn't faint, but she was light-headed and it was all she could do to keep her arms wrapped around him.

They felt like overcooked spaghetti noodles.

He went to pull away, but she held him to her, discovering energy she didn't know she had. "Please, it's wonderful. So special. Don't leave me."

"I am too heavy."

She clung. "No. You aren't."

"I am, but I too enjoy the closeness and have no wish to move." His smile was so gentle, she could be forgiven for believing it held more than simple physical satiation.

He kissed her.

Moisture burned her eyes, but she refused to let it spill over. She would not spoil this moment, even with happy tears.

His lips slid to her temple and he placed a kiss there that was no less than a benediction to her soul.

"Oh, Damian."

Holding their bodies as tightly together as possible, in one deft move he reversed positions and she was on top of him. He was still inside of her.

She looked down into his face, the quiet approval she saw there touching her more deeply than she'd ever allowed another human being to touch her. "I love you,

Damian. So very much. Thank you for helping me to be a real woman."

His expression turned fierce. "You have always been a real woman. *Thank you* for sharing your body with me."

He hadn't responded to her avowal of love, but she hadn't expected him to. He might not love her, but he'd given her more than Toby ever had, or anyone else who said they loved her had, in her whole life.

He pulled her mouth to his for a long, lingering kiss and then caressed her back with soft, soothing strokes until she fell asleep.

She woke up with him making love to her sometime in the night and cried with joy when her body accepted him without having to use the dilators.

The next day, Lia bubbled with joy, the only cloud on her horizon the fact her husband did not love her. But he wanted to be married to her and that counted for a lot. He also desired her and enjoyed her company. He was committed to her well-being and that of her daughter. She wasn't sure even love would carry with it anything more than what he so generously gave.

He didn't trust love and she could understand why, but one day, he would change his mind. She would show him that loving her was not wrong or risky.

He was working in his study when unexpected visitors arrived. Toby's parents.

The housekeeper showed the elderly couple into the sunroom where Lia and Kaylee worked on an art project together. Kaylee's squeal of delight brought Lia's head up with a quick jerk and then a smile of welcome spread across her own features.

She jumped up along with Kaylee and they both rushed across the room to hug the tiny woman and big barrel of a man that reminded Lia so much of her late husband.

"Edna, Bruce…this is a wonderful surprise!"

"We thought we'd give you a little while to get used to being married again before showing up on your doorstep, but I finally couldn't wait to see my baby girl." Edna hugged Kaylee close. "The phone just wasn't enough."

Guilt assailed Lia. She should have had her former in-laws flown to Seattle to be there during Kaylee's procedure. "I didn't think of arranging for you to come. I should have."

Bruce shook his head. "No need to worry about us, young lady. You've had plenty on your plate lately."

But she should have worried. She was so used to living on a tight budget, her new circumstances had not sunk into her thought processes yet. Three months ago, paying for the plane tickets for Kaylee's grandparents to come visit would have been as impossible as financing the little girl's surgery.

She shook her head. "I can't dismiss my thoughtlessness so easily. I am sorry."

"You kept us up on the news by phone," Bruce reminded her.

"But a hug is worth a thousand phone calls," Edna said, making Kaylee giggle as she tickled the little girl.

Lia's smile was forced as she invited them to take a seat. She loved these two people and no matter what they said, she'd let them down.

Bruce and Edna took up the chairs on either side of Kaylee at the table covered with art supplies.

"I'll get something for you two to drink." Lia turned to do just that and stopped abruptly at the sight of her frowning husband standing in the doorway.

"I was told we have visitors."

"Grandpa and Grandma came to see me, Papa!" Kaylee yelled excitedly from the other side of the room, practically bouncing in her chair.

Bruce flinched at the word Papa and Edna's smile dimmed a little, but they both rose to meet Damian and shake his hand.

"We owe you a debt of gratitude," Bruce said, his emotions close to the surface. "Lia told us that you made it possible for her to pay for Kaylee's procedure."

Nothing could be read in Damian's expression, but he shook the older man's hand. "Kaylee and Lia are my family now. Rest assured, I will always look out for their needs."

Bruce's smile was tinged with sadness. "Yes."

Lia wished she knew what to say to ease the obvious burden of pain in the man who had been her only real father figure since the death of her own at age fifteen. But everything she considered saying would sound disloyal to Damian. Conflicting love and loyalty twisted her insides just as her hands twisted together in front of her.

Damian noticed and reached out to gently disentangle them, folding his big hand around one of hers. His eyes asked if she was all right and she tried to reassure him with her own, but guilt and sadness weighed on her heart.

He narrowed his eyes and then turned to Bruce and

Edna. "I owe you and your son an even greater debt, however. Tobias Kennedy fathered my precious step-daughter. I am honored to be Kaylee's papa, but your son will always be her father. Since his death, you have taken care of Lia and Kaylee as only family can. For that, I am forever in your debt."

"Nonsense," Bruce blustered, but Edna's eyes filled with tears and she choked trying to get words out.

"You are very important people to both my wife and my daughter and I hope you will see your way to spending a great deal of time with us here in New York."

"We would like nothing better," Edna said, obvious tears in her eyes.

Lia couldn't help it. Her own eyes filled with tears and she gave Bruce and Edna a watery smile. "Is it any wonder I love him so much?"

"You've found yourself another good man," Bruce said. He met Damian's gaze square on. "We were both worried about Lia marrying again. She deserved the best and I'm glad to see she's gotten it."

Damian's thanks was obviously sincere.

The rest of the visit went smoothly and the elderly couple was convinced to transfer their belongings from a nearby hotel to Damian's home for the remainder of their stay.

"You were tense when I first arrived in the sunroom this afternoon." Damian spoke from where he sat on the bed removing his shoes.

As always, when her husband began undressing, Lia's brain had a hard time focusing on anything else. "I was?" she asked absently.

"You looked unhappy."

And he sounded bothered by that fact.

She forced herself to remember. "I felt guilty. I could have made sure they were there when Kaylee had her procedure, but I didn't even think of it. They offered to sell their house to pay for the surgery we all thought she needed, but it wouldn't have been enough money. Yet they were willing to make the sacrifice and I let them down, even if they don't see it that way."

"I am sorry. I should have considered this as well."

"You can't think of everything."

"I usually do, but if you want the truth, I did not like the thought of your former husband's family having a claim on you."

"But you were so kind to them."

He continued undressing, the sight of his muscular chest coming into view doing things to her breathing. "Your loyalty to me came first and I saw this. It was enough."

"You are so special."

His expression wasn't one she recognized. Sometimes she wished she could read her husband's complex mind.

He stood up and unzipped his pants. "They are older than I expected."

She had already changed into a satin robe and she busied herself hanging up the dress she'd worn for dinner. "They had Toby late in life. He was an unexpected blessing after years of trying and finally giving up on having children."

"It must have been very hard for them when he was killed."

She sighed and turned to face Damian again, her mouth going dry at the sight of his naked body. "I-it was," she stuttered out, having to concentrate on what had been said before she could speak. "They latched on to Kaylee and me, but they supported us as well. I owe them a lot and I really appreciate you being so sensitive to them."

"I am not the most sensitive of men, *querida,* but family is family."

She begged to differ on the sensitivity part, but she just smiled. "Well, I'm glad you don't mind them being a part of our life. They're very special to me."

"They were bothered that Kaylee calls me Papa."

"That's to be expected, but I think they were ultimately okay with it. You did a tremendous job of setting their minds at rest."

"And you, are you ultimately okay with me being her Papa?"

How could he even need to ask that? "I'm more than okay with it. I'm grateful she has a daddy again. I'm thrilled that man is you. I love you, Damian." The words got easier to say even though he never said them back.

He sat down on the side of the bed again. "Gratitude is not love."

She settled into his lap and looped her arms around his neck. "No, it's not, but then what I feel for you is so much bigger than gratitude. I passionately want you. I adore spending time with you. You make me feel like a complete woman, even when we're just together like we were in the sunroom this afternoon. I love you, Damian. Believe me."

He picked her up and carried her to the en suite. "Bathe with me."

"Yes."

But it bothered her a little he had not said he believed her. Did he really think she could mistake gratitude for love?

He made a production out of removing her silky bathrobe while the water ran to fill the spa bath. Scooping her up, he stepped into the hot water and sat down with her in his lap once again.

"I love you," she whispered over and over again as he kissed her neck, along her collarbone, her shoulders and the tops of her breasts.

She wanted to imprint the words on his soul.

Finally his lips swallowed her continued whispered avowals and within minutes they were straining together in the bubbling water. She touched his hard length and he shuddered.

Smiling with feminine delight, she stroked him into complete readiness. Willingly she allowed her legs to be pressed apart and his hand to trespass on her most feminine place. When she felt her body tighten around his finger, she refused to accept it was happening at first. But no amount of denial could stop the truth from crashing through her like a marauding stampede of cattle, trampling her heart in their wake.

A cry of despair rose up, but he cut that off with his lips, too, giving her a hard, possessive kiss. "Hold that thought, *mi esposa.*"

He climbed out of the bathtub and walked sleek and naked back into the bedroom. He returned seconds later with a small, familiar plastic case.

She stared at the case with a mixture of despair and

bitter knowledge. "You can't want to go through this every time we make love," she wailed.

He stopped with his foot on the edge of the bath and looked down at her in all his naked glory. "Do you think it bothers me to kiss your breasts, to take their peaks into my mouth?"

"No."

"And yet, I do this every time we make love."

"It's not the same thing."

"Is it not?"

She opened her mouth to speak, but he overrode her.

"Who is to say what a man enjoys doing with his woman?"

He climbed into the tub and pulled her back into his arms. She tried to resist, but he would have none of it and she was no match for his strength. She ended up on his lap, his erection pressing against her hip.

The plastic case that produced such ambivalent feelings in her sat on the oversize spa's tile edge, right in her line of vision.

His hand trespassed the intimate heart of her again, his finger gently caressing her sweetest spot. "You are so soft here, so silky and it excites me to touch you."

Her breathing splintered. "Ye-es."

The knowing finger went lower and touched the flesh closed to him. "I love touching you here."

"I love it, too…" Her voice trailed off in breathless delight as he pleasured her with his hand.

"It matters not to me if the touch is to put a dilator in to stretch you so we can make love, or it is simply to run my fingers over your tempting feminine flesh. *I enjoy it all*. Would you deny me the right to touch you as I wish, in the ways that give me pleasure as well as pleasing you? Each touch excites me and fills me with satisfaction that you open yourself to me so completely."

She desperately wanted that to be true, but could it be?

The doubt must have reflected in her eyes because he growled in obvious displeasure at her disbelief and then kissed her in a way that dared her to deny him anything.

She didn't. She couldn't.

When he finally lifted his mouth, her lips pulsed with need for more. But she had to say, "There's still my sexual dysfunction."

His hand traced her breast in the water. "For me, you function perfectly sexually."

"But we have to use the dilators…"

"And that excites me."

He didn't look like he was kidding and she knew he would never lie to her. "It *excites* you to use them?"

Wasn't that a little kinky?

"It is something private and special between us. A thing I do for you that no one else can do. Preparing you to receive me in this way is as intimate as the act of love itself. Of course it makes me want you more."

If she tried to speak, she would choke on her emotion, so she kissed him, trying to infuse her lips with the huge love she felt for him and the overwhelming gratefulness to God that this man was her husband.

He took her through the dilation and then made love to her, all of it there in the hot waters of the spa. And the whole time, he praised her for her passion, told her how much he loved the way her flesh swelled around him, that he couldn't wait to be inside her and share the pleasure together.

When they did make love completely, it was every bit as earth-shattering as it had been before.

Damian worked in his study while his wife entertained her and Kaylee's guests. At least he was supposed to be working. He was thinking about her avowals of love instead.

She said the words often, as if she hoped that by repeating them he would accept them. She had to sense his reservations about the reality of her gift. For her love would indeed be a gift. A necessary gift. One he was not sure he could continue to live without.

If only he could be sure that it was love. She said often how much he had given her, implying she owed him some immeasurable debt of gratitude for each thing. He did not want gratitude masquerading as love. He needed the real thing.

Kaylee's grandparents stayed a week and left with the assurance that Damian would bring Lia and Kaylee to New Mexico for a visit very soon.

That night, Lia walked into her and Damian's bedroom to find a carved wooden heart sitting on her pillow. It was about four-by-six inches and the laced carving in the dark, polished wood looked both intricate and lovely.

She walked forward slowly, hope and love and fear, swirling together in a heady mixture inside her.

Could this mean what she so desperately wanted it to mean? Hearts meant love, didn't they? Romantic love. Man-woman, forever after love. Valentines and sentimental romance. Everything she wanted from him. She lifted the heart, enjoying the sensation of her fingertips against its smoothly polished sides.

This close up she could see the top was covered in tiny carved roses and rosebuds, intertwined by vines with delicate leaves. Only in the center, the roses seemed to fade away, leaving an opening in which the words, *Tu tienes mi Corazon* had been carved in a scrolling script.

Her eyes burned with moisture as her heart contracted. *You have my heart.* Did she? Could she? The possibility stole every other thought from her head.

Two strong arms came around her and she gasped.

He didn't say anything, but his hands covered her own. He lifted the lid from the heart. Inside, on a bed of rich red velvet was an assortment of dilators.

"Are you ready to make love to your husband?" he asked, his voice seducing her every bit as effectively as the proximity of his body.

She smiled, feeling feminine and strong, while hope beat a wild tattoo in her heart. "Yes, but I don't think we're going to need those." She indicated the dilators. They hadn't at all the past three nights.

"Can we use them anyway?"

She looked at him startled, her breath suspended in her chest.

He was saying something important here and it wasn't about wanting to make love with accoutrements.

He turned her around and cupped her face in his hands. "I love *you*, Lia."

The tears spilled over and he smiled, not in the least bothered by her emotional reaction.

"When I first met you, I wanted you. You were too

young, but I never forgot you and when your grandfather suggested a merger marriage, I was intrigued. When I saw you again, the desire you sparked in me almost sent me to my knees."

"Desire is not love."

His smile turned incredibly tender. "You told me you felt more for me than gratitude."

It almost sounded like a question and she had no hesitation in reassuring him. "I do. So much more. I can't deny my thankfulness for all that you have given me, but the greatest gift in our marriage to me has been yourself. I love you, completely."

"I also feel this love you speak of. I do desire you. More than any other woman in the world, but I feel so much more for you than mere physical need. Love is the only word that can describe the way my soul belongs to yours."

She had hoped. She had wanted. She had desperately needed this to be true, but one doubt remained.

"Even with my problem?" she asked with aching vulnerability she could not begin to hide.

"It is not a problem for me. *I love you.*" He pressed a soul caressing kiss to her more than willing lips. "This means I love your body and *everything* your body does."

He picked her up and carried her to the bed, laying her down so she faced him. Then he tugged the wooden heart from her hands and tipped it over, pouring the set of graduated cylinders on the comforter between them. "These represent your trust in me, our desire for each other and the will to bridge any gap to keep our marriage strong. To me, they are beautiful, just as you are beautiful because in a way, they are part of you, but they are part of me also."

"Yes." She understood and the understanding filled her with more joy than she'd ever known.

That joy was reflected in his amazing dark eyes. "I love you, *all of you,* for all time."

She looked at the small cylinders he'd used to help her reclaim her womanhood then into the eyes of her tycoon husband. She had married him looking for a way to save her daughter's life, but he had given her so much more. He had given her a new life of her own. "I love you, Damian, all of you, for all time," she repeated.

"I know." His hand curved possessively over the indentation of her waist. "It took me time to accept it, but I believe you now. What we have is nothing like what I have ever known and you are a woman unlike any other."

"It's not gratitude," she reiterated.

"*Sí.* No more than what I feel for you is mere lust. It is love, pure and strong."

More tears filled her eyes and she let them fall. Her heart was so full, she couldn't stop them. "I'm so glad."

"I also, *mi corazón.*"

He pulled her into his arms and she eagerly snuggled into him. "You are the very air that I breathe. I will never let you go."

She remembered how hard he had fought to keep their marriage viable from the start. "You've given me so much."

"You have given me more. You have given me a family again. To be Don Damian Marquez holds no importance beside the titles of husband and father. You have enriched my life beyond measure."

"Oh, Damian…" She kissed him, letting every bit of

emotion inside her flow freely from her heart to his. When she pulled back, they were both shaking. "I love you."

"Until the last breath in my body and then into eternity." His kiss sealed the vow.

Lia gently laid her tiny son in his crib. It was the same one his brother had used two years ago. She could not believe the changes in her life three years of marriage to Damian had wrought. She had a closer relationship with both her grandfather and mother. She also had three children and Damian loved them all with the same fierce, possessive tenderness he felt for her.

The box of dilators still resided on her dresser, dusted daily by their maid, but it had not been opened since before the birth of their first son. Damian refused to get rid of it, saying he wanted her to remember he would always be willing to bridge whatever gap might emerge in their marriage.

And he had, too, lovingly participating in parenthood as only a reformed workaholic tycoon could do.

"Is he sleeping?"

She turned and smiled, her heart catching as it always did at the sight of her gorgeous husband. "Yes."

"Then you are all mine?"

"Always."

He swept her into his arms and carried her through the connecting door to their bedroom. He made love to her whispering a litany of love and need that grew richer as time went on, but did not diminish.

He was her world and she was his and their love grew stronger with every passing year.

Neither one of them would ever take that love for granted, either, because they knew it was too much of a miracle.

A note to readers from Lucy: One in three women has a physiological sexual dysfunction, which means her body physically responds to lovemaking in a negative way. The most common of these dysfunctions is vulvadynia, but vaginismus is not nearly as rare as many medical doctors would like to believe, nor is it always the result of sexual trauma, although pain related to sexuality is the leading identifiable cause. I wrote this book for the tens of thousands of women who suffer in silence believing there is something wrong with *them*. Only one in ten will seek treatment and of those, less than thirty percent will be willing to undergo physiological treatment such as the dilation procedure for vaginismus. I hope that if you are one of the women suffering in silence, you will be silent no longer, but most of all that you will realize that it's not your fault—no more than it was Kaylee's fault in the story that she was born with a heart defect. She got her happy ending and I hope you get yours, too.

BEDDED BY BLACKMAIL

by

Julia James

Julia James lives in England with her family. Mills & Boon® were the first 'grown up' books she read as a teenager, alongside Georgette Heyer and Daphne du Maurier, and she's been reading them ever since. Julia adores the English and Celtic countryside, in all its seasons, and is fascinated by all things historical, from castles to cottages. She also has a special love for the Mediterranean – 'The most perfect land-scape after England'! – and she considers both ideal settings for romance stories. In between writing she enjoys walking, gardening, needlework, baking extremely gooey cakes and trying to stay fit!

Don't miss Julia James's exciting new novel,
The Greek's Million-Dollar Baby Bargain,
available in March 2009 from
Mills & Boon® Modern™.

For my long-suffering, fabulously patient
and above all inspiring editor, Kim –
all my thanks for everything.

CHAPTER ONE

'Now, that one there. She interests me. Who is she?'

Diego Saez indicated with his wine glass before sweeping it back up to his lips to take another mouthful of the extremely expensive vintage wine. He lounged back in a stiff-backed chair, long legs extended under the damask-covered table. He looked relaxed, despite the formality of his evening dress. One hand lay on the tablecloth, the natural tan of his skin colour accentuated by the white linen. His dark, hooded eyes were very slightly narrowed, and his strong, compelling features held a considering expression.

The man beside him looked across the large, crowded dining hall. Stained glass windows pierced the outer wall, emblazoned with the arms of the City livery company where tonight's banking industry dinner was taking place. A wash of people, predominantly men, all attired in black-tie and evening dress, sat at the fifty or so tables filling the room. There was an aura of expensive wine, port and brandy, and faint fumes from cigars, for the Queen's toast had already been given so smoking was now permitted, as the several hundred guests relaxed for a while after dinner, before the evening's guest of honour—a senior politician—rose to give his speech.

'Which one?' asked the man sitting next to Diego Saez, craning his neck slightly to see where his companion was looking.

'The blonde in blue,' replied Diego laconically.

An unpleasant smile appeared briefly on the other man's narrow face.

'Not even you, Señor Saez, could do the business for

5

Portia Lanchester. And even if you did get up her skirt you'd just meet iron knickers!'

Diego took another mouthful of burgundy, savouring the bouquet a moment, and ignoring the comment. Its coarseness did not strike him as incongruous, merely repulsive. Upper class Englishmen might talk with plums in their mouths, but the sentiments they expressed—like that one— were by no means unusual amongst a certain type. And Piers Haddenham was definitely that type. His background might be moneyed, but his soul came from the gutter—and that was to insult the gutter. Diego had no illusions about him, or the rest of this collection of comfortably privileged company.

But then he had no illusions about anyone.

Especially women. They might play coy for a while, but they all came round in the end. Their reluctance never lasted long.

Diego's dark eyes narrowed again, studying the woman who had caught his attention.

He could only see her profile, but it was enough to tell him that he'd like to see the rest of her. She had those classic English rose looks—fair hair, translucent skin, and facial bones that told her bloodline as clearly as if she'd been a racehorse.

'Lanchester...' he murmured.

'Loring Lanchester,' supplied Haddenham.

'Ah, yes.' Diego nodded.

Loring Lanchester. Merchant bankers to Victorian industrialists and colonial expansionists. Now, a hundred and fifty years later, a complete anachronism. They should have been taken over by a global bank years ago if they were to have the slightest chance of long-term survival.

His razor-sharp mind worked rapidly, filing through the complicated landscape of the City's financial institutions, long since meshed into a global nexus that spanned the UK, Europe, America and the Pacific Ring like a spider's web. And one of the most skilful spiders, who could sense and exploit to his own unerring advantage every tremor in that delicate, complex web, was Diego Saez.

Quite who he was no one seemed to know. He was South American—but his Hispanic background, hinted at in the strong features was as far as anyone got in identifying him. Self-made; that much was evident. There was no Saez dynasty backing him, bankrolling him, opening doors for him. But then Diego Saez opened his own doors.

He'd opened them in New York, Sydney, Tokyo, Milan and Frankfurt, and any number of the less influential financial centres. Now he was busy opening them in London.

Not that he needed to exert any pressure. Doors opened magically for him the moment he expressed the slightest interest in any kind of venture or investment. His reputation as one of the most astute financiers operating on the global stage had gone before him. Saez made money. A lot of money.

Out of everything he touched.

And that made everyone—from chief executives to bankers, investment houses to industrialists—very, very keen to know what he was up to, and to get in on the act if they could.

Frustratingly, Diego Saez had a habit of keeping his cards close to his chest.

Piers Haddenham, despatched by his chairman to woo Saez during what seemed to be an impromptu visit to London, was doing his best to get a glimpse of those cards. But so far Diego Saez had done little more than make enticingly ambiguous remarks—possibly leading, more probably misleading—and sport a sardonic look in his eye whenever Piers tried to steer the conversation towards what might or might not be attracting his interest right now.

Apart from Portia Lanchester.

Piers looked at the woman again, this time with a different mindset. He'd assumed Saez was simply thinking of the night ahead, who he would warm his sheets with, but perhaps he was still running on his daytime agenda.

Loring Lanchester. Was that the name on one of the cards Saez was thinking of playing during his visit to the UK?

He decided to see if he could draw Saez out.

'Not in the best of health these days,' he observed. 'Old man Loring lost his marbles years ago, but won't give up the chairmanship. And young Tom Lanchester, the nephew, is even more useless.' He paused a moment. 'Took some reckless decisions recently, so I heard. Wouldn't like their asset book myself.'

He glanced at his dinner companion, to see whether his fishing line would twitch, but Diego Saez was merely looking bored, waiting for him to stop speaking.

'So...' mused Diego, flexing his legs slightly under the table—his chair was quite inadequate for his tall frame. 'Why the ironclad underwear?'

Piers's face relaxed. His initial assumption had been right after all. Saez was simply after sex. Not that he'd get any from Tom Lanchester's cold bitch of a sister. No one did. Certainly not that poor sod Simon Masters, who was sitting next to her and just about panting. Piers didn't know anyone who'd got their leg over Portia Lanchester.

His brow furrowed momentarily. Hadn't she been engaged once? A few years back? Who the hell had volunteered to get his tackle frozen in that glacier? He'd bolted, anyway, whoever he was, and married someone else, and since then her name never came up when the brandy came out—well, not unless the subject was ice maidens.

Not even Diego Saez could heat her up, thought Piers dismissively. Not that he didn't roll an enviable number of women, but none of the ones he'd ever been seen with could have been described as cold. Hot ones, yes, like that Latino singer—Diana Someone—and the Italian opera diva, Cristina Something. Plus a French countess, a Moroccan model and a Hungarian tennis ace. And that had just been this year. A sour look, of male envy, lit his eye.

Women fell over themselves to drool—and drop their knickers.

The sour look vanished. Malice gleamed briefly. No way would Portia Lanchester go for Saez.

He leant towards Diego and said confidingly, 'Frigid, that's why. Listen—' he slid his hand inside his tuxedo and drew out a card that looked like an ordinary business card '—don't waste your time on her. Phone this number and you'll have someone waiting for you in your hotel suite. Tell them your spec and they'll deliver whatever you want—and your choice of equipment.' He proffered the card to Diego. 'They're all clean—I use them myself. And they take credit cards, of course.'

Diego drew his arm away and suppressed an instinct to slam his fist into Haddenham's corrupt, narrow face. Instead, he drained the last of his wine and reached for the port bottle, which had stopped its circulation conveniently to hand. He decanted a generous measure into the appropriate glass.

'I believe we are about to suffer for our supper,' he remarked, looking towards the top table, where the scarlet-coated Master of Ceremonies was stepping forward, gavel at the ready, to call for silence—and then the dreaded speeches.

Diego lifted his port glass and prepared to be bored, instead of revolted.

Then, as the politician was introduced and stood up to give his prepared speech on the state of the UK economy, his eyes drifted back to where Portia Lanchester was sitting. Ramrod-straight, her well-bred chin lifted, she displayed no emotion on her fine-boned, aristocratic face.

Diego sat back again and wondered what she looked like naked.

He had every intention of finding out.

*   *   *

Portia sat motionless, hands in her lap, her face blank to conceal her acute boredom, as the speaker droned on, immensely pleased with the sound of his own voice.

But then the whole evening had been exquisitely tedious. God alone knew why she had given in to Simon's endless cajolings to come along as his partner. She'd done it out of a combination of exasperation and pity. Simon kept thinking that if only he didn't give in she would take him seriously. His dogged determination to woo her both irritated and softened her. Though she would never be stupid enough to go out with him on a real date, lest he get hopeless hopes up, tonight's stuffy City do, with wall-to-wall bankers, had seemed innocuous enough.

She hadn't realised just how incredibly dreadful it would be. Money and politics dominated the conversation, and she was interested in neither. She was also the only woman on her table—one of little more than a few dozen women in the whole room—and as the wine had gone down so the awareness of the several hundred men in the room to the presence of any females at all had increased accordingly. She had begun to be on the receiving end of some very open assessment—something she had always loathed.

She had reacted by adopting her usual defence—total and deliberate freezing. By refusing to acknowledge how they were looking her over she could pretend they were not. Simon's presence did not seem to deter them sufficiently—but then he was not particularly put out by the attention she was getting. Irritatedly she knew that he was actually enjoying having his escort lusted after—it made him feel envied, and he presumably liked the idea of that.

Suppressing a sigh, half of annoyance, half of boredom, she reached out and took a sip of mineral water from her glass, then idly nibbled at a *petit-four* from the plate in front of her. The politician droned on, talking about interest rates and invisible earnings and fiscal instruments, none of which she had the slightest interest in.

Poor Tom. She thought instinctively of her brother. He

has to know all this stuff. Not that he liked it either. But the wretched bank needed him, so he had to put up with all this boring finance-speak. At least he was escaping this shindig tonight—from the looks of him he was coming down with flu, and he was keeping indoors. She didn't blame him.

She stared into the distance and let her mind drift away to something she *was* interested in—producing a definitive catalogue of the Regency portraitist Benjamin Teller. She still needed to trace several missing paintings—plus *Mr Orde with Gun Dog, 1816* was proving tricky to attribute conclusively. And she still needed to identify the woman portrayed in the *Young Lady with Harp, 1809.* She was pretty sure she was Miss Maria Colding, of Harthwaite, Yorkshire, but needed proof. She would have to visit Harthwaite, she suspected, and check out what other family portraits were still hanging there, then sift through the county archives to see if there was a commissioning letter or bill of payment still in existence.

Finally the speech concluded and the politician resumed his seat to polite applause.

Talk broke out again at her table, and Simon leant across, patting her hand.

'Phew, what a number! Were you completely bored?'

He sounded so anxious she hadn't the heart to agree too acidly.

'Does anyone actually listen to these things?' she asked, putting a slight smile on her mouth.

'Lord, no. Well, only the hacks on the press table, I suppose. They'll pounce on anything they can turn into a headline.'

She reached for her water again, and took another, longer drink.

'Are you up for a liqueur now?' her escort asked attentively.

She shook her head. The last thing she wanted was any more alcohol. She'd drunk champagne at the reception, then both white and red wine over dinner.

'Coffee would be lovely. Is there any left in that pot there?'

Simon immediately reached across to where the silver coffee pot hid behind the flower arrangement in the centre of the table. Portia slid her cup towards him. The back of her neck was stiff. It must be the effort of holding still for so long during that speech. Gracefully she twisted her head to the left, and then to the right, to ease the stiffness.

And froze.

A man was looking at her.

Correction. A man was looking her over. His hooded eyes were resting on her with lazy assessment.

Something like a hot thread of wire drew through her stomach.

As if in total slow motion she felt her pupils dilate.

She stared, unable to move her gaze away.

He was sitting a few tables away, right in her eyeline through the mesh of heads and bodies at the other tables in between. He was tall; she could tell that even with him sitting back, lounged in his seat. His skin was dark for a European, but with a deep, natural tan. Mediterranean? Not quite. Too big to be Italian or Greek, anyway. High cheekbones. Strong nose. Deep lines running to the edges of his mouth. Eyes dark. Very dark.

And still looking her over.

As her eyes met his, she felt the hot wire draw out through her spine.

Liquefying it.

For one endless moment she could not move, and then, with an effort of will that made her weak, she averted her face.

'Cream?'

She jumped minutely, forcing her eyes to focus on the cream jug held in Simon's hand over the cup of coffee he'd just poured her.

'No, thanks.'

Did her voice sound different? Shaky?

She reached for the cup and lifted it to her lips. The caffeine jolted her, and she was grateful. As she sipped, she recovered her composure.

Oh, for heaven's sake, she snapped to herself—he just took you by surprise, that's all.

Usually she was careful never to make eye contact when a man looked at her in that way. She'd just been caught off guard this time. That was all. A mistake, and one she must ensure she would not repeat. She schooled a look of blankness to her face, the one she usually fielded to members of the male population unless she knew she could trust them.

She drank more coffee, trying to listen to whatever Simon was saying to her.

But she felt uncomfortable still. Her nape was prickling now—and she knew why.

Unbidden, his face leapt in her mental vision again—those strong features, that expression of cynicism mixed with an open sexual appraisal.

The wire began to pull slowly through her again.

Stop this!

Her mind snapped away, concentrating on Simon. He was a nice enough escort, and certainly never pushed his luck with her or tried it on. She was easy enough with him, in a casually indifferent way. He didn't threaten her.

Not like the man watching her...

Now that that the wretched speech was finally over, surely she could get away? She would finish her coffee and then get Simon to put her into a taxi. She wouldn't let him come with her—he would probably get desperate and try to pounce, and she didn't want that. She liked him, and didn't want to hurt him. Better by far to end the evening in public and escape on her own.

She wondered if Tom would still be up. She hoped not. He needed an early night. He hadn't looked well at all.

A faint furrow of concern marked her brow. Was it just flu? He'd seemed under the weather for a good few months now. She hadn't seen a great deal of him recently—she'd been off in the States last month, tracking down some of the Tellers that had got sold to American buyers years ago. He ought to get out of London, spend some time at Salton. Catch up with Felicity.

They really ought to get on with it and marry, Portia found herself thinking—a familiar refrain. They were so obviously ideal for each other. Neither liked London, and both were far happier at Salton. Felicity would be ideal for Salton, Portia knew. She had an instinctive feel for the place. She wouldn't muck it up. She'd leave things alone.

Portia had lived in dread that Tom would marry some woman who would summon an army of ghastly fashionable interior designers and turn Salton into some vile 'show-piece'—but Felicity Pethridge would never do that. She'd just settle in, be devoted to Tom, give him a brood of tumbling children, and take her place as one of the long, long line of châtelaines who had kept Salton going through the centuries.

A poignant look softened Portia's clear grey eyes. It was one of the painful ironies of the English land inheritance system that daughters never got to live in the houses they grew up in—not unless there was no son to inherit, of course. Daughters had to go off and look after someone else's place. A guilty look entered her eye. That had been the main appeal of Geoffrey Chandler, she knew—not him, but the prospect of running his vast Elizabethan pile in Shropshire, which came complete with an art collection.

But although the art collection had been to die for, it hadn't proved sufficient to marry for. Poor Geoffrey. If he hadn't managed to persuade her—against her better judgement—to pre-empt their wedding night, she might have gone ahead and married him. As it was, a month in Tuscany with him had made her realise she couldn't possibly go ahead with the wedding. Not even holing up in the Uffizi for sanctuary during the day had been compensation for the ordeals of the night.

Instinctively her mind shied away from the memories. He'd tried so *hard*, and she'd still hated it. And even though she'd tried desperately not to let her revulsion show, of course he had realised—and that had just made things even more unbearable.

Ending the engagement had been awful too—painful and embarrassing, and making her feel so guilty. And when Geoffrey had announced a whirlwind engagement to one of her own schoolfriends not two months later she'd felt more than guilty.

She'd felt totally inadequate.

A shiver went through her. After the disaster with poor Geoffrey she'd simply given up on sex, and had found abstinence a huge relief. She knew that the men of her acquaintance thought her frigid, but she didn't care. She just wanted them to leave her alone.

She didn't even like them looking at her.

The nape of her neck prickled again. That wretched man was still over there, keeping his eyes on her.

Dark, hooded eyes…

She straightened her back and pushed her coffee cup away. For one extraordinary, inexplicable moment she'd wanted to turn her head and check whether he was, indeed, still keeping her in his eyeline.

Instead, she turned to Simon.

'I don't mean to be a wet blanket, Si, but I've got quite an early start tomorrow. Do you think you could get me a cab? I'd better make a move.'

Disappointment showed in his pale blue eyes.

'Must you? I thought we might be able to take in a club...'

He sounded so hopeful she hated to turn him down. But what was the point of going on anywhere with him? He'd just get ideas. Hopes.

She laid a hand on his sleeve. 'I don't think so, Simon— I'm sorry.'

There had been pity in her eyes, and she saw him flinch and hated herself for it.

She got to her feet, and the rest of the men at the table, realising she was leaving, stood up as well. She took her leave, bidding them all goodnight, and one of the younger ones asked her to give his regards to Tom.

'No show tonight, I see,' the man said. 'Well, it's understandable.'

'He's got flu,' said Portia.

Another of the men laughed. 'He's certainly caught a cold, all right!'

The others laughed, exchanging glances. Portia frowned. She hadn't a clue what they meant, and didn't want to know. She just wanted to head for home.

She bent down to retrieve her evening bag from under her chair and stood away from the table. Simon took her arm and they started to make their way to the exit, on the far side of the room. With the speeches over there was a lot of movement, with people heading out to the restrooms or to the bar in the reception lobby, or just to go and catch up with diners at other tables.

As she made her way on Simon's arm several people stopped to greet him and chat innocuously. Dutifully she paused, making whatever responses were called for. Their progress was slow, however, and at one point she realised they had become stalled just beside the table occupied by the man she had intercepted looking her over. A faint prickle of unease went through her and she felt herself tensing, then becoming irritated by her own reaction. She risked a brief glance towards the table.

His place was empty, and she felt an irrational spurt of relief. Then, as her eyes swept back to Simon, engaged in conversation with a man who appeared to be a former colleague at another brokers, she stiffened abruptly.

He was talking to two other men. One was slightly built, with a narrow, fox-like face she didn't like. The other was in his sixties, portly, smoking a cigar and red-faced. She heard the narrow-faced man call him 'Sir Edward' in obsequious tones.

The man who had been looking her over said something. It was deep and laconic, with an accent that sounded more American than anything else, though there was definitely something foreign about it. English, even American English, was not his first language, she guessed.

He was tall, all right. Easily over six feet, with broad shoulders. He made the narrow-faced man look like an unhealthy weasel, and the older man like an overweight bear.

But then, Portia found herself thinking, he would make any man look disadvantaged.

For all his height, and breadth of shoulder, there was an innate grace about him. As if his body were under perfect control.

It was certainly in good shape, that was for sure. His torso was lean, his legs long and muscled...she could see how the material of his dinner suit was pulled taut over his thighs.

What on earth am I doing? she suddenly thought. She tried to drag her eyes away, but they swept over his face as she did so. She wished they hadn't, because all over again it had the same impact on her as it had before. The deep, curving lines from his nose to his mouth drew her eyes, the high cheekbones, the plane of his jaw. Those hooded eyes...

Suddenly, and without warning, his eyes flickered to hers.

The hot wire jerked through her.

For one long, unbearable moment he held her gaze.

Heat flushed her skin, and she was suddenly vividly aware of her bare arms and shoulders. Even though her dark blue evening dress was not in the least décolleté she suddenly felt hideously, horribly exposed.

She wanted a shawl, a wrap—a blanket!—anything to cover herself up under that gaze.

But she had nothing. Nothing to conceal herself with.

Automatically, unconsciously, her chin went up and she looked away, back to Simon.

Three feet away from her, Diego Saez smiled.

Seducing Portia Lanchester was clearly going to be an amusing enterprise.

And different, very different, from his usual affairs.

Typically, the women he selected for his bed required nothing more than an indication on his part that he found them desirable. His problem was getting rid of them, not getting them in the first place.

Not that he envisaged any serious problem with Portia Lanchester.

Her reaction to him demonstrated that amply. She was aware of him, all right, and that was the first step of the journey for her. The journey that would end in his bed.

Not tonight, however. There was no point hurrying her. He wanted to take his time over this one. Enjoy every stage of the seduction. By midday tomorrow he'd have a complete dossier on her, courtesy of his security agency, and then he'd take it from there. For now, he would just enjoy continuing to make her aware of him.

He flicked his attention back to what Sir Edward Porter, a former but still influential chairman of a major bank, was saying about the current level of merger and acquisition activity in the City, and made some appropriate comment.

With more animation that she was feeling, Portia joined in the chit-chat with Simon and the other man. Then, as she recovered her composure, she decided enough was enough. Taking ruthless advantage of a momentary pause, she spoke up.

'Simon—my cab?' she prompted.

Reluctantly he moved off, or tried to, but suddenly, and she didn't quite see how, her way was blocked. The trio ahead of her seemed to have shifted somehow, and now the man who'd been looking her over was right in her path.

'Excuse me.'

Her tone was clipped.

For a moment he did not move. She levelled her gaze at him—though it meant looking up at him.

The dark eyes swept over her face one last time, and for one last time she felt that hot wire jerk.

Her lips pressed together. Anger spurted through her. She moved to step around him, and then immediately he had stepped away, clearing the way for her.

'Thank you,' she said, her voice even more clipped, simultaneously dropping her eyes. She marched forward, still angry.

Behind her, Simon hurried to catch up.

Diego let his gaze linger on her receding form for a few more seconds, then cut back to Sir Edward.

'Loring Lanchester...' he said speculatively. 'Are they as vulnerable as they look, do you think?'

At his side, Piers Haddenham's eyes gleamed. So, not sex after all, then. He listened with acute attention to Sir Edward's reply.

'Sinking faster than the *Titanic*,' the older man said succinctly. 'Unless they get a tow—and by a pretty damn large ship!' His shrewd eyes met Diego's speculatively.

Diego's expression did not change.

Far across the room, he could see the elegant, slender form of Portia Lanchester walking out.

CHAPTER TWO

'NEXT Thursday at two? That would be wonderful. Thank you so much!'

Portia put the phone down. Descendants of the Coldings still lived at Hathwaite, and were happy for her to inspect their remaining portraits and compare them with the photos she'd taken of the mysterious *Young Lady with Harp*. Their family papers had been deposited with the county records archive years ago, and she would do a search through them the following day if her suspicions about Miss Maria Colding proved well-founded. With a feeling of satisfaction she tidied the papers on her desk.

Her work at a small but prestigious art history research institute never failed to fascinate her. She knew she was very fortunate to have been taken on, though she was also well aware that the institute director, Hugh Mackerras, considered it a definite plus that she possessed an ample private income of her own. It meant not only that he could pay her very modestly indeed, but that she was more than ready to fund her own travel expenses. But she was pleased to do so—she knew she was fortunate not to be financially dependent on her salary, which meant she was able to pursue a career that really interested her, rather than one that kept body and soul together.

A slight pang of guilt assailed her. She enjoyed her substantial private income thanks to Loring Lanchester—and it was thanks to poor Tom, incarcerated there, that the family merchant bank kept going. Poor Tom. He really wasn't cut out to be a banker—he was much happier tramping through fields in his gumboots and Barbar, getting stuck in to the muddy side of agriculture.

Thinking of Tom made her remember that awful dinner the night before—and that brought another memory in tow.

A shiver went through her.

That wretched man had disturbed her, whether she wanted to admit it or not. There had been something about him that had seemed to threaten her.

In her mind's eye she saw him again, lounging back in his chair, cradling his wine glass, his hooded eyes resting on her, looking at her.

Even as it had last night, she felt her skin begin to prickle.

With a shake of annoyance at such a ridiculous over-reaction to a man whose name she did not even know she returned her attention to her notes. As she did so she realised she was suppressing a slight yawn. She was not surprised. She had not had a good night. The wine had made her sleepy, but although she'd slept as soon as her head hit the pillow, she'd had dreams she wished she hadn't.

Dark, intent eyes had haunted her dreams.

Dreams of being watched, assessed.

Desired.

The phone rang, jolting her out of an unpleasant train of thought.

She lifted the receiver and cleared her mind.

'Yes?' Her voice was crisp and businesslike.

'May I speak to Portia Lanchester?'

She stilled disbelievingly. The voice at the other end of the phone was deep, with a distinct foreign accent, plus echoes of American. The line was distorting the voice, changing the balance of the mingled accents, but she recognised it.

Think of the devil and he'll come calling…

The words leapt in her mind and she pushed them aside. For a second only she paused, getting back her composure.

'Speaking,' she answered. The breath seemed tight in her chest.

'Miss Lanchester? My name is Diego Saez—I noticed you last night at the dinner. Are you free for lunch today?'

Her chest tightened even more.

'I beg your pardon?'

Her voice chilled the line.

'Are you free for lunch?' he repeated. She heard a trace of amusement in his voice, as if her answer had been predictable.

For the briefest second she paused, then, in crystal-cut accents she said succinctly, 'I'm afraid not.'

She put the phone down.

Her heart, she realised, seemed to be beating most unevenly.

She'd been rude, she knew she had, but she excused herself. She had just wanted to get him off the line.

Urgently. Instinctively.

Slowly, deliberately, she let the breath out of her lungs. Her eyes rested on the phone. She wondered if it was going to ring again. But it stayed silent.

Diego Saez.

So that was what his name was.

Her mind ran automatically. Spanish—or Hispanic at any rate. South American? Latino?

How did he know my name? My work number?

She pursed her lips. It didn't matter how he knew, he wasn't going to get anywhere with her.

Why not?

The question slid into her brain like a stiletto knifeblade. In answer, her lips pursed even more. Why not? What kind of question was that? The man had eyed her up like a slab of meat and she had to ask Why not? about him?

Angrily, she flicked through the papers on her desk, looking for the one she wanted. She found it and started to read. Within minutes she was back in the world of early-nineteenth-century portraiture.

Two hours later a massive bouquet of flowers arrived—exotic scented lilies and tropical ferns. The accompanying card simply said 'D.S.' on it. She fetched a vase from the kitchen in the basement of the old Georgian house in Bloomsbury that housed the institute and plunged the flowers into water. Their scent filled her small office—rich and overpowering.

As she left the institute that evening she took the vase downstairs with her, and left it in Reception. She didn't want it in her office.

The scent disturbed her.

A mile or two west of Bloomsbury, Diego Saez glanced at the ticket that had just been couriered to his hotel suite. It lay on the glass coffee table in the suite's lounge, next to a freshly typed dossier that had been delivered before noon that day. It outlined in considerable detail a great deal of personal information about the individual who was the subject of investigation. Although Diego had been in meetings all day he'd had time to peruse it and take action accordingly.

He had the main facts that he required, from her age— twenty-five—to her employer, her home address, family connections and key friends, and social interests.

That Portia Lanchester had not jumped at his invitation to lunch neither surprised nor bothered him. On the contrary, it pleased him. Had she proved, like other women, to be eager for his attentions after all, she would have already started to bore him.

A leisurely pursuit of her would be far more enjoyable.

He gave a slight, self-mocking smile. Even if it meant enduring an evening spent in surroundings even less congenial than last night's City dinner. Still, the evening would have its compensations.

He strolled off to his bedroom, ready to shower and change.

Portia eased her way through the crush of people in the foyer, following her old schoolfriend Susie Winterton and her mother as they crowded into the auditorium. The two-minute bell was sounding and she wanted to get to her seat. In the pit the orchestra was already tuning up, and she glanced around at the familiar red and gold glory of the Royal Opera House, Covent Garden. A sense of pleasant anticipation filled her. *La Traviata* was one of her favourite operas. But as she reached their row in the front stalls, and started to thread her way along it, her sense of pleasant anticipation drained away totally, replaced by cold shock.

Diego Saez had the seat next to her.

He stood up as she took her place.

'Miss Lanchester,' he said politely. His eyes were mockingly amused.

On her other side, Susie, leaning forward, said brightly, 'Oh, do you two know each other?' Her eyes gleamed with curiosity.

'No,' said Portia tightly, and opened her programme.

'We met the other evening,' he contradicted, and bestowed a smile on Susie. She, treacherously, reacted predictably and returned the smile with an openly questioning look on her round face.

'Diego Saez—' He held out his hand.

There were introductions all round, and a lot of speculative looks cast by Susie at Portia. Portia continued to bury her head in her programme as much as she could, uttering the barest monosyllables as Susie chattered away to the man she obviously found fascinatingly masculine. The arrival of the conductor and the dimming of the house lights as the overture started was a blessed reprieve.

But throughout the performance Portia was punishingly aware of the tall, dark frame beside her. He seemed to intrude into her personal space, though his long legs were slanted away from her, and not even the sleeve of his tuxedo touched her arm. But it was more than her body space that seemed threatened—it was her mental space too.

She was aware of him. Horribly, inextricably aware of

him. She could feel him beside her, inhale the scent that had to be him—a mix of subtle, faintly spiced aftershave and his own masculinity. She wanted to pull away from him, but wouldn't. But as the evening wore on awareness sharpened into hyper-awareness. The second interval was even worse than the first had been.

In the first, Portia had at least had the company of Susie and her mother. Diego Saez had managed to take over, somehow, though she hadn't the faintest idea how he'd done it. He'd simply ushered them all along to the bar and sorted drinks for them in an instant. Then he'd stayed, chatting courteously to Susie and her mother, hardly saying a word to Portia. Not even looking at her. He had smiled down at Susie, and Portia's lips had thinned as she sipped her gin and tonic. Susie had chattered away like an idiot, and her mother had smiled benignly, clearly equally impressed by this imposing, attentive male.

But now, in the second interval, Susie proved even more treacherous. As they took their drinks, she suddenly squealed, 'Oh, look, there's Fiona and Andrew—*do* let's say hello!' She dragged her mother across to the other couple, pointedly deserting Portia.

Diego Saez glanced down at her.

Her lips tightened, fingers pressing on the stem of the glass holding gently fizzing mineral water—a second gin and tonic would be unwise, she knew. She steeled herself. He was probably going to try and invite her out again, suggest post-theatre dinner, or make some reference to the flowers he'd sent, or explain how he'd managed to find out she'd be here tonight and get the seat next to her. She instinctively knew—accident it had *not* been!

But he did none of those things. To her stunned disbelief, she felt his fingers stroke along the nape of her neck.

'I'm told,' said Diego Saez, in a low, considering voice, 'that you're frigid. Is that so?' His fingers moved on her skin, then stilled, feeling the instant trembling, quivering reaction to his touch, and rested. 'No, I think not,' he drawled, and dropped his hand away.

She couldn't move. Not a muscle. Her anger was so great that for a second she thought she would not be able to stop her arm swinging up and her palm swiping right across his face.

Something moved in his eyes.

It was amusement.

'Try it,' he murmured. 'It should go down well in a place like this.'

She turned on her heel, but in that instant her wrist was caught and held. 'Sometimes,' he told her, his voice quiet, 'a delicate courtship is…inappropriate.'

He let her go. Then abruptly he walked away, heading for the foyer. She stood watching him, staring blindly, anger washing in icy waves through her.

And something else. Something she wouldn't think about.

Wouldn't.

For the rest of the evening her stomach churned, as if she had swallowed live worms. It was a horrible feeling.

There was only one source of relief. Diego Saez had left before the final act. Portia could only be grovellingly grateful—though her gratitude was severely curtailed by the fact that his absence only meant that Susie felt free to interrogate her thoroughly in low, excited tones, all the way out to the taxi at the end of the opera.

'Portia!' Susie gripped her arm. 'He's gorgeous! *So* sexy!' She spoke in a low voice, so her mother wouldn't hear. 'I'm going to phone you tomorrow and you've got to tell me *all* about him!'

Portia eyed her balefully. 'There is nothing to tell. Susie, please don't make anything out of this. I don't intend to have anything to do with the man.'

Her friend stared at her.

'You're mad,' she said roundly. 'Completely loopy.

Anyway—' she glanced sideways at Portia '—I don't think it's really going to matter what you intend or not. He doesn't look like a man who's used to being turned down.'

'Well, he'd better *start* getting used to it!' Portia snapped.

CHAPTER THREE

HE WAS haunting her. There was no other word for it.

No, that was wrong. Diego Saez was *hunting* her.

Portia had never felt strongly one way or the other about blood sports. She'd grown up with them, as part of country life, but, being arty rather than horsy, had never hunted.

But now, for the first time in her life, she knew what it felt like to be a hunter's quarry.

Diego Saez was relentless. He had her in his sights and he intended to bring her down. Other men had pursued her in her time, but none like this. Others she had frozen off and eventually they'd given up. Anyway, since Geoffrey she'd stuck to totally safe men, like Simon and a couple of Tom's friends, if she ever needed an escort anywhere or simply a partner for a dinner party and so on. But she made sure it was understood by any man who accompanied her that sex was not on the menu.

When it came to Diego Saez it was perfectly, glaringly obvious that sex was the only thing on the menu. A man like that wasn't going to exercise the slightest self-restraint.

She pressed her lips together. Why the hell couldn't he go and get sex from someone else, in that case? Good grief, it hadn't taken her long to be informed by a blatantly fascinated Susie that most women were only too keen to get his attention in that way. Not only was he *fabulously* rich, and *exotically* South American, he also, Susie confided avidly, when she turned up the next day to drag Portia out to lunch, had a reputation for flaunting one fantastic-looking female after another.

'Bully for him,' Portia answered tartly.

'You should be flattered he's keen on you,' Susie reprimanded her reproachfully. 'I mean, compared with Simon Masters the man is just sex on legs! He's as rich as anything, and I mean, *look* at him! Simon's totally wet in comparison!'

'Simon's very sweet!' Portia retorted.

Susie groaned derisively. 'Oh, *sweet*—you don't want *sweet* in bed. You want someone like Diego Saez. He just *drips* sex!' She gave a delicious shiver. 'God, Portia, even you must feel it!'

Portia speared a green bean viciously on her plate. Feel it?

Her fingers gripped her fork. Oh, yes, she felt it all right. She felt those hooded eyes on her, appraising her—waiting for her.

Waiting for her to give in to him. To let those long, skilful fingers brush across her bare skin, as they had already done so devastatingly last night at the opera. He had touched her for only a few moments, but it had been enough—enough to make her realise how very, very dangerous Diego Saez was to her.

Her anger at his insolence—touching her, *daring* to ask her if she was frigid. Daring to make such a personal, intimate comment to her—had been a relief.

A refuge.

She worked hard to keep her anger at him going. She had to. Had to keep it as her primary response to him when she encountered him—yet again—wherever she seemed to go.

Suddenly, out of nowhere, it seemed, Diego Saez had developed an interest in being an art patron. The London art world was delighted—Diego Saez was too rich for them not to be eager for his interest.

She started seeing him everywhere—at private views, art auctions, sponsors' events and even, worst of all, at private parties. To find him intruding into her own social circuit appalled her, but how could she tell a hostess that if her latest guest was the rich and magnetically attractive South

American financier Diego Saez then she, Portia Lanchester, unspectacular art historian, would decline the invitation?

It didn't matter that he never invited her out again, never even singled her out for conversation. He was just there—everywhere. She couldn't escape him.

He was like a hair shirt, she thought. Her own personal hair shirt—mortifying her flesh. Making her, with every amused, taunting glance, punishingly aware of her own physicality. His considering appraisal of her—never overt enough to draw the attention of others, but always there, never turned off, even when he wasn't looking directly at her—made her hypersensitive to her own body. She saw the graceful twist of her wrists as she ate, felt the movement of her head on her slender neck as she turned to talk to someone, felt the brush of her dress against her breasts, the press of her thighs, one against the other…

It was a constant torment, making her feel like this.

How could he do this to her? How could he make her so aware of herself? And worse, much worse, aware of him?

Aware of the way his dark, knowing, heavy-lidded eyes would rest on her, aware of the strong width of his shoulders, the lean, hard-packed lines of his body. The sensual twist of his mouth.

She'd never been so aware of a man in her life. And she didn't want to be aware of him—didn't want to feel this panicky, jittery rushing of blood through her veins whenever she saw him, didn't want to feel the heat flushing through her skin when she realised he was, yet again, looking at her.

Why couldn't she control her reaction to him? Why—she shut her eyes in despair—was she reacting to him in the first place?

He was the *last* kind of man she should want to have any interest in! Too rich, too arrogant, too blatant, too—too everything. She hated that type! The type that thought

they owned the world and could help themselves to anything in it.

Including all the women they wanted.

And she knew exactly how long he'd keep a woman—
a handful of weeks, a month or two at the most. During
their brief affair his mistress would be seen everywhere
with him, at one glittering event after another, his 'constant
companion' as the coy vulgarity of the tabloids loved to
put it, and then, when he was bored—dumped. The end.
Nada.

And he'd be on to the next one.

She'd got a rundown from Susie—uninvited, but that
hadn't stopped her friend from telling her—on just how
many women he'd been seen around with in Europe and
America in the last year alone. There'd been an opera
singer, a model and a tennis ace, just for starters.

All of them had been glamorous, high-profile and aston-
ishingly beautiful women, with fantastic figures and dramatic personalities.

So why is he the slightest bit interested in *me*? Portia
thought bitterly.

Susie echoed her question, but from a quite different angle.

'Honestly, Portia, you should be flattered he's keen on
you! He can pick and choose, you know!'

'Well, let him pick and choose someone else, then!'
Portia replied tightly.

Susie looked at her.

'You know, it would do you good to let him have his
wicked way with you.'

Portia stared disbelievingly at her friend.

'What?'

'I mean it,' said Susie doggedly. 'You need a man,
Portia. You haven't been out with anyone since you and
Geoffrey split up.'

Portia's face had gone rigid. 'I've been out with Simon
Masters—'

Susie interrupted her ruthlessly. 'I mean a real man, not a wet rag! This Diego Saez would be ideal for you!'

'*Ideal?* Are you insane?'

'No, just realistic. Look, I know you were cut up over Geoffrey, but you can't just shut yourself away for the rest of your life. It's ridiculous! That's why someone like Diego Saez would be so good for you. Boy, would he get you cured!'

Portia's mouth tightened.

'Thank you—but I don't consider myself to be in need of a cure.'

'Just a good, *hard* man—excuse the expression, but it's true. Someone who'll sweep away all those inhibitions and let you rejoin the female sex!'

Portia turned on her icily.

'Believe me, Susie, *when* I "rejoin the female sex," as you so charmingly put it, it will *not* be with some ruthless Latin Lothario like Diego Saez!'

Susie was unrepentant.

'Why not?'

'Why not? Are you mad? Do you seriously think any intelligent woman would want to humiliate herself like that? Be the latest idiotic *floozy* for Diego Saez to amuse himself with, and then get dumped two weeks later when he goes on to his next glorious conquest? And have everyone laugh at her when he'd dumped her?'

She shuddered.

Susie just laughed. 'Oh, don't be so negative! Think of the fun you'd have for a fortnight. And anyway—who knows?—Diego Saez might fall headlong in love with your blonde English looks, sweep you off to his million-acre ranch in Argentina and keep you in polo ponies for the rest of your life!'

'Very amusing,' Portia answered humourlessly.

She could see no humour in the situation at all. Susie didn't know what it was like. She thought it would be *fun* to have someone like Diego Saez pursue you. Fun? *Fun* to have his dark, heavy-lidded eyes seek you out across a room, make you feel, suddenly and shamingly, as if you were in your underwear, or, worse, make you stall halfway through a sentence and find the breath tight in your throat. *Fun* to know that of all the men in the world none had *ever* made her react like this.

It was terrifying, mortifying.

She didn't *want* to react to a man like Diego Saez. So why, *why* did she have to be so punishingly, *stupidly* aware of him the whole time? Why couldn't she just ignore him?

She did her best. Did her best to put him off her.

If she couldn't avoid him—and it seemed she couldn't, so intrusive was he everywhere she went—then she could at least try and make herself as inconspicuous as possible. As undesirable.

She tried concealing her body. At the next private view she went to she wore a dress that had a high, Chinese-style collar, long sleeves down to the backs of her hands and a hem down to her ankle, with flat slippers that did not lift her hips.

When her tormentor arrived, fussed over by everyone there, he let his glance rest momentarily on Portia, who lifted her chin and looked right through him—but not sufficiently to miss the mocking twist of his mouth as he took in her suppressed appearance.

When the opportunity came he strolled across to her.

'Very erotic,' he murmured. 'You must wear it for me some time—privately.'

Then, before she could say a word, he strolled off again. A redhead, poured into a clinging emerald-green cocktail dress, seized his arm and pressed herself against him blatantly, making it clear how attractive she found him.

Portia glared after him, rigid with fury.

And something even worse.

The jittery, panicky feeling filled her again, and to her disgust she found that she was watching him, seeing how he smiled down at the redhead, who was rubbing up against him now, his mouth giving that sensual twist that disturbed her so much.

She felt that hot wire tug inside her, and forcibly turned her head away so she could not see him.

Why? she thought despairingly. Why was he getting to her like this?

Why couldn't he just clear out? Go back to Wall Street, Geneva, Buenos Aires—wherever he came from!

And leave her alone.

That was all she wanted. Just to be left alone.

She got some relief when Susie reported—reproachfully—that he had started being seen around with a well-known actress currently starring in a West End hit.

'Good,' said Portia tightly.

She took the opportunity to get out of London herself. She'd already taken two days out to visit Yorkshire, in search of the elusive Miss Maria Colding. Now she booked a flight to Geneva. She wanted to check out a painting sold thirty years ago to a wealthy Swiss, listed only as 'School of Teller'—with luck it would prove to be by Teller himself.

She mentioned her plans to Tom that evening. They shared a house in Kensington, which had been divided into two generous flats, with a guest flat in the basement. The arrangement suited them both—it gave them enough privacy, but each other's company when they wanted it.

Tom seemed to be over the flu, but he looked haggard and heavy-eyed, and definitely not firing on all cylinders. Portia frowned, feeling guilty. The last thing she wanted to do was to complain to her brother that she was being pursued by Diego Saez. Tom might feel he had to impose some kind of brotherly protection around her, and, little as she knew the world of high finance, she had nous enough to realise that for Tom to be on bad terms with a man like Diego Saez was not a good idea.

'You need a break,' she told him. 'Can't you get away

from the bank and go down to Salton for a while? It would do you good. You know you hate London.'

'I can't get away right now,' her brother answered shortly.

She looked at him. Everything about Loring Lanchester bored her stupid, but poor Tom had to deal with it, like it or not. As the son and heir, he'd had no option but to step into his father's shoes. She, a mere daughter, had been free to follow her own consuming interest—the history of art.

'Is everything all right?' she asked suddenly. 'I mean at the bank.'

Tom's grey eyes shifted away. 'Just the general economic downturn, that's all. It's hitting everyone.'

Not Diego Saez, she thought acidly. The man had just bid a record sum for a Dutch still-life at auction. It had left everyone gasping.

But she wasn't going to think about Diego Saez any more than she had to.

'Well, don't work too hard anyway,' she told her brother. 'Do you want me to invite Felicity to stay for a while? She'd cheer you up! You know, you really ought to get on with things and fix a wedding date. What on earth's keeping you?'

Tom's expression changed. 'There's no rush, you know. And anyway...' He paused, then went on, 'Maybe we're not right for each other.'

Portia stared. 'Not right? I've never seen two people more right for each other! Felicity's crazy about you—and I should know, it's me she confides in whenever I'm down at Salton.' She frowned suddenly. 'Don't tell me you've gone off her, Tom?'

He looked uncomfortable. 'I'm...very fond...of Fliss, but—well, she could probably do a lot better than marry me, you know! Rupert Bellingham would marry her like a shot!'

'Yes, but she's not in love with Rupert Bellingham— she's in love with you!'

'She'd be a lot better off marrying him,' Tom said doggedly. 'And he's got a handle!'

'Felicity doesn't want to be Lady Bellingham—she wants to be Mrs Lanchester. So I simply don't see why you don't agree a wedding date and get on with it!'

Tom looked hunted suddenly. 'For God's sake, stop nagging me!' he bit out.

She stared, both astonished and shocked. Tom never lost his temper at her, or indeed anyone. He saw her expression and looked apologetic.

'I'm sorry—it's just that—well, like I said, there's a lot on my plate at the moment at the bank.'

She was immediately sympathetic—and indignant. 'You really ought to get Uncle Martin to pull his weight more. He *is* still the chairman after all—and he makes such a *point* of it. He shouldn't leave everything to you.'

Tom made no reply, just looked tireder. Not wanting to plague him any longer, let alone about the inertia of their late father's friend and partner Martin Loring, she simply bade him goodnight and went off up to her own flat.

The trip to Geneva proved to be a waste of time. The painting was, indeed, nothing more than a work from Teller's studio.

Her mood when she returned was not good, and what she wanted to do was stay in that evening, have a long bath and an early night. But she had promised Hugh Mackerras she would go with him to a select reception to launch a new exhibition at one of the prestigious private London art galleries, and, knowing that he valued her for her social contacts, she felt obliged not to let him down.

Would Diego Saez be there that evening? she wondered. Surely to God he ought to be leaving London by now, instead of tormenting her!

But in case he hadn't, in case he was still haunting London and the art world, she dressed with particular care that evening. She did not make the mistake of wearing that

over-concealing outfit again, but she did, all the same, select her attire deliberately. This time she wore a heather-
coloured cocktail dress that she had realised was a mistake
the moment she'd got it home. It had languished in a corner
of her wardrobe ever since. The colour made her look
washed out, and the cap sleeves cut her upper arm at just
the wrong point.

But it made her feel safe.

Hearing her cab at the door, she set off.

The gallery was in a large, double-fronted Georgian man-
sion a street or so back from Piccadilly, and the rooms
where the reception was being held were already crowded
with familiar faces. Portia's progress towards Hugh on the
far side of the room was inevitably slow as she was caught
up in greeting and being greeted along the way. Her eyes
rapidly scanned the space for the man she did *not* wish to
see there, and to her relief she caught no sight of his tall,
broad-shouldered, olive-skinned frame. She started to relax,
paused to engage in some social chit-chat with a female
acquaintance, smiled politely after the requisite length of
time, and turned to continue on towards Hugh.

And realised that Diego Saez was standing right beside
him.

Immediately, without her volition, she felt that wire tugging through her, felt that jittery, panicky feeling jump inside her. She could feel her heart-rate increasing, her lungs
tightening.

Desperately she fought to regain control of her reactions,
subdue them, force them down below the cool, composed
surface she liked to present to the world.

It was so obvious that she'd been heading for Hugh that
she could hardly change course now. As for latching on to
someone else to talk to until the danger was over and Diego
Saez had moved on—suddenly there was no one else within
chatting distance. With a fateful feeling of helplessness, she
bowed to the inevitable and continued to head towards Hugh.

Deliberately she did not look at the man with him.

But she had to fight herself to stop herself doing so. Something inside her made her *want* to look, made her want to let her eyes go to him, see those dark, heavy-lidded eyes, that strong nose, the high-cut cheekbones and that sensual mouth that so disturbed her...

Her feet reached Hugh. He greeted her in his customary fashion and then immediately said, 'Mr Saez was expressing an interest in Regency portraiture. I told him you were something of a specialist.'

She lifted her chin, realising she would have to look at Diego Saez because social convention demanded she did not cut him, as she longed to do.

Nevertheless, it took a distinct effort to keep her voice cool as she made her reply.

'Hardly. Benjamin Teller, in whom I specialise, was a very minor artist in comparison with the likes of Lawrence and Romney.'

She took refuge in prosing on, trying hard to look at a point somewhere over Diego Saez's tall shoulder.

'Is he increasing in value?'

The deep, accented tone of his voice jarred through her. So did his question. Typical of a financier, she thought acidly.

'For someone of your means, Mr Saez, Benjamin Teller is nothing more than small fry. Quite off your radar.'

She could see that her offhand reply had both taken Hugh aback and displeased him.

'Teller would be an astute investment,' he contributed smoothly. 'He's considerably under-appreciated, I believe.'

A caustic look lit Portia's eye. 'You sound like a dealer, Hugh,' she said dryly. She turned back to Diego Saez, who had singled her out to torment her with his disturbing attention. 'Dealers,' she said, with malicious lightness. 'They see art only in pound signs—or dollars or euros. As do investment buyers, of course.' She smiled pointedly. 'As worth nothing but money.'

She looked right into her tormentor's face.

A strange, measuring look entered his eye. And something more.

Dangerous—

She put the thought aside. Ridiculous! Of course Diego Saez wasn't dangerous. He was just an over-rich, sexually spoilt man who wanted to take her to bed simply because she'd made it perfectly obvious she did not want him to!

'You consider money something of little value, then, Miss Lanchester?'

The deep voice was probing.

'In comparison with art, yes,' she answered tartly.

He smiled. Deep lines indented around his mouth. She felt something tug at her internally. Then, as he spoke, she noticed that the expression in his eyes did not match the one on his face.

'But then you have never been without money, have you? Or, indeed—' there was a sardonic tone to his voice '—without art. I notice that at least two of the paintings in this exhibition are on loan from your family.'

She ignored both the tug that had come again inside her, and the tone of his voice, merely glad that the subject was still the relatively safe one of British landscape paintings. If she *had* to have a conversation with Diego Saez at least let it be about something that innocuous.

'Yes—my brother has loaned a Gainsborough and a Robert Wilson.'

'Show me.'

There was a command in his voice that put her back up automatically. But before she could reply his hand had come around her elbow, and with a brief, dismissive smile at Hugh he started to lead her away.

Her stomach clenched, and she had to force herself not to jerk away from his hold on her. As if he knew it, and it amused him, he merely continued to lead her inexorably away from Hugh.

She wanted to make a fuss, detach herself instantly, but

knew that she could not. Not here. Had it been any other
man who had commandeered her like that she might have
made the attempt, but something about Diego Saez told her
that he would not be easily dislodged. Schooling her expression, she let him guide her away, wishing that the touch
of his hand on her bare elbow was not making the tugging
feeling in her insides ten times worse.

'The Wilson is through here,' she said, in a voice sounding as uninterested in what was happening to her as she
could make it. She'd checked the catalogue earlier on, to
see where the two paintings had been hung.

'I'd prefer to see the Gainsborough,' Diego Saez replied,
and altered direction, his frame leaning very slightly into
her path to make her change course. Not wanting the
slightest contact with him, she moved instantly.

On top of everything else that was wracking her nerves
by this wretched encounter, she was conscious of a reluctance to show him the Gainsborough. It was of Salton, and
suddenly—she could not tell why—she did not want him
seeing it. It was too…intrusive.

But short of making an unacceptable scene she had no
option. Stiffly she walked beside him to gain the room
where this section of Gainsboroughs was hanging.

'Which is yours?'

'My brother's,' corrected Portia. 'Over there on the far
wall, third from the left.'

He walked towards it, dropping her elbow. She followed
beside him.

He stopped a few feet from the painting and stood looking at it.

Portia gazed too, and felt a familiar emotion well through
her. It was so powerful that it even, for a moment, blanked
out the disturbing presence of the man beside her.

She gazed in familiar pleasure at the painting, which usually hung in their entrance hall at Salton.

Very little had changed since one of the greatest artists
in the English canon had captured the likeness of Salton's

honey-coloured South façade. Some of the trees framing the lake from where the view had been taken were now gone, and some were far mightier than the saplings they had been two hundred years ago and more. There were more flowerbeds now, and her great-great grandfather had planted an azalea arboretum to the east of the house a hundred years ago, but otherwise she felt she might as well step straight into the picture for all the difference the intervening centuries had made.

She felt her expression soften. Though she would never live at Salton she had grown up there, and it was as beloved to her as her brother was. As for Tom—he *was* Salton. It was his home, and the place he belonged to. He held it in trust for his son to come, and for his grandson. For future generations of Lanchesters, just as past generations had held it in trust for Tom. An uninterrupted inheritance for over four centuries.

A voice beside her spoke.

'Is it for sale?'

Her head swung round. She was totally taken aback.

'Of course not!' There was shock in her voice. 'And nor is the Wilson!' she added, before he could ask about that, too. 'This is an exhibition of paintings for public view, a temporary exhibition gathered together from museums and private collections around the world, Mr Saez—it is not a saleroom!'

'I was not referring to the paintings. I mean the house—Salton.'

The sardonic look was back in his face, but she ignored it. She was simply staring at him in total disbelief.

'Salton?'

'Yes.'

She took a deep breath. 'Mr Saez, I appreciate that not being English, or indeed European, you may not understand that country houses traditionally continue within the same family unless adverse circumstances dictate otherwise. In the mid-twentieth century, for example, there was a great selling off of country estates for that reason, and many of those now do change hands fairly regularly—I'm sure any of the country house specialist property agencies could help you if you are interested in buying an estate in this country,' she finished quellingly.

'Thank you for the information, Miss Lanchester.' The deep voice sounded even more sardonic, and she felt a flush go through her. 'However, the concept of ancestral property is not unknown in South America—nor are the sentiments that accompany that concept.'

There was a bite in his voice that she could not fail to detect.

She felt colour flare in her cheekbones. Of course a man of his background—the South American megaplutocracy—would know all about vast inherited estates! But she ignored it. 'In which case I can only be astonished that you thought to ask such an extraordinary question!'

'Extraordinary?' There was suddenly a flat note in Diego Saez's voice. 'You yourself concede that "adverse circumstances" can make selling an attractive proposition.'

She went on staring at him.

'There are no "adverse circumstances" surrounding Salton, Mr Saez,' she bit out. 'And therefore no possibility whatsoever that it will ever come on to the market! It is not for sale, nor will it be—please disabuse yourself of that idea!'

Something showed in his eyes, and was veiled. Then, with a twist of his mouth, he said 'Everything is for sale, Portia. *Everything*. Don't you know that yet?'

There was mockery in his voice now, an open taunt. And more—derision.

She felt for a moment as if something had crawled over her flesh.

Then, recovering, she lifted her chin.

'In your world, perhaps, Mr Saez. But not in mine!'

There was something strange in his eyes.

'Do you think not?' He paused. 'Are you really the innocent you look?' The expression in his eyes changed, and suddenly Portia felt that hot wire drawing through her again. 'You look so extraordinarily *untouched*—and yet I'm told you were engaged for nearly two years.'

His hand reached out, the backs of his fingers drawing down the side of her throat, her jaw. She could not breathe. Could only feel the hammering of her heart. She wanted to move, but she could not—*could not*.

CHAPTER FOUR

WITHOUT her realising, without her even being aware of it, he had moved in on her. His body was closer to hers now, shielding her from the doorway on the far side of the room that led back to the reception. There was no one else here, it was just the two of them. She could inhale the scent of him, that mix of masculinity and expensive, exclusive aftershave. She could feel the heat of his body—and the heat of her own, as her skin flushed.

'Don't—' Her voice came on a faint breath. The panicky, jittery feeling was shivering through her, her breath was shallow.

'Don't? Is that what you told your fiancé?'

There was mockery as well as questioning in his voice. And taunting too—she could hear that loud and clear.

She could feel his breath fanning her face, hear the husk in his voice. 'They tell me you're cold, Portia, as cold as the snow. But you're not—I can feel it—here...'

His fingers pressed lightly, oh, so lightly, against the pulse in her throat. It leapt at his touch, flushing blood through her already heated veins. She was gazing up at him, eyes dilating.

Watching, breathless, helpless, as his mouth descended. 'I can feel it here,' he murmured, and his mouth took hers.

It moved with slow, leisurely movement across her lips, as his fingers splayed out across her throat, imprisoning her.

Blood drummed through her, blood and faintness and a sensation so blissful she wanted it to go on and on, as his mouth moved on hers.

It was a different world, another universe. Never, ever,

had any man kissed her like this. She didn't like being kissed much—even by those few men she had liked enough to let them do what they had so evidently wanted to do, even though she'd wished they hadn't, had wished they'd been content, as she had been, with a comfortable brush of the lips—swift and soon over and done with.

This kiss was neither.

It was cool—with possession, with casual tasting, with an assumption of intimacy, of pleasure, that dissolved the very bones in her body.

He let her go, lifting his mouth from hers, slipping his fingers from her skin, and she stood there, swaying, blinded, dazed.

'Fools,' he mocked. 'To call you cold...' He touched along her parted lips with the tips of his fingers. 'At my touch, for me, you are not cold...'

He dropped his hands away from her face to her bare upper arms and put her away from him. She would have stumbled but for his hold, steadying her. He stood looking down at her a moment, his hands still around her arms, surveying her.

His eyes lit with amusement—and more—as he looked at her unflattering attire.

'Did you really think that you could disguise your beauty in a dress like that?' His voice dropped, 'Do you think that you can run from me? It's time,' he said softly, and something in his voice sent shivers down her spine. 'Time to stop running, Portia. It has been amusing, but...' His voice changed again, becoming nothing more than its familiar accented timbre. 'Now...' His left hand slipped down to cup her elbow and he let go of her other arm, steering her from the room. 'We had better return to the reception or our absence will draw comments.'

The heat in her skin flared, and she realised suddenly, horribly, just what had happened. Diego Saez had kissed her. A man who represented *everything* that she hated most—the kind of man who treated a woman like a conquest and herself as his quarry. Stomach churning, she stalked at his side, back into the crowded reception. Her breath was coming and going sharply in her throat and she had to fight down her emotions, slam the lid of social conduct down tightly upon them—and make her escape as soon as she could do so.

Emotions chewed through her. Outrage at what he had just done so supremely casually, helping himself to her as if she were a fresh, ripe peach on a market stall! But worse, far worse that the stinging outrage, was the melting, dissolving weakness that was still echoing through her body, a physical memory of what she had just experienced.

Then, overlaying both, a new emotion thrust up into her. Blind panic.

A sense of danger pressed down upon her, so intense it was almost frightening.

But she could not get away. As if sensing her feelings, Diego Saez merely strengthened his hold on her elbow, walking her through the reception, pausing as he went to exchange social chit-chat with others as they passed.

And as they made their uneven progress Portia, through the emotions panicking her, became aware of yet something else.

People were looking at her. She could see it in their eyes—speculation, some covert, some blatant, over her presence at Diego Saez's side.

And she realised with a horrible, hollowing sense of horror that finally he was making his move on her. He was not going to let her evade him any longer.

She heard his words in her head, terrifying her.

Time to stop running...

But she *had* to run—had to get him to leave her alone! To accept that however many other women were stupid enough to fall into his bed for a month or two, she would not be among them!

However much he calmly intended to have her.

Diego Saez, hand still at her elbow, holding her at his

side, was proclaiming to all the world that she was the woman he wanted—and was sublimely confident of getting.

Feeling as if she were some kind of conquered slave, trailing along with the triumphant Roman general, she could do nothing except let herself be steered through the room. Her lips were smiling, as if in a rictus, her voice was murmuring the required niceties, and all the time she was feeling the heat flushing through her like a ghastly wave machine, over and over and over again.

Heat and memory—memory of that kiss...

He did not move from her side—nor let her leave. As if in some kind of nightmare she had to talk, and smile, and endure the worst ordeal of all—the knowing looks, the pointed remarks, that Diego Saez's constant presence at her side inevitably drew. She ignored them doggedly, desperately, calling on all her reserves of self-control to get her through to the end.

But was it going to end? After what seemed a perpetual eternity it came to her, with a new wave of horror, that they were progressing slowly but surely towards the exit. And then, through the blankness in her head, she heard that deep, accented voice saying to whoever he was speaking to at the time, 'Another evening, perhaps. Tonight I have a prior engagement.'

He glanced down at her, and whoever it was gave a knowing laugh and moved away. And then one of the gallery staff was there, proffering her jacket, and the man at her side was slipping it on her, his hands drawing it up over her shoulders. Her face and her body were as stiff as board as, making smooth, bland farewells, Diego ushered her out on to the pavement.

She was like a zombie, without will or volition of her own. Diego Saez had taken her over.

Her heart slugged in her chest, panic prickling all through her body, as she climbed into the waiting car, where a chauffeur was holding open the door, and Diego Saez folded his long, lean body in after her.

This can't be happening, she thought. *It can't!*

She sat ramrod-straight in her seat, staring doggedly in front of her through the dividing glass at the back of the chauffeur's head as he took his place, pulling the limo out into the street.

She wanted to scream, to shout, to leap from the car. But she could do none of those things. Something had taken control of her—something more powerful than she had ever felt in her life before.

Of their own volition—certainly not with her conscious will—she felt her head turn, her eyes rest on the tall, dark figure sitting beside her in the far corner of the wide rear seat of the limo. His long legs were stretched out.

He smiled. A slow, sensual smile.

'Well, Portia—here we are. Alone at last.'

His mocking tone sent shivers through her.

From somewhere deep inside she found the strength to speak.

'I would be much obliged, Mr Saez, if you would please drop me off at the next taxi rank or Underground station. I have no intention of spending any further time with you.'

She wanted her voice to sound arctic—but it merely trembled.

His presence overpowered her. It was like a physical weight—touching her, crushing the breath from her lungs.

'We're going to dinner,' he replied, his casual indifference to her rigidly civil request galling her. 'I've reserved a table at Claridge's.'

Her eyes flashed in disbelief at what he had just said. Outrage soared up over the panicky feeling that was flushing through her.

'Then you may *un*-reserve it, Mr Saez. I am not dining with you!'

Looking him in the eye had been a mistake. As she met that heavy-lidded gaze, resting on her, a feeling of hot, molten lava started to flow viscously through her veins.

Confusion churned in her.

What's happening to me? Why is he doing this? How is he doing this? I don't want him, I don't like him, I want to get out of the car and run, and run and run...

Danger pressed all around her. It was tangible—a dark, disturbing presence.

And more than danger.

Something she would not give a name to. Something that had leapt in her throat as she let his dark, dissolving gaze hold her.

He reached a hand out to her. Lightly—casually—devastatingly—he drew the backs of his fingers along her cheek.

She jerked away as if a thousand volts had just gone through her.

'Don't touch me!'

There was panic in her voice.

Long lashes swept down over his eyes.

'But you want me to touch you, Portia. And I want to touch you. Very much...'

He leant towards her. She could do nothing. Not even shrink back into the corner of her seat.

Her eyes fluttered shut.

His mouth moved on hers, long fingers tilting up her face to his. That slow, dissolving lava was molten in her veins, her body.

She tried to summon outrage, tried to want to push him away, shout at him—slap his face!

But she could not. She could only sit there, her body dissolving, at his touch.

I don't let men do this. But Diego Saez, who only wanted to amuse himself with her for a bare handful of weeks, she let him. Let him help himself—shamingly, humiliatingly, *totally*, to her mouth...

He pulled away and dimly, very dimly, she became aware that the car had stopped.

He drew a finger across her swollen lips. Her body was trembling. His eyes were dark, so dark.

'Tonight, Portia, it begins.'

He smiled at her. A long, sensual smile.

Absolutely confident.

Supremely expectant.

It was the smile that did it. Broke through the dissolving, weakening paralysis that was holding her in a helpless thrall. As if surfacing from a deep, drowning wave, she felt a new emotion surge through her. Virulent. Overpowering.

She was icy with rage.

Rage at Diego Saez for daring, *daring* to do that to her. For helping himself to her as if he had every right to do so, as if all he had to do was simply reach out and *sample* her...

And she had let him. Had let him do exactly that. Had offered no resistance—none—as he had made free with her as no man had ever done. And for a man like Diego Saez to do that to her—arrogant and spoilt by legions of women drooling over him, a hedonistic sensualist for whom women were an appetite, an indulgence. Everything, *everything* she despised in a man.

Good God, if she hadn't liked Geoffrey kissing her, touching her—a man she'd respected, liked...loved...how could she bear to have someone like Diego Saez kiss her...touch her...?

But she *had* let him kiss her. Touch her. Had let him walk off with her in front of everyone, signalling to the whole world what his intentions to her were. Portia Lanchester—ice-cold Portia Lanchester—was about to feel the heat...

About to be Diego Saez's next amusement.

The icy rage shot through her again. But this time it had a different target.

Herself.

Fear shivered through her. Somewhere deep inside, in a part of her she had never known existed but which, now she did, terrified her, she knew that Diego Saez could exert a power over her that she had never imagined.

With every ounce of her being she fought it. Rejected it.

Shame flooded through her. That of all the men in the world it should be a man like Diego Saez who could reduce her to such a condition.

She felt the rage against herself, her own weakness, her own folly, as ice in her veins. She clung to it. It was her saviour, her one chance of escaping with her skin whole. Because if she stayed…

She flung open the door of the car and climbed out. The chauffeur was still getting out of the driver's seat, but she didn't wait. She stood on the pavement, rigid with lashing fury. She had to keep angry—she *had* to!

Diego Saez got out and said something to the chauffeur. He nodded and got back into the limo. It began to pull away from the kerb.

'Come,' said the man at her side, and slid his hand under her elbow.

She jerked away violently. She was trembling with emotion that this arrogant man was simply assuming that she would fall into his bed like a ripe peach, just because he wanted her to.

'Take your hand off me!' Her voice was loaded with anger as she stepped back.

The rest of the world had disappeared. Somewhere in her mind she realised she was standing in Brook Street, outside Claridge's. There was a doorman not three feet away, and several other people disgorging from a taxi.

She had to get away.

Urgency overwhelmed her, overriding everything else. She started to walk away, heading past the hotel façade towards the traffic lights on the corner. Her heels clicked on the damp pavement. Her breathing was short. Heart pounding in a horrible, sick fashion. There was pressure inside her head.

She started to walk faster.

There were footsteps behind her. Rapid, heavy.

A hand clamped around her shoulder, halting her. Turning her around.

'Portia—'

His voice sounded impatient. There was a dark look in his eye. His prey was escaping, walking out on him. Diego Saez's prey for the night was daring to walk out on him...

Something, it might have been hysteria, started to climb in her throat. She crushed it down.

'Leave me alone!' she snapped at him, trying to jerk herself loose.

But this time it did not work. His fingers bit into her.

Panic stabbed at her. He wasn't letting her go. He was holding on to her. Touching her...

'How dare you manhandle me?' The words cut from her, clipped and furious. 'How dare you touch me? You *disgust* me!' A sharp, searing breath sliced through her throat and her chin flew up. He was standing there so tall, overpoweringly so. He seemed to loom over her. His face, as she threw her angry words at him, darkened. She didn't care. Didn't care that she was making a scene right outside Claridge's. Didn't care that she was finally venting that terrifying surge of emotion he aroused in her.

She stepped back. 'Did you think—did you really think—' her voice was icy with scorn '—that you could just *help yourself* to me?' Her eyes were cold grey pinpricks, flashing disdain, disgust. Outrage. 'Do you really think that I would even *consider* having an affair with *you*? Of *all* people? A man with *your* history? *Your* reputation? *Your* past? Do you really think I would *demean* myself with a man like *you*? Do you think your *money* makes you acceptable?'

Something changed in his eyes. Something that just for a second sent a shaft of fear through her. And then, like a metal gate slicing down, it was gone. His face was like a mask. Completely expressionless.

Her breath was coming in sharp, painful jags, like ice in

her lungs. Her chin had flown up, her hands clutching her open jacket across her, her shoulders rigid, eyes arctic with rejection.

He was standing quite still, she realised. Completely motionless. But it was the stillness of a jaguar poised in a jungle clearing, every muscle under complete, absolute control.

The still before the kill.

Fear stabbed through her again, countering the icy rage that still consumed her, which itself was forcing down yet another emotion—one that she could not cope with, could not admit or acknowledge or allow.

With one part of her mind she knew she had behaved disgracefully, lowering herself to speak in such a way to him—but she had had no choice. None. She *had* to protect herself from him—any way she could.

He was just so, so dangerous…he made her feel out of control.

He spoke. His voice was without emotion.

'In which case, if those are your sentiments, I will bid you goodnight.'

He turned on his heel and walked into the hotel. His pace was neither hurried nor slow.

He was gone.

Alone on the pavement in the chill spring night, Portia stood, face frozen, everything frozen.

Slowly, jerkily, she started to walk.

Diego Saez strode down the black and white squared hallway, away from the hotel lobby towards the bar. He walked in and up to the bar. The barman took one look at him and was there instantly.

'Whisky.'

There was a nerve working in his cheek.

A single malt was soon in front of him and he lifted the glass and knocked it back in one.

An image burned in his head.

Not of Portia Lanchester.

Another woman.

Chic, immaculately dressed, with inky blue hair coiled like a snake at the back of her head. Her lips were very red.

Her eyes were black, as black as sin. Nothing like the cool, cutting grey of Portia Lanchester.

But the expression in them was the same.

Disdain. Revulsion. Horror.

He heard the voice in his head again.

'*You?* The son of Carmita? It isn't possible!'

A stream of Spanish had followed. Foul, insulting, vicious. Her heavily beringed hand, flashing with diamonds and emeralds, had flown up, pointing dramatically to the door.

'Get out! Get out or I'll have you thrown out!'

Above everything from that scene, everything he remembered in coruscating detail, it was that—the absolute disbelief in Mercedes de Carvello's voice. She had been completely, totally unable to believe that the son of her maid had returned—through her own front door, walking into her drawing room—and told her that he now owned the *estancia*.

It had been the sweetest moment of his life.

And the most bitter.

For it had come too late for the two people for whom he had bought the *estancia*. His father—dead for fifteen years of a cancer caused by the carcinogenic agents knowingly used on the *estancia*'s banana plantations—and his mother, fatally knocked down on the *estancia* drive by Mercedes herself in her sports car, which she'd been driving at eighty miles an hour with a bottle of champagne inside her.

And that bitterness had made him stand there while Mercedes de Carvello, who had treated each and every one of the myriad staff who'd served her like the dirt she'd thought them, had tried to throw him from the house he had once never even been allowed to enter. But now, thanks to his own punishingly hard escape from the poverty he'd been born to, and thanks to the stupid, reckless extravagance of her dead husband Esteban de Carvello, he owned it—every last inch of it—and the vast estate that went with it.

His to do with as he liked. Whatever he liked.

A place Mercedes de Carvello no longer had any right to be.

Just as she had once told a twelve-year-old boy, his mown-down mother hardly cold in her grave, that he had no right to be there any more. She had thrown him off the estate, banning all the other workers from helping him. For he had dared, *dared* to call her a murderess to her face for killing his mother.

He had left, taking nothing with him—for he possessed nothing, she had told him—and had walked the long, weary miles, day after day, week after week, to the city, his feet bleeding, the flesh hanging from his bones, starving like so many other unwanted, surplus, valueless boys in his home country.

Taking with him nothing but the burning, punishing desire for justice.

A justice he had meted out those long, long years later, when he had ordered Mercedes de Carvello from the home she no longer possessed.

Slowly, very slowly, his eyes refocused. Came back to the present.

And saw another face—another image. Cool, blonde, English.

Filled with revulsion.

Disdain.

For him.

The barman had come back to his end of the bar. Diego pushed his empty whisky glass towards him.

'Another one,' he said.

His eyes were dark and shuttered. His face expressionless.

Silently the barman refilled his whisky glass.

CHAPTER FIVE

PORTIA stood by the sash window in the Morning Room, gazing out over the lawns. Splashed across the green, all the way down to the lake, daffodils nodded and danced in the breeze. Cloudlets scudded across the bright spring sky.

She gave a sigh of contentment. The Morning Room was one of her favourites at Salton—its delicate rosewood furniture with a slight sense of chinoiserie, the trellised, hand-blocked wallpaper, and, of course, the wonderful view down to the lake.

Slowly, as she stood gazing out over the sea of gold and green, a sense of peace, of safety, started to soothe along the edges of her torn, ragged nerves.

Here at Salton she would be safe.

She had driven down the very next day, leaving nothing but a terse phone message for Hugh to say she was catching up on some unused leave. Then she had set off, reaching Salton before lunch.

She had driven as if a devil were in pursuit.

And he is a devil, she thought. *Taunting me. Tempting me.*

She had not slept—had been tormented by dreams. Hot, disturbing dreams, where Diego Saez hunted her down a maze of corridors, pursuing her steadily, remorselessly, until he had her trapped...

Then he advanced on her. Pulled her into his arms.

Even now, standing here, gazing out over the timeless, peaceful view of the gardens, if she let her guard down for a moment, an instant, the memories were there, leaping into her mind, clutching at her.

I don't want him. I don't...

57

She repeated the mantra to herself, clinging to it.

It was insane that she should want Diego Saez. Insane to want a man like that.

She felt her breasts prickling beneath the cashmere of her sweater and turned away sharply.

No, she would *not* let herself be taken over like this. It was like an illness, that was all. A bug in her system. For some ludicrous, absurd, ridiculous reason Diego Saez, with his heavy-lidded eyes and his sensual mouth, had got past her defences. Defences she had erected painstakingly, doggedly, ever since she had realised so devastatingly that for her sex was a disaster—it left her cold. Untouchable.

In her mind, she heard Susie saying impatiently, 'Oh, for heaven's sake, Portia, Geoffrey was just wrong for you, that's all! That's why you didn't like sex with him. And *that's* why you need someone like Diego Saez! There isn't a woman alive who wouldn't enjoy sex with a man like him!'

For a hot and shameful instant she saw a vision of herself in a bedroom, with Diego Saez advancing on her. His hands were unknotting his tie, shrugging off his jacket. His eyes were focused on her, dark and knowing. And with one intention only…

She suddenly felt the sensual quickening of her own body. Then, like a lid slamming down, she regained control.

She would go for a walk. Out in the grounds. Round the lake. Pick some daffodils. Arrange some flowers in the afternoon. Have tea in the library.

Feel safe.

Be safe.

Resolutely, she walked out of the room.

The long, blowy walk did her good. She always went for a good long walk when she came down to Salton, whatever the weather or the time of year. It was a ritual, so that she could find the peace she knew she would always find here.

Even now.

She had not put Diego Saez out of her mind completely.

That was impossible. What he had done to her was so devastating, so frightening, that it would take a long, long time to get over it. He had broken through her defences and destroyed her peace of mind. How he had done it she still did not know.

And that made it even more frightening.

But here at Salton she was safe. Here she would find her peace of mind again. Here she would find the balm that she needed. Her safe, familiar world.

And so very precious to her.

Even more so to Tom.

But then Salton *was* the Lanchester family. Had been for generations and generations. She could not even begin to imagine not being part of Salton—Salton not being part of her, part of her family. It was a sentiment, she knew, that those who did not have the privilege—and it was a privilege, she was supremely conscious of that—of being so inextricably linked with a house, a place, found it difficult to understand. It was not a question of wealth—a Welsh hill farmer struggling desperately to survive against the hardships of the modern agricultural economy would feel just as passionate about the land he farmed, the land he owned. That sense of kinship, devotion, to a particular piece of the earth, for which no other place, however beautiful, could substitute, a kinship earned through time, hundreds of years, was something that was hard to understand if it had not been experienced.

She experienced it again now, as she experienced it every time, as she tramped in gum boots down across the lawns, around the lake, through the woods and across several fields to come back up to the house by way of the azalea arboretum. She made a swathe through the sea of daffodils again, gathering them up in a bountiful armful and going on to add sufficient greenery from the shrubbery plantings around the edge of the lawn.

By the time she came back indoors she was pleasantly tired—and spiritually refreshed. Her instinct to fly to Salton had been the right one. Here, she knew, she would find the peace of mind that had been ripped from her.

Here she would forget that face with the heavy-lidded, darkly knowing eyes, and the mocking, sensual mouth.

Here, Diego Saez could not endanger her.

She laid down her bounty of daffodils and greenery on the cool marble surface beside the old stone sink, and spent a happy hour arranging flowers in the flower room. It was a soothing occupation, and the sweet, fresh scent of the daffodils was familiar, her fingers working so deftly, that the time flew by.

It flew by for the next three days. Three days in which she succumbed to the peaceful, familiar, uneventful rhythm of life at Salton. She did not go out, did not even phone round her acquaintances to let them know she was there. She didn't want to socialise. All she wanted to do was stay safe at Salton.

She was not bored. She was never bored at Salton. Although Tom had a professional estate manager to look after the farms, the house and grounds were under his direct remit. And until he married she was, in effect, mistress of the house. While they were in London the Tillets, the couple who kept Salton running on oiled wheels, either phoned or faxed to stay in touch as necessary, but the moment she or Tom appeared in person they were always pounced on.

Now Mrs Tillet, the housekeeper, had a hundred things to check with her, that had cropped up since her last visit, from a spot of damp noticed in one of the upper bedrooms, to whether or not the sun-faded curtains in the music room needed to be relined yet. Outdoors, Fred Hermitage, the head gardener, needed decisions on a hundred more items on his list, from repainting the interior of the orangery to replanting the herbaceous border below the west terrace. And within the community there were regular matters to attend to.

With the summer coming, the list of Salton's regular open days needed to be decided, and that required her to liaise with the vicar's wife as to what the parish committee would prefer and which charities they would like proceeds to go to. The local cub pack had requested permission to hold their annual treasure trail in the woods that formed part of the demesne lands, the headmistress of the village junior school wanted the ten-year-olds to tour the house as part of their history curriculum, and the amateur dramatic group wanted to stage *A Midsummer Night's Dream* beside the Greek temple folly on the far side of the lake.

It was all safe, familiar, reassuring—a million miles away from Diego Saez and his powerful, disturbing presence.

Here at Salton she was safe from it. From him. He could not intrude, could not threaten her fragile peace of mind.

She was just heading upstairs to change, on the third afternoon after her arrival, when Mrs Tillet hurried out into the hall. Portia paused on the stair. She had come indoors after a vigorous session digging up the herbaceous border with Fred Hermitage, emptying wheelbarrows of discarded vegetation and mulching in fertiliser and humus, and her ancient, baggy corduroy trousers needed a good wash. So did she.

But her mood was good. She loved gardening, even when it left her with an aching back and tired muscles.

'Hello, Mrs T. What's up?' she asked with a smile.

'Your brother has just phoned, Miss Portia,' the housekeeper told her. 'He said to tell you that he'll be coming down tomorrow.'

Portia's smile widened. 'Oh, I'm so glad, Mrs T! Tom's been overworking horribly, and I've been telling him to take a break from that wretched bank and come down here for a while! He can relax and recharge before going back to town again!'

'He did say, Miss Portia, that he would be bringing a business acquaintance with him,' answered Mrs Tillet.

Portia's smile turned to a grimace. 'Oh, how wretched! I suppose he's going to stay the night. Is the Blue Room made up? He can go in there. Or is it a couple? Did Tom say? If so, then the Oak Room would be better.'

'A single gentleman, so I understand,' elaborated Mrs Tillet.

'The Blue Room it is, then, Mrs T. Do you want a hand getting it ready?'

The housekeeper shook her head. 'I've got Betty Wilkins and Marjorie Sanders coming up this afternoon and all day tomorrow. We'll see to everything. Would you care to choose the menu for tomorrow night?'

Portia shook her head. 'You can do menus blindfolded, Mrs T. I'll stick to the flowers—I'll have to go and raid the glasshouses and risk wrecking Fred's wrath upon me for taking his prime specimens!'

Later, as she sat curled up on the leather sofa in the library, in front of a crackling wood fire, she wondered who Tom was bringing down. Salton was often used for business entertaining, and Portia was no stranger to acting as hostess when she was here. She wondered whether she should phone Felicity, suggest she come over as well, to make it four for dinner, but decided it might be a bit too pushy on her part. She had not forgotten Tom snapping at her when she'd gone on at him to propose to the girl he was so obviously in love with.

She frowned. Was it just overwork that was making him so short-tempered? Or a persistent bug that made him look so haggard all the time? Or were things tricky at the bank? Trickier, that was, than they normally were, with Uncle Martin wanting to have all the privileges of his position and do none of the work.

Words uttered in a deep, accented drawl echoed in her memory. *Adverse circumstances.* She pressed her mouth tightly. Diego Saez was being absurd. There were no 'adverse circumstances' surrounding Salton. Salton had belonged to the Lanchesters for hundreds of years, through thick and thin. The bank, Loring Lanchester, provided a hefty boost to the family wealth, but Tom was not dependent on it. If necessary Salton could be self-sufficient—there were the farms, and, like so many other stately home owners, he could always go into the heritage business. Besides, both she and her brother had investment portfolios which yielded generous private incomes.

So why, deep in her bones, did she feel a frisson of fear go through her, and that dark, deep voice echo again in her head, laconically enquiring whether Salton was for sale?

More words echoed in her mind.

Everything is for sale, Portia.

A scornful look lit her eye. Yes, in Diego Saez's world everything had a price! A man as rich as he was, with a spoilt, pampered background as he had—a prince of the pampas, or whatever part of South America he came from!—*would* think like that, she thought condemningly.

Into her mind's eye came the image of his face—those hooded, knowing eyes, that cynical, sensual twist of his mouth.

That mouth, moving on hers...

Out of nowhere, like a wolf at her throat, memory gripped her. So vivid it could be happening now, again. Diego Saez helping himself to her mouth.

Shudderingly she pushed the memory away. She would not remember. She must not!

Diego Saez was gone from her life. She had got rid of him. Disposed of him. Made it very, very clear to him that his attentions were repugnant to her, his generous invitation to add her to his charming collection of temporary bedwarmers unwelcome.

She did not want Diego Saez.

And she had told him so. Spelt it out to him loud and clear, voicing all her contempt, her revulsion, for the life he lived.

He had got the message, all right. Walked away from her. Taken his dismissal and walked off.

A shiver went through her.

I got off lightly...

The words formed in her brain, and even as they formed she felt a shimmer of unease go through her.

Did men like Diego Saez walk away from what they wanted?

Tight-jawed, she reached forward for the teapot. Well, this time he would just have to accept defeat.

Portia slid the black jersey silk dress over her head, and smoothed it down over her body. It was a particular favourite for dinner parties here, whether large or small, social or business. Its graceful boat neck flattered her shoulders, and the elbow-length sleeves made her forearms slender and graceful, as did the on-the-knee hemline She slipped her feet into a pair of modest high heels, clipped a necklace around her throat, put on matching drop earrings, strapped her evening watch around her wrist, then applied her lipstick, checked her hair was still immaculate in its chignon, and headed downstairs.

Tom and his business guest would be here any moment. Even though it was unnecessary she did a quick walk around the twelve-foot mahogany table, glittering with crystal and silver, and with one of her floral arrangements centred on its length, flanked by silver candelabra. In the grate a wood fire added to the background warmth of the central heating, and on the walls an array of family portraits, landscapes and still-lifes complemented the long dark blue velvet curtains, the blue and gold patterned carpet and the mahogany sideboards and console tables. The scent of beeswax polish mingled with the freshness of the flowers and the fragrance of the burning wood.

It was a familiar and beloved scene, and Portia found herself wondering, with a smile, just how many dinner parties this room must have seen in its time, presided over by whoever was head of the house at the time.

And how many more it still would see.

She moved on to check the drawing room where, as in the dining room, everything was in perfect order. She paused in front of the fireplace, shielded from the blaze by a firescreen, and gazed at her own reflection momentarily in the glass over the mantel.

Why had Diego Saez pursued her the way he had?

Surely he could see from looking at her that she was not the type to indulge in the kind of sordid little affairs he clearly specialised in? Nor was she *his* type either—from all the photos in the celebrity magazines that Susie had insisted on showing her it seemed Diego Saez went for the sultry type. She gazed at herself a moment longer, taking in the cool, classic features that looked back at her out of clear grey eyes. She was a million miles away from the spectacular, flashy females he obviously had a taste for!

So what on earth did he see in her?

Certainly Geoffrey Chandler, she thought with a sudden pang, hadn't found it hard to find another woman to marry him, and his chosen bride was a very pretty brunette.

She turned away. She must not think about Geoffrey. It had all been such a mess. Such a horrible, painful mess. She'd hurt and humiliated him, and though it had superficially been a very civilised parting of the ways, the wound had gone deeper than she wanted to admit.

A thought drifted across her mind. Was Susie right? Did she need some kind of drastic 'cure' for her messy broken engagement? Such as a passionate, physical affair with someone like Diego Saez?

No! She wouldn't even *start* to think like that! The man's attitude to her—to sex—appalled her. Disgusted her. Treating it as if it were nothing but an appetite—to be sated on any female he decided to select, as if he were choosing from a wine list.

Her lips pressed together and she turned away from the looking glass.

As she did so she realised she was hearing the sound of a car coming along the long drive from the road, a good mile and a half away. Tom and his business guest were obviously about to arrive.

She performed one last rapid scan around the room, and waited while the car pulled up in front of the house on the gravelled forecourt. The engine cut, there was a sound of car doors slamming, feet crunching on gravel, then voices out in the hall, indistinct and muffled—Mr T taking coats, Portia assumed, as she stood, poised in front of the fire, ready for her brother and his guest. Then footsteps approached the drawing room. The double doors were opened, and in walked Tom.

Her eyes took him in, but only for the barest handful of seconds. Darkness seemed to be swirling around her. Her eyes were dragged over Tom's shoulders to the man who had walked in behind him. She felt the blood drum in her ears, her chest tighten.

It couldn't be. It just *couldn't be*…

From far away she heard Tom's voice, but it came dim, inaudible. The only sense that seemed to be operating was her vision.

And all she could see, like some horrible dream, was a tall, dark, dangerous figure that she had hoped, prayed, never to have to set eyes on again.

He was walking towards her. That same lithe, purposeful gait. The same dark, heavy-lidded eyes and strong, arresting features. His expression was shuttered, unreadable. He stopped in front of her, holding out her hand.

'Portia—' said Diego Saez, and took her nerveless hand in his.

It was like something out of a bad dream. A very bad dream. A nightmare.

It couldn't be true, it just couldn't! Diego Saez could not be standing here, in the drawing room at Salton, right in front of her.

She wanted to snatch her hand away. Was desperate to do so. But the fingers holding hers were like steel pincers. As if he knew her intention, her desire, her overwhelming instinct to pull away from him. His hand was hard, his grip unshakeable.

Then, abruptly, he let her go.

She was fighting for air. It was thick in her lungs, unbreathable. She could hear Tom speaking and with sheer force of will she turned her head towards him.

'Have you two met already? You didn't say, Señor Saez.'

There was polite surprise in his voice, and Portia was incapable of answering. Incapable of doing anything other than try and get breath into her lungs, stay upright in front of the hearth.

'Several times,' Diego Saez replied, his voice deep and accented. Portia felt the slightest shiver go through her, as though she were cold. Yet she could feel the heat from the fire diffusing through the fireguard on to the back of her stockinged legs.

'I've been buying art,' he continued, as if that was by way of an explanation.

'Ah.' Tom nodded. 'Of course.'

'In fact,' Diego Saez went on, in that same smooth, deep voice that was sending chill shivers along Portia's rigid spine, 'only last week I chanced to be at the opening of an exhibition on British eighteenth-century landscapes. The Gainsborough of Salton was very...' he paused minutely '...memorable.'

His eyes rested expressionlessly on Portia, and she knew it was not the Gainsborough he was referring to as memorable. Memory of his kiss bleached through her. She looked away.

Shock was still ricocheting inside her.

What was he *doing* here? She cast her mind about desperately. Surely Tom could not have invited him here deliberately?

Reason came to her rescue. Why shouldn't Tom have invited him? They moved in the same world of high finance, even if Diego Saez operated on a vast global scale. Desperately she found herself hoping that Tom would not

have business dealings with the man! Let alone discuss
them here, at Salton. At the same time she knew, with a
ghastly hollow feeling that was opening up inside her, that
the very last thing she could do was tell Tom just why she
objected so much. How could she possibly tell her brother
that, actually, Diego Saez was not welcome at Salton on
account of the fact that he was trying to get her into his
bed and she'd had to make her objections to his ambitions
very, very plain indeed?

Of course she couldn't tell Tom. She couldn't do anything—anything at all except accept, with a trapped feeling
of horrible inevitability, that she would have to spend the
evening playing the gracious hostess to a man she wished
to perdition! For some hideous reason Tom had seen fit to
invite Diego Saez here, to Salton, on some kind of banking
matter, and there was nothing, *nothing* she could do about
it.

It took every ounce of her poise and self-control to get
through dinner with some semblance of normality.

Throughout the long, excruciating meal—at which she
did nothing more than pick—she took as little part in the
conversation as she could get away with. Unfortunately,
though she longed for her brother and his unwelcome guest
to immerse themselves in banking talk, so she would not
be required to join in, Tom insisted on making general conversation. She tried to support him out of loyalty, and also,
as she belatedly realised, because he was clearly under visible stress himself. His face was still haggard, and to her
own sense of anger at Diego Saez's presence at Salton was
added yet more indignation that he should have accepted
an invitation from a man who was so clearly unwell.

Tom was manfully trying to get through the evening,
lurching from one innocuous topic to another, with Portia
doing her best to behave as though the man sitting between
them were nothing more than a business acquaintance. Yet
all through the meal the undercurrents swirled at her feet.

She could feel the pressure of Diego Saez's presence as if it were a tangible force, was supremely aware of him seated only a few feet away from her. Desperately she tried not to watch the way his long, tanned fingers curved around the stem of his wine glass, or the silver fork he was using. Tried not to look at the lean strength of his wrist, banded with a slim gold watch, at how white the gleaming cuff looked against his skin.

But at least, she realised, he was not looking at her the way he usually did. When he spoke to her his eyes rested on her with a shuttered expression. It took her a while to realise she was finding that even more oppressive than the usual sensual assessment he subjected her to.

Her nerves started to stretch unbearably, and she longed for the meal to be over, so she could finally escape and leave them to their business discussion over the port.

She headed straight upstairs. Urgency drove her. She had thought herself safe at Salton, but Diego Saez had walked in as if he had the keys to the place!

Why? The question circled in her brain, as it had all evening, but now she could give free rein to it. He was not here because of Tom—he was here because of her. She knew it with every fibre of her being.

And she knew why.

He was angry. Angry with her for having dared to reject him. She had dared to heap scorn on him for his arrogant assumption that she was his for the taking, dared to be revulsed at his libertine lifestyle.

Well, so what? Anger lashed through her. She had spoken nothing but the truth—why should she care that he was angry at it?

Because he's dangerous...

The voice in her head stopped her restless pacing around her bedroom.

She stared, blank-eyed, ahead of her. A deep foreboding filled her. Diego Saez was here for a purpose.

Surely to God he did not think he could still succeed

with her? Did he think he could pay some midnight visit to her under her brother's own roof?

And if he does, what will you do? If, in the middle of the night, you hear the bedroom door open?

The sly, insidious question slipped past her defences. Even as it formed she stilled totally.

And into her mind came an image—heavy, sensual—of Diego Saez walking into her bedroom, taking off his tie as he advanced upon her, shrugging off his jacket, his hands going to his belt...

And her, lying back on the sheets, waiting for him...

She felt a slow, viscous heaviness subsume her body, flow through her dilating veins. Felt a flush of low, building heat mount through her, licking like a slow, sensuous flame.

Then, as if she were deep underwater, she fought her way back up to the surface. To sanity. To reality.

The reality of standing in the middle of her deserted bedroom, trying to fight down the dark, oppressive feeling of foreboding that shimmered all about her.

She slept fitfully, waking often from heavy, unremembered dreams which left a heavy feeling of dread in her heart—and something other than dread, something she would not give a name to. The knowledge that in the other wing of the house was Diego Saez, beneath the very roof of Salton, filled her with disturbing emotion. Although her room had no lock, she had placed her dressing table stool in front of the door—a frail barrier against a man such as the one who had pursued her.

But there was no nocturnal visitation, and when, finally, she fell into a proper sleep it was as dawn set the birds into their early chorus. She did not wake until gone ten. As she realised the lateness of the hour a sense of relief went through her. She had missed the ordeal of breakfasting with her brother and his unwelcome guest. With any luck he might even have left by now.

But when, after she had gone cautiously downstairs, she

enquired of Mrs Tillet, it was to learn that her brother and his guest were incarcerated in the library. Well, at least she could have her breakfast in peace, and count the time until Diego Saez took himself off.

She helped herself to tea and toast in the Morning Room, but found she was incapable of eating. Her ears still strained for sounds of masculine voices emerging from the library, and she had scarcely finished her cup of tea when she pushed her plate aside and stood up.

Instinct made her head outdoors. She didn't bother with a jacket, and her feet in their short suede ankle boots were fine for the pathways, even if the dew-wet grass would get them sopping wet. She scrunched rapidly over the gravel, heading for the Italian garden. On the far side of it a paved path led down to a little sunken garden that was always a sun-trap in the morning, with a bowered bench set there for that very purpose. After mopping the ironwork seat dry, with some tissues brought for the purpose, she sat down.

Her eyes gazed blindly over the spring flowers bobbing in the light morning breeze. The leaves of the rose bushes were dark red, still furled. Blossom from the ornamental tree in the centre shone palest pink against the blue sky. The tiny bite of cold she had felt when she first sat down stung and made her shiver.

She was waiting. She knew she was. She was waiting and waiting for it to be safe to go back indoors. And as she waited that same oppressive sense of foreboding stole over her.

Despite the brightness of the spring sunshine, and the warm shelter of the sunken garden, she shivered. Her ears strained for the sound of a car engine starting up, signalling that once more Salton was safe.

There was a footfall on stone. Her head flew up.

Diego Saez had walked into the sunken garden.

CHAPTER SIX

PORTIA had frozen again, he could see, just the way she had last night, when he'd walked into her drawing room. Going completely rigid as only an outraged woman of her class could. It was as if an invisible layer of ice had settled over her whole body.

As he strolled towards her his eyes flicked over her again, taking in the fine bones of her face, the slender wrist, the discreet swell of her breasts beneath the softest cashmere that made him want to hold her in his hands…

But if the thought of caressing her breasts heated him, the look on her face was designed to do just the opposite. Yet the icy disdain in those grey eyes merely acted like a spur to the anger which he held, like a jaguar on a leash, beneath the surface of his conscious mind.

She had come here to avoid him—she might as well have written it in letters a metre high! Just as she had left the dining table last night and disappeared. Making her aristocratic disdain for him so obvious he'd have had to be a clod of earth not to recognise it. He felt the leashed jaguar growl silently as it crouched, waiting to be given the order to surge forward.

But he would not loose his anger on her. Would not reduce himself to her level—lashing out at him like that, her eyes flashing with contempt for him for all the world to see, dismissing him like some peasant!

No—he stilled the tensing jaguar—he would not loose his anger on her.

He would play a far, far more enjoyable game with her.

* * *

72

Portia felt ice fill her veins. It was a mix of rage—and dread.

Rage because how dared, how *dare* Diego Saez persecute her like this?

And dread because there was something about the way he was walking towards her, something purposeful in his long, rhythmic stride, that crushed the breath from her lungs.

It did something else too. Something she pushed away blindly, urgently, as if she had suddenly seen a poisonous spider on her bare leg. But not before she had felt its fatal bite. Felt the poison enter her flesh.

Heating it.

She wanted to leap to her feet, wanted to turn on her heel and rush out of the garden, away from him as fast as she could. But the ice filling her veins kept her frozen in position. All she could do was let her fingers clutch at the sides of the cardigan at her throat, as if that might free the choking sensation in her throat.

In a voice as tight as steel she heard herself speak. Sharply. Cuttingly.

'I don't know why you came here but I want you to leave! I have nothing more to say to you!'

He stilled. He was about six feet away from her and seemed to be twice her height. Again she urged herself to stand up, and again realised that it was quite beyond her power.

For one long, paralysing moment he simply went on standing there, looking down at her. He was wearing a business suit, immaculately tailored, and it seemed to make him look taller, darker than ever. His obsidian eyes surveyed her, and she felt the breath stall in her lungs.

'I have something to tell you,' he said, in his deep, accented voice, 'which you would be advised to listen to.'

Her lip curled.

'I can't imagine that there is anything in the world I want to hear you say!'

His face was expressionless. Then, with a slight turn of his head, he indicated the pale gold mass of the house across the lawn rising behind her. Slowly his gaze came back to her, and what she saw in his eyes hollowed her out.

Then, his face still completely expressionless, he spoke.

'If you want to save your precious family home you will listen to every word I have to tell you.'

He had her.

Every synapse in her brain, every nerve in her body, was focused on him. Instantly. Totally.

A cold sense of pleasure went through him. Again, the years split away, and there was Mercedes de Carvello, her black, mascaraed eyes totally focused on him—her disbelief instant, her denial total—as he informed her of the new state of ownership of her home.

Now, in a different place, beneath a different sun, Portia Lanchester, who considered herself too good for his bed, had exactly the same expression in her eyes.

'Are you mad?'

The clipped, upper-class tones cut through the morning air, carrying every gram of her disbelief, her denial.

He looked down at her. Saw the fingers digging into the soft cashmere at her neck. The soft gleam of sunlight on the row of pearls at her throat.

He had a sudden vision of her wearing nothing but those pearls. Walking towards him. Towards his bed. To do there whatever he wanted her to do.

And she would do it. He knew that. Knew it with every fibre of his being.

Knew it because it was what Mercedes de Carvello had done…

He dragged his mind away. He would not remember. Would not remember how the woman who had killed his mother, mown her down like a dog beneath the wheels of her car, had come to him that night he had returned to San

Cristo, his heart heavy despite the cold pleasure of having taken possession, with the full panoply of the law to endorse him, of the *estancia* that had ground his parents into the dirt. Would not remember how she had come to his penthouse suite in the de luxe American hotel in the city, stripping the clothes from her body, offering herself to a man she had thrown from her house as a boy—the house he now owned, the house she was prepared to do anything, *anything* to get back…

He had thrust her from his room, his whole being filled with disgust, with loathing.

But this woman here, now, in front of him, her well-bred chin lifted as if she could smell the dirt of his former poverty in her delicate nostrils—her he would not reject…

What was it, he found himself questioning yet again, that made Portia Lanchester a woman he wanted so badly? She was nothing like his usual women. He had always preferred the voluptuous type—enticing, alluring, fully aware of their own sexuality, and of his.

Portia Lanchester was quite different. He had assessed that instantly, the first time he'd lain eyes on her at that bankers' dinner. She had looked so *apart*. So completely oblivious to the regard she was gathering from male eyes.

Except his.

The memory of how she had realised he was looking her over replayed in his mind, and he savoured the moment, as he had done so often before, when she had met his eyes and recognised in them the look of his desire.

For that briefest moment she had let him look at her, knowing he was looking at her. And then all that chill had flowed back into place, freezing him out.

It hadn't bothered him. It had interested him. Had she returned his assessment with the kind of knowing satisfaction with which women usually received his attentions then he would have been swiftly bored.

But Portia Lanchester had merely made him want her more.

And he would have her.

The desire to possess her was incontrovertible. The more she sought to evade him, the more he knew he was going to possess her.

And the more he wanted her.

Wanted to loosen that fine spun-gold hair and let it cascade over those slender, elegant shoulders. Wanted to reveal those high, soft breasts and feel them harden in his hands. Wanted to skim his hands down over those pale flanks and part her white thighs, take her, possess her.

Her constant evasion of his pursuit had merely made him more determined. He had hunted her down.

And then, like a deer at bay, she had turned on him. Lashed back at him with weapons that had been deadly.

To herself.

Until that moment outside the hotel he would have had infinite patience in his pursuit of her. Relishing every moment, assiduous in his inexorable wearing down of her resistance to him, until the moment came when she finally, gloriously yielded to what he wanted—and found her own satiation in that infinite fount of pleasure which he would release in her.

But at that moment when she had turned on him, rejecting him with words that doomed her, patience had become—unnecessary. He need exert no sensitivity towards her now, no consideration for her reluctance to let him ignite in her the passion that he knew was buried deep within her. Now he need only exert the pressure he knew she would respond to—the pressure that would make her do what all her kind did. Protect her possessions.

And so he would take her. Not against her will. For she would consent to him—consent to the deal he would offer her, the deal that would protect the possessions her kind thought most precious. And she would consent—oh, much more than merely *consent*!—to the pleasures she would find with him. And to make her feel such pleasure, even while her conscious mind would know that she had come to his bed merely to protect her possessions, *that* would assuage his anger.

His anger that a woman who had so beguiled him—so eluded him—had in an instant plunged him back to the sickening memory of the moment when he had taken his revenge on those who had destroyed his family and cast him onto the streets like a dog.

He felt that anger lick at him like black flame and he doused it. He did not need to feel angry with Portia Lanchester for despising him for what he was. He need only desire her—and enjoy her.

He shifted his weight minutely from one leg to the other. At another time he might have enjoyed playing with her a little longer, as a cat with its prey. But, abruptly, he wanted now only to go in for the kill. He would break her arrogance, her aristocratic disdain, with a single blow, as a cat would break the neck of the prey caught in its claws.

He spoke briefly and brusquely, not bothering to soften the blow he aimed at her.

'Your brother has got himself up to his neck in debt—he's put Salton up as security.'

The words fell with killing force.

She heard them, but she didn't hear them. They seemed to come from very far away, and then right up close. For a long, timeless moment she just went on sitting there, ice all the way through her, wondering what it was she had just heard Diego Saez tell her.

Only three words registered—debt, Salton, security.

Then behind the words came a kind of sickness, like some huge, overwhelming tidal wave, engulfing her.

'No—'

Her voice was so faint it was scarcely audible. But he heard it. His face remained expressionless. When he spoke he was merciless.

'Loring Lanchester has become a byword for bad investments. It's sinking faster than a stone in water. Your brother hasn't a hope in hell of dragging it clear. He's put Salton up as security because no one will bail him out. But it won't be enough. It will go. Along with the rest of the bank.'

She stared at him. The obsidian eyes were looking down at her. There was no expression in them—nothing. They might have been the eyes of some Aztec statue—indifferent, blank.

She tried to gather her thoughts, picking them up like bits of paper gusting in the wind. She realised she had got to her feet, but had no conscious memory of doing so. And she still had to look up into those eyes, those dark, shuttered eyes set in that dark, sublime face.

He had just said something so absurd, so ridiculous, that she could not find the words to refute him. As if explaining something to a child, she spoke.

'Mr Saez, I appreciate that you are used to the extreme volatility of the economy of South America, where banks crash and currencies become worthless overnight, but I'm afraid you must appreciate that here in England things are very different. Loring Lanchester is one hundred and fifty years old. It is one of the most highly regarded merchant banks in the City. There can be no question, no question whatsoever, of it being in trouble. Loring Lanchester is one of the soundest, most financially secure—'

'Loring Lanchester is broke.' Diego Saez's voice cut across her clipped tones with harsh brutality.

Something stabbed at Portia. It was fear—a slicing, shearing stab of fear. She thrust it aside.

'Mr Saez, I simply don't think you understand how business is done in this country!' Her voice had risen slightly in pitch. Her hands tightened on the edges of her cardigan.

His face was still blank. For some reason that made the fear slice at her again.

His voice was a dark drawl. 'I understand that when a bank makes loans that are massively defaulted on then it is broke. Loring Lanchester has done just that. Your brother has made a series of disastrous decisions, resulting in a loan portfolio that hasn't a chance in hell of paying out! He's loaned the bank's money to every no-hope venture going—from Eastern Europe to Africa to the most tin-pot banana republic you can name! He'll have to write off just about all of it! And he doesn't even have any income to begin to cover him—the last two years of recession have seen merger and acquisition activity plummet, and bankers' fees with it! M&As may be picking up now, but it's not going to be enough to bail out Loring Lanchester. Nothing can. Your brother has been trawling the City for cash—but no one's about to bail him out. No one! He's going to lose it all. And Salton.'

She was reeling. Reeling as if a hurricane had caught her in its pitiless teeth.

'Salton belongs to Tom outright! It's not part of the bank!'

His eyes flashed derisively.

'You weren't listening, were you? He's already put Salton up as security. It will go with the rest of the bank. The house and estate are just about the only solid assets he's got!'

She shook her head. There was a muzziness in her brain. This wasn't true. This wasn't happening. It couldn't be...

She had to get away. Had to. Had to find Tom. Get him to tell her it wasn't true. That this awful, awful man was simply telling lies—vile, ugly lies. It wasn't true. Wasn't true!

She stumbled away. A hand whipped out, securing her arm.

'I've already told you. There's no point running, Portia.'

His voice was too close. His body was too close. She could smell, with an overpowering sense of nausea, the scent of his aftershave, could feel the crushing presence of his body, too close to hers. She tried to tug away, but she was powerless.

'There's no point,' he said again, and she could feel his

breath on the back of her neck. His other hand reached up and closed over her shoulder. She was held still, almost within the cradle of his arms, but her whole body strained away from him.

'And there's no need to panic the way you're doing. Your brother has found his white knight. The bank is safe.' He paused. 'Salton is safe.'

She should feel relief sagging through her at his words, but she did not. Only the teeth of the hurricane again, biting at her the way Diego Saez's hand was biting around her forearm. She strained away from him.

'Wh—who…?'

She got the word out somehow.

And knew the answer even before he spoke.

She could hear the smile in his voice. Feel the sickening plunge of her heart.

He turned her around so that he could look at her. Look at her hearing what he was going to tell her.

'Why do you think I'm here, Portia? Why do you think your brother brought me here?' He looked down at her, savouring the moment. 'He thinks I'm going to save his skin.'

Time had stopped again. The world was motionless around her. Not even her heart was beating. Her eyes were fixed on his; she felt them spear her. Her voice was a husk.

'And are you?'

It was pointless asking. Because she knew—dear God, she knew what the answer was going to be. What it could only be. Because why else would Diego Saez be here, telling her that her world had just crashed around her ears?

For one purpose. One purpose only.

He went on holding her, looking down at her.

'Of course,' he told her. 'I've thrown him a lifeline. I'll sort out the bank's debts—I'll even let him stay on. It wouldn't be good for the bank right now for him to leave. Martin Loring will have to go, of course—your brother should have cleared him out when he took over. He's the worst liability the bank possesses. If your brother had got rid of him he might have stood a chance. He could have brought in a team of directors who knew one end of a balance sheet from the other! Who could have sold out to one of the global majors for a good price—because then it would have been a profitable deal, not a salvage sale! But your brother let Martin Loring behave as though Queen Victoria were still on the throne and he could order gun-ships to go in and secure British assets in the world's rough spots!'

Her eyes fell, squeezing shut.

'He wanted Uncle Martin to retire,' she whispered.

'He should have kicked him out on his useless backside! There's no room for sentiment in business, Portia.'

Her eyes flew open and she forced herself to lift them to his again. Her body strained, rigid in his grip.

'So why are you bailing him out?'

It was another pointless question.

And she answered it herself. Her eyes slid past him, out over the little sunken garden, through the archway in the yew hedge at the far side, down the path that wound back along to the lake, which lay like a glittering diamond in the emerald grass of the lawns that lapped around the jewel that was Salton. Her home. Tom's home. It would have been Felicity's home with him, and their children together, and their children's children...

But it would now belong—her heart crushed like a rotten fruit inside her, oozing poisoned bile—to the man who was pinioning her, holding her immobile, powerless.

The man who had looked at the Gainsborough painting of Salton and wanted it there and then. Asked whether it was for sale...

'You want Salton.'

Her voice was dull. Dead.

Her eyes went on gazing. The breeze was moving the branches of the trees beyond the garden, winnowing in the branches of the ornamental tree within it, showering blossom to the ground like a blessing.

She could feel nothing. Nothing at all.

Then, slowly, as if surfacing out of insensibility, she felt something. His hand moving on her shoulder, his fingers stroking the softness of her cashmere.

'No.' His voice was low. Accented.

Her eyes dragged back to his, as if each were bowed with unbearable weight.

She saw what was written there in his eyes, and knew instantly, mortally, just why he had done this. Come to Salton, sought her out, told her that her world had been destroyed.

And he was telling her now, in the depths of those dark, obsidian eyes, just what the price would be to save it.

His hand smoothed over her shoulder again. Hard. Warm. Heavy.

Possessive.

'I want *you*, Portia,' he said.

CHAPTER SEVEN

HER interview with Tom was painful. Agonisingly painful. She had to wait over an hour before seeing him. Diego Saez had walked away from her, there in the little sunken garden where her world had ended, and closeted himself with her brother in the library. Then a chauffeur-driven car had arrived at the front door, a fast, powerful, expensive saloon, and Diego Saez had climbed inside and been driven off.

Portia had given Tom five minutes, then walked indoors. What had struck her first, like some ghastly bad joke, was that he no longer looked ill.

Ill? The sick humour of it struck at her. Tom hadn't been ill—hadn't been coming down with flu. He'd been sick with worry, with fear! And she'd been blind to it! Totally, completely blind!

Guilt coursed through her. Her own brother, floundering in despair, and she hadn't even noticed.

Yet now, seeing his face clear of that haggard, drawn look only made her lungs squeeze. Because there could be only one reason for Tom no longer looking at death's door.

Diego Saez had offered him his lifeline.

As she stood, hovering on the entrance to the library, he surged towards her.

'Portia! Come in! Listen—I've something I've got to tell you!'

She listened, trying desperately hard to conceal her own emotions, as he poured out to her, at last, the situation at the bank. He was so full of self-recrimination, constantly berating himself for having let it get so bad, excusing everyone but himself, that Portia could not bear it.

Even less could she bear him extolling Diego Saez.

'If he'd ridden up on a white charger I couldn't have been more relieved!' he exclaimed. 'He's giving me the breathing space we need. Oh, he'll take the majority holding—I can hardly expect anything else—but the main thing is that the bank will keep going. He'll sort out the situation, get everything in order, and use his massive financial muscle to knock heads together. He'll get us clean, and then he'll organise an orderly sale to one of the US giants. He's happy to wait to take his profit then, and he will, too—I wouldn't begrudge him a penny of it!'

He frowned slightly. 'Uncle Martin will have to go. I knew he'd insist on that—and if I'd had more gumption myself I'd have done the same. Trouble is—' he looked at his sister wryly '—it's pretty difficult to tell the seventy-year-old man who taught me how to bowl that he's not wanted on voyage any longer. I always knew he lived in the past, but I thought—well, I thought I could carry him.' His face took on a guilty look. 'But I couldn't. And I damn near ruined everything, thinking I could!'

She took an unsteady breath. 'And what about you, Tom? What happens now with you?'

He gave a shaky smile—but at least it was a smile. 'Well, Saez wants me to carry on for a bit—though he'll find a good man to underpin me, and he'll be taking all the decisions. Then, when he thinks the time is right, I'll resign. Yes, I know it's a comedown, but, Portia, for me it's like the end of term! You can't believe how much I've come to loathe that damn bank! And now I'm going to be free of it.'

He made a face and looked her in the eyes. 'I'm going to live here, marry Felicity, look after Salton and be a countryman at last! It's what I've always wanted to do.'

His expression was like that of a reprieved prisoner.

She returned his shaky smile with one even shakier. 'I know. And hearing you say you're definitely going to marry Fliss is brilliant! She's hopelessly in love with you, you know, Tom.'

His eyes shadowed for a moment. 'But till now I couldn't ask her. How could I, when I had all this fiasco hanging over me? But I'm clear now—as soon as Saez takes over and the contracts are signed!'

She swallowed, and forced the words from her.

'When's that going to be?'

'Well, all the paperwork will have to be drawn up first. There's a whole bunch of legal stuff that has to be gone through, and then the banking regulators have to give it all the OK and so on, but it's all just a formality.'

'Can he pull out?' Her voice was sharper than she intended.

Tom shook his head.

'He's got no reason to. He's already gone through the bank's books with a fine-tooth comb, and there's no more bad news to come—he's got the lot! So why would he pull out?'

Why indeed? thought Portia, with a hollowing of her stomach.

She walked across to the window, her stomach roiling. Outside the long library windows the lawns stretched for ever, it seemed to her. And a path stretched before her. Dark, and paved with sharpest glass. It was the path she would have to walk.

She had no choice. None.

Behind her, Tom was speaking. She strained to hear his voice.

'I know this has come as a shock, sis, and I'm really, really sorry. But thank God it's all worked out all right! I was just about suicidal...'

His voice trailed off.

Guilt crushed her. *She* had been distraught at the thought of losing Salton—but for Tom, for her brother, the guilt would have been a hundred times worse! Guilt at having failed to guard his inheritance, which he had been handed on trust for his son, as Salton had been passed, father to son, for nearly half a millennium.

She stared out over the grounds. In every life, she knew, there was a test—an ordeal to be endured.

This was to be hers. The ordeal of knowing that she had no choice. She could not, *could not*, give Diego Saez any reason to pull out from saving her brother. He had made it totally, utterly clear what he wanted. The price he was exacting.

And she would have to pay it.

Her eyes gazed over the sunlit gardens. For her brother's sake she would pay the price that Diego Saez demanded of her.

Whatever it cost her.

A terrible urge to laugh hysterically almost overcame her. She fought it back. From now on she must do everything to suppress her emotions. She must allow herself none.

Because the price she was going to pay to protect Salton was far more costly than even Diego Saez intended her.

For him, taking her to bed was simply a matter of appetite, a passing, easily sated desire. She had defied him, refused him—scorned him. So he had found a way to change her mind. By offering her brother his only chance to save Salton.

He knew she could not refuse. Knew that finally she would now come to him—give him what he wanted. Her body.

He thought he was breaking her pride, her self-respect, but she knew with a terrible sense of foreknowledge that he was going to break something far, far more precious to her. Something that she had known all along would be in the gravest danger if she succumbed to what he wanted from her—a brief, fleeting, meaningless affair. That would be all it was for him. But for her—

She shut her eyes in anguish. Now that she knew she could not escape him, she also knew that she could no longer deny why she had run from him.

Diego Saez was going to take her to his bed—and break her heart into the bargain.

'Mr Saez's suite, please.'

'Certainly, madam. Whom may I say is calling?'

The voice of the hotel clerk was polite, but Portia knew he would insist on a name.

'Portia Lanchester.'

Her own voice was rock-steady. She would allow no tremor in it. None.

She had driven up to London that afternoon, grateful that Tom had told her that as he was at Salton he would stay a while, now that his fears for the bank, for Salton, were put at rest.

'One moment, madam.'

The line went quiet for a few seconds. Then the clerk spoke again. 'Just putting you through now, Ms Lanchester.'

There was a click, and then a strong, masculine voice spoke.

'Portia.' Just her name, that was all.

She felt the constricted passageway of her throat tighten. After all the chasing he had done, now he was going to make her do the running.

'I'm—I'm at my flat. I... I...wondered whether you might be free for dinner tonight.'

She could feel the seconds pass, each one an eternity.

Then down the line came that same voice.

Her fingers clutched at the phone so tightly her nails were white. He gave her her answer.

'I'm flying out tonight, Portia. But if you wish you could come over now.'

Her throat closed completely.

'Now?'

It scraped through her lips, scarcely audible.

'I think so. Don't you?'

The voice was controlled—very controlled—but she

could hear emotion beneath it. It would be satisfaction, she knew. The satisfaction of a rich, spoilt, powerful man who had just achieved what he had wanted.

She put the phone down, feeling a wave of faintness going through her. Was she really going to go through with this? Give herself up to Diego Saez? Take a taxi to his hotel at this hour and…and… *Go to bed with him.* That was what he wanted. He was flying out tonight, and he wanted to make sure he'd had his before he went. After all, who knew when a busy international financier like him would be back in London again?

A shiver went through her. Would Diego Saez expect her to be waiting for him when he came back to London, whenever that was? Was she supposed to be his woman in London for the time being?

Stop it! She tore her mind away. What was the point of tormenting herself like this? Didn't she have enough to feel anguished about? Tom was in danger of losing Salton— and the only lifeline being held out to him was Diego Saez's.

And it came with a condition.

She was going to have to put aside all her principles about not indulging in a brief, physical affair with a man whose attitude to women, to sex was abhorrent to her.

A word came into her mind, ugly and vile.

Was she *prostituting* herself? To save Salton for her brother?

A bitter expression lit her eyes. What did it matter what you called it? She could not—could not—let Tom lose Salton just because she did not want an affair with Diego Saez. A man who with a single look could make her tremble...

A deep, abiding sense of inevitability swept through her. She had run all she could, denied him and defied him, scorned him and condemned him. But it had all been in vain.

Diego Saez would possess her, enjoy her, and dispose of

her. What she had most feared, most fled from, would happen, after all.

She had no choice.

Slowly she walked into her bedroom and started to get changed. To adorn herself for Diego Saez.

Diego stood by the window of his penthouse suite and gazed out over the traffic on Park Lane and across to the dark mass of Hyde Park beyond. Through the soundproofed windows the roar of the traffic was silent, the endless procession of red tail-lights and white headlights streaming along the busy road.

His mind slipped away to another city.

Another time.

The stench. That was what he remembered most about San Cristo. The stench of poverty, destitution, despair. The stifling heat of the day and the chill of the nights as he lay, arms crossed over and hands tucked into his armpits, knees drawn up, sleeping in filthy doorways, with the perpetual gnaw of hunger in his belly.

And blackness in his soul.

Like a shutter, he closed the past away from him and turned away from the window. He never allowed himself to remember. Never.

All he ever allowed himself to do was send money to Father Tomaso, who spent his life gathering up the unwanted street children, day after day, little by little earning their trust, reaching out to them until they turned to him and came with him to the refuge he offered them. Shining the first ray of light into their unbearably dark lives.

Now, thanks to money from the Saez coffers, more and more street children could be taken into refuge, given the chance that he had been given so long ago to become something other than human detritus thrown away on the midden of unspeakable poverty—as he had been, before Father Tomaso had found him and rescued him.

Deliberately he summoned another memory, a far more

recent one, to replace the dark horror that lay haunting him, deep within his mind. As he crossed the room on long legs, heading for the drinks cabinet, he saw in his mind's eye the stately proportions of the dining room at Salton—two hundred and fifty years of gracious living, frozen in time. His expression hardened. How could anyone born to that have been so careless with it? Tom Lanchester was a fool. It had taken a single glance at the bank's books for him to know that. Still, he should be glad of it. After all, thanks to Lanchester's financial idiocy he now had within his reach something that he intended to possess to the full.

He poured a shot of whisky into a glass, feeling his body enter that most pleasurable state of imminent sexual arousal. She would be here soon.

Another memory slid into his mind, mingling with the sensations beginning to stir in his body. Portia Lanchester, wearing that classy, understated black number last night as he'd walked into her ancestral home. It had been her face he'd concentrated on, relishing the expression of outraged disbelief on her well-bred features, but it had not blinded him to her body. The material of the dress had been silky, but slightly stretchy, grazing her breasts and outlining the delicate sculpture of her shoulders. Her pearls had leant their sheen to her skin, giving it a translucence that had been almost tangible.

What would she be wearing when she came to him now? As he lifted the whisky glass to his mouth he found himself hoping that she would not signal her intentions too obviously. She would come, of course, to offer him her body in exchange for safeguarding her family's wealth—and he would, of course, accept her offer. But he did not want her to do so dressed for that role.

The glass stilled at his lips, and he found himself lowering it slowly. Something moved in his mind. Some emotion. He wondered what it was, and then he realised.

It was regret.

His eyes darkened minutely.

Regret, he knew, that his pursuit of Portia Lanchester should end in this fashion.

It was not what he had intended.

He had intended a quite different affair. One in which Portia Lanchester succumbed to his desire for him simply because—

Because all women he desired did so.

He cast his mind around. Had there ever been a woman who had resisted his desire for her? He could remember none. He had only to indicate his interest and she was his. Nor was it just his wealth that made them so responsive. All his life, even while clawing his way out of poverty, women had come easily to him.

Except Portia Lanchester.

That, of course, had been part of her allure—that she had resisted him.

A frown entered his darkening eye.

But she had gone on resisting him, and allure had begun to turn to impatience. So he had called time. And then— his mouth tightened into a grim line—she had revealed the reason for her resistance outside Claridge's.

Her contempt for his origins.

Dismissing him as not worthy of her illustrious breeding and ancestry.

Not good enough for her.

And in that instant the game had changed.

He lifted the whisky glass to his lips and took a generous mouthful, letting the complex fiery liquid burn around his palette, savouring the sensation.

Portia Lanchester had changed the game, and now it was being played out with new rules. She had made clear her values to him—all that was important to her was her money and her social status. To protect that she would do whatever she had to.

Including coming to his bed.

Slowly Diego let the whisky glide down his throat, kicking into his system. It felt good. His body felt taut, and fit, the first tightening of sexual anticipation was tensing through him.

He glanced at his watch. The gold gleamed in the lamp-light.

She would be here soon.

He took another mouthful of whisky, and waited.

He had waited a long time for Portia Lanchester.

But soon, very soon, the waiting would be over.

Portia could hear her heels click on the marble floor of the luxury hotel fronting Park Lane. Once the site had been the lavish townhouse of an aristocratic family, torn down after the First World War to be replaced by an even more lavish art deco luxury hotel. Park Lane was lined by such hotels, from Marble Arch to Hyde Park Corner.

The one that Diego Saez patronised was one of the very best—in fact, one of the best hotels in the world. Well, for a man of his wealth—who could afford to buy a failing bank just to make sure of a woman he wanted—the outrageous cost of a suite here would be negligible.

She reached the front desk.

'Mr Saez's suite, please,' she announced.

If there was a tremor in her voice she would not acknowledge it. She stood, poised and elegant, in a pale blue cocktail dress just right for this early hour of the evening. In the tea lounge opening off the main lobby she could hear a grand piano playing quietly. Chopin, she recognised absently.

She listened to the nocturne as the reception clerk phoned up to Diego Saez's suite, then, a moment later, a bellboy was hovering attentively, ready to show her up.

She felt strange. Frozen somehow. Dissociated. As if none of this were real. For a moment, as she stepped out of the lift and the bellboy went ahead to rap on the door of the suite, she could not even remember what Diego Saez looked like.

Then the door opened and he was there.

She walked in.

Behind her, Diego Saez pressed the requisite note into the bellboy's hand and closed the door. It closed silently, with only the barest click.

It was a very final click.

Somewhere deep, deep inside her, she felt her heart begin to thud.

Diego Saez let his eyes rest on the woman who had come to him, as he had known she would, to offer him her body in exchange for her family's wealth. A sense of satisfaction went through him. She looked exactly the way he wanted her to look. She had resisted the temptation to come on too obviously to him, by wearing some seductive, sexy number. Instead she was wearing a dress that was the very opposite of that.

It was the colour of pale water, very plain, but beautifully cut, gliding over her fine-boned body, revealing nothing, baring only her arms. Her hair was dressed exactly the way he liked it. A low, elegant chignon nested at the nape of her neck, the hair swept back from her face, exposing her sculpted features, her wide-set grey eyes. She had used minimum make-up, and he liked that too. It was subtle, like the scent she wore. In fact, he mused, he doubted she was wearing perfume at all. The fragrance was so faint it was probably just soap and face cream.

Her lipstick was barely there, just a slight gloss, and there was nothing more than a sweep of mascara and the merest hint of shadow to deepen her eyes. There was no foundation or powder on her flawless skin.

He went on looking at her, taking in her whole appearance—from her freshly washed hair, down over her slender body to the cool blue material of her dress, down her slim legs to her small feet in modestly heeled shoes that exactly matched the colour of the dress.

She looked exactly what she was. A woman born into a world of Old Masters and vintage port, of landed estates and old money, of heritage and bloodlines—privileged, protected.

Protected from men like him.

His eyes rested on her, and for an instant so brief it was hardly there darkness clouded his gaze. Then it was gone.

Instead, he turned his mind to the physical sensations that had been releasing slowly inside him as he had looked at her.

She looked as cool, as untouchable as white marble. He felt his body surge. He had waited for her for so long—far longer than any other woman he'd wanted—and now, finally, she was here.

That pang he had felt earlier came again. For an instant, like a blade on his skin, he felt regret that it should be on terms such as this.

Then he put the thought aside. She could despise his lowly origins all she liked, but if she wanted to save her precious family home she would overcome her revulsion to him.

Something burned briefly in his eyes. Oh, yes, she would overcome her revulsion, all right. Portia Lanchester would enjoy every moment of her time in his bed...

He would make sure of that.

It was as if she had stepped into an abyss.

Yet it was very strange. She was not falling. Instead she seemed to be sort of held motionless, as if suspended. She could feel nothing. There was nothing to feel. Diego Saez was there. He was looking at her. The way he always looked at her.

Up to now she had always felt oppressed whenever he looked at her. Felt haunted, hunted. She had wanted to get away, to escape from that gaze that rested on her, dark, assessing, *knowing*.

Wanting her.

Yet now, when she was here, standing in front of him,

knowing that she had fled from in vain, it was as if a fine film of ice had formed all over her.

With part of her mind she realised it was a form of self-protection. She thought back to the first time she had seen Diego Saez's dark, knowing eyes resting on her. Making her aware, as she had never been so aware in her life, of her own body.

Yet now she felt as if she were almost a ghost. Or an inanimate statue. As if her blood were suspended in her veins.

The reality of what she was doing opened up around her. She had come to Diego Saez—now he would take the clothes from her body, take her to his bed, make her his own.

She knew it, but she could not believe it. It was so unreal, surreal.

Her eyes went to the huge formal arrangement of flowers on a gilded pier table across the wide reception room of the suite in which she now stood so motionless. The exotic scented blooms were like those he had sent her—a million years ago, it seemed—that morning after the bankers' dinner.

Did I think then it would come to this?

No—how could she have?

And yet—

Deep inside her there came a sense of inevitability about what was happening. It went through every fibre of her being. It was as if, right from that first moment when her gaze had intersected his, this moment had been waiting for her.

Dispassionately she stood still, let herself be looked at. Suspended, immobile. And quite, quite passive.

When he finally spoke she turned her face slightly to look at him.

And as she did so she felt a shaft of emotion pierce her. She could not name it, only feel it.

It was powerful, overwhelmingly powerful. It knifed

through her, slicing through the blankness, making it suddenly, instantly non-existent.

Her eyes met his. Out of his poured something that was almost tangible, as if it were streaming over her, touching every pore of her body.

It possessed her, possessed her utterly.

The knifing, overwhelming emotion came again, and for a long, endless moment it occupied her totally, as if there was nothing else inside her.

Except the touch of his eyes.

'So, tell me, Portia—what is it you want?'

His voice was low, with the deep, accented timbre that seemed to resonate through her body.

Want? The word seemed to mock her.

She dragged her eyes from him as if she were caught in a force field, a vortex, and hauled them back to the vase of flowers in their ornate vase. Safe from that sucking, knifing emotion that had possessed her when she experienced the touch of his eyes.

She took a breath. The air seemed cold in her lungs. Chill.

'I want Salton to be safe.'

Again her eyes met his, but this time she was better prepared. The knifing sensation came again, but she was expecting it. She let it pass through her body and then empty out again.

'And is that all you want?' Something had fired in the depths of those dark eyes, but she could give no name to it.

She could not answer him.

She turned her head away, walking towards the vase of flowers. She seemed so calm still, and yet inside her something was happening to her that was not calm at all.

She stopped, and reached out her free hand to touch one of the petals. It was heavy and waxy to her touch. There was a mirror behind the vase, and she could see, although she was not looking directly into it, that Diego Saez was walking towards her.

He stood behind her. She did not lift her eyes from the flower, nor move her hand. Only when she felt his hand curve around the nape of her neck did she still completely. Her finger touching the petal hovered immobile, her unvarnished nail gleaming pale against the vivid magenta of the bloom.

But the flowers had disappeared.

The whole world had disappeared.

Only one thing still existed.

The touch at the nape of her neck.

His hand was warm, encircling, resting on the bared skin beneath her chignon. She could feel the tips of his fingers, moving slowly, exploratively, hardly at all. With such a slight movement, how could they engender such sensation?

Because sensation *was* dissolving through her, wave after slow wave, shimmering down her spine, fanning out across her shoulders, easing along her neck, her throat.

She could not move, only stand there as still as a statue while the press of his hand on her nape, the slow moving of the tips of his fingers, became the whole world of existence to her.

Was she still breathing? She did not know. Knew only that the world had become focused minutely, consumingly, on his touch.

The tips of his fingers reached further, spreading out to splay around her throat. His thumb found the small hollow behind her ear, stroking into it gently, so gently, that she thought she must faint and fall, as the shimmering sensation became focused on that one point of being.

Then it shifted, and his thumb and forefinger closed over the tender lobe of her ear, feeling the fullness of that delicate flesh. Slowly, so slowly, she felt her head droop and turn, so that his long fingers could span further, stroke yet more of her throat, while his thumb feathered at the softness of her earlobe.

It seemed to last an eternity. An eternity that dissolved around her as she stood helpless, immobile, while Diego Saez touched her, stroked her. She had no will left, no strength, no resistance.

She was nothing, nothing except sensation. Slow, drugging sensation.

Slowly, as if it were infinitely heavy, she lifted her head to let her eyes gaze ahead. Through the mesh of vivid petals she saw her own reflection, a pale, slight figure, and behind her, as if caging her, Diego Saez's tall, imprisoning darkness.

She stared, eyes unblinking. His hand was still at her neck, but it was motionless now, merely holding the base of her head, watching her watching herself—and him.

Her gaze moved away from herself, shadowed by him, and moved to meet his.

For one eternal moment he held her gaze in the glass, his eyes dark, and hooded, and unreadable.

She felt her lungs tighten. For the briefest instant an urge so great she thought it must overwhelm her shook silently within her.

She should have run. Because if she did not, if she did not run now, something terrible would happen—something that would cost her more than she could pay.

More logic sliced through her mind.

You can't run. If you run now Salton will be lost, your family destroyed. You will have to live with that all your life, the fact that you ran and Salton was lost.

What did she count for compared with that? Whatever price she paid, Salton would be saved—for Tom, for his sons, for his grandsons.

She could not run. Could do nothing—nothing except go on standing here, caged by the man she was going to yield her body to, the man who was already putting his mark on her, with his hand resting on her bared skin.

So it was with complete, absolute acquiescence that without a word, with only the sliding of his hand down over her shoulder, pressing her around, she turned away from the mirror, trailing her fingers away from the vivid waxy petals. And with that same acquiescence she let him guide her forward, his hand splayed now across the small of her back, hardly touching her, but for all that controlling her—totally.

The bedroom was vast, and as opulent as the reception room. The floor-length curtains were already drawn, bedside lights already lit and turned low. She walked into the room, and halted.

Her heart slewed in her chest with heavy, uneven strokes. He shut the door behind them, then came up to her.

He touched her hair with his hands. Not stroking, simply drawing his fingers lightly back from her temples. That same quivering sensation that had shivered through her when he had touched her nape, her earlobe, her throat, shimmered through her again.

His hands were cupping her chignon now, drawing out one by one the pins that held it. He let them fall to the floor, indifferent to their fate. Long fingers loosened her hair, threading through it until the coils unwound and layered down her back.

Something was happening to her. It was that same sensation again but more, like tiny ripples of water, merging together into larger ripples.

He was speaking—indistinct words. It was Spanish, but none that she could understand. His voice was low. There was a husk in it. She could feel his breath softly on her neck. He had moved the heavy fall of her hair to one side, smoothing it across the material of her dress.

His fingers were at the top of her zip, and with a sudden swift glide he pulled it down the length of her spine, using both hands to part the material. His hands were flat on her bare shoulderblades. The heat in them burned like a brand.

He is branding me. Branding me as his possession.

She felt the breath rise in her throat. The ripples were spreading, growing more and more. Quickening.

The tips of his fingers threaded under the straps of her bra and she realised that not only was the zip of her dress undone, but the clasp of her bra as well. Silently he pushed the material of her dress, the straps of her bra, down over the cusp of her shoulder.

Then, with the same pressure on her shoulders, he turned her around to face him.

She lifted her eyes to him.

His were narrowed, lit with a dark intensity that seemed to pierce her, deep and penetrating.

Again that slicing sensation knifed through her, but now it was a thousand times more potent.

He lifted a hand from her shoulder, and lightly, very lightly, ran the backs of his fingers down her cheek.

She felt weakness flood through her, and that shimmering, shivering sensation again. But she couldn't move. Was trapped utterly in the rippling, emotions cascading through her.

She went on gazing at him, unable to move. Helpless. Helpless with sensation.

Slowly, very slowly, she watched his mouth lower to hers.

She tasted of cool water on a hot day, like scented nectar. He opened her mouth and drank deep from the sweet well.

She did not respond, simply stood there as passive as she had been as he'd stroked her, and for an instant a biting emotion went through him. A low, viscous anger.

Did she really think that she could simply offer him her body as if she were a puppet? Did she really think that she could stay *uninvolved* while she bought her precious stately home for the price of her body in his lowly hands?

Those hands pressed against the bare skin of her back, folding her into him. His kiss deepened.

For an instant, a moment longer, she still resisted him, and then, as if every bone in her body had suddenly melted she responded.

Triumph surged through him! She could *not* stay uninvolved! No, she would be trembling in his arms, clinging to him—*aching* for him, for his possession!

And he would possess her all right! *Dios*, but he would possess her. She would be his—entirely, consumingly.

He tasted her mouth one last time, then drew back.

He wanted to see all of her.

Portia was drowning, drowning in sensation. The ripples which had been widening suddenly swirled into a white whirlpool, sucking her down.

For an instant, when he had first bent to kiss her, she had felt paralysed, her heart surging into her throat. And then as his kiss deepened the whirlpool of sensation had flooded through her.

He was kissing her as she had never, ever been kissed before. She had never responded like this before. The kiss he had given her at the art gallery had been as a gentle stream. This was a drowning whirlpool, extinguishing everything around her. Nothing else existed except the touch of his lips, his tongue.

And then, just as suddenly, when time had stopped and all meaning, his mouth moved from hers.

She felt bereft, as if she had lost something infinitely precious.

But even as the sense of loss washed through her a new realisation took its place.

He was stripping her.

She could feel the material of her dress slip from her shoulders, taking her loosened bra straps with it, and then suddenly, shockingly, she felt her breasts engorge, her nipples harden.

Slowly, seductively, he slid the dress down her arms. The touch of his hands moving over her bare skin ignited another intense sensation that shimmered through her again. She sought to still it, but it was beyond her power. Everything was beyond her power—except to yield to the exquisite, magical feelings that were rippling through her body.

But as she felt the dress slip completely from her, her bra tumbling to the floor, revealing the swell of her breasts, instinctively, protectively, she shut her eyes.

Immediately she felt the stroke of the backs of his fingers along her cheek. His voice as he spoke was low, commanding.

'Oh, no, Portia—not that way. *This* way—'

She felt the trail of his fingers glide downwards, softly knuckling the line of her throat, and then continue to descend. Softly, very softly, he stroked the side of her breast.

The breath stopped in her throat. He repeated the movement, and this time he brought his other hand to her other breast, stroking outward and downward from the topmost swell of each engorged orb.

The world disappeared. Disappeared completely, utterly. Just as it had when he had stroked along the nape of her neck, so now the entire world simply became the touch of his hands at her breasts.

Sensation dissolved through her.

Her body dissolved.

Into a feeling and emotion she had never, ever in her life felt before. Had never even known existed.

Wonder took over. How, *how* could such feeling exist? Her drawn-down lashes quivered on her cheeks and she gave herself to his soft, exquisite exploration.

She thought she heard Diego Saez say something, but she paid no attention. Her whole being was focused, unseeing, on what she was feeling. That soft, feathering touch, she realised in confusion, was making her breasts feel so strange, so heavy. An extraordinary lassitude was sweeping through her. She felt weak, boneless—his.

She gave a low, helpless moan, deep in her throat.

Her breasts were just as he had wanted them to be. High and pale, with a soft swell to them peaked by small pink tips. As he stroked them to ripening fullness, watching the nipples tighten, he felt his own body echo that hardening in response.

She was giving that low, helpless moan again, her eyes still shut, lashes like silk against her flushed cheeks. Satisfaction scythed through him. Portia Lanchester might not have wanted to soil her fine, aristocratic hands on him, but she was responding to him all the same—completely.

He had known she would. Known from the moment her bored gaze had been speared by his the first time he had set eyes on her, known from the way her body had tensed, signalling its awareness of him, that she would be helpless against him.

Now the pleasure he felt in her response to his touch was more than sensual, lending an edge to his possession of her that quickened his appetite.

He stroked her breasts again, hearing again that soft, blind, helpless moan.

It pleased him, pleased him very much, but he wanted more. Much, much more.

He wanted her naked.

And more—much more.

His hands slid down her silky flanks, feeling the slenderness of her body. As he did so he pushed down the fabric of her dress until it slithered free over her hips and cascaded to the carpet. He rested his hands on her, splaying his fingers around her soft curves.

He looked down at her. Her eyes had opened, and they were staring, wide, dilated, up at him.

For a moment, just a brief, fleeting moment, an emotion jerked through him that had nothing to do with the powerful, throbbing urgency of his state of arousal, nothing to do with the low anger banked down inside him.

It had everything to do with the expression of helpless, wondering vulnerability in her wide grey eyes.

Then, as the needs of his own body surged again, he felt his hands tighten over her hips. And Portia was lost, lost—in a world so wonderful she never wanted to leave.

He scooped her up and carried her to the bed.

CHAPTER EIGHT

THE low throb of the jet engines seemed to vibrate through every cell in Portia's body. She shifted slightly in the wide leather seat.

It did no good.

Her whole body throbbed.

But not because of the vibration from the powerful engines.

She pressed her eyelids shut more tightly, trying to blot out memories as she blotted out vision.

But she could not.

Her body was one entire sensate memory. Every centimetre of her skin bore its imprint. Even the most intimate folds of her body.

Especially those.

Between her thighs the low, insistent throbbing was witness to her folly.

How could I? How could I have responded to him like that?

The rhetorical question mocked her. She knew exactly how—why—she had responded as she had. Because she had been taken somewhere she had not even known existed—an exquisite, ecstatic place of wonder, of enchantment and mystery, a revelation so intense it had transfigured her.

And the person who had taken her there, step by shivering step, had been Diego Saez.

He had lowered her down onto the bed, peeling away the rest of her clothes and then doing likewise with his own. Her eyes had been dazed in wonder when she'd seen his strong, planed body emerge from the dark veneer of his suit.

Geoffrey's body had been slim, almost boyish. There was nothing boyish about Diego Saez's body. Broad shoulders, powerful chest, muscles smooth and gleaming. She had wanted to graze her hands over them, feel their strength, their power. Her arms had reached up to him, touching almost with fear, with wonder, with the tentative tips of her fingers, the contours of his shoulders, his arms.

He had folded down on her, his weight so heavy that she had almost gasped, and then the gasp had turned to a moan, as with shock, with piercing pleasure, he had lowered his head to suckle her.

From that moment on she had been lost, utterly carried away on a tide so strong, so irresistible, she had been able to do nothing but be sucked into the white swirling maelstrom of sensation. No part of her body had been secret to him. He had explored, caressed, *possessed* every part of it. And she had lain beneath him, helpless, swept away by what he was doing to her. Time had lost all meaning. Reality had slid away. All that had been real was her body—and what he was doing to it.

It had been a revelation, a miracle. She had never *known* that she could feel like that, feel such hunger, such wonder—such gasping pleasure. Her body had been hers no longer. It had belonged to him, totally to him, the man who had consumed her, possessed her.

And she had been his. She had given herself to him without restraint, without caution—with a yearning, straining ardour that he had drawn from her with every caress, every skilled, arousing touch, until she had been a mesh of sensation.

And when he had possessed her fully, powerfully, surging within her with all his strength, she had gasped at the wonder, the pleasure of it all, exploding all through her, again and again.

But that was nothing—nothing to what she had gone on

to feel as, stroke by powerful stroke, he had brought her inexorably, relentlessly to the topmost peak. And then out of nowhere, it seemed—for she had not known her body was capable of it—she had been convulsing around him, crying out, a tide of ecstasy engulfing her in wave after wave of pounding, threshing pleasure.

It had gone on, as if it would never stop, *could* never stop, as if she were one entire fusion of endless, endless bliss.

She had cried out his name, helpless with wanting, with wonder, then cried it out again, wrapping herself around him, holding him to her, because she would never let him go, never...

And then, as she had come down from her ecstasy, her eyes blind, her vision slowly clearing, she had gazed, weak, panting up at him.

He had been looking down at her, shock in his eyes.

She had reached a trembling hand to cup his face.

'Diego...'

Her voice had been a whisper, a last caress.

For an instant longer he had stayed, with her hand curved around his jaw, and then suddenly, as if a bullet had been fired, he'd pulled free from her, put her from him and risen from the bed.

He had walked to the bathroom, and she had seen the play of muscle and sinew in his powerful, sculpted back, had felt again for one fragile, fleeting moment the wonder that had consumed her, and then, at the door to the *en suite* bathroom, he had turned, glancing back at her, his expression blank, indifferent.

'Use the other bathroom, Portia. And then get dressed. Be ready in fifteen minutes—don't keep me waiting.'

Then he had shut the bathroom door.

And in that moment, that sickening, hideous moment, she had realised with punishing, brutal clarity just *why* she had always run from Diego Saez...

Shame had burned through her. Hot, coruscating shame at her own blind, unforgivable folly.

That feeling was with her still now, as she sat, silent and strained, in the first-class airline seat.

And the same question burned through her mind, round and round.

How—how could I have responded to him like that?

To her, the experience had been wondrous, magical. A revelation so exquisite that she had been consumed by it.

To Diego Saez it had been nothing more than a quick lay with a woman he'd had to blackmail into bed with him...

And when it was over, he was done with her.

Until the next time he wanted sex.

Tightness garrotted her throat as she sat in the plane, feeling the low, betraying throb of her flesh, hating herself.

Desperately, brokenly, she had gathered to her the only armour that she had been able to find, like tattered rags to cover her shaming nakedness. And by the time she had walked out into the reception room of the suite, showered and reclothed, her hair redressed in its chignon, only the faint stain of colour along her cheeks and her swollen lips to betray what her state had been such a short time earlier, she had donned that armour, her only frail defence

He'd been standing at the table, immaculately attired in a dark business suit, freshly shaved, white cuffs gleaming against his tanned skin. He'd been closing down his laptop, clicking down the lid and zipping up the case with swift, decisive movements.

Something had gone through her as she'd watched his tall, powerful frame.

She had crushed it down.

It had no place in what had been between them.

He'd turned round.

His face had been shuttered, the way it had been when he'd walked into Salton.

'We'll stop off at your flat on the way. You can pick up

your night things and your passport. Don't take long. The flight won't wait.'

She'd stared.

'Flight? I...I don't understand.'

His mouth had tightened.

'You're coming to Singapore with me.'

'*Singapore*? But—but I—'

He walked to the door and opened it, pointedly waiting for her to walk through.

She took a breath.

'I have a job,' she said in a clipped voice. 'I can't just go...go off to Singapore!'

'You swan off from your job whenever you want,' he replied dismissively. 'Geneva—Yorkshire—America.'

'But that's for my work!'

'And when you disappear down to Salton?'

Her face tightened. 'I have leave owing to me.'

He looked at her impassively. His face was as closed as a book.

'Take some leave now.'

'But—'

He lifted a hand. 'Portia. Save the debate. I'm a busy man. I have more to do in my life than bail out third-rate merchant banks in exchange for sexual favours.'

She whitened like chalk, the breath freezing in her throat.

For a second, so brief she did not see it, something changed in his eyes. Then it was gone.

'I'm flying out to Singapore tonight, Portia. You come with me—you don't come with me. It's your choice.'

His voice was flat. His face expressionless.

So was hers as she walked out of the suite in his wake.

Choice? The word mocked at her, just the way Diego Saez had mocked her with it. She had no choice. If she walked away from him now, when he had indicated that he wanted her to come to Singapore with him, for when he wanted sex again, would he go ahead with his bail-out of

Loring Lanchester? Would Tom lose Salton, everything that meant anything to him?

No, she had no choice. No choice.

She barely had time to collect her passport from her bureau, throw together a small hand valise of essentials, and leave voicemails for Hugh and Tom to say that she had gone abroad at short notice. She did not specify her destination. It was not Hugh's concern—only that she was highhandedly helping herself to yet more leave—and as for Tom…what could she possibly say?

Diego Saez's brutal words seared in her mind—*I have more to do in my life than bail out third-rate merchant banks in exchange for sexual favours…*

Cold flushed through her.

And when Diego Saez has had his fill of you—he'll leave.

Her mind sheered away. She must not think of that. Must not feel. From now on her only salvation was that frail armour she had donned.

She wore it now, as she sat beside him, separated only by the inset drinks table between their seats. He was working, rapidly scanning through dossiers, papers, making marks every now and then with a gold fountain pen. He was utterly self-contained. He had spoken to her only when necessary, in a terse, closed voice. She had done what he had told her—silently, obediently.

A heavy numbness descended over her. The throb of the engines resonated with the throb of her body as the plane ate through the night towards the eastern dawn. She turned her head to stare out of the dark porthole. No stars, no moon visible. Only blackness.

All around her.

It was the late afternoon of the following day when the plane landed at Changi Airport. By the time the chauffeured limo pulled in under the portico of the *de luxe* hotel on Orchard Road the tropical night was already curtained around them, pierced by the jewelled brightness of the city lights. For a few brief moments as she exited the car Portia felt the heat and humidity close over her like a steam bath. The air felt thick to breathe, filling her lungs with warm dampness. But when she walked into the chill of the air-conditioned lobby the cold made her shiver. Or something did.

She walked beside Diego, his long stride making it hard for her to keep up with him. Her feet felt swollen from the long flight, her shoes tight, and she longed for a shower.

She felt dazed, disorientated. Her body clock was completely awry. But even without the time difference she would have felt the same.

If she had thought the suite Diego Saez had occupied in London luxurious, she had to reclassify the one they were shown to now. It was vast—the size of an apartment in its own right. Instinctively she crossed to the huge window. One of the staff was there before her, bowing and asking if she would like to go out on to the terrace. She shook her head and turned back.

Awaiting orders.

Inside her, sickness ate like acid.

Diego disposed of the hovering staff and looked across at Portia Lanchester.

She was as white as a ghost.

His mouth tightened.

'Go and lie down before you pass out.'

His voice sounded brusquer than he'd meant it to.

She seemed to flicker slightly, like a candle guttering before it went out, then, recovering, she looked around, clearly wondering which direction to go in.

'Take the second room. Get some sleep.'

He saw her tense visibly, and the movement irritated him. As she moved past him towards the door he indicated he caught her arm. She stilled utterly, going rigid. He stepped up to her.

'Don't start, Portia, what you aren't prepared to finish,' he said softly.

Then he let her go.

He watched her go into the second room. Then, abruptly, he turned and headed for the terrace.

As he stepped out from the air-conditioned interior of the room the heat enveloped him like a hot, sultry blanket. His breath caught. His hands closed over the warm surface of the balustrade. He stared out into the tropical night.

Memory drenched through him.

The thickness of the air, the instant sweating of the body, the enveloping, encompassing heat. But here, at least, in this clean, hygienic city on the equator, there was no stench—no foetid reek of drains and sewage and contaminated water, of rubbish rotting in the heat, infested with vermin, picked over by the human detritus searching for anything to keep them going in the hell in which they lived out their lives.

His knuckles whitened as they pressed the top of the railings, his shoulders tensing.

Why the hell was he thinking of that stinking cesspool of a slum in San Cristo? He never allowed himself to remember. Never.

But these days the memories intruded more and more. He knew why. He gave a tight, savage smile.

Portia Lanchester. Portia Lanchester with her white skin and her fine bones and her wide, cool grey eyes.

She was opening that gate to the past that he had thought locked for ever.

Portia.

He didn't want to think about her.

The smile vanished, replaced by a closed, forbidding expression.

What the hell had gone wrong?

His stared out into the hot, jewelled night, oblivious to the noise of traffic coming up to him over the tops of the ornamental trees in the hotel grounds.

Portia Lanchester had thought she could offer up her pale, soft body and then get up from his bed without a hair out of place in her chignon!

He had showed her otherwise. *Por Dios*, but he had shown her!

He had wanted her pleading for him—and he'd got what he'd wanted. She'd lain beneath him, hair loosened and tangled on the pillow, eyes wide, dilated, giving those low, moaning gasps in her throat, her straining body arching up to him.

He felt his body tightening even as memory swarmed in his head.

And when she'd come—

Cristos—it had been her first time! It had to have been The shock on her face had been absolute. She had stared up at him incredulous, disbelieving, for one brief second, before orgasm had convulsed through her. She had cried out—a high-pitched sound of anguish and ecstasy—and in that instant, that fraction of a second, it had all gone totally, terrifyingly wrong.

His own body had flooded with her.

A sharp intake of breath knifed through him as he stared blindly out into the dark.

How could it have happened?

He'd been totally, completely, out of control. Unable to halt that sudden, unstoppable surging of his body. The total, absolute need to fill her.

Become one with her.

Roughly he pushed away from the balustrade and strode back inside.

I should have left her in London.

A mocking smile parted his lips. He knew exactly what he'd brought her to Singapore for. Portia Lanchester had sold herself to him, and he was still in the mood to buy her wares.

And next time he took her he would be in total, absolute control.

* * *

The sun was high when she woke. For a good half an hour she just simply lay there, unwilling to go out of her bedroom in case Diego Saez was there. But eventually she realised she couldn't just go on hiding for ever in her room.

Dressing was simple. She'd managed to grab a single sundress and a change of underwear from her flat, and, after her shower, she put them on.

Heart in her mouth, she went out into the suite's sitting room.

It was deserted.

Clutching her handbag, she went out. She had no key, but assumed that the hotel would let her back in if need be.

There was a coffee shop downstairs, off the huge lobby, and she sat there a while, sipping coffee and nibbling a pastry. She didn't feel hungry.

She didn't feel anything.

That total sense of blankness had descended on her again. She could feel nothing.

Deliberately she kept it that way. It was the only way she was going to survive this. She knew that. By keeping that frail armour around her. By recognising, admitting, that there was nothing else for her to do. She had no choice any more. She was here to save Salton—not herself.

And to do that she had to be what Diego Saez wanted her to be.

A body for his bed.

Nothing more.

And when she was not in his bed, then she would have to keep that frail armour around her—the armour that kept the rest of the world away from her, kept her within a blank, insensate cocoon.

It was the only way to get through.

She paid for her breakfast with her credit card, and wandered out into the lobby again. Outside, through the revolving doors, she could see hot sunshine beating down.

She wondered what to do. Presumably she ought to stay in the hotel.

And do what?

The place must have a pool, she supposed, and went across to the desk to make enquiries. The smiling assistant also indicated the small interior mall of shops and boutiques, stretching in a wide corridor beyond the bank of lifts. Using her credit card again, Portia bought herself a swimsuit. It was not her usual style, but it came with a filmy sarong in a matching gold and turquoise print.

Even through the shade of a thick parasol Portia could feel the sun beating down on her back. She would need to cool off in the pool again, but right now she was too tired to move. Although she'd slept till late she still felt exhausted.

It must be the heat...

But it was more than exhaustion of the body, she knew, even after the long, unexpected flight and the change in time-zones.

It was exhaustion of the spirit.

Effortlessly she dragged herself up off the lounger, feeling dizzy and disorientated as she stood up. She was on one of the layered roofs of the hotel, in an airy garden lush with potted palms and raised flowerbeds, with a sort of green felt carpet laid everywhere except for on the vivid blue tiling around the pool. As she stood in the sunshine, the heat hit her again, like a blast from a fire. After another dip in the pool she would have to go inside again—she felt weak from the heat.

The cool of the water closed over her like a blessing, and she sighed in pleasure. It was not crowded—just a few women, like her, lounging around the poolside. The hum of traffic from busy Orchard Street below could hardly be heard above the music piped out of speakers hidden in the greenery.

She dunked her head under the water, letting her hair

flow out like a mermaid's, floating back bonelessly, limbs splayed.

Eyes closed, she let the sun beat down on her face.

What am I doing here?

The question echoed around her brain, pointless, rhetorical.

She was there because Diego Saez wanted her to be there.

With him.

As she waded out of the pool, patting herself dry with one of the towels provided, wringing out her hair, she again felt the need to get back into the air-conditioned interior. Wrapping her sarong around her still damp bathing suit, she headed indoors.

She let herself into the suite with the key the reception desk had given her when she'd requested one, and stopped dead.

Diego was there.

He was sitting on one of the pair of sofas, legs extended, remote control in his hand as he watched stock prices flicker on the huge flat screen television in the room.

He looked up.

His face was shuttered.

But something flared deep in his eyes as they ran fleetingly over her scantily clad body, draped in the filmy sarong, dampened from the bathing suit beneath.

She stood there, incapable of speech.

She'd assumed—wrongly, it seemed—that he would be out all day—off downtown to the business section of Singapore, west of the harbour, where all the international banks and corporations were.

His voice, when he spoke, was dry.

'Did you sleep well?'

She swallowed, and nodded infinitesimally.

Inside her body, her heart suddenly seemed to have got too large. It was choking her. Her skin felt clammy, despite the chill of the room.

'Pleasantly rested?'

She gave that minute nod again, as her breath froze in her throat.

She could feel panic starting to mount, coursing into her bloodstream.

He got to his feet. It was a single, smooth, limbering movement.

She stood stock still, frozen to the spot.

He came towards her.

Her heart was racing. Like a stricken deer, fleeing for its life.

And finding itself at bay.

He reached a hand out. She tensed, her breath solidifying. He fingered the filmy material of the sarong.

'Very pretty. Have you been out shopping as well as enjoying the pool?'

She shook her head. He let his hand fall.

'You'd better go out this afternoon, then. You'll need clothes while we're here. Especially evening wear. There's a reception tonight. Buy whatever you think appropriate. Do you know Singapore?'

She shook her head again.

'Well, simply mention your preferred designers to the concierge, and they'll direct a car to take you. Obviously you will charge all purchases to me. Do you want a personal shopper?'

This time she managed to answer.

'No—no, thank you.'

He nodded cursorily. His eyes were frowning now.

'Did you bring any jewellery?'

For a moment she wondered if he was being sarcastic, but then he was speaking again.

'Then make sure you buy a dress that goes with diamonds.'

Words blurted from her. 'You're not buying me jewellery!'

He gave a derisive smile.

'I don't need to, Portia. I've already bought *you*. And the family bank, of course—and the stately home to go with it. You sold yourself to me, remember? Speaking of which...'

He reached forward again and flicked loose her sarong. It fluttered to the floor.

His dark eyes flickered over her. She felt as if she were naked. The damp swim suit outlined every curve of her body, clinging to her breasts, her stomach, outlining her pubis between the high-cut legs.

'Such a pity,' he said softly. 'I have an appointment with a government minister in forty minutes.'

He turned and walked away, back to his screen full of stock prices.

'Buy something—interesting—to wear tonight.'

She bolted for the sanctuary of her room.

CHAPTER NINE

THE car wound along a long, curving drive. On either side flambeaux flared, extravagantly lighting the way to a huge house set back in manicured grounds off the exclusive Tanglin Road. It was ablaze with light and people thronged within, visible through the acres of glass windows.

As always, as Portia stepped out of the limo, the heat of the tropics hit her after the air-conditioned cool of the car. Her high heels scrunched on the gravel as she lifted her long skirt minutely to make it easier to walk the short distance into the house. At her side the tall tuxedoed figure of Diego Saez kept pace.

The evening passed in a blur. The majority of people at the reception were Singaporeans, but there was a sizeable sprinkling of other nationalities, from European to African. She must have been introduced a hundred times, she realised, but she had taken almost nothing in. Apart from some of the younger European women, whose eyes openly speculated and who reached their own conclusions about what she was doing in Diego Saez's company, no one was interested in her. Diego Saez was the one they wanted to talk to. She was profoundly grateful.

Habit got her through the evening. She made polite chit-chat, dutifully admired Singapore's achievements, talked a little about opera and art, and sipped at her champagne. Inside her the knot of tension tightened with every passing moment. She was continually aware of the dark presence at her side.

Dreading the moment when he would take her back to the hotel suite.

No, don't think. Don't think about that. Don't think about anything.

She took another mouthful of champagne.

Diego listened impassively as the chairman of one of Singapore's largest shipping companies commented on the growing cost of marine insurance. He was paying no attention whatsoever to the subject under discussion.

He didn't want to be here.

The fact that he had conducted a sizeable amount of profitable business already, with more in the offing, was of no interest.

Only one thing was of interest to him.

Getting Portia Lanchester back to his hotel suite.

She was wearing a long, classic-cut dress of deep blue. Had she done it deliberately? he wondered. Picked the colour he had first seen her in? She had dressed her hair the same way as well, in a tight French pleat that exposed the bones of her face, the line of her neck. The dress was high cut, very nearly a *cheongsam*, but with a round neckline, not a high standing collar. It was sleeveless, however, and every now and then his own sleeve would brush against her bare arm.

He could feel her tense whenever it happened.

He glanced at her profile. Her cheekbones were stark, her jaw set. Her skin looked ashen.

Around her neck, the diamond necklace he had hired for the evening looked garish. She had accepted it passively, making no comment as he fastened it around her neck before they set out. Only the sudden tensing of her whole body as he stood behind her had revealed her reaction to him.

Anger bit through him again. What the hell business had Portia Lanchester to flinch away from him like that? She had sold herself to him—and he had every intention of ensuring he got value for money from her.

And that included a willing woman in his bed.

He shifted his weight uncomfortably from one leg to the other. Thinking of bed and Portia Lanchester right now was not a good idea. It was close on forty-eight hours since he'd first had her, and it had simply whetted his appetite. He wanted her again—now—badly.

With scarcely contained frustration he tuned back into the conversation about global shipping.

At his side Portia Lanchester stood, stiff as a piece of wood, repeatedly sipping her champagne, her face a mask of tension.

All the way back to the hotel Portia leant into the corner of the back seat of the limo and stared out of the tinted window. Despite the hour, Singapore was still awake. People thronged the wide, litter-free pavements, tourists evident by their shorts and the cameras slung around their necks.

She looked out at them, dissociated, dispassionate.

She had drunk too much champagne, she knew. It creamed down her veins, flowing like an insulating blanket over her ragged nerves.

But she needed it. Needed something, anything, to keep her going.

To protect her through the ordeal that she knew awaited her.

Diego Saez would want to take her to bed again.

And when he did she would be unable to stop her body responding to him, catching fire, igniting with the flame he lit in her.

And she knew it would be a torment that would be unbearable.

But she would have to bear it. That was the very, very worst of all.

Don't think! Just don't think.

She went on staring out of the darkened car window.

When they walked inside the hotel everything seemed very far away. Unreal.

The swoop of the lift as it bore them upwards hollowed her out.

Cocooned in her haze of champagne, she walked into the suite and halted. What did he want her to do? Go into her room? His?

She stood, waiting for instructions. The room seemed to be moving in and out.

'Portia?'

Diego's voice seemed to be coming from very far away. She turned around to look at him and the room swirled around her.

She could see him looking at her, frowning.

'How much have you had to drink?'

She looked back at him. He was so tall, she thought, and those eyes were looking at her, making her feel faint and weak. His mouth had a sensual twist to it, for all it was set in a straight, tight line. The dinner jacket sat on his broad shoulders, superbly cut, the white of his shirt front strained across his broad chest.

She wanted to splay her hands across it. Feel the hard muscle beneath. Press up against him.

Weakness washed through her.

She gazed at him, drinking him in.

This was desire, she knew it. An emotion she had never before experienced.

Until Diego Saez.

She didn't know why fate had played so cruel a joke on her. Didn't know why of all the men in all the world it had to be this man—this man and only this man—who could do this to her. Reduce her to such weakness. Such desire.

But it was. And there was nothing she could do about it. Nothing at all.

Except yield to her desire, shed the frail armour she had tried to clothe herself in during the day, and give herself to the flame that he, and only he, could light within her.

So that she could burn for him.

It didn't matter that she would pay a price more terrible

than she could yet imagine for what she would have of him. And this was all she would have of him—this time, this brief time, when all he wanted of her was her body, though she wanted far, far more of him…

Slowly she walked towards him, swaying. Her whole being was focused on him. Nothing else existed any more.

He stood stock still. There was tension in every line of his body. His face was like stone. Except for one low pulse at his cheekbone.

The champagne creamed in her veins. How much had she had? She gave a slow, sensual smile.

'Just enough,' she whispered, and wound her arms around his neck and drew his mouth down to hers.

For one brief, rejecting second he resisted. Fighting for control.

But as the softness of her lips met his he was lost.

His mouth opened, opening hers with it.

He heard her sigh, felt her sink against him. Automatically he caught her body, holding her at her waist. Her breasts pressed upwards against him. His hands tightened on her waist.

Her mouth was honey. Honey and champagne. Nectar to his lips, his tongue. He kissed her deeply, consumingly, possessing her mouth, one hand sliding up her spine to mould her against him. The other slid down over her rounded bottom, pulling her into him.

His arousal was total, instant.

Waiting no longer, he twisted her round in his arms and lifted her up, then carried her through into his bedroom.

She was velvet and silk. The fine fall of her loosened hair was a pale swathe across the pillow. Her small, high breasts were tipped with coral, her white skin like pearl, flushed with the opalescence of desire. Around her throat the diamond necklace burned with blue fire in the lamplight.

On the floor, in a pool of sapphire, her dress lay discarded. Nearby his clothes were flung—carelessly, urgently.

He stroked her hair and tasted her mouth again, caressed the softness of her breasts, her slender flanks, the slim columns of her thighs. She arched beneath his hand like an arrow. He moved his body over hers, parting her thighs, honeying the dew from her, hearing the little moans she gave in her throat.

He wanted to fill her, sink deep within her, possess and spear the body spread wide for him, open and defenceless. He stroked her hair one last time, holding her wrists above her head, and entered her slowly, watching her face. Her eyes were open this time, denying him nothing, yielding him everything.

His control was absolute. This time he would set the pace, he would take her and enjoy her, watch her flood for him, helpless beneath him, pulsing for him, supremely vulnerable.

She came. He saw it happen. Saw the flush of her orgasm redden her breasts, sweep up along her throat, suffuse the lines of her cheeks. Her throat arched and a high, soundless cry came from it, parting her lips.

Triumph surged through him.

More than triumph.

But with a sense of cold, disbelieving shock he realised that he, too, was about to climax.

He could not stop himself. It surged through him—powerful, ruthless with its own need, its own urgency for satiation now, right *now*.

He climaxed in a single thrust, rearing over her, filling her, flooding her. The release was exquisite, and for a few timeless seconds nothing else existed. Then, as swiftly as it had happened, it ebbed away.

Exhaustion gripped him, and satiation—and something else that he could not recognise.

He didn't care.

His heart hammered, slumping in his chest, and he drew a long, harsh breath of relief. Relief—release—such as he had never known before.

For a few seconds longer he held himself over her. Then with a swift, withdrawing movement he disengaged. He did not look down at her.

For some reason—something he would not admit to himself—he did not want to look at her. Did not want to see the expression in her eyes.

Instead he rolled out of the bed and headed for the bathroom.

'The day is your own. I'm in meetings until the evening. What will you do? More shopping?' Diego's voice was clipped, almost curt.

'Why not?' Her voice was equable.

Indifferent.

She had her armour on. It kept the world away. Kept her inside a blank, numbing cocoon.

They were eating breakfast at a table set by the window. Portia was picking at a slice of papaya. Diego was polishing off Eggs Benedict. He seemed to eat with a huge appetite.

But then he was a large man. Tall, broadly built. He would need feeding.

No, don't think about his body—what it does to yours...

That was for night-time. The night-time, when she had no armour to wear. When her naked body bared its aching vulnerability to his.

And he took total, ultimate advantage of it.

She pushed her plate aside.

A frown crossed his brow.

'Why aren't you eating?'

'I'm not hungry.' She reached for the coffee pot and poured out some more coffee.

Something flashed briefly in his eyes. It looked like anger, and she wondered why.

Diego watched her. She wasn't hungry. His mouth tightened. She would never have felt hungry in her life. She wouldn't know the meaning of the word.

He did.

He knew hunger, all right. Knew it like a dog gnawing at his guts.

He slammed the memory away. He would never feel hungry again—not unless he chose to.

He forked the last piece of the Eggs Benedict and sat back. He should be feeling relaxed, but he wasn't. Sex always relaxed him. And he had had a lot of sex last night. And more just now, on waking.

But he wasn't relaxed.

Maybe I'm going off her. Had enough of her.

His eyes flickered over her, sitting opposite him. She was wearing an emerald-green silk kimono, embroidered in gold. She must have bought it yesterday, when he'd sent her out to get the evening dress.

The wide sleeves made her hands seem smaller as she lifted her coffee cup with a graceful gesture, cupping it between her pale fingers. The emerald silk fell back slightly, revealing slender forearms.

As she lifted the cup to her lips the folds of the kimono shifted slightly, outlining her breasts at either side of the deep vee.

He felt his body stir faintly, despite its satiation.

No, he hadn't had enough of her.

Abruptly, he got to his feet. Whatever he might feel inclined to do, he had to make a move. He had a lot to get through today.

Suddenly the day ahead seemed very long. And tedious. He wanted it over.

Irritation nipped at him. Usually he enjoyed his pursuit of wealth, stalking new opportunities, harvesting existing ones. And here in the Far East there was a whole lot of both. Asia Pacific was wide open—the money to be made here was breathtaking.

He liked the attitude to money out here. It was open and

honest. These burgeoning economies wanted money—and they were prepared to work their backsides off for it.

The way he had.

But not everyone worked for their money.

He glanced down at the blonde head, bowed slightly as she drank her coffee.

Portia Lanchester thought she could stay rich just by offering him her body. Even though it meant soiling her lily-white hands on him…

A hard smile curved his mouth.

She wasn't so fastidious about him now. No lying back and thinking of her precious stately home! No, she shuddered with pleasure in his arms, her body pulsing, unable to stop her response to what he did to her.

His smile deepened, and there was a dark glitter in his eyes.

Making her take pleasure in what she was offering him was his own particular pleasure.

And shocking her with his demands—that added to his pleasure too.

He'd made a lot of those demands in the night.

And there'd be plenty more tonight, too.

But first he had to get through the day.

It stretched ahead of him endlessly.

I'm being a tourist, thought Portia. She had taken a taxi and gone down to the old centrepiece of Singapore, the wide green Padang, where British colonials had once played cricket in the days of Empire. Now the red-roofed cricket pavilion was dwarfed by the giant high-rise blocks that were modern Singapore. She'd seen the greystone Merlion, rising from the sea by the harbour, half-lion, half-fish, symbol of a city called into existence by Victorian merchants and now the busiest port in the world and a global financial powerhouse.

She was lunching at Raffles, the legendary hotel named after Singapore's founding father Sir Stamford Raffles, flanked by flat-leafed palms, gleaming white in its restoration as a tourist attraction. She sat at a table on the inner veranda, overlooking a pretty courtyard garden, picking at delicious food. She felt bad, because much of it would be wasted, but she could not force more of it down. She set it aside and went back to sipping her iced water.

She felt suspended. A fly in amber. Time was moving, but she was not. Her body ached, as if she'd done too strenuous a workout.

Inside her head pressure seemed to be building.

She knew, with a certainty that was like a knifeblade slicing through her, that what was happening to her was destroying her.

And there was nothing she could do about it.

She had become an addict, one who both craved and hated her addiction.

And her addiction was Diego Saez, who could take her to a paradise of the senses she had never known existed—and then abandon her.

She meant nothing to him. Nothing but a body.

Somewhere, very deep within her, a slow pulse throbbed. In her head the pressure swelled, seeking escape.

But there was no way out. No escape from what Diego Saez was doing to her.

She went on sipping her water, and staring out over the tropical plants of the central courtyard.

In the afternoon she went shopping, drifting through one mall after another along Orchard Street. She bought a few small items—some toiletries to keep her going, some underwear, a few more clothes, a handful of magazines and some books. She didn't know how long Diego Saez would be staying here in Singapore, or where he would go afterwards.

Or how long he would keep her.

She knew only that she had made her choice, and that from that choice there was no going back.

She would have to see it through to the bitter, bitter end.
Whatever the price she was paying.

Diego lounged back against the pillows. A whisky glass
was in his hand, and the sheet was half pulled up over him,
riding low on his hips. In his lap, Portia's head rested, her
fine silken hair spread over the curve of his thigh, her body
stretched out across the wide expanse of the bed. Though
he was spent, the pressure of her head on his groin was
faintly pleasurable.

Idly he stroked her hair.

He took a sip of his whisky.

He felt—replete.

This time had been the best yet.

It was, he knew, because this time he had stayed in total
control the whole time. There had been no more disastrous
going over the edge at her first orgasm.

He had had to adopt several methods stay in control, but
they had brought their own rewards.

Not least the satisfaction of seeing just how far—and
how fast—he could extend Portia Lanchester's sexual rep-
ertoire.

And she was learning—oh, she was learning, all right.
Learning just how infinite the pleasures of the flesh could be.

Tonight he had taught her just how much pleasure she
could feel even without his possession of her.

She'd been reluctant at first, seeming to expect that he
would want his own fulfilment, but he'd soon dissolved that
away. It had not been long before she was giving those low
little moans he liked to hear so much. He'd lain beside her,
propped on one elbow, looking down at her, enjoying the
way her nipples were like ripe red cherries. He'd brought
them to fruition first, gently teasing and squeezing them,
each upon each, until her breasts were a matched pair, each
a swollen, rounded orb, their peaks suckled to ripeness.

Then he had let his hand glide further down, to tangle
awhile in the tight curls at the clenched vee of her thighs,

until, with another little moan, she had slackened and given him access. And there, touch by touch, stroke by stroke, he had teased her to pulsing, flooding readiness.

She had pleaded with him, gasping his name in her arousal as she never did otherwise, her breath shallow, her hands kneading supplicatingly into the sheets, eyes closed in inward focus on the sensations rippling exquisitely through her body. But he had ignored her pleas, only continuing with his task, his eyes half closed, merely dipping his head every now and then to suckle one breast or the other, keeping both at engorged ripeness.

He had felt the pressure rising in his own body, known that had he followed his own appetite he would have come down on her and taken his satiation. But he had resisted, letting his fingers and not his body arouse her, sometimes halting quite deliberately, so that her closed eyes had flown open, anguish in them, until he had laughed softly and continued. And with a long, sensual sigh her eyes had fluttered closed again and she had given herself to his caressing.

Only at the last, when the flush had already started to stain across her breasts, and his forefinger had poised over the quivering nub of her delicate aroused flesh, had he paused one final time.

Her eyes had flown open again, gazing up at him with imploring disbelief.

He had leant forward, kissing her languorously on the mouth.

'Tell me, Portia, would you like me to stop?'

A smile had played about his mouth.

Her expression had been worth every word of scorn and derision she had ever thrown at him.

She had been beyond speech. Only a low, agonised moan in her throat, and her hips straining upwards to try and catch his touch again.

'Well?'

There had been the merest exhalation of breath. He'd had to strain to hear it. But it had been enough.

'Please… Diego….'

He had smiled again.

'My pleasure, Portia. Or rather, yours…'

His finger had lowered to her, vibrating, and he had watched her spill, the tide of her orgasm flowing out from that one supremely sensate point of her being.

It had taken her a long, long time to come down from it.

He had made sure of that.

And then, and only then, had he sheathed himself and taken his own enjoyment.

He lay back now, supremely relaxed, still stroking her hair. The second time, just now, had been even more pleasurable—and had shocked her even more.

Until, of course, she'd given herself to it and experienced, he was sure, a sensual banquet surpassing every other.

He smiled reminiscently, taking another sip of whisky. The complex fiery flavour overlaid quite a different taste. Portia—the very heart of her.

His fingers trickled softly along the tender line of her neck and he felt her move minutely in response. The movement altered the pressure on his groin, and he felt himself start to tighten.

After feasting on her he had given her subsequent orgasms in the traditional way—and himself. But now… He moved his hips a fraction and felt his arousal quicken. Now he felt in the mood for what he had given her.

He set down his whisky. He stroked her hair one more time, then brought both hands to cradle her head, turning it gently inwards. She resisted a second, as if she did not know what he was doing, or why. Then, as he murmured to her, at the same time sliding back the sheet, she finally seemed to realise his intent. Drawing up a little, to rest her weight across his now bare thighs, she dipped her head again.

Diego sighed pleasurably, and relaxed back more deeply into the pillows.

Her hair fell like a veil around him. Her lips were like velvet.

Portia took one more mouthful of the duck, and then set down her chopsticks. The plate seemed very far away. So did the gleaming white linen tablecloth, and the people around the table.

Everything seemed far away. Remote.

Unreal.

'The duck is not to your taste? It is a speciality of the house, but we can easily order something different for you if you prefer.'

The speaker, a petite, elegantly dressed Singaporean woman, sounded concerned. Portia gave a slight shake of her head.

'No, thank you. It's delicious. But I'm not very hungry, I'm afraid.'

Dark eyes narrowed at her from across the table. She looked down at her plate, where the almost untouched duck lay.

'Perhaps it is the heat,' said the woman. 'It takes a little while to acclimatise—especially the English. Your... partner...' She hesitated fractionally, then went on, 'He is more fortunate. You must be more used to higher temperatures. Señor Saez?'

Diego moved his eyes from Portia to his hostess, the wife of the president of an Asian telecoms company with whom he was discussing opportunities to invest in the developing communications infrastructure of China.

'San Cristo is further north than Singapore, but, yes, the summers are probably as hot as the climate here.'

'San Cristo?' said Mrs Ling politely.

'The capital of Maragua—one of the more inconspicuous countries in Central America.' Diego's voice was dry.

'Very little happens there to bring it to the attention of the rest of the world.'

'Wasn't there some turmoil there a year or two ago? Over elections?' Mr Ling enquired.

'Yes,' his guest conceded. 'A new popular front government was elected. It was not popular with everyone, however.' Diego's voice was even drier, but there was a grim tone lurking beneath.

Mr Ling gave a slight laugh. 'No, I would imagine not. Still—' he glanced across at his guest '—your interests, of course, Mr Saez, are global. And increasingly so.'

He went back to the topic of investment in China.

Portia reached for her cup of green tea. It was all she could face. The smell of the fragrant food made her feel ill. She took another sip of her tea and found that her hands were trembling. She tried to steady them, and could not.

She felt Diego's eyes on her, lancing at her.

'Are you all right?'

His deep voice cut through the miasma that was netting around her.

She looked at him. He was frowning.

'Perfectly, thank you.'

For a moment he held her eyes, and as he did so she began to feel pressure welling up inside her.

The expression on his face changed. He went back to talking to Mr Ling.

Mrs Ling made some remark to her about sightseeing in Singapore, and Portia forced herself to respond. But that same sense of dissociation started to float through her. Mrs Ling's voice seemed to drift in and out.

The pressure began to well up again inside Portia from very deep. Very slow, but inexorable.

She let her eyes rest on Diego. He was talking, completely absorbed in what he was saying to Mr Ling, who was listening attentively and nodding from time to time. As she looked at him she heard his words echo in her mind—*Not popular with everyone*... Heard the grim tone of his voice.

Nor popular with men like him. That was what he meant, she thought distantly. Maragua was probably one of those countries run by a dozen families, solely for their own interests, as their own personal fiefdom. They would resist any change of government, any threat to the power they wielded. When political changeover came men like him would pull out their capital and clear out, putting it somewhere much safer, like Swiss bank vaults and property in Mayfair.

Or invest it in telecoms in China.

With enough to spare for buying up ailing merchant banks and women who would not go to bed with them otherwise...

The pressure swelled in her head.

She set down her teacup and it clattered on the tiny saucer.

Mrs Ling paused in what she was saying. Portia had no idea what she had been talking about.

'Are you sure you are all right, Ms Lanchester? You seem a little—feverish.'

Portia forced herself to drag her eyes from Diego.

'I'm quite all right, thank you.' Her voice sounded clipped.

Across the table, Diego's eyes flickered over her.

There was a frown in them once more.

'I asked you if you were ill?'

There was a hectoring tone to his voice.

Portia turned away.

They were back in the hotel suite. Not answering, she walked across to the recessed section which housed the bar area, opening up the cabinet with its beautiful contemporary marquetry. She took out a bottle of gin and a tin of tonic, then opened up the concealed freezer to take out some ice, dropping a couple of cubes into a tumbler. The ice crackled as she poured the gin over it, and the tonic hissed and fizzed.

'Answer me!'

She took a sip of the drink, watching her hand shake slightly, and turned back to him. That strange, ballooning pressure that had swollen inside her in the restaurant had gone. It had disappeared as they'd come up here in the lift.

Something else had taken its place.

'Of course I'm not ill,' she answered.

'Then what the hell is wrong with you?'

She looked at him. The question was so unbelievable she could only stare at him.

'Portia—'

There was an odd note in his voice. She said nothing, only went on staring. He gave a rasp.

'Are you so incapable of speech?' he demanded.

She looked at him. From somewhere, she did not know where, the invisible armour slid over her.

'What would you like me to say?'

'What did you do today? Where did you go?'

She wondered why he was asking. What did he care what she did in the daytime? She only existed in the night-time. In his bed.

But she answered him all the same.

'I went to Sentosa.'

'Sentosa?' He looked taken aback.

'It's the island beach resort south of Singapore,' she answered indifferently. 'You get there by cable car from Mount Faber.'

'I know where it is! What did you go there for?' He seemed to be controlling his voice.

Her expression did not alter.

'To get away.'

His eyes narrowed.

'From what?'

From you. From this. To find, for a few brief hours, my sanity again.

She kept silent. It was all she had left.

She took another mouthful of her drink, and stood looking across at where he stood.

He was in a lounge suit tonight, the superb line of the tailoring moulding around his shoulders. She felt a kick go through her that was nothing to do with the gin.

And everything to do with her helpless, shameful addiction to him.

She wanted him.

Wanted to feel his body, hard and demanding against her.

Wanted him to strip the clothes from her and tumble her down on the bed.

Possess her.

Consume her, body and soul.

She took another mouthful of the gin and let her eyes wander over his tall, powerful frame.

His face darkened. He strode up to her, hands clamping around her upper arms.

She felt sexual excitement bolt through her. The sexual excitement he unleashed in her, night after night, that she had never known existed, that would never exist again once he had done with her.

He took the glass away from her, roughly setting it down. His eyes never left her. Something flared, deep in their depths.

'I don't want you drunk. I want you very, very sober...'

He pulled her against him, and lowered his head, spearing her hair with his hand.

And she was lost, sucked down into that vortex that sucked everything out of her. Everything except the consuming need to sate herself on him. And sate him with her naked, inflamed body.

'I need to speak to you.'

Portia's voice was clipped.

Diego looked up from the morning paper he was reading at the breakfast table.

Her face was expressionless. But then it always was.

Except in bed. Then and only then did that mask of indifference fall from her. Then, when he caressed her, possessed her, her face would show everything—everything that he was doing to her. She was helpless to resist her reaction to him.

He looked at her; his mouth tightened automatically whenever she had that face on her.

'So speak.'

A frown flickered in his eyes. Her face was looking almost gaunt. Her cheekbones were standing out and there was a stark look about her mouth.

She'd lost weight.

Her body was thinner, he could tell. It was hardly surprising. In the week they'd been here she'd eaten like a bird.

And it was starting to show.

She'd said she wasn't ill, so what the hell was wrong with her?

'How long are you planning to stay in Singapore?'

Her enquiry was cool, with that same edge of indifference that always got under his skin.

'Why do you ask? Do you think I've had enough of you yet?'

The skin seemed to tighten over her cheekbones.

'At the moment I'm taking unscheduled leave from my work. I need to know how much more I need to request.'

He laid down his newspaper

'Tell me, Portia, what if your request for more leave is turned down? What then?'

His eyes baited hers.

She didn't miss a beat.

'I would take unpaid leave. If necessary I would resign my job, effective immediately. Why do you ask?'

'To make sure,' he spelt out, 'that you understand the

terms and conditions of your presence here. You are with me until I say otherwise. Do you understand?'

For one long moment she looked at him. There was nothing in her eyes.

'You started this, Portia,' he said softly. 'And I promise you, I will finish it.'

He held her gaze a moment longer, then let it drop and went back to his paper, a tightness lashing inside him.

She reached for the coffee pot and poured herself another cup. As she set the pot back on its stand she found her hands were shaking again.

Kuala Lumpur, Manila, Taipei. The most prestigious hotels, the most luxurious suites. Days to herself, to do the round of the tourist spots, wander the shopping malls, sleep by the pool. Shut down her mind.

Endure.

And wait.

Wait for the night-time. Not the formal dinners or the business socialising that she did at Diego's side every night—poised, well-dressed, well-bred, with a flow of social chit-chat, trying not to drink too much, trying not to look at the tall, dark figure of the man of whose presence she was always, constantly aware. No, that was not what she waited for.

It was midnight. The midnight hours when she could finally sate her addiction for Diego Saez in what he did to her, what she let him do, what she felt in his arms, his bed. Addicted to his touch. Addicted to his possession.

It was a fever in her blood, in her body.

And it was burning her away.

Down to the bone.

Because, like every addict, she knew with a sick, hideous despair that there was a poison, destroying her.

But she had no choice. No choice.

Except to endure what he was doing to her.

*   *   *

Manila, Jakarta, Hong Kong.

He was pushing himself at a punishing pace. Something was driving him to it. He was doing business at a relentless speed, occupying every minute of the day.

Racing to get to the night.

When he could have Portia to himself again.

Not ringed around by other people, not with that cool, polite social smile pinned to her face, talking inanities because social convention demanded it, being that uptight, reserved, oh-so-English upper class female with her cut-glass accent and her *sang-froid*.

His mouth twisted. Cold blood?

Not when he had her under him, with the flush of her climax coursing through her! Not when she wound herself around him, feverish with desire.

Then—then her blood was hot…

That was the Portia he wanted—the one he got in the dark reaches of the night, when she belonged to him and him alone. When she yielded to him and him alone. When he feasted on her like a starving man.

Who could never have his fill of her.

He wanted her more with every day. His was a hunger that could not be sated, that grew with every passing day.

Consuming him.

Devouring him.

His mouth twisted into a savage, mocking smile.

How had it got like this?

How had Portia Lanchester reduced him to this?

Worse, how had he let it happen?

He did not know—knew only that soon, very soon now, he must find the strength to finish with her, sever her from his life.

Be free of her.

Before it was too late.

Portia leant on the balustrade of the balcony of a suite in a world-famous hotel in Kowloon, watching the *Star Ferry* ply its way across from Hong Kong island. The day was cloudy, the Peak wrapped in a white mist. She wondered what she would do today. She had already been sightseeing for three days. There wasn't much left of Hong Kong to see.

Perhaps she would go across to Macao, that strange, hybrid city, half-Chinese, half-Portuguese, with architecture to match. Or perhaps she would just stay here in this luxurious hotel.

The glass door slid open behind her.

'Portia?'

Diego's voice was brusque. She was used to it being so.

But as she turned and saw him standing there, hand splayed on the door's edge, those dark, hooded eyes resting on her, she felt, as she felt every time, the same surge of longing.

He met the hunger in her gaze and for a moment his eyes blazed with an answering hunger.

Then it was gone, blanked out with that familiar, shuttered look.

'Yes?' she answered enquiringly. Her voice was schooled to its usual level of steady indifference, which she always used when she had to talk to him.

He did not speak for a second or two, just went on looking at her with that closed expression on his face.

He looked tired, she thought, registering the observation with a sense of slight surprise. Though freshly shaved, and looking as superb as he always did in his hand-tailored business suits, the white shirt brilliant against the dark tan of his skin, his face looked drawn.

For an instant so brief she almost could not believe she had felt it, she had an urge to go to him, soothe her hand along his brow, wrap her arms around him to shelter him..

'I'm going to Shanghai for a few days.'

The curtness of his voice brought her back to reality. She looked at him expressionlessly.

Again something that she could not read shifted in his eyes.

Shanghai, she thought. Would there be a tourist agenda there? It wasn't exactly a tourist hotspot, just an industrial and financial showcase for the new, expanding Chinese economy.

'You can go back to London.'

His words fell into the air.

She went on staring at him, her expression unchanging. Again there was that movement in his eyes. She still could not read it.

'Did you hear me, Portia?'

'Yes.'

Her voice came from very far away.

'Your flight has been booked. A car will take you to the airport.'

She could only go on staring at him.

His mouth tightened.

'Portia—'

Her name hung in the air, and then without a word he slid the glass door shut and went inside.

She went on standing there, entirely, totally motionless. She could not see through the tinted glass of the balcony door. He had gone, disappeared from view.

For a long, long time she went on standing there.

When she finally lifted her hand from the balustrade to go indoors she found it was shaking.

CHAPTER TEN

HER flat was unchanged. Everything exactly as she had left it.

Yet she was completely changed. A different person.

As she set down her valise in the bedroom, her eyes caught her reflection in the looking glass on her dressing table. They slid away as quickly as possible, but not before she had seen the gaunt, thin figure in the glass.

She turned away, looking around her blankly.

She didn't know what to do.

Her mind did not seem to be working. She was still encased in the same deadening blanket that had surrounded her since she had walked back into the hotel room in Hong Kong from the balcony and realised that Diego had gone.

For want of something to do she went into the kitchen, running cold water and filling the kettle, staring about at the familiar units and appliances.

A cup of tea. That was what people had when they came back home after a journey. They had a cup of tea.

With immense effort she went through the motions of making tea in a mug with a teabag, then took it through into the sitting room. She switched on a table-lamp and sank back into the sofa. She felt so tired she thought she would never move again.

It was nearly midnight. The flight had deposited her at Heathrow some time after nine o'clock, but she had only been able to move in slow motion through the airport, and there had been a long queue for taxis.

She rested her head on the back of the sofa, shutting her eyes.

She wanted to feel something. Anything.

But all there was was that thick, deadening blanket, all around her.

She was home.

Home after a journey that had taken her far further than the other side of the world. A journey from which there could be no return.

She was no longer the person she had been.

Diego Saez had seen to that.

She felt that sense of pressure build up inside her again—the one she had become so familiar with. It seemed to balloon through her body, pressing outward. It threatened to break through, to explode her into fragments.

She clenched her fingers on the hot surface of the mug, willing the pressure to subside.

Suddenly, on impulse, she set aside her tea and stood up abruptly. With jerky, urgent steps she headed for the door, hurrying down to the bathroom. She stripped off her clothes, letting them fall, and yanked back the door of the shower, stepping inside.

The water rushed down over her, cold first, then warm, then finally hot. She reached for the soap and started to wash herself.

But she could not get clean.

Her doorbell went.

For an instant Portia froze, her hands hovering over the keyboard in the middle of the difficult—impossible—letter she was writing to Hugh. Then, pushing her chair back from her desk, she went into the hall from the second bedroom of the flat, which she used as a study. She opened the door into the outer hallway, which she shared with her brother's flat upstairs, and there was Tom, standing there, ready to ring again.

'Portia!'

He walked in.

'Where on earth have you been? You just about disappeared off the face of the earth?' He sounded both exasperated and anxious.

She was prepared for this. She had known Tom would realise she was home at some point and come calling. Though they did not live in each other's pockets, she did not usually vanish for such a long period merely on the strength of a brief message left on his voicemail.

'I took a holiday,' she said. 'It was all rather short notice.'

She did not look at him, merely led the way into the sitting room. It was hard to see him—very, very hard.

He followed her in.

'A holiday?' He was staring at her. 'Good God, sis, have you been ill? You look awful! Did you pick up one of those foreign bugs?'

She didn't answer him.

'Would you like a coffee? Or are you in a rush?' she asked instead.

He shook his head.

'I phoned Hugh to ask if he knew any more, and he said that all he'd got was a voicemail, same as you left me. Left late at night, too, like mine.'

'Yes, well, like I said, it was short notice.'

Tom was looking at her. She wished he wouldn't. There was concern in his eyes, worry.

'Portia, are you OK?'

She tensed.

'I'm fine,' she said automatically. Her voice sounded too brittle. But then her whole body felt brittle.

But she was functioning; that was the main thing. She had got up this morning, had gone out shopping to replenish her stores. It was a drizzly day—very English for summer. Quite normal. Everything was normal, in fact. The houses, the streets, the supermarket, the red London buses, the hurrying people. Quite normal.

Except that everything was happening through a thick, impenetrable, transparent glass wall.

Tom was behind the glass wall as well. She could see him, but he was very far away.

Or perhaps it was her who was very far away.

'You don't look fine,' he said bluntly. 'You look bloody. I think you should see the quack—get him to check you out. Some of those foreign bugs can be really nasty. Where did you say you went, anyway? Anywhere tropical? That's where the worst bugs are.'

'I'm fine,' she said again. Then, to get him to stop looking at her like that, she said abruptly, 'How are things over here?'

The moment she'd asked she wished she hadn't.

'OK,' he said. And then, expansively. 'In fact, never better. I've been given my "Get Out of Jail Free" card and I couldn't be happier! The takeover's forging ahead, and it's all a matter of paperwork now. Saez's man is in place, and he's just about running the show now—and I'm effectively on gardening leave. All I have to do is show up every now and then, just for appearances—I'm still a director, obviously, but I don't take decisions any more, thank God! Uncle Martin is out—pretty miffed, I can tell you. I got an earful from him about "jumped up foreign financiers"— you know what he's like! He rang a peal over me for my general incompetence and irresponsibility and went off in a huff. I don't care. He's not out of pocket, and he's still got all his non-exec directorships in the City to play with.

'You know,' he said, in a more serious voice, 'this takeover is the best thing that could have happened. It's extraordinarily fortunate that Saez thought it worth his while to bother with us.' He glanced at his sister. 'He's a seriously big wheel financially, you know. Still, maybe Loring Lanchester is just some sort of stepping stone for him—a lever to get to something else.' He shrugged. 'Who knows? I'm out of it now and I am just incredibly grateful.' His face sobered. 'I very nearly lost Salton. I came within a hair's breadth. Out of everything else that's all I care about—that Salton didn't go under the hammer. I've had a reprieve I didn't deserve, and by God, sis, I'm not going to mess things up again. I've managed to hang on to Salton, and now it will go on to my son.'

He rested his gaze on Portia, an almost sheepish expression on his face.

Waves of coldness were going through her. *A lever to get to something else...*

That was, indeed, all Loring Lanchester was to Diego Saez. A lever to get what he wanted—her in his bed.

The enormity of it made her faint.

Tom was talking again, behind that thick, transparent glass wall that still separated her from him.

'Speaking of which—son and heir and all that—I went to see Fliss this week. I've just come up from Salton now, actually, and it's all settled. We're not going to rush. Her mother wants a couple of months to buy her hat and all that malarkey, so it's likely to be September. In the meantime, I'm afraid I'm going to take advantage of this gardening leave and buzz off with Fliss somewhere. She deserves it—I've been a rat, letting her stew down there, not having the courage to tell her that with the bank about to crash I could never ask her to marry me. So I'm going to whisk her away somewhere really gorgeous. What's the Maldives like at this time of year? Is it the monsoon season now?'

He looked questioningly at Portia.

'I've no idea,' she managed to say.

'Oh, well, I dare say the travel agent will recommend somewhere suitable. Where did you go, by the way? Wherever it was we won't be going there! You've come home looking like a wet rag.' He frowned again. 'And you've lost weight too, Portia. You're thin as a bone! You really should see the doctor, you know.'

'I'm fine. Just jet-lagged.'

Her voice was short, but it was all she could manage. That pressure was building up again inside her head. She just wanted Tom to go—leave her alone—leave her inside her glass capsule.

But he wouldn't go.

'Jet-lag doesn't make you lose weight,' he retorted. 'You've got a bug, you know. You must have, because the only other reason girls lose weight is either because they're trying to catch a man or they've just been dumped by one. Neither is likely to apply to you, because I know there's been no one since you got so cut up over Geoffrey so—'

He broke off, staring at her.

She was holding herself together. It was hard, excruciatingly hard, because she was like a porcelain vase with hairline cracks running all over its surface. Inside the pressure was building up, and building up, and the cracks were widening...

'Oh, my God, sis,' said Tom in a hollow voice. 'Is that it? You ran off with some man and it all came to grief?'

He came towards her as if to take her hands, give her a comforting fraternal hug.

She stepped back. He mustn't touch her!

Or she would break.

The glass wall that was holding out the world, cocooning her inside it, would shatter.

And so would she.

'No! Don't! I'm quite all right, Tom. It—it wasn't anything serious. Just—just a fling.'

He shook his head, contradicting her.

'You don't do flings, Portia. So if some man persuaded you to go off with him there must have been something pretty deep going on for you.'

Yes, she thought, as the pressure ballooned inside her. I had to save Salton for you.

'He must have been pretty important to you,' Tom went on, his voice rich with sympathy.

'No! He wasn't important at all. He was no one.'

She could feel the cracks widening further. Any moment

now, the pressure would burst through them, shattering her into fragments.

He was still looking at her, pity on his face.

'I know how cut up you were over Geoffrey, and I've always hoped you'd find someone you could settle down with and marry and all that. I'm sorry this man wasn't it. Look,' he went awkwardly, 'you really do seem to have been badly hit by it, and although I know you're probably all set to go straight back to work, why don't you take a few extra days off and go down to Salton for a while? Mrs T would feed you up, and—'

'No!' The word shot from her like a bullet. 'I'm...I'm sorry, Tom, but I just want to be left alone. I...I can't go down to Salton.'

She could never go to Salton again. She had saved it for Tom, for his children, for his future with his wife, but the price she had paid meant she could never go there again.

Grief filled her, a huge welling up of grief. But she knew she could never go there again. She had exiled herself from it.

She turned away. She wanted Tom to go.

If he knew—if he knew what you've done! If he could see what you did with Diego Saez! If he could see what you let him do to you—night after night. And you craved it. You couldn't get enough of it. Couldn't get enough of him...

Her brother's voice came from very, very far away.

'I just want to be left alone, Tom,' she said in a thin, strained voice. 'I just want to be left alone.'

But being alone was no comfort. It was worse, far, far worse. Alone, by day and by night, she had to face her demon. The demon that tormented her,

Guilt.

Guilt for so much.

For giving her body to save Salton.

Guilt for having craved the man who'd bought it.

And, worst of all, pincering her with red-hot tongs, guilt at craving him still...

Because that was the worst, that was the ultimate guilt—that after all he had done to her she wanted him still.

The torment of it convulsed her. To want a man who had treated her like that. Who could take her, night after night, with nothing more than lust.

Memory flooded through her. Hot and humid and shaming.

Shaming because she had responded to him, trembled at his touch, burned beneath his skilled, remorseless caresses. A man who had blackmailed her into his bed because she would not come on any other terms.

But slowly, very slowly, out of the crushing burden of the guilt that pressed down upon her, another emotion began to stir.

Crushed long since by necessity. Repressed deep inside her. Because to give vent to it would be to lose the very thing she had sold herself for. An emotion that was so dangerous she had never once, not once, allowed it to surface. But it was there, like a slow, welling pressure, in the very core of her being.

And now it began to surface.

And as it did, as it made its relentless journey to the surface, she knew with a deep, abiding certainty that she must give it voice.

Or lose her mind.

Diego Saez sat back in a leather seat in the lavish chairman's office at Tencorp, an unreadable expression on his face. The chairman continued with his spiel, wondering whether he was catching his fish or not. With Saez you could not tell. What he did know was that if he did catch Saez for the joint venture he was proposing he would have caught himself a barracuda.

Across the room, on a wide black leather sofa, a third

figure was seated, the eyes in his narrow face flicking between his chairman and Diego Saez.

It hardly seemed yesterday that his chairman had despatched him to sound out Saez when he'd first appeared in London, yet in that time there had been a whirl of activity surrounding him. Piers Haddenham could have named half a dozen deals that had been set in motion between various City institutions and corporations, but the one that irritated him most of all was the Loring Lanchester takeover.

His mind flipped back to that bankers' dinner, and Saez looking over Tom Lanchester's iceberg sister. He hadn't shown his hand then as to whether it was the bank he was after or Portia Lanchester's frozen assets.

And all along it had been both.

Piers's mouth tightened. Typical of Diego's type to get them both—the bank and the cold-hearted bitch! Not that anyone knew about the latter—not here in London, anyway. If it hadn't been for someone he knew out in KL mentioning that Saez had turned up to a reception with the ice queen on his arm he'd never have known what was going down.

The meeting drew to a close.

Piers glanced at his chairman's face. He was not pleased, he knew. Saez was being evasive, and he'd brought up a whole load of time-wasting rubbish about insisting on running an environmental audit of Tencorp's proposal before signing up to any joint venture. It was just a tactic, obviously. Piers knew the deal being offered would make money hand over fist—what the hell were a few native settlements and some mangy animals in comparison with that level of profit to be made?

He watched Saez stand up and take his leave. As his gaze ran over the other man's tall, powerful frame, a familiar flush of envy went through him. The bastard had everything! Money, looks, and women throwing themselves at him. You'd have thought, mused Piers sourly, that he could have looked a bit more cheerful! As it was, his expression could have sunk a ship.

He stood dutifully aside to let Saez leave the office first, then followed him down the wide corridor towards the bank of executive lifts.

On the way down he attempted various pleasantries appropriate to the situation, but drew a blank response. As the lift doors sliced open, and they walked out into the huge, echoing lobby of the Tencorp reception area, Piers could not resist an unwise jibe. He felt like riling that self-contained bastard.

'So, turned up any golden nuggets in the empty coffers at Loring Lanchester?' he remarked.

His shaft got him nothing more than a silent look of unsmiling derision. Stung, Piers let fly another arrow. He hadn't sweated blood sucking up to this get-rich-quick merchant to get him to bite at the Tencorp proposal just so he could go back up to his chairman's office and get an earful about not having talked Saez out of that environmental audit garbage!

'Of course,' he went on smoothly, quickening his pace to keep up with Saez's long stride across the marble floor, 'you did get a personal sweetener, so I'm reliably informed. Tell me, was it worth buying a failing bank just to get inside Portia Lanchester's iron knickers—?'

He did not even see the fist coming. One moment he was taunting Diego Saez, the next he was sprawled flat on his back, blood pouring from his broken nose, hand clutching his dislocated jaw.

Without even pausing in his pace, Diego kept on walking to the door.

Rage consumed him. Cold, hard rage.

It snarled in him like an angry jaguar.

Not just at that loathsome piece of ordure he'd left groaning in agony on the floor.

At everything—the whole world.

But most particularly at two people.

Himself.

And Portia Lanchester.

His anger at himself was absolute. Unforgiving.

As he got into the chauffeur-driven car waiting for him at the entrance to Tencorp, his face darkened.

How could he—how *could* he be in this condition? How the hell had it happened?

He'd tried other women. They were never hard to come by. The ones he'd already had were always eager to come by for more, and every mixed-company social event he went to inevitably had a selection happy to make themselves available to him. Since returning from China and touching base with his European headquarters in Geneva he had deliberately run through half a dozen—old and new, in a variety of physical types—but every time, *every* time, he'd either sent them home or walked out himself.

They had done nothing for him. Nothing.

No woman did.

Only the memory of one.

Rage spurted in him again.

Why the *hell* did he still want Portia Lanchester? He'd had her—*Dios*, but he had had her!—so why the hell did he still want her?

Why was it only *her* body that he wanted beneath him, above him—any damn way so long as it was *her*?

Why was it only *her* face he kept seeing, by day and by night, intruding into business meetings, festering in his dreams?

How could he still want her?

A woman he despised. A woman who thought herself too good for his touch.

Except when his touch could save her family wealth…

Anger seethed in him.

How *could* he still want a woman like that?

*   *   *

The car pulled up in front of the Park Lane hotel. He would spend one night here, and then fly on to New York tomorrow. The Tencorp proposal he'd flown in to hear had been a waste of his time. They were not a company he wanted to do business with. Their environmental record was abysmal. He'd known it, but had stopped off in London all the same. It had been weakness to do so. He did not ask himself why it was a weakness he'd succumbed to.

It certainly didn't have anything to do with Loring Lanchester. The bank was being run now by someone who knew one end of a balance sheet from the other, and it might, given some proper management, be showing a decent profit by the time he sold it off to one of the multinational banking houses for a worthwhile price. He would not be out of pocket on Loring Lanchester.

Liar! The word mocked in his brain as he headed up to his suite.

Money was not the only currency in the world…

He walked into his suite and tossed his briefcase down on the coffee table. He needed a workout. Perhaps some heavy expenditure of muscle power in the hotel's health club would drain out some of the anger eating away at him.

More than just anger.

Frustration.

He was not used to going without sex for this long.

Three weeks since he'd got rid of Portia.

Three weeks of celibacy forced on him by his own crushing inability to summon the slightest interest in another woman.

How the hell long is this going to last?

How long before he was free of wanting Portia Lanchester?

With an impatient gesture he loosened his tie and headed into his bedroom.

The phone rang on the sideboard.

He picked it up as he went by.

'Yes?' he said curtly.

'I have Ms Lanchester in Reception, Mr Saez,' said the deferential voice of a hotel clerk.

He stopped dead. Had he heard right?

There was a long, long pause. The clerk at the other end waited politely.

Then, in a slow voice, Diego heard himself say, 'Tell her to come up.'

Déjà-vu, thought Portia, as she pressed the button for the penthouse floor. Or should that be *déjà-fait*? She wondered absently what the correct French would be for doing the same thing second time around.

But this time it was a very different thing she was doing.

The first time she had come up in this lift she'd been about to sell herself to a man.

This time—

Her mouth pressed into a tight, hard line.

This time a different transaction would take place.

The lift slowed and the doors sliced open. She stepped out into the quiet, hushed corridor. Diego Saez still had the same suite.

Definitely *déjà-vu*, she thought.

She hadn't known when he would be back in London. She'd kept a request open with Tom's secretary at the bank. She would, Portia knew, be able to find out from the new Saez-appointed chief executive's secretary when Diego Saez was passing through again.

The call had come this morning. Mr Saez, she had been informed, had an afternoon meeting scheduled, but nothing thereafter. Yes, he was booked into the same Park Lane hotel as last time.

Portia had dressed carefully. The business suit was freshly dry-cleaned, her court shoes newly polished. Her hair was drawn back into a French pleat. Her make-up was the bare minimum.

She knocked on the door.

It opened at the first touch, drawing back wide.

For one long, hideous moment she just stood, motionless, then with Herculean effort she stepped inside.

Diego Saez stood there.

His tall frame seemed to tower over her, his dark presence dominating her vision.

She felt weakness sweep through her, as if every bone in her body were incapable of holding her upright.

'Portia.' Diego's voice cut through her. 'How—unexpected.'

His voice was as deep as ever. But there was something else about it.

A jagged edge to the voice, leashed under tight control.

She didn't let herself look at his face, just looked past him as she walked forward slightly, moving into the room as he shut the door behind her. She heard it close with a final sound.

She clicked open her handbag and drew out a piece of paper, placed it down on the surface of the glass coffee table.

This time she looked at him.

His face was a mask, eyes like slivers of obsidian.

'This is for you,' she said in a steady voice. She clicked her handbag shut again.

She watched him pick up the paper, watched him register that it was a cheque, watched him register the sum it was made out for. And the payee.

He seemed to still. Then, expressionlessly, his eyes went from the cheque to her.

'And this is—?'

His voice was as expressionless as his face.

She looked at him. She was calm—completely calm.

Only somewhere very deep inside that bubble of pressure had started to build.

'For you,' she said. 'You were good. Very good indeed. I'm afraid I don't know what the market rate for stud services is, but I'm sure you'll agree that this sum represents a generous recompense for your time.'

She turned to go. A hand clamped down on her shoulder, hauling her back round again.

His face was a savage snarl.

'What the *hell* do you think you're playing at?'

She could feel that bubble of pressure rising inside her. It was starting to balloon through her.

'I'm paying you,' she spelt out, 'for the all the sex I got. There was such a lot of it, and it was so very—inventive. And certainly very educational.'

'*You* are paying *me*?'

She might have laughed out loud. Laughed at the expression on his face. It was outrage, anger, disbelief—and something more that she would not think about.

But she had no time to laugh. Nor inclination either. The feelings ballooning inside her made no room for laughter. No room for anything. Except its own swelling volume, which was growing inexorably, unstoppably.

His other hand closed over her shoulder, crushing her bones. The cheque fluttered to the ground.

'You *dare* to do this? You sell yourself to me like a whore and you then *dare* to offer *me* money?'

The pressure exploded through her.

Throwing up her hands, she pushed his arms away, stepping backwards.

'You bastard!' she cried out. 'What did I *ever* do to you for you to treat me the way you have? To do to me what you did? All I did was say no to you! Say no to going to bed with you! But you wouldn't take no for an answer, would you? You had to go on and on and on at me! Hunting me down because *you* wanted me and I didn't want you! And for that crime, the terrible, heinous crime of not wanting to go to bed with you, have the cheap, meaningless, sordid little affair that you wanted to have, for that *unforgivable* crime of saying no, you had to resort to blackmail! You played with my brother's *life* just to get me into your bed!'

His face was black as thunder. The rage was ripping through him.

'You came to me—offered yourself to bail him out!'

Her face contorted.

'I had no *choice*! You gave me no choice! You spelt it out in letters a mile high when you told me you might— *might*—buy Loring Lanchester! I got the message all right—you had to have what you'd been wanting from me or you wouldn't go ahead with the takeover! What choice did that give me? Tell me that! What did you think I would do? Do you think I would stand back and watch my brother lose Salton? Do you think I could have lived with myself if I hadn't paid the price you demanded? I did what I did for his sake. I didn't want to. Dear God in heaven, I didn't want to!' Her voice choked.

He laughed—a harsh, mocking sound that flayed her.

'No. You made that clear enough. You thought you were going to get away with lying back and thinking of your ancestral pile. You'd have kept your gloves on if you could—to stop yourself having to touch me!'

Her eyes were venomous with loathing.

'You're right. I would have. Your touch contaminated me. I didn't come to you a whore—but I left as one! You made sure of that! I had to take what you handed out or my brother's life would have been destroyed—but now, now I'm clearing my account with you! Not his! And *my* account is that cheque!'

'A million pounds?'

His voice was scathing, still black with anger.

'Why not? My body was worth even more to you! You bought Loring Lanchester just to force me into your bed! But a million is all I can raise in cash. It's nothing to you, of course. I know that, with all your money. And it galls me even to give you that, because if I think *I'm* privileged then it's nothing compared with you! Look in the mirror and tell me if you're proud of what you see! I might have been born with a silver spoon, but you were born with a golden one!

'God knows how much of your poor benighted country you own, how many wretched peons slave away for you on a pittance while you gad about the world on your merry way, making more and more obscene amounts of money—enough to buy banks as toys and buy sexual favours! So that's what that cheque is for. And you can cash it or tear it up or choke on it. I don't care! You bought Loring Lanchester, Mr Saez, but you didn't buy *me!* And now I'm rid of you!'

She turned away. Stumbling. Unseeing. The room whirled around her dizzyingly. Bile rose in her torn throat. She reached the door and pulled it open.

He watched her walk out. Standing stock still, every muscle frozen, immobile.

The door shut behind her.

CHAPTER ELEVEN

'THAT'S good, Jaime. Well done!'

Portia leant over the young boy's rickety desk, reading what he had written.

'Thank you, miss!'

A flashing white grin came her way, splitting the dark face looking up at her.

She smiled back. 'Now, copy the next sentence,' she said encouragingly, hoping she had got it right in her tentative Spanish. 'Maria, let's see what you've done so far.'

She moved on to the next child.

It was hot in the classroom, with not a trace of air-conditioning, not even an electric fan. But the children were used to the heat, and the money that keeping cool would cost was better spent on other things.

There was an ever-present need for money. For, however many children the refuge could take in, there were always more. They came from the punishingly poor slums of the city, where poverty and ill-health made their parents—if they had any—indifferent or incapable of caring for them. The refuge, Portia now knew, offered them the only chance most of them would ever have of getting off the streets, giving them some kind of education—some kind of hope for the future.

It had been a photo that had brought her here. An illustration in a charity fundraising leaflet that had arrived in the mail. It wasn't a charity she subscribed to, but mailing lists were passed around. This one had been from some kind of third world orphanage, or so it had seemed. She'd placed it in her in-tray. She would write out a cheque some time.

She had picked up the next envelope in the day's post, ready to slice it open with her paper knife. Her movements had been mechanical, unthinking, but doing something as banal as opening the post had kept her going.

It had been a week then, since she had confronted Diego Saez. A week since the venom had been drained from her in that maelstrom of emotion that had poured so unstoppably from her.

But it had not brought her any peace. How could it?

The old life she'd lived had gone for ever. She could not go back to it as if nothing had happened.

Diego Saez, what he had done to her, had changed her for ever.

Hugh, when he had received her painfully worded resignation, had been on the phone immediately, trying to argue her out of it. She had been terse, uncommunicative about her reasons, merely insisting that she would not be coming back to her job. The very idea of spending her days tracking down the identities of long-dead sitters for minor portraitists had seemed pointless.

But everything had seemed pointless. Nothing had had meaning.

Tom had taken Felicity off on holiday, and somehow she had bade them farewell. Somehow she had endured the other girl's open happiness, somehow she had reassured a still anxious Tom that she was perfectly all right and did not need to go to the doctor, despite being as thin as a rake.

But though her hands had not shaken any more, though she'd been functioning perfectly well, had been quite capable of going to the shops, cooking for herself, getting through the days, still she had been surrounded by that strange, muffling layer that kept the rest of the world very far away.

Until that charity brochure had arrived. As she'd slid her paper knife into the back of the next envelope in her hand her eyes had dropped to the photo on the leaflet again.

It had been a photo of a boy. Not more than twelve or

thirteen. Wearing a ragged pair of trousers, no shoes, a torn
shirt. He was lying in a doorway, legs drawn up, head
tucked in, arms wrapped around his body, asleep.

There had been something about it. Something that had
made her want to stare. The photograph was grainy, she
could not see the boy's face, only the long dark hair of his
head. But there had been something about seeing him sleeping in that doorway that had made her look at the photo
for a long time.

Then, putting down the envelope in her hands, and her
paper knife, she had picked up the leaflet and opened it up.

It had been about a street children's charity in Latin
America. An organisation dedicated to providing a home,
shelter and safety for children who had none of those
things. There had been more photos inside. Tiny children,
dirty and barefoot, picking over a rubbish heap. A family
cooking a meal outside a shanty, the mother's eyes dead,
the children all painfully thin, staring blank-faced at the
camera..

She had started to read. At the end there'd been a heading: *How you can help*. She'd placed the leaflet on her desk
and opened the drawer to reach for her chequebook. She
wouldn't be able to give now the way she'd used to, but
she would still give something.

She had thought of the money she'd paid to Diego Saez.
It had come from her private income and her shares, sold
off despite the shocked protests of her broker, who had
advised her strongly that this was not a good time to sell,
and in such quantities, subject to such punitive taxation.

'I want to raise a million pounds cash, immediately,' she
had told him, and hung up.

A million pounds for sex.

An obscene amount to pay.

But it had been the only way to lance the poison in her
veins.

Poison he had injected there.

She'd given a bitter smile. He had so much—and now

he had a million pounds more. Another handful of gold on his towering heap. While children like those lived in filth and hunger and homelessness.

In the very country he had come from.

Maragua.

The charity rescued children from the streets of the capital, San Cristo.

Did he even know they existed? she had wondered, with bitterness in her soul. Their wretched lives were as alien to his lavish gilded existence as if he'd come from another planet.

Her eyes had dropped to the heading again: *How you can help.*

She had read on.

And as she had read she'd closed the drawer again.

And had reached for the phone to dial the number printed in the leaflet. A silent revenge on Diego's way of life...

Father Tomaso murmured grace, made the sign of a blessing, and sat himself down at the supper table. At all the tables in the room the seated children started to chatter as the eldest at each table dished out the food.

'So,' said Father Tomaso, addressing the adults around him, 'how are our latest crop of volunteers coming along? Have we made a good harvest this season?'

He smiled encouragingly. Though old, he was still vigorous, with a determination and a dogged dedication that inspired all his flock.

'Can you say that again in English, Father?' quipped a young man of twenty or so, in an American accent.

Many of the volunteers who supplemented the Maraguan house parents and teachers at the refuge came from America or Britain, and most were students, coming here in their vacations or gap years. Portia felt old in comparison—but never unwelcome.

She looked around her. The dining room was a plain whitewashed room, its plainness brightened by a vivid mural that ran around the four walls, painted by the children. It was a waving rainbow that wove in and out of an arkload of animals, some rather unlikely-looking from an anatomical perspective, but all painted with enthusiasm and verve. Every child who came to the refuge added an animal.

This was their ark, thought Portia. Their shelter from the storm.

And mine too...

The storm had almost destroyed her. The storm that Diego Saez had unleashed over her life.

She would never recover. *Could* never recover.

Because although the anger and the guilt had gone, assuaged in that final excoriating denunciation of him, what remained was more agonising still.

A pain that would be with her all her life.

The pain of having fallen in love—despite everything he had done to her—with a man as ruthless as Diego Saez.

Father Tomaso was talking again.

'Tomorrow we have a visitor—a new volunteer! He cannot stay long, but while he is here I hope you will get good work out of him! He is strong, so I think we should corral him into helping with the building project. The walls of the new clinic grow high, but they must be higher yet, and there is still the roof to put on.'

'Who is he, Father?' asked one of the volunteers, curious.

'He is a most remarkable man,' answered the elderly priest. 'He lived here once, in this very home. He came here, half-starved from the streets, but he was not from San Cristo. He had come here from the country, a vagrant without family. With nothing. Yet now...' he paused. 'Now he has everything that money can buy.' Father Tomaso's dark eyes saddened. 'But nothing that it cannot.'

'He's rich, but he's going to work on our building site?' The volunteer asking the question sounded sceptical.

'He does not know it yet,' Father Tomaso remarked dryly.

There was some laughter.

'I have merely persuaded him at last to make an inspection of what his money is building—he does not yet know that his hands are going to make an equal contribution. In fact—' he paused again '—it will be a much greater one. For some, giving money is easy. For them, the real act of *caritas* is much harder.'

His eyes flickered over the table, resting briefly on Portia. She held his gaze minutely. He knew that, unlike the majority of volunteers, she came from a privileged background. But she knew he accepted that she had come here to battle her demons—demons that must shrink to insignificance compared with those that preyed on the lives of the children he rescued.

Portia's thoughts slid to the tale of the boy he had taken in, who had become so rich now. In her mind's eye she saw the photo that had brought her here, of the boy sleeping rough in a doorway.

She felt her heart squeeze with pity.

Father Tomaso went on.

'But, for all that, I am grateful for what his wealth can do. Thanks to him we can reach out to more and more who need our help—not just here in San Cristo but throughout Maragua and beyond, in other countries, for his generosity is great.' He gave a tired, defeated sigh. 'I only wish that he could find the time to come back and see what his money has done...'

'But you said he *is* coming back,' said someone.

'Yes.' The priest's eyes brightened, taking on a resolute gleam. 'Finally he has accepted my constant invitation. I must be glad he can spare the time—he is a man of great affairs now, with many calls upon his time, and he no longer lives in Maragua. Indeed,' he mused, 'I do not think he has been back here since he left to seek his fortune.'

'What changed his mind?' one of the house mothers asked.

'I do not know,' replied Father Tomaso simply. 'But—'

His voice broke off suddenly, as an indignant squawk sounded from one of the children, followed by a voluble protest from his neighbour.

'José? Mateo? What is the matter?' Father Tomaso enquired.

As the children simultaneously vented their grievance— a dispute over the last piece of corn bread, resolved by sharing it—Portia resumed her meal. The spicy vegetable soup, with slices of sausage in it, was simple fare, but she ate it with appreciation out of the pottery bowl. An image slid across her mind, of herself pushing aside the gastronomic delicacies served up to her in one expensive restaurant after another across the Far East.

Memory opened its jaws and swallowed her.

She was there again, sitting opposite him, dressed in a gown the price of which could have clothed a score of refuge children for life, her eyes sucked to him without volition, without consent, but with a hunger that had ached within her like a famine.

A hunger that was still inside her.

That she would never sate again.

Why the hell had he said yes to the old man?

Diego swirled the brandy around in his glass and stared moodily across the hotel room. The hotel was new, and held no memories, but memories crowded all the same. He tried to banish them, but he could not.

They had invaded his mind since the moment he had stepped foot inside the first-class cabin of the plane that had brought him here across the Atlantic, on a journey he had never thought to make again. Never wanted to make.

But something had brought him back. After so many years, something had made him do what he had vowed never to do.

Go back to Maragua.

He had never gone back, not since he had slammed shut the door in Mercedes de Carvello's face. He had left the next day, never to return. Not even when the new popular democratic party, to whose funds he had so handsomely contributed, had swept to power. There had been no need for him to go back. He could invest his money in fair trade ventures and environmental projects, make his extensive charitable donations, as easily from Geneva or New York as from San Cristo.

So why was he back now? Because an elderly priest had invited him?

Father Tomaso had invited him a hundred times—and he had always refused. Had refused to read the reports Father Tomaso had sent him about what his donations were accomplishing. Had refused to do anything more than give what was easiest for him to give—his money.

So why had he said yes now?

He took a mouthful of the brandy. It burned as it slid down his throat.

So did the truth.

He lifted his head. Looked into the mirror that faced him across the room.

Words stung in his mind. Scathing. Scornful.

Look in the mirror and tell me if you're proud of what you see!

The taste of the brandy turned to gall in his mouth.

Guilt seared through him.

And something worse than guilt.

Loss. Loss of something he had never even had. Because he had never had her—never had the woman he had hunted down remorselessly, determined to possess her simply because he wanted her. And when his usual means had failed he had resorted to other methods—despicable ones.

And he had tried to justify himself for using them.

And that was the most bitter gall of all. There had been no justification for what he had done to her.

His mouth twisted. She thought him born with a golden spoon—one of the very kind he despised so much, who treated those like him as if they were trash, worked them to death, ran them down like dogs beneath the wheels of their fancy imported cars.

I thought she was like that—rotten and corrupt. Caring only for her money. Ready to sell herself to protect her wealth.

But she had sold herself to protect her brother—had paid for the privilege. A million pounds. Paid to claw back from him some shred of what he had stripped from her even as he had stripped the clothes from her body.

No! He mustn't think—mustn't think of that! Must not think of the worst, the very worst torment of all.

He looked into the face staring back at him and mocked it with a bitter, jeering look.

He had lost her for ever.

And his life had no meaning any more.

'Diego! What shall I say to you? The prodigal returns?'

The welcome in Father Tomaso's voice did not hide the dryness in it.

Diego cast a twisted smile down at the elderly priest. Father Tomaso had aged—that was not surprising—but he had not changed.

'Then you must allow me to pay for the fatted calf myself, Father,' he replied, matching his dryness.

'I'm sure you can make it tax-deductible,' came back the priest, his voice even dryer.

No, thought Diego, the old man had not changed.

Emotions churned in him. As he had got out of the car—despatching a visibly relieved chauffeur back to the rich side of town—they had assailed him, twisting like snakes inside him.

The past and the present slammed one into another. Memories into reality. Time collapsing in on itself.

He cast his glance around. The place looked just the same—the same brave flowers, assiduously watered, by the front door, the same white walls, the same brightly painted door.

And inside the same smell.

That hit him the hardest, making him pause in his long stride beside Father Tomaso's brisk pace.

The years dissolved.

It had been the smell that had hit him the first time Father Tomaso had brought him here, with hunger gnawing like a dog in his empty, hollow belly. It was the smell of food. Hot food. Spicy food.

It was there still. He felt saliva run into his mouth, as it had done over twenty years ago.

The priest did not pause, continuing his brisk and busy pace, leading the way out into the central courtyard. Diego followed him. They must be cooking the midday meal right now, for when lessons ended. He found his mouth twisting again as memory sliced beneath the skin.

He had fought against those lessons long and hard. He had not wanted to waste his time with letters, with numbers. Had only wanted, once his belly was full, to go back out into the streets again, away from all the relentless good cheer and pious charity. But Father Tomaso had spelt it out. No lessons, no home. No home, no food.

And besides, only cowards ran from what they feared, the priest had told him. And if it was ink on paper that he feared—well, then it was a shameful thing. For there were boys here, girls too, who were half his age and yet they were not afraid of ink on paper…

So he had endured the lessons. Endured the good cheer and the pious charity.

Neither had changed, it seemed. As he walked past the classroom block in the wake of Father Tomaso he heard a burst of laughter, childish and adult together, and then, from the next classroom, the sing-song chant of a prayer.

His eyes roved around. There was much more here now than when he had been living at the refuge. Everything was larger, with a second storey built on, and extensions. The plot size seemed doubled, too. He started to listen to the commentary that Father Tomaso was giving, indicating with swings of his arms what had been done with the money Diego had given.

They rounded the end of the classroom block. Another plot of land lay across the narrow road, and Diego saw a building site behind the perimeter wall.

'This is the clinic. It will serve not just the children, but their families and their neighbours. With the physicians and nurses you are paying for we can provide the more basic treatment. For anything more we must persuade them to go to that fancy hospital you have built for the city.'

'Tell me, Father,' said Diego, his voice still as dry as the priest's, 'would you rather I hadn't given the people of San Cristo a free hospital?'

The priest headed across the road, avoiding an old truck that jerked and jolted past him.

'I would rather you gave from your heart, not your wallet—the wallet you spend your life stuffing with more and yet more money! Your wallet is fat enough, Diego. But your heart—your heart is as thin as a starving boy.'

Emotion stabbed in Diego—it might be anger. Or something else.

He caught Father Tomaso's black sleeve and stayed him by the edge of the road.

'My wallet pays for this! It pays for a hundred places like this!' He swept his arm around. 'It pays for a hospital in the city, and in half a dozen other towns in Maragua. It pays to stop our forests being logged to the ground, our rivers poisoned with pollution. It pays for farmers to buy the machinery they need, for village tradesmen to buy their stock. Its weight even helps to remind our esteemed president that he would be *unwise* to listen overmuch to the self-pitying whines of those who think the taxes they pay are wasted on running schools to educate peasants who have no function other than to slave in their factories and on their *estancias* and ranches!'

Old eyes looked up into his, saddened.

'You have come so far, Diego. So very far. You have

achieved so much. The world is yours. So why, then, is your face as gaunt as an old man's, your eyes like a hunted animal's?' He paused, his gaze questioning. 'Why have you come back, Diego? Why now? Why have you stepped aside, even momentarily, from your gilded, glittering life?'

Heat beat down on Diego's head. The air was perfumed with the exhaust of the jolting truck. He let go of Father Tomaso's cassock sleeve and looked away. There was stone inside him, as heavy as the blocks of concrete neatly stacked inside what would become the gateway of the clinic his money was building.

'So,' he asked, gesturing at the site, 'when will it be operational?'

'Well, that depends,' said the priest, the dry note back in his voice, 'on how much labour is available. Fortunately, for today at least, we have an extra labourer to hand.'

He looked blandly at the man beside him, who could count his wealth in billions.

'I am glad to see, my son, that those doubtless extortionately-priced health clubs you belong to all over the world have kept you fit. Now, give me your jacket and tie, and those fancy gold cufflinks, and that watch that tells you the time in every time zone you are making money in, and off you go. The others will tell you what to do.'

Diego stared at him, disbelieving what he had just heard, the bland expression on the old priest's face.

'Do you not think it a shameful thing,' murmured Father Tomaso softly, 'to be a grown man afraid of honest labour when there are children here who are not afraid of it?'

He nodded at the building site, at a relay of children passing roofing tiles along a chain, grinning and shouting to each other as they did so.

For a moment longer he held the younger man's eyes, and then grimly, mouth tight, Diego Saez took off his hand-made jacket and his silk tie, removed his gold cufflinks and gold watch and silently handed them to Father Tomaso.

The priest took them, that bland expression still on his

face. But beneath the blandness his heart lifted for the first time since the boy whom he had once found sleeping in a doorway had arrived that morning, in his gleaming chauffeur-driven limousine. Diego Saez might be looking at him with a glare that could strip paint, but his eyes no longer looked like those of a hunted animal.

Merely an irate one.

As he watched his former charge stride onto the building site, rolling up the sleeves of his immaculate white shirt, he hoped he had done the right thing. Salvation was never easy—but if ever a man was in need of it, it was Diego Saez.

The devil was riding on his back.

Consuming his soul.

Diego strode up to the half-completed building. The chain of children stopped their relay and stared at him.

'Are you our new helper?' one of the boys asked him. 'Father Tomaso told us we would have one today.'

'Did he?' echoed Diego grimly. 'I might have guessed.'

A girl spoke up, maybe eleven or twelve.

'You look too rich to work. Your shoes are polished.'

'Don't worry—they'll soon get scuffed. Tell me, where do these tiles go?'

He picked up an armful, hunkering down on his haunches to do so.

'You take them round to the other side, where the grown-ups are working. Do not drop any—they cost good money,' the first boy warned him.

'I shall try not to,' answered Diego. He stood up, bracing his weight.

One of the younger boys was staring at him.

'You speak like us,' he said.

Diego stilled. He had answered them in their own street accents. He had not even realised he had done so. Had not even realised he still knew such patois.

He looked at the children. They were staring at him.

'I lived here once,' he said slowly.

Their stares of curiosity turned to open disbelief.

'But you're rich,' said the girl who had spoken.

'I was not rich when I lived here,' he answered.

Another child spoke.

'Father Tomaso says we are all rich. We eat every day and we have a bed to sleep in and clean clothes to wear. That makes us rich, he says.'

Diego looked at them, at their neatly cut hair, their bright eyes, not dulled now by hunger, or by alcohol, or solvents.

'Yes,' he said, nodding slowly. 'I think Father Tomaso is right.'

'He's always right—he tells us he is,' said the boy who had warned him against dropping any of the tiles. 'Are you going to take those tiles to where they are needed, or just stand with them all day? They all have to be moved today.'

'Whatever you say, boss,' said Diego, and set off with his load.

It did not seem to be as heavy as he had thought.

Portia heard the call for the midday meal—a wooden spoon being noisily banged on the back of an iron pot—and drew her lesson to its close. Dismissing the children with an adjuration to wash their hands before going into the dining room, she put away her well-worn teaching books and headed for her own small bedroom. She needed to freshen up and change her top—she was sticky with heat.

The volunteers' rooms were in a side block across the courtyard to the rear. As she emerged into the bright sunlight she blinked, momentarily blinded. When her eyes cleared she saw the morning shift of volunteers and children come across the roadway from the building site.

She blinked again.

And then froze.

Faintness drummed through her. Denial seared in her head.

No! This isn't true! It can't be!

Diego Saez was walking into the courtyard.

She felt her body sway and found herself clutching at the doorjamb. The breath was sucked from her body.

It can't be him! It can't be!

But it was—his height, his broad shoulders, his dark hair, his features. Him. Diego Saez.

Frozen, the blood draining from her, she leant motionless against the doorway.

Sweat was running down his back, soaking his shirt and his waistband. It was just as soaked at the front, and his hair was damp. Father Tomaso's dig about health clubs might have been accurate, but there was a definite difference between working out in an air-conditioned gym on top-of-the-range equipment and labouring on a sun-drenched, baking hot building site. Yet he wasn't about to complain. Not when he was working hard so to keep pace with a bunch of denim-clad students, some grizzled locals and a bunch of eager kids.

But by the time the signal to down tools was called he'd been ready for a break.

As he came into the courtyard—which, judging by the rusting basketball hoop on one of the walls, still served as the children's playground as well—he found himself wondering what other surprises Father Tomaso had up his sleeve for him.

His mood was strange. Overriding everything was a sense of physical depletion from two hours of unaccustomed labouring. But there was more than that. There was a sense, he knew, of cussed satisfaction that he had kept up with the other labourers. And there was more as well. There was a sense of satisfaction—completely alien to him—from working in harness with others, of his own free will, for something that was important.

The others were wary of him, he could see—the local hired workers were openly chary, and even the volunteers had been awkward about his presence at first. But there

was nothing, he realised, like working with people on a
task for breaking down barriers. Especially when some of
them were children. Now, as he headed across the courtyard, he looked down to answer something that one of them
was saying to him.

As he looked up again his eyes roamed around the buildings. Again that crushing sense of time collapsing in on
itself came over him, of the past rushing up to collide with
the present. For a second he felt the years dissolve, like
copper sheet in acid, etching out the contours of the boy
he'd once been, so long ago, in a different lifetime.

He could feel his heart thump in his body—and not just
because of the physical labour he had done.

And then, as his gaze swept past the open door leading
into the classrooms, it stopped altogether.

Portia Lanchester was standing in the doorway.

He stood rooted to the spot, and slowly, very slowly,
lifted up his arm to wipe away the sweat running into his
eyes.

He was seeing things. Hallucinations. Visions.

Memories.

Ghosts that haunted him, tormented him.

It could not be Portia. It could not. She was six thousand
miles away, in that beautiful eighteenth-century house
where she belonged. As distant from him as if she had been
locked away behind glass—like a precious jewel that was
forever beyond his reach.

Then, as he stared, he watched the figure in the doorway
that looked so like Portia but could not be—*could* not be—
turn and grope her way indoors and disappear.

And in that instant he moved.

She staggered back indoors. Dear God, it was him!

Not a vision, not a mirage. But Diego Saez. Here. Now.

Blindly she walked back down the corridor that ran
alongside the row of classrooms. Her heart was pounding,
her breath short.

Disbelief still flooded through her.

'Portia!'

She stopped dead.

It was his voice.

Harsh, demanding.

He said her name again, and this time it was not harsh, nor demanding, but strange—very strange.

As if he, too, were deluged by the flood of disbelief that was dissolving through her.

Slowly, very slowly, she turned.

And as she did so, her gaze fastening on him, she felt her heart squeezed in a giant vice.

'How can you be here?' he said.

His voice was strange, so very strange.

And yet so familiar.

She felt her knees begin to buckle and reached out a hand to steady herself against the wall.

She stared at him.

It was Diego Saez—but not Diego Saez.

He was jacketless, and his white shirt was smeared with terracotta dust. It was also soaked in sweat, and his hair was damp with sweat as well.

She stared, bewildered—bewildered by his appearance, by his presence.

And then into the silence came another noise—footsteps walking briskly.

Father Tomaso came around the corner.

When he saw the tableau in front of him he stopped dead.

Then, his eyes moving between the two frozen figures, he spoke, the blandness in his voice quite at odds with the keen, assessing look in his eye. 'Ah, Portia, let me introduce our latest, if somewhat temporary, volunteer. This is who I was telling you about last night.'

Breath hissed into her lungs and her eyes widened.

She dragged her eyes to the priest.

'It can't be! I know this man. He owns millions! He—he—'

'He used to live here,' said Father Tomaso simply.

She shook her head.

'No. It can't be true. It can't.'

'I found him in a doorway when he was twelve,' Father Tomaso said, his eyes never leaving her. 'He was sleeping. I had some food with me. He woke, sensing danger, perhaps smelling the food as well. I offered him the food but he would not take it. He ran, suspicious, wary. I watched him run. He had no shoes; his bones stood out with hunger. I found him again the next night, in another doorway. I offered him food again and told him I was simply a priest, no one to harm him. This time he ate the food I gave him— wolfed it down, tearing into it. And then he ran again. It took me weeks to bring him here, and he ran away several more times. But eventually, he stayed. Until...' He paused, and this time he glanced at Diego as well. 'Until he ran for the very last time. Out into the world he conquered.'

His eyes rested on Diego's face. 'But did you conquer the world, Diego? Or did it conquer you?'

Diego's face was set, as tense as steel. He did not answer.

Instead he turned away, making to go.

'Running away again, Diego?' came the voice behind him.

'No,' he answered, and his voice was harsh, self-mocking. 'Merely rejoining the ranks of the damned.'

'You're not damned, Diego.'

The priest spoke with a calm assurance that infuriated its target.

Diego turned back, a snarl on his face. 'What do you know about it? You stand there taunting me, but you know nothing. Ask *her* if I'm damned. Ask her!'

His voice was harsh, tearing from his throat.

The blood drained from Portia's face.

The light in Diego's eyes was vicious.

'Ask her what I did to her,' he said, his voice low.

The priest turned to Portia, studying her stricken face.

'Is he damned?' he asked her, almost conversationally.

Her eyes slid past the old priest, back to Diego Saez. Her heart was slumping in her chest, her breathing ragged. She stared at Diego's face. It was stark, pulled tight with tension.

It was him—and it was not him.

An image laid itself in her mind. The Diego she knew. Sleek, powerful, rich—reaching out for her to peel her clothes from her, lower her down beneath him on the bed…

Possessing her. Buying her.

Another image intruded. The photograph of the boy sleeping rough that had, for some reason she had never understood, so worked on her that she had walked away from everything she had once thought she had to come out here. A world away from all she knew. All she took for granted.

A world Diego Saez had destroyed for her.

The two images collided, then dissolved, one into another.

The man and the boy.

The vice around her heart squeezed unbearably.

Something poured into the space around her heart, filling it. An emotion so powerful she could not block it.

'Portia—' Diego said her name, his voice low, cracked. 'Don't look at me like that. *Por Dios!* Don't look at me like that! After everything I did to you I don't deserve your pity! Only your contempt!'

She couldn't speak. Could only slowly shake her head.

He closed his eyes, then opened them again.

'Don't make excuses for me. I did what I did to you knowingly—I thought you deserved it. I thought you were like—'

His voice broke off. Then, 'Like Mercedes de Carvello.' His voice was flat. His eyes dead. 'She was the wife of the man who owned the *estancia* I was born on—where my parents worked. They poisoned my father. She killed my mother. Ran her down like a dog in her sports car, when she was drunk. I accused her of murder and she had me

thrown off the estate. I walked to San Cristo. Father
Tomaso found me, living on the streets. Years later, a lifetime later, when I'd made money as I'd *vowed* I would do,
I bought the *estancia* from Esteban de Carvello—he'd run
through all his money. His wife came to me in my hotel
room and offered herself to me—the son of her maid—to
persuade me to let her go on living at the *estancia*. I threw
her out.'

His voice shuddered to a halt. Then he spoke again.

'I thought you were like her—willingly giving yourself
to protect your wealth. I thought your reluctance was because, like Mercedes de Carvello, you thought yourself too
good for me—you didn't want to soil your hands on me.
So I...I made you *want* to soil them...'

Faintness drummed through her.

Diego's voice came to her from very far away. 'They
say that deeds bring their own justice. I can attest to that.
I wanted you so much—wanted you for my bed. But you
would not come. You thought yourself too good for me.
So I gave you an...incentive.' He took another painful, ragged breath. 'But justice had been meted out to me—a terrible justice.' He fixed his eyes on her. They were dark and
hollow. 'Content yourself, Portia, in your contempt for me,
for what I did to you. What I thought you were. Content
yourself and know that justice has been done. I have my
punishment for what I did to you.'

He looked at her, his face like death.

'I fell in love with you, Portia. Fell in love with you
who can only loathe and hate and damn me for what I did
to you. And every day, every day of my existence, I wake
knowing that you hate me—can only ever hate me. All my
life. That—' he let his eyes rest not on Portia but on the
still face of Father Tomaso '—that is damnation. So whatever I do now with the rest of my life—here or anywhere
else—it means nothing to me.' His face was shuttered.
'Nothing.'

He turned away.

A sound broke from Portia. A tight, broken cry.

Father Tomaso's eyes went to her.

Questioning.

'And now,' he said quietly, his eyes steady on her, 'it is up to you. You hold the key to his prison. Will you release him? Or keep him in his hell? The choice—' his voice was even quieter '—is yours.'

He started to walk away.

She wanted to call him back. Run after him. But he kept on going, and her feet would not move, her throat was paralysed.

She heard his voice toll in her brain.

The choice is yours.

Choice. She had had no choice. When Salton had been threatened, her brother's home threatened, she had had no choice. No choice but to do what she could—whatever it took—to save it. No choice but to accept the devil's bargain that Diego Saez had held out to her. No choice but to go to him. No choice but to let him peel the clothes from her and take from her what she had refused him. Refused because she would not be one more woman that he simply picked up, enjoyed, and discarded again, to move on to the next one.

And when he had peeled her clothes from her and taken her to his bed she had had no choice—no choice but to accept the shame, the coruscating, burning shame, of discovering so devastatingly, so annihilatingly, that Diego Saez—who was buying her, possessing her—could light in her a fire that she could not quench.

And when he had finally thrown her out, terminated that devil's bargain of his, she had had no choice but to endure the greatest shame of all.

She craved the man who had done this to her.

More than craved.

The silence stretched all around her. The sound of Father Tomaso's footsteps had ebbed away. Time had stilled to this one point.

The choice is yours…

The words tolled again in her brain.

She looked at Diego. He stood there still, turned away from her, shoulders hunched, hand splayed out on the door. He started to push it open, started to move forward.

The choice was hers. Now. Here.

To let him go. Let him live out the rest of his life damning himself, hating himself.

Or—

She thought of what he had been—that lost, wandering boy. Without family, without a home. With nothing. Not even shoes. Sleeping in doorways. Like the boy whose photo had brought her here.

Here. Now.

As he started to walk out she reached out a hand to him. It trembled as she did so. And as it touched his stained shirtsleeve he froze.

She took a step forward.

'Diego.'

Her voice was a husk. She could see the tension strapped along the lines of his shoulders, the curve of his back, outlining every muscle.

She spoke again. 'Diego—I—'

She couldn't go on. Her throat was choking, pulled so tight it was like a band around her breath.

She gave a tiny broken cry.

He turned. Faced her. Her hand dropped away from him and she just stood there.

Her eyes fastened to his and her throat worked.

His face was stark, emptied of everything.

His eyes were dead.

Her heart was crushed again in its vice.

She took a faltering step towards him. Holding out her hands to him.

Making her choice.

And as she did so the emotion that had flowed in around

her heart seemed to swell and flood, flood out all through her, like a great, cleansing wave. Washing everything away.

Her shame. Her guilt. Her anger. Her hatred.

She went to him. Wrapped hers arms around him, holding him so tight, so very tight against her, leaning her cheek against his dust-stained sweaty shirt.

For a moment, so long it felt like an eternity he stayed frozen, immobile. And then slowly, very slowly, she felt his arms come around her. Haltingly at first, and then suddenly with a desperation that crushed her to him, bands of steel fastening her against him.

She felt him shudder, the breath raking through his body. She held him tighter, and more tightly yet. How long she held him she did not know. Knew only that she would never let him go. Could never let him go.

She felt tears spill from her eyes. That high, broken sob came again.

'Portia! No—don't cry. Dear God, don't cry!'

But she cried all the more, an ocean of tears.

His arms around her loosened. Gentled. His hand slid up to her head, stroking her hair.

'Don't cry, Portia. Please don't cry.'

She lifted her head. Blindly, instinctively, she reached upward.

He could not stop himself.

He kissed her, taking her uplifted mouth, crushing her to him.

The heat of midday made her little room an oven. She didn't care. The fires of hell could have burnt around her and she would still have been in heaven. She smoothed the sweat-stained shirt from him, kissing his body. She felt him shudder.

She drew him down onto the narrow bed, her arms winding around him.

'Portia—' The hoarseness in his voice tore at her.

'I want you so much,' she told him. 'So much...'

The little bed could hardly hold them both. They did not
care. With slow rapture they found each other's bodies. He
spoke to her in Spanish—soft, wondering phrases that she
only half understood, and yet she knew he had never spoken them before.

This was a new world for them both.

Only as he lay within her, and her body glowed like the
sun, did he pause and tense, his voice grating as he gasped
aloud, the words torn from him.

'I can't! I can't hold back—'

He surged within her and she arched to meet him, igniting at his flame, burning in the same golden purifying fire.
An eternity of ecstasy.

Later, much later, they lay together in each other's arms.

For a long, long time they said nothing, only lay in the
sheltering cradle of their embrace. Then slowly, haltingly,
Diego spoke.

'You are my life, Portia. For all my life, you are my life.
Whatever happens now, whatever my fate is to be, it is in
your hands.'

She pressed her lips against his throat. A peace filled
her—a peace she had never known.

'I love you,' she told him. And knew it was the truth.
The only truth.

His arm tightened around her.

'After all I did to you?'

'It's gone now. Over. Washed away.' She lifted her head
to look down at him. 'I understand now the demons that
haunted you. Made you think me like that woman. And I'm
not proud of what I did—but I didn't do it for myself. I
swear to you I did it for my brother's sake. That's why I
paid you that money—to buy back my self-respect.'

Her eyes clouded.

'I thought you worthless. Spoilt, arrogant, selfish. And I
hated you. But I hated myself more—because I had fallen
in love with you despite everything you had done to me.
So I knew...' Her breath caught painfully. 'I knew I had

to change my life completely. When I saw that photo in the charity leaflet, of the boy sleeping rough in a doorway, something about him caught at me so powerfully. And I knew then that this was what I must do. That it was the only way I could heal, find some meaning to my existence from then on. But I never dreamt—how could I?—that *you* could have been such a boy. I never dreamt, that I would find you here—the real you.'

A troubled look crossed his face.

'I am everything you thought me, Portia. Spoilt, arrogant and selfish. I am guilty of everything you accused me of. I wanted you—and I wanted you on my terms and for my purposes. I wanted—just as you said—one more fleeting affair, one more sexual indulgence of the kind I had filled my life with. But justice found me, Portia. Found me, punished me, and mocked me.'

He paused.

'I denied what was happening to me. Denied that I felt anything more for you than some kind of endless craving. But however much I had you, I wanted more, and still more. And I finally realised just how dangerous you were to me. Because I thought you a woman to despise—a woman like Mercedes de Carvello. So—so I ended it.'

His arm tightened around her shoulder, betraying his tension.

'I thought I'd ended it—but it hadn't finished with me. You went on echoing in me. I could not silence you. I reached for other women, but I could not touch them. I wanted only you. A woman who'd sold herself to me.'

He took a heavy, ragged breath.

'But I didn't care. I didn't care—I just wanted you. And I knew it was bad inside me—very bad—the day you came, throwing your cheque in my face. I had just smashed my fist into the face of a man who had insulted you. I knew then just how much danger I was in. Loving a woman who hated me.'

His eyes gazed unseeing at the low ceiling.

'Then you came calling, and held up to me a mirror that made me realise I had damned myself—and lost all hope of you. Lost all hope of everything. My life was as empty, as worthless as a dried husk. Then...' He paused. 'Then Father Tomaso got in touch, as he always does twice a year, to try and get me to come back here. I never had. Never. Not since the day I threw Mercedes de Carvello from my hotel room. But this time…this time I came back.'

She pressed her cheek against his chest, just holding him.

'You came home, Diego,' she said softly. 'And I was here, waiting for you—but I did not know it. Waiting for the real Diego Saez—not just the boy who slept rough in doorways, but the man now, who gives back so much of his wealth to those who still need it.'

He scooped her tight against him.

'They can have my wealth—but you—you, my Portia—you have my heart.'

'It's all I want,' she answered.

Salton lay bathed in sunlight. The honey stone was warm, with sunshine dazzling from the myriad windows.

Portia stood on the south lawn, Diego's arm around her. She leant into him, tilting her head so that her wide brimmed hat was not crushed. A happiness so profound that she could not measure it filled her completely.

There was no marquee. The late-summer weather was too fine. The wedding breakfast was laid out on tables in the dappled shade of the oak trees. She took a sip of champagne from the flute in her hand.

A vision in sunshine-yellow was making a beeline for her, champagne glass waving precariously.

'You see—I told you, didn't I?' an exuberant, if slightly inebriated Susie Winterton cried volubly as she came up to them. 'Didn't I just *tell* you that he was *exactly* what you needed?' She beamed up at Diego, standing so close to Portia. 'I told her, you know—straight after the opera! I told her you were just what the doctor had ordered—*and I* told her you'd marry her and whisk her away to your fantastic polo ranch in Argentina!'

She sighed romantically.

'It's Maragua, Susie. And it's in Central America, not South America,' said Portia.

'Wherever.' Her friend shrugged haphazardly, still beaming at them both as she took another mouthful of champagne.

'Nor is it a polo ranch,' pointed out Diego, with a twitch of his lips.

Susie was undeterred.

'I'm sure it's gorgeous, wherever it is and whatever it is, and I'm sure you'll be ecstatic and blissful and so ridiculously, wonderfully happy that people will stand up and applaud! And,' she added lavishly for good measure, 'you'll have gorgeous, adorable children! Lots and lots.'

Portia felt Diego's arm tighten around her.

'Yes,' he said, 'we'll have many, many children, Susie.'

'We've got a good few already,' added Portia. 'And there'll be many more to come.' There was a husk in her voice she could not hide.

Susie's eyes widened, confused.

'Diego's going to turn his *estancia* in Maragua into a children's home, Susie,' Portia explained. 'He already funds refuges for street children, but this will be a place out of the city, with clean air and no pollution and no slums.'

Admiration glowed in Susie's eyes.

'Oh, I think that's *wonderful*!' she enthused. She gave another romantic sigh. 'You've got it *all*, Portia! A man who's sex on legs, has got buckets of money and is generous as well. You've definitely, *definitely*, got it all.'

She reached to kiss Portia's cheek, and then, with a beneficent smile, Diego's as well. They watched her head off, and Portia leant her head deeper against Diego's shoulder.

'I *have* got it all,' she said. 'All—and so much more! More than I ever knew existed.

Diego's hand came up to tilt her face towards him.

'Then we are alike,' he said softly, brushing her lips with his, his eyes warm. 'For with you I have everything my heart can desire.'

For a long, timeless moment they gazed at one another, and then into their silent communion came the tap of a knife against a glass. A voice called for attention.

'The bride and groom!'

Glasses were raised, the toast drunk. Portia drank too. And standing on their own, beside the towering white wedding cake, her brother and his bride, resplendent in morning suit and yards of white satin and lace, accepted their toast.

Diego looked down at her, his eyes questioning.

'This should have been your wedding. This is where you belong.'

His voice sounded troubled.

She shook her head.

'I belong with you,' she said simply. 'Nowhere else. And I have had my wedding—and it was perfect. Perfect in every detail.'

As if it had been yesterday she saw again the tiny chapel at the refuge, saw herself walking down the narrow aisle wearing a wedding dress the teenage girls had made for her, and all the under-tens following behind her in a vast procession of flower girls and pageboys, until she reached the man waiting for her by the altar rail. As they had both knelt they had looked up into the wise eyes of the priest who was to marry them.

'You chose well,' he had said softly to Portia.

Tears pricked in her eyes now, at the memory. Yes, she had chosen well—for her heart had chosen, and her soul and body too. All the elements of her being. She looked up at Diego, the man she loved and who loved her. Despite everything that had happened.

Or because of it?

It did not matter.

All that mattered was that they had come through.

Come through to this state of perfect happiness, perfect understanding.

Perfect love.

He held her gaze, and her heart swelled and overflowed. She slipped her hand into his and held it tight.

'The bride and groom,' said Diego softly, and lifted his glass—to his own bride.

His own true love.

To marry a sheikh!

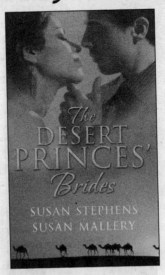

The Sheikh's Captive Bride by Susan Stephens

After one passionate night, Lucy is now the mother of
Sheikh Kahlil's son and Kahlil insists that Lucy must
marry him. She can't deny her desire to share his bed
again, but marriage should be forever.

The Sheikh & the Princess Bride by Susan Mallery

Even though beautiful flight instructor Billie Van Horn
was better than Prince Jefri of Bahania in the air,
he'd bet his fortune that he was her perfect match
in the bedroom!

Available 19th December 2008

M&B

Celebrate 100 years of pure reading pleasure with Mills & Boon®

To mark our centenary, each month we're publishing a special 100th Birthday Edition. These celebratory editions are packed with extra features and include a FREE bonus story.

Plus, you have the chance to enter a fabulous monthly prize draw. See 100th Birthday Edition books for details.

Now that's worth celebrating!

September 2008

Crazy about her Spanish Boss by Rebecca Winters
Includes FREE bonus story
Rafael's Convenient Proposal

November 2008

**The Rancher's Christmas Baby
by Cathy Gillen Thacker**
Includes FREE bonus story *Baby's First Christmas*

December 2008

One Magical Christmas by Carol Marinelli
Includes FREE bonus story *Emergency at Bayside*

Look for Mills & Boon® 100th Birthday Editions at your favourite bookseller or visit www.millsandboon.co.uk